Dear Lee,

Thank you so much
for finding and holding
my phone ... part
of my next book
is in my phone ...
You rescued it!

"all stories of life
are stories of love..."

Leo Harrell Lynn
april 10, 2018

The Stone Heart

LEO HARRELL LYNN

THE STONE HEART

iUniverse books may be ordered through booksellers or by contacting:

iUniverse
1663 Liberty Drive
Bloomington, IN 47403
www.iuniverse.com
1-800-Authors (1-800-288-4677)

Because of the dynamic nature of the Internet, any web addresses or links contained in this book may have changed since publication and may no longer be valid. The views expressed in this work are solely those of the author and do not necessarily reflect the views of the publisher, and the publisher hereby disclaims any responsibility for them.

Any people depicted in stock imagery provided by Thinkstock are models, and such images are being used for illustrative purposes only.
Certain stock imagery © Thinkstock.

ISBN: 978-1-5320-0647-0 (sc)
ISBN: 978-1-5320-0661-6 (hc)
ISBN: 978-1-5320-0650-0 (e)

Library of Congress Control Number: 2016916330

Print information available on the last page.

iUniverse rev. date: 08/02/2017

All stories of life are stories of love.
All stories of love are tales of heartbreak.
All tales of true love are tales of tragedy.

Critical acclaim for *THE STONE HEART*

"Emotionally charged and hauntingly evocative, *The Stone Heart* from Leo Harrell Lynn explores the complex nature of family, love, and hope, and is at once both delicate and resilient."

"On the craggy cliffs of Mendocino overlooking the waters of the Pacific, a solitary man contemplates the twisted, tragic path his life has taken and his decision to end it once and for all. After years of searching for true love, forty-four year old Shell Stone Lyon has finally given up. Love found, love lost, death, despair, and misfortune seem to shadow his family's attempts at living happily ever after."

"A romantic and poet at heart, Stone attempts to capture his last thoughts and reflections in a journal that becomes a testament of the Lyons' strengths and shortcomings, beginning with their southern roots in Alabama and the Florida Gulf Coast and spanning generations."

"In a true character study, Stone records family dynamics—not at face value, but by exploring the complex relationships of mothers, fathers, sons, and daughters, and how each shapes the next generation in their quests for love and acceptance. This is a narrative that delves into the psychology of behavior and emotion."

"Stone himself is an intriguing study in contrasts, by turns sensitive and cruel, heroic and cowardly, bold and afraid. He is an antihero who struggles to make sense of his feelings and desires. Drawn to beautiful things, words, and music, he expresses himself through poetry. His journal is lyrical as well—descriptive and flowing, passionate and engaging..."

"Heartbreaking but still hopeful, Stone's journey is a winding one, full of unexpected stops and turns, and the possibility of second chances."

"Not a typical love story, Leo Harrell Lynn's *The Stone Heart* is unique in its intensity and focus on examining the heart of the relationships that shape young boys and girls into the men and women they become."

--PALLAS GATES MCCORQUODALE, *FOREWORD CLARION REVIEWS*

"Reminiscent of the dysfunctional family sagas of Pat Conroy..."

"Chapter 1 starts well when an enterprising, elementary-school age Stone, hunting for fallen treasures beneath stadium bleachers, is blind-sided by a fetching little girl. The next chapter skillfully details an unexpected friendship between Stone and a black boy that briefly overrides the segregationist Sixties South. Another early chapter, titled "Butch," stands out, illustrating Stone's realization that a one-time schoolyard bully is actually struggling against tragic odds."

"Lynn's prose...is cleanly written and includes some terrific descriptions, depicting a face's off-center features, for example, as a chess piece slightly askew from its square."

--BLUEINK REVIEWS

"A debut novel details love lost through the voice of a compassionate but jaded writer...The story is rich in detail and intricate character development..."

"Beginning the poignant novel with Stone's ultimate expectation of committing suicide, Lynn sets a tone of palpable tension that propels the plot forward. The journalistic narrative is engrossing, and readers should find themselves absorbed in Stone's retelling of his countless misfortunes, driven by their curiosity and the desire to find the reasons that he has decided to kill himself."

"A captivating, heart-wrenching mosaic of life experiences encompassing family, tragedy, mental health, and fortitude."

--KIRKUS REVIEWS

ACKNOWLEDGMENTS

*W*riting a book can be a solitary pursuit and the loneliest of journeys. In my case, this path was made easier by the inspiration and support of family, friends, and so many others.

My mama and daddy, Nona and Leo, laid the foundation for everything I am, and this novel is a remembrance of all they did for me.

My brothers and sisters, Larry, Vickie, Mark, and Carol, have provided guidance and support throughout my life, including reinforcing the importance of making memories and keeping them alive in our hearts.

Love and sweetness to my wife, Mary Arios, who gave me the space, time, and patience to finish this seemingly never-ending project. Thank you so much!

Special thanks to Josie Carter for keeping Mary sane when my passion for this novel bordered on selfish obsession.

A toast to my best buddies, Jake and Jim, who stood up for me at my wedding and on so many other occasions. Also to Dave Chairez, Mike Bond, and Mark Mortimer—you all helped in more ways than you know.

Respectful nods to my literate pals who guided my way on this novel trip by constructively deconstructing my book: Eva Yablonsky, David Jordal, Robbie Arios Wallace, and Arnetta Lee. Special shout-outs to Robbie, whose intelligent guidance in the art of words straightened my course, and Arnetta, who provided uplifting cheers, pats on the back, and creative insight that helped me over the mountain of molehills I had made at the end.

Thanks to Donn Miller, my English teacher at Bella Vista High School, who gave me the freedom to write to my heart's content for an entire semester of independent study. His generosity and belief helped me discover my passion for writing.

Thanks to John Mahoney, my high school soccer coach, who gave me a job at Bella Vista shortly after I graduated. Coaching those boys for 12 years prompted my direction toward working with youth.

Thanks to Jack "Slippers" Murphy for giving me my first writing job, at Sacramento Sports Magazine, and showing me both the technical and descriptive beauty of the perfect sentence. He was also a helluva man.

Thanks to Howard Brown Jr., who taught me the heartbreaking power and depth of passion, and Doyle Minden, who modeled selfless dedication.

And heartfelt thanks to Linda, Jane, Mary Mac, Tani, Robbie G., Glenna, Margene, J. Mary, Elise, Rebecca, Stacy M., Kim, Barbara, Frances A., Amy (Ms. Moo), Patricia H., and Avneet for your lessons in friendship, compassion, and love. And thanks to Corinne, just because.

Thanks to my "family" at River Oak Center for Children—you all have been my inspiration for what the human heart can do for others.

Loving thanks to sweet Bobo, for giving all your Stone Heart could give and letting us think we were rescuing you when the reverse was true.

For my Mama and Daddy—Nona and Leo—who showed me the way simply by how they loved each other.

PROLOGUE

*T*oday is no different than yesterday.

I sit crumpled into a weathered wooden chair on a weather-beaten deck, a broken man examining the broken pieces of his life. It's only morning but I'm already tired. More to the point, I'm still tired. I barely recall sleeping, a common occurrence in my restless forties.

I look out at the scene before me, the view of the jagged Mendocino coastline and sullen blue-green water of the Pacific Ocean greeting every one of my mornings, and it's one of unparalleled splendor. Crashing waves toss frothy foam and particles of life toward the shore, then take it all back, leaving only the briny, salty smell of the sea. A potion mixed of salted water, gritty sand from million-year-old rocks, winds of all the world's storms, and energy from its relentless tides, the scent of the sea is my sensory elixir of life, the aroma reviving the dying cells of my spirit.

Though the smell of the Pacific awakens each of my days with hope, the shells I see scattered on the beach reflect my ultimate fate.

The third and last son born to Shell Stone Lyon, I was blessed with my daddy's name but not his love of working with his hands. On days like this, I feel more akin to my namesakes on the beach below—the shells and stones tossed about in the sea and cast upon the shore, dried out by the unrelenting wind and sun, and left hollow, weathered, and half-buried in the sand. A familiar voice—mine, I think—echoes from the cavities, but no one but the gulls are there to hear. And they are not listening, just picking at the shells and bones sticking from the sand.

All I seem to have these days are questions, the same old questions I have often asked myself but never fully answered. I'm scared to hear the answers and fearful of what they might reveal. But these questions cannot be avoided—they are as constant and continual as the dryness of my chapped skin from the relentless, scathing coastal winds.

What legacy will I leave to what is left of my family? How will I be remembered by my friends and lovers, and the others who in reality barely knew me? Will they look upon my body of language and find pearls within the remains? Will they read between the lines and find the truth amidst the lies? In the silence of my departure, will they hear the echoes of pleasure I gave to others? Will they dwell upon the money I never made or all my hopes turned to masquerade? Will they understand the voice that lives on in these pages, where my heart still rages?

Most likely, they will merely pick my bones or sift my ashes—and find nothing of substance either way.

Many people would say my life has not been one to lament. In many ways, they are right. I have walked barefoot in green grass every spring and summer. I have breathed fresh air and known the freedom of nature's beauty most every day, from the lush greenery of my Southern upbringing and the rolling golden foothills of my Northern California years, to the rugged majesty of the Mendocino coastline that has captured my heart most recently.

I emerged from childhood unscathed and idealistic. I met ordinary people who achieved extraordinary things, and was privileged to communicate their stories to the world. I helped shape troubled young lives into ones with hope.

And I have known the greatest of loves.

Yet it is all I didn't know about love that haunts me.

The past year has been a bad one. I have lost much of what I loved and seen the lives closest to me die or spin into ruin. After a lifetime of running, I cannot escape the truth about myself. I can no longer accept my choices and who I've become. As I enter my forty-fourth and final year, it's time for me to write down all the painful, gory details.

I lived a fairytale existence for my first eighteen years. Since then, death and loss have been sobering facts of my life. This is not only my story, but the tales of my family of passionate eccentrics, and follows our tireless and tragic search for true love. Our sojourn is a remembrance of romance and regret, hope gained and lost, and love fought for and forsaken.

We all sought true love with the awkward thrill and trepidation of babies learning to walk, trembling with excitement at our first steps but unsure about how or when to turn the corner. The path we walked was crooked and broken and not well marked by those who came before, and the end was not easily reached. Along the way, we found truth rarely kept company with love. Still, we stumbled upon love's grace one way or another. We all lost it for a time, with some never finding it again. But we never stopped trying.

My family of Lyons is a weak clan, many who know us would contend. In many ways, they are right. We haven't been achievers, at least not by society's standard of the American Dream. Only two of us attended college and just one finished. None of us have made much money. We aren't noteworthy in either the best or worst of anything we have accomplished—except in one area.

Our passion is close to unmatched. Though losers in the material game, we have often been gallant in matters of the heart. Though each of us used varying strategies, we have all been tenacious battlers on the field of love and always put up a fierce fight.

Too often though we lost.

Our love stories had a single storybook beginning. My mama married the only man she ever kissed and my daddy married the only woman he ever loved. A blue-collar worker and a housewife, there was nothing spectacular about them except the love they shared. This love would define their lives and shape the romantic relationships of their children.

My oldest brother was the hero in our household. Christened "Henry" at birth, he became Hank days later when his huge hands and feet suggested he should be known by a more adult name. A leader on the sports field as a youth, he would later save the lives of my mother and others. Despite his heroic qualities, Hank was never meant to be the oldest son. He wore the mantle of first born at a tilted angle. After Daddy died, this mantle became a cross he dragged through much of his life.

Peter, the second oldest son, was a natural-born leader. Charismatic, fiercely outspoken and independent, Peter would have fit better into his older brother's shoes. The responsibilities related to being the number one son that ultimately buried Hank would have barely slowed Peter. As it was, his second-born status allowed development on his own terms and outside the realm of others' expectations. He flourished without these restrictions, embarking on a search for eternal truth at an age when the main goal usually was to entice a redhead into the backseat of a Chevy Nova.

Peter's quest would lead him to the highest ground of spiritual consciousness and leadership. Along the way, he discovered that true love was elusive in the real world, and truth and falsehood were determined by humans in all their fallible ways.

My sister Christine sought a fairytale life, embracing true love before her teen heart could discern the falseness of her choice. Her devotion to the sanctity of love threatened to come at the ultimate cost to herself and her family.

I searched for love with all my romantic heart. I viewed true love as God's greatest gift, a spark of life energizing like a lightning bolt from the heavens. Belief in love was all I needed—as nourishment for my soul and food for my mind. I believed what Christine once told me, that true love gives beauty to the soul and the heart its reason to exist.

But true love wears two faces, and the second one, the false one, is an evil visage. Love is Satan's scythe, and in the wrong hands, it cuts clean or jagged through foolish hearts to the bone deep inside where all hope lives and breathes. The pursuit of true love often leads to the purest form of tragedy—nothing enthralls and enlightens more, and nothing rips out the heart and destroys the soul more.

Behind most human devastation there exists a love lost but not forgotten. I have found this to be true in my life and the lives of my flawed family. The quest for true love led to the death of one of us, the ruin of another, and the broken spirit of a third. The last one—this one—is standing at cliff's edge.

I didn't understand until too late that finding true love costs more than anything and losing it carries the ultimate price—the end of dreams and the beginning of the long loneliness of the heart.

I carry the scars of my failures in love not jagged on my arm or slashed across my face, but deep in my heart. Ragged piercings from the searing cuts remain unhealed through the years. I have tried to forget the lovers who left the widest gapes in my chest and the deepest tears in my heart. But every time I recall their faces or words, my wounds open anew. When I expose my heart to test the winds of hope, the coldness stings the cut inside. Each time I close my eyes, I can still see theirs, and I feel that old familiar pain.

At night, I yearn for sleep to escape the weight of my memories. But sleep does not come easily on most nights and not at all on others. I close my eyes and cover my ears but cannot still the voices or obscure the faces of the love I have lost or squandered. A tape runs backward day and night through my head, recounting in my conscious and unconscious minds the details of my failed loves. I live a version of Dante's Inferno—though it's more like Cupid's Hell, for I am burdened by faces of beauty and feelings of love I cannot forget.

Maybe I could forget these memories if only they were general in nature. But I have two different yet equally enchanting visages that never go out of focus. I try to close my eyes to the images but the negatives are imprinted in my heart and cannot be erased by mechanisms of the mind.

Living in the past, especially one filled with such exquisite memories, would not seem to be a regrettable hell if not for the life I'm wasting in the present.

I live on the fringe, allowing ready escape when my fears warrant change. The edge of reality has been my refuge, my harbor of the soul. Only one constant exists—the search for true love. I leave behind everyone— friends, family, and former lovers. When I lose the feeling, I try to wipe the slate clean by running away. But I can never flee fast enough to avoid lost love's fallout or far enough to leave behind the baggage of my heart. Sensitivity is my virtue, but also my prison, for I have kept my feelings trapped inside. The steps leading out are treacherous from tears of those who left broken hearted.

Now though my window view is filled with pristine symmetry, I remain imprisoned behind the pane—where darkness is my companion, doubt is my guide, and fear the path I have chosen. Dreams I have abandoned, forgotten, and lost along the way, but reality has been a poor substitute. And though my sight is intact, my vision is obscured.

Elk has been my temporary home for the past several months. A small fisherman's cabin, abandoned long ago but revived and well-taken care of by a diligent caretaker, has been an ideal writing den to draw out my despair and put it down on paper.

Written by hand shaky not from age but from mental failing, this manuscript might be difficult to decipher by those who find it. The art of handwriting, fading like my energy for living, is my stubborn choice to share this story.

These words are the only way out of my self-built dungeon. I am not seeking redemption or salvation—I long ago traded God's grace for pride and praise. This journal is meant for those who still fall for the fairytale of true love, to educate them in the folly behind this mindless faith by revealing the ravages that come from believing in hopes and dreams, passion and love. My only hope is that readers of this diary discover what I found out too late—that believing in the lie that is true love leads to a dead end.

Maybe then, those who read these words will understand why I threw myself into the restless azure waves 150 feet below my front window.

My journal, bound in a cover made from a burlap bag that once held oysters my daddy shucked and ate, lies wedged between two rocks on the cliff's edge, so it will not blow over the side and join my body amidst the shells and stones below.

I start at the beginning.

I tell the truth, even about the lies.

Part **1**

ALL STORIES OF LIFE
ARE STORIES OF LOVE

Chapter *1*

THE BEGINNING

*T*here is something to be said for having crappy upbringing. You always have a past to explain why your present is screwed up and your future will be even worse.

I am cursed by a happy childhood. None of my errors and misjudgments date to troubled early years wrought with conflict, abuse, and neglect. I have only my adult self to blame for my wrongs and misdeeds.

My childhood was one of splendid isolation, surrounded by parents, two brothers, and a sister who shared a mutual misunderstanding of each other. I was alone in my thoughts and goals, and my aspirations were tightly held secrets. I took pride in the loneliness of my aloneness. I felt safe living in the shadows, hidden from even those closest to me and knowing no one could invade my space. Not until much later would I comprehend that my sensitive heart, not the world, was my true enemy.

I grew up in two worlds as different as planets in separate universes. My first world was shared between the incessant rain and moist greenness of the Alabama seaport of Mobile and the withering humidity and crystal white beaches of the Florida Gulf Coast. I would later land with my family on a separate plane of existence—the mother lode country of Northern California, countering with dry, blistering summer heat and rolling foothills of waxen gold.

There were connections between my two worlds—the abundance of sun, trees, and water—but even these natural staples were as different as moon dust and earthen soil. The sun's rays in the South burned lower, but had a hidden agenda—they lured you outside with lower temperatures, only to cover you in a blanket of sticky discomfort. The California sun was lively and perky, announcing itself with gusto over the Eastern ridge. Unrelenting in its dryness, Western heat was at least straightforward in its impact and message: "Stay inside or in the shade, you will be okay; venture directly into my path, prepare to face my wrath." I adapted to the directness of this sunshine over time and have never again been as comfortable with the furtive nature of the Southern rays.

Trees were everywhere in both my lives—the South's straight and stiff longleaf pines, standing tall and stout and stately even in their old age, contrasted with the Gold Country's stooped, twisted, and curved valley oaks, their bent and gnarled branches looking arthritic and misshapen, but their wide trunks hinting at comfort and wisdom.

I never found a tree anywhere, though, to rival the pecan tree that dominated our back yard in Mobile. Though the tallest of many large pecan trees in our neighborhood, its toughness was what I admired. As a kid, I was told the tree had a cannon ball lodged inside that dated back to the Civil War. Before I had a good grip on math and history, I believed the Yankees had overrun our area a hundred years before, pelting the orchards with cannon fire and leaving a permanent memorial to Rebel toughness in our wounded, but unbowed tree.

What I remember most about my years in the South was the simple wonderment of being a child, a time when freedom was measured in summertime stanzas, morning recesses, and final afternoon bells. Freedom's uniform was bare feet, plaid shorts, and any old white t-shirt. Water for swimming was never cold and rainfall held all the mysteries of afternoon play. I didn't know until much later that my hometown was the rainiest city in the United States outside of Hawaii and Alaska. But the rain never seemed bothersome, as it opened up all kinds of play opportunities, from racing homemade wooden boats down the street gutters and playing in vast vats of mud, to collecting tadpoles in the huge runoff ponds and gingerly grabbing crawdads that had crawled into the submerged areas around our water meters.

My first sports dreams and fantasies were played out in the "Circle," a patch of grass surrounded by a concrete curb that sat in the center of our cul-de-sac. As a kid, it looked longer than a football field; on subsequent return visits, I noticed it getting smaller and smaller, as if by magic, until it was about forty yards long and twenty yards wide.

On this field of glory I made my first catch of a baseball in a game that mattered. I fell for the game from that day forward, but it proved to be a love-hate relationship. The "hate" part involved my time at bat. Hitting was not my forte, though I was a decent batter—no power but I always hit the ball somewhere. I didn't like the thinking needed, the myriad of choices on where to hit the ball. As the ball traveled plate-ward, my mind became defensive in its approach and doubtful in its execution. I had epic conversations during every at bat. "Should I swat it between the shortstop and third baseman? Wait—the third baseman is playing off the line, maybe I can spray it down the third base line. But look at the right fielder. He thinks he knows me, believes I can't hit it over his head. If the next pitch comes inside, I'll turn on it and whack it over his head. Then again, the first baseman is playing back, behind the runner. I could drag bunt the ball down the line and beat it out. Or..."

And so on and so on, until I was mentally exhausted. I usually popped out.

Fielding was a different story. Catching a baseball was the only doubtless passion I possessed as a boy. If someone hit a ball, nothing would stop me from trying to catch it. Nothing at all. Not a fence, a wall, a rose bush, or another fielder. To this day, diving headlong for a ball remains the only totally unconscious act for me.

Baseball represented a parable of my life to come. Just as I was defensive about the baseball hurtling toward my bat and worried about where to place it, I have been tentative about my decision-making as an adult. And even my one passion—catching any darn ball hit my way—was simply a reaction to what someone else was doing. This defensive approach has remained my entire life.

Baseball, I have found, is a lot like life. The game is tough, and often long and lonely for those positioned away from the main action. The best batters only get about three hits in ten tries, while pitchers aren't perfect either, succeeding maybe seven out of ten times. With all the hopes and expectations thrown at us, we fail more times than not. Learning to deal with this failure is the most important aspect of life.

In my life, failure was a failing I never handled well.

I enjoyed watching baseball almost as much as playing it, especially when my brothers were involved. I was drawn to the geometric smartness of the game, with dirt and grass arranged at ninety-degree angles and boys dressed in bright uniforms of Sunday-best white and candy cane stripes. I remember the infielders spitting into their gloves and chattering, "Humm Baby" and "Thatta Boy," and the "thump" of the pitch as it snaps into the catcher's glove. I can still hear the sound of the ball hitting the bat, the "craaack" of wood smashing horsehide, which back then always returned my wandering attention to the diamond, where kids played under the watchful eyes of daddies who were dreaming in reverse.

Most of all, I recall the smell of the leather gloves. My brothers let me try them on and play catch before their games. I held the glove to my face, chewing on one of the loose, salty cowhide lacings while breathing in the leather's rich, earthy aroma, a mixture of dirt and sweat and spit, all the things that brought the senses of a young boy alive.

Still, my attention wandered outside the chalk lines more often than not, as the countless diversions around the ballpark held my rapture. As my brothers played the National Pastime, I pursued my own perennial favorites—chasing fire flies, playing tag, and ducking under the bleachers.

The metal catacombs beneath the descending layers of lead paint-chipped wooden slats opened a special world that I was drawn to by the search for lost treasure. My small frame and nimble feet moved me stealthily through the steel girders unnoticed by those seated above, though their legs often dangled inches from my head.

My treasure haul included enough change to keep me supplied with candy, ice cream, and sunflower seeds throughout the summer—or at least for that night. Sometimes, I skipped the snack bar middleman, finding unopened candy bars, cokes, and baseball cards. My card collection was filled with ones I didn't pay for, including my prized Bert "Campy" Campaneris rookie card. The diminutive Cuban became my hero as a minor leaguer, when he dazzled as a visiting player for the Birmingham Barons against my Mobile Bears. In the first professional baseball game I witnessed, he hit a single, double, triple, and homerun—the "cycle"—and stole three bases. He caught my eye mostly because he was the tiniest player on the field. As a four-foot six-year-old, I could relate to him.

I picked up fascinating objects I could neither use, sell, nor identify. I stuck these in a cigar box until I figured out a use for them. I showed some of this stuff to my brothers, who usually brushed me off with some half-real or imagined definition. Once, I showed Peter a strip of three connected pouches, each containing a thick yellow balloon rolled up into a ring. Peter gave me an odd look, then smiled. He handed the balloons to Hank, who shoved them in his pocket. "I can use them at a party later on," he said, winking at Peter.

I shrugged, thinking it wasn't gonna be much of a party with stupid balloons like those.

I had a rationalized set of ethics regarding my found items. I never picked up anything just after it fell. I usually made a couple of sweeps through the subterranean metal jungle, only picking up things that had fallen earlier. I figured it was fair to give people first shot at their dropped stuff. But after a while it was their bad luck and my good fortune.

One night, I stumbled upon the Holy Grail of bleacher treasure.

Out of the corner of my eye, I saw something fall from the bleachers, but could not readily identify it in the shadows below. As I turned toward where it had fallen from about twenty feet above, I could tell it was a wallet by its shape and leather material. But the uneven, dirty-brown yellowish color suggested a rare, exotic type of leather and wallet. Whatever its leather type, the billfold looked stuffed and I envisioned a lifetime of ice cream, baseball cards, and bubble gum.

Keeping true to my paper-thin ethics, I walked past it after giving one last look. I made my way to the far end of the bleachers, where my buddies Joey Brown and Scottie Vandenburk and a trio of kids I didn't know well were milling about in their quest for kid riches. Though we often split our treasures, I hadn't yet told my friends of the potential gold mine descending from bleacher heaven. Maybe I felt entitled to my treasure in its entirety by rule of luck, for want of a better reason.

I am not sure if it was guilt or camaraderie—or the fear the three kids I didn't know would stumble onto the treasure, but I eventually clued in Joey and Scottie to my secret. Joey, a jumpy kid who would run crying into his house when thunder sounded, started breathing hard. "We gotta pick it up now or we're gonna lose it," he said, his face flushed sanguine with excitement. When his pacing began, I knew he was becoming agitated.

I also knew he was close to pounding the iron girders in frustration or sprinting willy-nilly toward the unguarded wallet, alerting the people above or the other kids with us below.

I motioned with my hand for him to relax, but he was already headed out of control. "Wait," I whispered, trying to keep the world above interested in the game, not us. "We have to follow the code; we can't take it until the man has a chance to find it."

I said this even though I wasn't quite sure about the specifics of these unwritten rules, or why they needed to be followed. I just knew, somewhere in the back of my mind, there was a structure involved, a way to give balance to things so they could work out fairly. In our own crude, weird logic, giving the man in the bleachers first shot at recovering his wallet was a way to equalize the unfairness of us finding and keeping it.

Though Scottie had an uneasy understanding of structure and balance, he had a clear-cut way to enforce the rules, one he inherited from his old man and was reminded of each time he put on his belt. The marks permanently imprinted on Scottie's back, the ones he could see in the mirror when he looked over his shoulder, were the same width as his belt.

So when Joey ignored my suggestion and started his run, Scottie put his hard-earned lessons into action. He tackled the smaller Joey in one quick, efficient motion, stifling Joey's yell with his right hand as if he were using one finger on a TV's "off" button. He whispered something I could not hear, and Joey quieted his struggle. Joey retained a measure of wildness in his eyes but his overall look more closely resembled fear.

I was never quite comfortable with Scottie's aggressive nature, but I did not argue with his method this time. With Joey neutralized, we turned our attention to the intruders in our midst. They had seen the struggle and appeared to know something out of the ordinary was up. I had to redirect them without compromising our treasure site. As I look back, I am still amazed at the quick-thinking deceitfulness my seven-year-old mind was able to conjure. My chicanery involved an old-fashioned sleight-of-hand baseball card trick.

I knew Benji, one of the kids now headed in our direction, loved baseball cards. I had found three packs in my sweep, so I decided to throw him off track by tossing a few loose cards on the ground leading away from the wallet site. I was hoping Benji and his buddies would follow the trail of scattered cards like birds chasing breadcrumbs.

I enlisted Scottie and Joey to distribute the cards while I discreetly moved toward the wallet. I made sure my two friends made enough of a commotion to draw our rivals in their direction. Scottie and Joey played their parts perfectly, making it loud and clear they had found some cards but didn't care to keep them.

With Benji and his cohorts distracted, I slipped over to where the wallet lay waiting. I figured the man above had ample opportunity to determine his wallet was missing. The wallet felt slick and rough when I picked it up, and I noticed the yellowish leather looked like sections of animal hide. I wasn't sure at my young age, but I thought it looked like a chunk of crocodile. "Whew," I said to myself, as I guessed this crocodile stuff didn't come cheap. "This mister must be loaded."

The extent of his load was confirmed when a peek into the wallet revealed a thick wad of twenties, tens, and fives inside. I looked closer and saw the first $100 bill in my life. The numbers spun in my head and when they stopped, the total was nearly $300, the most money I had ever seen at one time. I was staggered, both by the wealth in my hands and the avarice in my heart. This wasn't just a five-dollar bill lying on the ground or a single ten or twenty rolled in a billfold. For us, finding the wallet was akin to stumbling upon Fort Knox.

Suddenly spooked by the realization of what I was holding, I looked up toward my unwitting benefactor. Momentarily blinded by a stadium floodlight slanting through the wooden bleacher slats, I thought it might be God sending down a strobe from heaven to remind me my every move was being watched.

I wasn't too far off my estimation of a divine presence. After I refocused my eyes and glanced back up a moment later, the blinding glare had been replaced by a most heavenly vision. Filling the space was the face of an angel.

I realized this angel was looking straight into my eyes. She had huge blue eyes and flowing blonde curls. But it was her face that made my kid brain jump a decade into the future. Compared to this little girl's beauty, my dream girl, Judy Garland's Dorothy from the *Wizard of Oz*, looked more like her dog Toto.

"Hi, I'm Michelle," said the *new* girl of my dreams.

I didn't know what to say. I had managed to slip the wallet behind my back, but I wasn't thinking about much else besides the little girl peering down at me.

"Didn't you hear me?" she asked. "What's your name?"

I realized she was repeating a question I totally missed the first time around.

"Stone."

"That's a mighty interesting name," she said.

"Named after my daddy Shell but I go by my middle name," I shrugged. "Don't really know the why of it. My Mama just called me that since I was a little boy. Said 'Stone' was a name in a fairytale she liked."

Usually creative with my comebacks when asked about my name, I cringed at my rambling remarks—especially my use of "little boy." I just stood there looking up, my mouth drooping like a basset hound's jowls. Then it dawned on me she hadn't seen the wallet in my hands. I saw her look away for a moment to talk with the man who had dropped the wallet. I guessed he was her father. The impetus for my next move popped out of nowhere.

"Does this belong to you?" I asked, holding out the billfold.

What?" she asked, and I could tell by the way she was scrunching her cute little nose that she was squinting into the darkness trying to determine what I was holding up.

"This wallet," I said. "I found it down here. Does it belong to your daddy?"

"It sure looks like my daddy's," she said, tapping her father on the shoulder. "Is that your wallet, Daddy?"

Her father looked over his shoulder in an uninterested manner, hardly looking down before turning back toward the field. As if by instinct, though, he reached for his back pocket, and when he didn't feel the familiar padding, his head jerked back around.

"Sir, is this yours?" I asked, in a faint voice.

"Oh my God, yes!" he exclaimed. And before I could even blink, the little girl named Michelle had scrambled down the bleacher bars like a monkey on the loose and was standing next to me. She took the wallet and skipped her way around to the front of the bleachers, climbing the stairs two at a time until she reached her father's row.

I turned to see Benji and his pals scowling at me. Scottie and Joey stood shaking their heads. Though unhappy I had given away their riches, they had already forgiven me. They, too, were just discerning the overwhelming power of the female allure.

I spent the rest of the night exploring the bleacher catacombs with my first girlfriend.

I don't know if it was my conscience or love at first sight that prompted my honesty that day. But I never kept another misplaced wallet after that evening, figuring I got all the good fortune I needed when I looked up and saw the prettiest girl I would ever see as a boy.

⁓

A great joy of my Alabama childhood was the twice-monthly trek to the supermarket.

Mama, who always led these expeditions with two or three kids in tow, shopped at either Delchamps or the Piggly Wiggly. She chose Delchamps more often than not—even though it was further across town and charged a bit more—because, she said, it had "fresher fruits and vegetables, and nicer folks working there." I think it was because she thought Piggly Wiggly was a silly name for a store. Mama hated saying the name out loud, preferring to call it "the supermarket that isn't Delchamps," or, if pressed, "PW."

Occasionally a sale at the Piggly Wiggly came along that was too hard for Mama to pass up. She would announce to me and my sister that we were going to "that other supermarket." I always played dumb, asking her where we were going and repeating the question until she became exasperated enough to blurt out the full name. Just hearing Mama say "Piggly Wiggly" made me all giggly—the goofy name alone signaled something fun and exciting was on its way. Mama actually came to look forward to our little game. She always had a little smile after hearing my laughter and soon took to calling the store "Stone's Giggly Piggly Wiggly," which made me laugh even more. Over time, she stopped going to Delchamps and shopped exclusively at the GPW around the corner.

I suspected most kids despised the chore of accompanying their mother to the supermarket. At first, I hated it too. It was demeaning to sit facing your mother, the bottoms and insides of your thighs receiving freezer burns from the cold steel basket as you were wheeled up and down the rows. You prayed none of your friends caught you in this helpless position. However, the aisles with their seemingly limitless possibilities never failed to excite me. My joy increased exponentially when I weaned myself from the frigid basket and could run ahead to explore all the mysteries of this enchanting, bountiful world.

I was enthralled by the toys lining the top shelves of the store's walls. Huge plastic dump trucks and tractors, packaged Wiffle ball sets, first-edition GI Joe figures and green plastic machine guns (with blood-red barrel tips) drew my wide-eyed attention.

I was more intrigued by a soda shop and grocery store located just around the corner. The soda shop fed my inexhaustible desire for ice cream. I also liked its bright, snappy appearance. The black and white tiles quilting the floor were always shiny, as were the chrome poles leading up to the red Naugahyde seats. I used to spin around in my fountain seat as I waited for my chocolate soda, coming to a dizzying stop just long enough to grab my foam-topped drink and sip it down in seconds, giving me another dizzying headache. Then I would repeat the entire head-shattering experience.

But it was the adjoining grocery store, with its dim, moody lighting and bright green and red letters on its windows spelling out Romano's Deli, which grabbed most of my attention. Mama didn't shop in this store, and when I asked her why, she would sigh and roll her eyes. "It's just too fancy and they only sell strange, funny-smelling foods that come from all the way across the Atlantic Ocean," she explained. "*European* foods."

Even to my immature mind, the drawn-out way she said, "European," emphasizing each of the four syllables as if they were separate words, suggested stuff in this store was so alien to our way of life it might as well have been from another planet. My mother believed anything so far removed from our frame of reference was to be feared and avoided.

Mama liked to leave my sister and me in the soda shop while she walked around the corner to get sewing supplies. She didn't want her kids to wander through the fabric store with dripping ice cream cones and sticky hands. She left strict orders to stay put, and told Freddy, the teenage "soda jerk," to keep his eye on us.

In those days, with four kids and a million things to do before Daddy arrived home from work, Mama had her day scheduled to the minute. She knew how long it took us to eat our ice cream cones, so she was gone for that exact amount of time.

My sister and I had a growing suspicion something interesting was going on at the deli. Walking by, we could smell rich, curious mixtures of odors and see rows of curvaceous, smoky-colored bottles and bright, colorful cans and packages. It fueled a lust in my tender body I could not yet fathom

One day we decided to find out what was in this mysterious place. We accelerated our eating schedule by slurping our ice cream sodas down in seconds. On the move before recovering from our ice cream headaches, we staggered through the side door and into the savory, seductive world of Romano's Deli.

Immediately, we knew we were in a different place from any we had previously known. Oh what an exotic variety of sensory sensations it offered—crackers with little seeds on them and cookies with jelly in the middle; hard candies in seemingly millions of fruity flavors and costumed in bright, colorful wrappers; big, puffy biscuits with swirls of whip cream inside; curved, pimply pickles half as long as my arm, and chocolate bars from faraway lands. *European* chocolate bars!

At first, the store *did* smell funny. But as we wandered the aisles, distinct odors were greeted pleasantly by our noses. I had never liked the burnt, harsh smell of the canned coffee my parents drank. But there was a sweetness to the aroma of the freshly ground coffee lingering from the end of one row. My sister liked the smell of the tea selections lining the entire length of another row, saying they reminded her of "a garden of all kinds of flowers."

Raised on tasty, but boringly uniform Oscar Meyer wienies, I was amazed at the shapes and sizes of the sausages and wieners filling the meat case that stretched the store's entire back wall. Tiny white wieners no bigger than my pinkie were dwarfed by fat, elongated red sausages with blunt ends and strange veins running their entire length. Skinny sausages linked together by thin pieces of skin dangled overhead. Hanging nearby were thick sausages in colorful green-red-and-white packages that my sister said you could "eat right out of the wrapper, right then and there."

Used to the synthetic, perfumy smell of processed American cheese slices Mama fed us, I was initially taken aback by the earthy, sour odors coming from the section filled with foreign cheeses. Some of them disgusted me, especially the white cheese with the blue and gray chunks and the really stinky "burger" cheese. It reminded me of what I smelled after a few weeks of shoving dirty socks and half-drank glasses of milk under my bed.

I was drawn to the odd shapes and sizes of the packages and varying textures and colors of the contents. My favorites were the thick triangular cheeses colored a bright orange, which I didn't think existed outside of Mighty Mouse cartoons. What I loved most about this tiny, stinky store were the free food samples that seemed to be everywhere. My sister liked the white linen table cloths, and the way the "mini-meals" were dished out on flower-shaped doilies. I simply liked the grub.

However, I had to endure cold-blooded blackmail from my sister. I was well known for my picky eating habits at home. Mama was forever begging me to try this or that new food, with little success. "Better hope Mama doesn't know you're trying all those cheeses and funny-looking meats, let alone any vegetables," she teased, as I grabbed a fistful of free food I had never seen before in my life. "She'll make you try everything she puts in front of you." Her teasing ended with, "I might have to tell her what you've tried, unless…" I caved in to her threats, spending that evening scratching her back and playing dolls with her.

I could not explain why I sampled things in that smelly store I would not touch with a ten-foot fork at home. Something about this mysterious place made me want to try all sorts of funny foods I would not eat if they were placed in front of me by Mama.

I was also intrigued by the store's foreign, unfamiliar nature because I knew it made my mother uncomfortable. I suppose it was a natural part of my maturation, a growing need to stretch the boundaries of my young world. It also signaled the beginning of my tendency to be drawn to all things—especially women—dark and mysterious.

Energized by some new source I could not identify, I rushed outside to play after returning home on this day. I made incredible diving catches of balls bounced off my roof and shot expertly at birds with rubber-tipped arrows. Something awakened inside me that would lead to grand adventures in the future.

For now I would play and dream, holding this mysterious new feeling inside until the time was right for further education. I would later solve many of these mysteries and discover and enjoy the realities hinted at by these early wonders. But this knowledge would be earned in return for a grievous payment of painful emotional currency.

Chapter 2

THE DITCH

My daddy was the gentlest of men, at least from my own memories. He never made a cross statement nor said a curse word in my presence, though he liked to kid about his own piousness. Upon seeing massive Hoover Dam for the first time, during one of our family's cross-country summer vacations, he joked, "Damn, that's a big darn," drawing out the first word so long I felt uncomfortable. I had formed an idealized view of my daddy, and his joking in the hallowed area of cussing sounded alien to me.

He raised his hand to me once, when I was seven and had ventured long after dark without telling Mama. She sent Daddy to find me, telling him to search along the cement canal I often frequented with my buddies. The canal, known as The Ditch longer than any kid in the area could remember, ran along the outskirts of our neighborhood and was the unofficial line separating the undeveloped woods from the suburbs in which we lived.

By the time the sun raised the following morning after my disappearance, I would learn the full nature of my parents' caring. This realization would be tempered by evil's introduction into my world, a lesson in humanity at the cost of my childhood innocence.

Mama warned me about going into these woods. To her, this undeveloped area was the cutoff point for civilization. "It's wild and dangerous," she cautioned. "There are wild animals and snakes, and opossums and wild dogs with rabies. There are even worms that crawl into your toes when it rains. And there are those undesirables who gather there."

I wasn't sure what she meant by "worms that crawl into your toes," but I had an inkling the "undesirables" she referred to weren't animals. They were the black kids—Negro boys, as my friends and I called them back then—who lived in broken down shacks on the other side of the woods, suggesting Mobile's development was not moving in a universal direction.

Mama probably knew her warnings wouldn't stop me from exploring these "jungles," but she wanted to plant a healthy fear in me. She understood The Ditch, which separated the woods from our neighborhood, was the closest thing to a melting pot in the segregated Mobile suburbs of the Sixties. Representing the only watering hole for miles and the last vestige of wildness left in our rapidly developing area, The Ditch attracted kids from both the black and the white sides of the tracks.

My mother needn't have worried. Though my friends and I occasionally ventured into the woods to play cowboys and Indians and to build makeshift forts, we were more interested in the watery world of the Ditch than socializing with the Negro boys.

The Ditch held all the mysteries that transfixed boys our ages—be they white or black, rich or poor. A narrow, intimate waterway, The Ditch was home to crawfish, hand-sized bream, polliwogs, frogs, and wonderfully gooey, sticky mud. With our cane poles and cans of worms, we all must have thought that we were Huck Finns and Tom Sawyers, and The Ditch was a tiny tributary of the mighty Mississippi River.

The Ditch also served as the line of demarcation between us and the Negro kids, who mostly hailed from the shantytown on the other side of the woods. The Ditch, itself, was an open zone split by an imaginary line that neither white nor black crossed.

The entire separation issue piqued my inquisitiveness. I couldn't understand why we were supposed to be so different. As I watched the young Negroes bent over in the distance—doing exactly what we white boys were doing—I wondered what they were thinking and what their lives must be like. I wanted to ask them, but my friends' attitudes made me hold back. They had already formed hard and fast impressions, handed down to them by their parents and grandparents. To them, the black boys were simply "niggers," and they wanted nothing to do with them. I followed their lead, not knowing why.

"Nigger" had been part of my vocabulary from the moment I walked outside as a small child and conversed with kids and adults in my neighborhood. I didn't realize, until later, that I never heard the word inside my own home, from either my mother, father, sister, or brothers. Actually, Peter said "nigger" once and was met with a cold, hard stare from Daddy. I never heard my brother use the word again.

My parents were not free from the bias and ignorance associated with their Deep South affiliation. My mama had no affection for the "Black Movement" or Dr. Martin Luther King Jr. "That man ain't no doctor," she often said. "He's a communist who wants to turn all the Negroes against us white folk."

I didn't know what being a communist meant back then, but I had an idea it wasn't a good thing, at least in my parents' eyes. So I had my suspicions about this Mr. King and all, but I did not hate him or other Negroes. I was taught to be wary of Negroes, but not to despise them. My parents, as usual, left the ultimate choice of feeling to my own heart.

I used the word "nigger" freely out of sound from my parents, though I had little knowledge of what it meant past the vague idea it was something or someone bad. I called my friends "niggers" because that's what they called me in jest or in anger, but I didn't know it had anything to do with the Negro boys I saw almost daily in The Ditch.

I had never spoken to a Negro, including any of the black boys in The Ditch. But this would change on the same summer day my Daddy spent an evening searching for me. That day, I talked to a boy whose skin was the color of Hershey's dark chocolate and learned the real meaning of "nigger."

Here is the story of that day, just as it happened.

I am excited as only a kid on summer vacation can be! The thunderstorm that hit this morning has passed, leaving The Ditch filled to its capacity and jostling its numerous creatures into heightened activity.

Defying the burning rays of the mid-day Southern sun, I have my shirt off and my Mobile Bears cap turned backward. I throw myself into my Ditch-time fun more intently than usual, chasing tadpoles into a plastic bag and turning over rocks looking for crawfish that have scrambled for cover to avoid being swept downstream by the steady post-storm current.

I succeed gloriously! Along with my full load of tadpoles and a personal record-tying nine crawfish, I catch and let go three chunky Southern toads displaced from their nocturnal burrows by the storm. Add to that the sighting of three fence lizards, two green anoles and even a frisky marbled salamander scurrying along a fallen tree branch.

With the sun dropping toward the Western horizon, I think about heading home. I reach down to turn over one last, dark rock.

I jump in startled amazement when the rock moves on its own. Closer inspection reveals the "rock" is actually a foot. As I straighten up, I look into the whitest eyes and blackest face I have ever seen close up.

The Negro boy's eyes grow larger until they resemble two pearl onions, but neither he nor I say a word. Neither of us move toward retreat, as we eye each other with more curiosity than fear. I figure he has been looking for crawdads with the same head-down focus as me and wandered over the invisible line in The Ditch separating the black boys from us white ones. Then I realize I was the one who stepped across the unofficial dividing point, marked by a single spindly longleaf pine on each side of the canal.

As I search for something to say to this wide-eyed boy, I spot a huge crawdad—the biggest one of the day—settling on a rock near his foot. I dunk my hand in the water and grab the crawdad by its tail, evading its massive pinchers. I lift it gingerly out of the water and am about to triumphantly place it in my bucket when it slips from my grasp. Before the crawdad even hits bottom, the black boy swoops his arm underwater in a blinding flash, grasps the freshwater crustacean behind its head using his thumb and forefinger, and holds it aloft with the flourish of a maestro finishing a symphony. He smiles and two rows of crooked, broken teeth light up his face like a lighthouse beacon. As I look on dumbfounded, he plops the crawdad into my bucket.

I don't know if I'm more surprised by his speed and technique or his generosity. Being a kid, I'm more concerned with action than feeling, so I ask how he did what he just did. "I ain't never seen nobody catch no crawdad that fast or grab them behind the head. Don't ya know what they can do to you with those pinchers?"

"So is t'at why ya was grabbin' t'is one by the tail?" he asks. He seems relieved I spoke to him first. I get the feeling he wouldn't have said anything had I not initiated the conversation.

"Yeah," I reply, suddenly feeling the need to defend my position. "Don't ya know if a crawdad clamps his pinchers on ya in the daytime, he won't let go 'til the sun goes down?" I don't tell him the source of this information is my mother, who instilled this fear in me the first time I found crawfish lurking near the water meter in our front yard.

"Ain't never heard of such a t'ing," he shrugs. "I's will be a pert mo' careful from now on." He hesitates a moment, as if deciding if he should say what he is thinking. "My name's Willie-Mays Simpkins," he says. "What be yours?"

"Stone," I say. "Stone Lyon. Huh. Willie-Mays. Your name sounds like I heard it somewhere before."

"I be named for the world's bestest ballplayer. He be the cousin of my pappy."

While I digest his relation to a famous person, he takes another look at my crawfish. "T'ere t'ese fish with whiskers, when t'ey get plum tired of w'ere t'ey are, t'ey just git outa t'at water and walk on top of t'e ground," he says, T'ey keep on a walkin' 'til t'ey find mo' water. My pappy say don't try to ketch 'em on land 'cause t'ey'll give ya t'e ol' evil eye."

I don't know what part if any of this "walking catfish" tale to believe, and I can't understand all of what he is saying, so I just keep nodding and saying, "Unh huh," over and over. It's as if he's talking in a foreign language, but at least the subjects of the water and the wonders of The Ditch are something we can both understand and appreciate.

Then I notice Willie-Mays' body stiffen and his eyes grow bigger, as he glances over my shoulder. I turn and discover Scottie and Joey are standing behind me.

"Ya wouldn't believe what this boy can—" I begin, but stop when I see the ugliness in my friends' faces. I have seen my sister and brothers when they are mad, and have watched my mama's face darken with anger as she reaches for the switch, but I've never witnessed the look of hate I see now in the faces of my two best friends.

"Stone, what lies is this here pitiful nigger been tellin' you?" hissed Scottie, as his eyes move slowly up and down Willie-Mays' skinny frame.

Now, I admit to hearing "nigger" muttered a thousand times in my first seven years and have used the word quite a bit myself. I even yelled the word earlier today, at a friend in his parents' car after he called me one while I was walking. The word's true meaning never occurred to me until now, when I hear the way Scottie says it and see the way it makes Willie-Mays Simpkins' jolly face cloud over and his rounded, laughing eyes slide into narrow slits.

"Nigger boy, you know better than to come this far up The Ditch," adds Joey, disregarding the obvious fact I am the one who drifted further than normal—as if anything is wrong with either intrusion.

"We're just talkin' about ways to catch crawdads," I begin, before Scottie interrupts again.

"Yeah, I saw the nigger take your crawdad," he says, turning to me. "It's good ya made 'im give it back. We can't let niggers start to gittin' uppity."

The "nigger" talk between me and my friends had always seemed like harmless taunting. The meanness I was hearing now was the same as I had heard from other kids' mamas and daddies but hadn't really paid much attention to, like "niggers are startin' to think they got rights or something" and "we should run off all the uppity niggers we can, and take care of the rest who don't git the message."

Willie-Mays has fallen silent since my friends arrived, but I sense his anger seething just below the surface. Seeing the hate and anger in my friends' faces, I feel alone. I am standing on an island between two worlds, neither of which I understand.

I start to tell my friends to shut up, but something holds me back. I turn in time to see Willie-Mays, his head bowed, slowly wading away from us.

"The nigger's got a yellow streak on his ass," sneers Scottie in a voice loud enough for Willie-Mays to hear. He appears about to say something else, but I silence him with a look darker than Willie-Mays' skin.

As I watch Willie-Mays slosh through The Ditch, I notice his clothing for the first time. He is wearing a faded t-shirt and shreds of cloth that can barely pass for shorts. Kids don't really care what other kids wear, and I hadn't noticed his tattered clothing before he trudged away. For some reason, I think I will remember his for a long time.

Just before reaching his friends, he turns in my direction. Pausing a moment, he raises his hand in a quick wave. Even in the distance, I can see the half-smile that lights up his dark face.

I look down and see my bucket is filled with a dozen or so extra crawdads, gifts from my black friend. I wave back. I hope to remember this moment forever.

As the sun dips below the horizon, Scottie and Joey head home for supper. They ask if I want to meet them later to play hide-and-seek. I say maybe, but have already made up my mind I won't be playing with them again—at least not until tomorrow. It's time for me to go home too, but I decide to walk across The Ditch and into the woods to play—and think—a little longer. It hits me as strange that I can go into the woods any time, but a similar choice to step into "my" world doesn't exist for Willie and other Negro kids.

I crawl into one of our forts and find a flashlight we have stashed. I begin playing with plastic army men I keep on hand. I stick the flashlight in a slat above the dirt floor and line up the soldiers. Playing like it's a night raid, I pelt them with dirt clods. After knocking the last one to the ground, I set them all up again and repeat the bombing. As I throw dirt clods over and over, I replay all that has happened today. I don't notice the darkness settling in outside until the flashlight dims and burns out. Stepping outside the fort, I'm covered by a shroud of complete and utter darkness. "Geez," I think to myself. "It must be really late. Supper's got to be done and gone."

A voice calling out in the distance makes me jump. As the sound draws closer, I recognize it as my daddy's voice. About to answer, I remember my pledge to Mama that I will be home before dark. I have overshot this promise by an hour, probably two. I know the ramifications will include swift and painful punishment.

As my daddy approaches, I decide I need more time to come up with a reasonable excuse. Besides, I figure the consequences won't get worse if I come home a little later. I scurry behind a mound of Bermuda grass and crouch.

The intense light of the full moon lights up my daddy's face as he enters the clearing next to my fort. His scared, frenzied look startles me.

The novelty of seeing fear in my daddy's face is so foreign to me that I freeze in place. "This can't be good for me," I say to myself. So I stay still even when Daddy moves to within five feet of me. I can see the desperation in his eyes, and as he looks toward me I'm sure he can see the puzzlement in mine.

But he sees nothing, as the darkness of night forms a black shield between him and me. "Son, if you're here, come on out," he pleads. "Please. I'm not mad."

Now, every kid has heard his mom or dad say they weren't mad in situations similar to this one. We kids know better—they are always mad, and it's better to avoid their immediate wrath so their anger has time to dissipate.

But it's my father's use of the word "please" that confuses me. Daddy is a kind and courteous man, but isn't one to use conversational manners. At the dinner table he has only to say a name and follow up with a look, and what he wants is passed to him. In my recollection, he has never thanked anybody out loud, just nodded his head. This unspoken communication is accepted and understood by all of us except Christine, who always seems to need more assurance.

As startled as I am by his use of the word "please," I'm more alarmed by the pleading tone in his voice. My daddy is all about a slow and steady pace in everything. His actions are smooth and methodical, and his words are even and textured with a slight baritone drawl thrown in. But there is nothing smooth about his movements and voice this evening, as he stands wringing his hands together and saying "please" with the shrillness of an inexperienced tenor. I sense in the back of my young mind a different fear, not of me facing a whipping but of something deeper and far more dangerous.

But whatever concern I have cannot force me from the safety of the thicket. I wait, my heartbeats sounding like clangs from a Sunday morning church bell, until my daddy starts walking downstream along The Ditch. He looks in all directions upon discovering my pail of crawdads, which he must recognize as mine by the sigh he lets out. He takes one more look over his shoulder before disappearing into the night. I hear him calling out to me, his voice sounding like that of a wounded animal before fading in the distance.

His voice resembles the wailing I heard a few days ago while walking with Mama past funeral services at the Cottage Way Cemetery. She told me two brothers near my age were being buried and that it was their parents' shrill cries I was hearing.

I hope whatever is bothering Daddy will lessen by the time I make my way home along my "secret" route. This path, which I use after school to evade pesky girls and neighborhood bullies, is a winding, circuitous passageway through the edge of the woods. I will emerge from the woods behind the old Benton place, follow the fence rimming the property, and catch the county road back to Cottage Way, which I will follow to the tributary streets spilling into Farmington Court.

I soon realize why I never take this route after dark. Though I know the way through the woods like I know my own reflection, I am lost when daytime's mirror is blackened by night. Cursing myself for not having a backup flashlight, I make my way cautiously along the path, ducking where I can make out shadows of low-hanging branches of the southern pines and white-ash birches rimming the trail. As I paw through, I feel the full intensity of the Southern summer heat on this windless, breathless evening. The stifling humidity, which hovered unnoticed while I played earlier, is now held captive near the ground by the dense forest. The heat covers me like a prickly, woolen blanket. I alternate between wiping sticky sweat from my brow and scratching the mosquito bites on both legs and the back of my neck.

But what I can't see or touch bothers me most. I guess it's the yips, something a kid feels when he's scared for no good reason. The hair on the back of my neck stands on end and I don't know why.

Then I know what I didn't before—the reason the strange fear existed in my daddy's pleading voice. It was coming back to me like a dream—actually, a dream my brother Peter had a few nights before.

My brother has "light" and "dark" dreams, as he likes to call them, and he only tells me of the "light" ones. I once asked him why. "Good dreams can show the light to others and should be passed on," he shrugged. "The dark ones should be kept to ourselves."

I loved to hear my brother describe his "good" dreams because they were often adventure-filled sojourns pulsating with vibrant, heroic characters such as pirates, gladiators, cowboys, and Indians. Though he didn't talk about his dark dreams, I knew when he had them. He would call out in his sleep from the bunk below me, and sometimes I heard him scream. Often, Mama would come to calm him. She seemed to know what he was seeing in his dreams. My brother never described to me what he saw on those nights.

Well, almost never.

Two nights ago, I was under my covers, trusty Coleman flashlight in hand and deep into my third *Sgt. Fury* comic book of the evening. I heard his uneven, restless breathing stop, become interrupted, and then cease altogether. When it began again in accelerated, panting rasps, I knew he had awakened from a dream. His labored breathing suggested it wasn't a good one.

I leaned down from my bunk to see what was going on, expecting him to wave his hand and tell me to go back to Sergeant Fury. He was mouthing words but nothing was coming out. Finally, he noticed my face and raised himself to a sitting position. His words came out in raspy whispers, sounding as if they were individual secrets.

"Billy and John-Rooney were talking to me, but nothin' was coming out. They started motioning with their hands, pointing to something I couldn't see." His voice, though still a whisper, picked up speed. "They were in a cemetery standing near two freshly covered graves and looking down into a recently-dug hole in the ground."

My head, struggling to transition from Sergeant Fury to Peter's ramblings, finally locked into what my brother was saying. A week ago, the Wilkins brothers, Billy and John-Rooney, were found strangled and buried in shallow graves in a wooded area on the other end of town. The funeral services Mama and I had passed were theirs.

My brother was in the same sixth grade class as Billy, but I didn't know him or his brother, as they lived two neighborhoods away in a huge brick house among other big brick houses in the "rich" area of town. They might as well have lived on another planet.

But John-Rooney shared one part of this world with my friends and me—The Ditch. I had seen him in our communal canal but had never spoken to him. There was talk he disappeared on his way home from The Ditch; his brother had also gone missing after being sent out by his parents to find him.

Peter looked straight ahead at the bottom of my bunk as if I wasn't in the room, and continued his dream recollections as though he no longer had any control over them.

"Billy and John-Rooney disappeared from beside the freshly dug grave, and then a man appeared in the cemetery. I couldn't make out his face but thought I knew him. As I looked over his shoulder at the graves, I saw pictures of Billy and John-Rooney on two of them. The third grave, the freshly dug one, didn't have a picture on it.

"The man began to speak. I knew his voice but couldn't place it. 'I needed to bury them because God said they needed to be in the ground right away,'" the man said. "'But God wanted them to be found so they could get a Christian burial. I wanted them to be found.' I tried to get in front of the man to see his face, but the scene kept spinning so that his back was always to me. If I got just one more look, I knew I would know who he was."

Peter looked past me, lost in thought.

"But who'd ya think was in the third grave?" I asked, my words startling Peter out of his trance-like state. He reacted like it was the first time he knew I had been listening.

"What?" he asked. "What did you say?"

"The grave. Who was in the third grave?"

"It looked like…" he began, then stopped in mid-sentence. "I don't know. I don't know," he said, yelling his second denial so loud that we both lay there silently, listening to hear if either of our parents had awakened.

"I don't know," he whispered, his control, if not his composure, returning. "But I don't want you going into the woods, do you hear me?"

"Ah, I hardly ever go into the woods," I lied.

"And The Ditch. Stay away from it, too."

When Peter ordered me to avoid The Ditch, I knew something was up. My brother understood The Ditch's mystique, as he had practically lived in it when he was my age.

"Who was in the third grave?" I asked, one last time.

Ignoring my question, he repeated, "Stay out of The Ditch and woods, you hear?"

"But they were found in the woods across town," I said.

"It don't matter," he repeated, his voice almost a hiss at this point. "Stay away." The "big brother" tone in his voice made it clear that this discussion was done.

I thought about what he had said for a few minutes. I leaned over to ask him one last thing, about the face and voice of the man in his dream. My brother was still awake and lying on his side, his eyes wide open and staring at something on his nightstand. I looked down to see that he had turned toward him a black-and-white photo of two kids, the bigger one holding a fishing pole and the smaller one holding a stringer of fish.

A photo of him and me, he was looking at it like he may never see the scene again.

I didn't ask him any more questions.

I ventured to The Ditch the next day anyway. And the day after, I went again.

And here I am tonight, hunched over in the dark in the very woods Peter had warned me about. My stomach gurgles and rolls from hunger and anxiety, and I begin to hear the darkness come alive with odd sounds. I'm definitely feeling the effects of the yips now, caused by fear of the unseen in the unknown of the dark.

I convince myself that the mixture of creaks and rattles are just natural sounds of nature at night, when I hear a very *unnatural* nature noise—a voice.

"Where ya at, boy?" a man's voice calls out in a soft, almost sickeningly sweet tone. I think I recognize it but can't quite place it. It has a familiar ring but also something is foreign about it. Maybe it's time to give up and let this searcher take me home. I'm hungry, tired, and a little bit scared. I guess I can face a whippin' if I have to.

I make a move to stand up and cry out, when a bony hand clamps over my mouth and I feel something hard and wiry tighten around my chest.

"Suuu" is whispered softly in my ear. I guess "Suuu" means "Shhh," and I realize the missing h's have a familiar ring. My growing terror dissipates when my eyes focus in the moonlight and I am able to make out a black hand and arm, and then a pair of white bulging eyes. I'm about to call out Willie-Mays Simpkins' famous first name, until I notice his forefinger pressed perpendicular to his lips.

The man's voice sounds again, closer this time. "Shit, boy," he spits out in a different, darker tone. "Where are ya? I'm a runnin' out of patience. Come and git what I got to give ya, ya hear."

I turn to Willie-Mays and he is already turning his head back and forth. I understand then that the man is after Willie, not me. This is about as much as my seven-year-old mind can comprehend, but the scared look in Willie's eyes tells me I, too, have reason to fear this man whose voice wavers between sweet and scary.

We sit motionless in the brush, waiting for the man's voice to drift further away so we can run in the other direction—*any* other direction. Instead, we hear his footsteps growing closer in the dark. As I try not to breathe, I feel something crawling over my lower body and stinging my feet. I realize what it is right away.

I'm sitting smack in the middle of a mound of red ants, and they are angry about my butt being on top of them. I try not to react too much, but the stinging is quickly becoming unbearable. I wipe away a few of the ants as quietly as I can but the obedient soldiers signal for reinforcements, and they are coming at me in an attacking frenzy.

Willie-Mays is crouched just a couple of feet away but isn't affected by the ants. He gives me a helpless look matching my own, as he can do nothing to ease my distress without drawing attention to our position.

I glance through an opening in the thicket and notice the man is standing about fifteen feet away, his upper body hidden in the shadows created by the full moon. With ants now stinging the bumps that have formed, I cannot hold out much longer.

Willie-Mays realizes this too. He slowly reaches for a two-foot-long stick, and using a grenade-throwing motion tosses it in a high, half-moon arc to the other side of the clearing. I cannot help but think this skinny black kid must have played army in his neighborhood too. I guess all kids, black and white, dream of vanquishing their enemies and saving the world.

At this moment, Willie-Mays is trying to save *our* world. The man, facing us at the time, suddenly whirls in the direction of the crash in the bushes. Seeing him turn and move away, I twirl on the ground trying to shake the ants off my body and soothe the bites in the humidity-moistened grass. Willie-Mays leans over and rubs my legs and feet, helping to dislodge the last of the ants.

I look over Willie-Mays' shoulder and confirm that the man has disappeared into the thicket. He didn't hear us move—and he has gone away! About to whisper my thanks to Willie-Mays, I see in his eyes that he doesn't think the danger has passed.

I peer closer at his eyes and realize they look like they belong to someone older, someone who has seen a lot of danger. I recall the fear and hurt in them when my friends called him names and chastised me for "getting too close to a nigger."

Willie-Mays is right about the remaining level of danger. The man, only briefly thrown off-track by Willie's stick, bursts out of the bushes and charges in our direction.

I freeze in a crouching position, transfixed by the on-rushing figure coming at us like a run-away rhino. Willie-Mays grabs me by the front of my shirt and yells, "You's gotta run…we's got to go different ways, so 'e won't git us both. Git out of 'ere!"

My head spinning by all the commotion, I stumble to my feet and try to choose a path in the dark. Seeing my indecision, Willie-Mays picks a direction for me. But instead of running away from the man, he runs straight toward him. Willie-Mays wants to make sure the man doesn't see me and his ploy works.

Just before he reaches him, Willie-Mays makes a left feint and then a 360-degree whirl to the right, faking the man to his knees. As the man stumbles after him, I stand safely in the shadows, trembling uncontrollably despite the late summer heat.

I want to head in the direction of my friend's frantic flight, but have no energy to do so. In a zombie-like state I make my way home, arriving shortly after midnight. Tired, hungry, and bleeding from mosquito bites, I don't notice right away the hug Mama gives me when I walk through the door. I barely pay attention when Daddy takes me brusquely over his knee and paddles my bottom. Afterward, I notice his eyes are teary as he squeezes me to his chest in an embrace I wish will never end.

As I lay in bed, listening to my brother's uneven, dream-filled sleep, I think back to Willie-Mays, who was just another nameless "nigger" to me when the day started but had turned into my savior by nightfall. Will I ever get the chance to repay him?

I wish the above story ended with me meeting up later with Willie-Mays and thanking him for saving my life. I wouldn't get that meeting, at least not in this lifetime. Willie's body, with two broken arms and a splintered neck, was found the next day near where we confronted the familiar voice.

I didn't hear about Willie's death from anyone in our neighborhood, and I doubt it was mentioned in the newspaper. I probably never would have known what became of my black friend had I not talked to one of the black kids hanging out at The Ditch.

The kid, Sherman, approached me the first time I was able to sneak back to The Ditch, a few weeks after that sad night. He told me Willie-Mays had stayed out after everyone else had gone home so he could collect more crawfish for his family's supper. "He talk to me before I went and gone home, and said you wasn't like any white boy that had talk to him befo'. He say you was right pleasant."

Back then, I didn't know what lesson to take from meeting Willie-Mays Simpkins. I did begin greeting everybody with a "howdy," without the "h." Ever since, when people ask why, I simply say I learned it from a friend who taught me how to escape.

"Escape what," they invariably ask.

"From crawdad pinchers," I reply.

I bawled when I heard my friend for one day had died. I blamed myself. He had stayed out later to replace the crawfish he had given me. Then he stepped in front of the Boogeyman and gave his life to save mine.

It was the first time I had ever cried in response to creating someone else's pain.

It would not be the last time.

Chapter 3

PETER

$\mathcal{M}$ama liked to say Peter's war with conventional society began in his teen years, when he battled the church brass over his youth ministry. "Peter started his weird religious stuff after he couldn't get along with normal religious folk," she said, to anybody who would listen.

My brother never told me directly, but I believe his disenchantment with organized religion and general society started earlier. I think it can be traced to a memory made in a barbershop on the outskirts of Mobile.

Peter loved when Daddy took him to get his weekly haircut at "Ol' Tom" Gilley's two-chair shop down the road. Though he needed to have his hair cut at most once a month, Peter begged Daddy to take him more often. He relished everything about the experience—the whirring of the clippers, the little snipping Ol' Tom did around his ears, and the shaving of his neck (as the buzzing gave him goose bumps all over his body).

Peter especially liked the perks that went with getting his hair cut at Ol' Tom's shop. Ol' Tom catered to kids, offering discounts for cuts on Saturdays and handing out candy and toys afterward. Peter liked the soft, thick peppermint sticks the best, spinning them around in his mouth to emulate the twirling barber pole greeting customers outside.

Peter didn't mind the usual wait upon arrival at the shop. Peggy, who cut the girls' hair, took Saturdays off and Peter liked that no annoying girls were around. Ol' Tom had lots of toys and games for Peter and the other boys to play with while waiting their turns.

One particular Saturday, no other kids were in the shop when Daddy dropped Peter off and walked around the corner to Penn Boys hardware store. I wanted to stay, because Ol' Tom liked to give free candy and toys even if you weren't getting your hair cut. But Daddy had taken to keeping me near since my close call in the woods a few weeks earlier. As I was ushered out of the shop, I looked over my shoulder with envy at my brother.

Peter sensed something was different about Ol' Tom from the moment he sat in the barber chair. As usual, the barber and the entire shop smelled of Old Spice, the only aftershave Daddy used and a scent Peter loved. Peter recalled the Old Spice scent was especially strong on this day, "like someone had spilled it all over the place."

Peter watched as the old barber teetered a bit when tying the bib around his neck, and then noticed a sharp, pungent odor cutting through the Old Spice. He couldn't place it at first, but when Ol' Tom leaned closer—closer than usual—Peter recognized it as the same smell of whiskey his drunken grandfather's breath smelled of during family visits to Panama City. Peter had formed few opinions about adults but hated that Grandpa Lyon always reeked of liquor and spoke harshly to his grandkids.

A towering, rounded man of more than 300 pounds, Ol' Tom normally made Peter feel at ease with his jovial manner and congenial nature. But as Peter looked up this time, he noticed Ol' Tom's eyes appeared glassy and his smile was a bit too wide. There was something scary about him today, like an evil cartoon character. Peter closed his eyes to envision a matching cartoon.

"I eventually formed a picture of Simon Bar Sinister, that creepy old man from the "Underdog" cartoons. This vision of Ol' Tom looking like Simon made me feel more comfortable and reassured 'cause then he just seemed like a cartoon character."

My brother's comfort and reassurance lasted until he opened his eyes again and saw Ol' Tom leaning over his shoulder and looking at him with lazy, glassy eyes that were nevertheless focused and intense. A feeling of unease he had never felt swept over Peter's body. Peter recalled the old man's stare as one of hunger—"like he wanted to eat me or something. I had never had anyone look at me like I was a Colonel Dixie burger."

Tom's usual jovial, easy-going voice had been replaced by an unsteady, overly friendly tone. "I bet you like Daniel Boone, don't ya, Petey my boy," said Tom, who was slurring his words so much Peter squinted, hoping to open his ears wider to hear better. "I like his sidekick Mingo. Ya know what? I'm gonna cut y'ur hair just like Ol' Mingo."

The results of Tom's handiwork were not readily observed by my daddy when he returned from the hardware store. Tom was not in the room and Daddy was surprised that the open sign outside the shop said "closed" when he and I returned. He had to look twice before seeing Peter was still in the chair. Peter had curled into a ball, his hands and arms wrapped around his head. I watched Daddy pry his arms loose, and what we saw next would have constituted a major lawsuit and criminal charges had it happened today.

Peter's hair was cut in a crude, unsteady "Mohawk," with the sides shaved jaggedly on both sides, leaving a two-inch band of hair running from the front of his forehead to the base of his neck. The shaving was uneven, with tufts of hair sticking up from both sides and tiny cuts and small abrasions appearing in several places of his scalp.

Tom walked out of his back room just as Daddy was finishing inspecting the barber's hackwork. Peter cringed at his return and leaned back into Daddy's side. Tom had rinsed off his face and was wiping it with a towel. Peter noticed that the drunken man looked calmer and less wild-eyed.

"I guess I got a little carried away," Tom shrugged, darting a glance toward Peter.

Daddy's eyes, which usually held either a mischievous sparkle or a faraway gaze of sadness, had something different in them when he looked up at the barber. My brother recalled the look as "twin lightning bolts crackling amidst cobalt skies." My daddy's blue eyes narrowed in slits, the veins on his freckled neck bulged, and his hands slowly formed into clenched fists. His entire face and body seemed to contort into something unrecognizable as our father. My brother could not say a word.

"I wanted to yell and scream and tell Daddy what the bastard had done," recalled my brother, "but I was taken aback by Daddy's look. I had never seen him stare at anyone that way—it scared me almost as much as that drunken barber."

For the first and only time in his life, Daddy came close to hitting a man. If it had been a different era, he might have contacted the authorities or sought out his own vigilante justice. Instead he picked up his silent son, cradled him in his arms, and said nothing as he walked out the door. Bewildered, I trailed closely behind.

Had my quiet, demure daddy known what else the drunken barber did to his son, he might have killed him.

The worst of what Ol' Tom did to Peter showed up not atop my brother's head, but inside. My brother did not tell Daddy or anyone else until many years later, that Ol' Tom had stuck his tongue in his ear and his hand down his pants. Peter didn't say how the fear of this unknown ugliness had kept him frozen in his seat, while the 300-pound drunken barber licked him like he was a Popsicle. His limbs felt like rubber and he couldn't seem to get them to work. When Daddy returned, he couldn't tell him what the fat monster had made him put into his mouth.

Peter had memories made for him that day lasting long after the laughter stopped from the kids at school and his hair grew out again, covering the jagged scrapes. Peter would find the scars within took the longest to heal.

A few months later, my brother and I had the answer to the familiar voice and smell we had associated with the "Back Woods Killer." Ol' Tom Gilley was pulled over by the local sheriff for suspected drunken driving after he was observed shakily steering his station wagon toward the Back Woods. After giving Ol' Tom the customary five-minute talkin' to and directing him to "drive straight home," the sheriff spotted rope, a shovel, and a large hunting knife on his back seat. Not so unusual during the deer hunting season occurring at that time. But a brick-red child-sized handprint facing out the side passenger window prompted an investigation of the home Tom shared with his blind elderly mother. Evidence gathered there led to his arrest and conviction in the murders of the Rooney brothers. I never heard mention of Willie-Mays Simpkins in connection with the case.

None of our family returned to Ol' Tom's shop during the months before his arrest and subsequent closure of his barbershop. Daddy felt the best answer to someone's insult was to stop doing business with them.

"There was no such a thing as suing anybody back then, at least not in Alabama," recalled Mama. "Why, if there was, we'd been suing each other all the time in our old neighborhood."

Peter took Daddy's boycott announcement a step further. "Somebody we know better know how to cut my hair, 'cause I ain't ever goin' into another barbershop as long as I live," he said. "And when I'm older, I'm gonna grow my hair as long as I want."

"Your brother sounded awfully calm and stubborn for a kid his age," Mama said, as she related the story to me several years later. And though Mama and Daddy tried to calm his fears and change his mind—initially cajoling him with bribes and later threatening him with grounding, Peter stood defiant and resolute in his position. My parents could not fathom why Peter did not trust other barbers, but gave in when they realized their son would truly die before letting a barber touch his head.

So Mama learned to cut hair. She developed her own style, and pretty soon we were the only kids in school and the neighborhood who had slick pompadours like her idols James Dean and Elvis Presley.

And my brother, true to his pledge emanating from a deep burning anger, never stepped into another barbershop, and he allowed his hair to grow long and unchecked when he reached adulthood. And when he had kids, he never let them go to a barbershop or beauty salon, or to a regular school or anywhere else for that matter, without him being on site or in close proximity. He rarely let his kids out of his sight, and on those few occasions when they were he became overwhelmingly nervous. He told me once that this anxiety regarding his children was the only thing prayer didn't seem to help.

Peter also developed a repulsive feeling toward Old Spice aftershave, never using it. I wore it later after my daddy died, causing his memories to come wafting back. I remembered our times fishing, when the Old Spice mixed with his sweat created a briny, almost feral scent as we sat in our twelve-foot aluminum boat.

I was also reminded of our Saturday night family outings to my daddy's favorite steakhouse. Daddy would be freshly scrubbed after a day working in his garden or tinkering with his car. His thick, reddish-blond hair, its waves combed casually to one side, would be lightly gleaming with a thin coat of Brylcreem. Mama would have on her best (and only) pearl necklace and her favorite homemade perfume, a combination of honeysuckle and lavender roses grown in her back yard. But her delicate, lovingly made scent would be overwhelmed by Daddy's freshly applied Old Spice. The aroma of the captain's clipper ship cologne filling our Chevy station wagon seemed to solemnize the Saturday night ritual, and triggered my Pavlovian salivation for the dollar-ninety-nine one-pound T-bone awaiting me at the Steak Warehouse.

Peter, though, continues to request I not wear it around him, and on those occasions I forget, he simply leaves the room.

There are memories made for us we would just as soon make go away, if we could.

Chapter 4

MAMA AND DADDY

$\mathcal{M}$ama and Daddy, the two people we knew first and longest, were our biggest strangers.

When I was a child, I could tell my parents loved each other. It wasn't so much what they said to one another, for they were both reserved in the language of love. If not closely observed, their silent messages of love could be missed. I watched them closely.

Their love existed in the simple things between them—the looks they gave each other on Saturday mornings as they drank coffee and smoked cigarettes at the kitchen table; the way Daddy ran his hands through the ends of Mama's black hair when he was going to work or leaving to go fishing; how Mama playfully scolded him for eating too many fried foods, while handing him a plate full of fried fish, fried potatoes, and fried okra.

Or the times, usually on Mama's birthday or their anniversary, when I would see a single lavender rose in a vase on the kitchen table. Daddy had forty or fifty rose bushes planted in the back yard, so my mama always had fresh roses of many colors in the house. But one bush was off-limits to anything but special occasions for Mama. A hybrid my daddy grafted from three different bushes, it produced a rare, possibly even unique silver-tipped lavender rose. Blooming rarely during the year, its flowers were alone in their beauty and as fragrant as concentrated French perfume.

Anna Lee and Shell Lyon modeled how a wife and husband should love one another, giving us a lofty ideal we would all aim for during our love lives. The love and commitment I witnessed between my parents would prove to be an elusive target at which I fired blanks most of my life.

I had little idea, though, what they were thinking, what their hopes and dreams were (beyond my daddy looking forward to retiring so he and Mama could run a camping park). Though I watched them like a scientist observes butterflies in a closed jar, my two closest people were complete and total mysteries to me.

Mama and Daddy didn't seem to have a clue about us, either. They struggled to support and shape their children's destinies. It wasn't that they didn't lay a solid foundation braced by moral virtue and sound work ethics, seeing to it we attended church regularly and treated others with respect. Often reserved and taciturn toward us, they made sure we had festive birthdays and merry Christmases, along with camping trips and family vacations. They didn't feel the need, though, to understand what was going on inside of us.

My parents were products of the generations before them, sturdy people who saw the world in cold, practical terms. Living was not easy, Mama and Daddy had learned growing up on the impoverished Florida panhandle, and they still believed life was a battle for survival even after they had left behind their poverty-stricken times. Mama believed the key to a happy life was avoiding what could hurt you and surviving what did. My parents instilled a fear of the unknown to discourage us from sticking our necks out too far. By doing this, they hoped we were exposed to as little disappointment as possible.

My mother and father were not engulfed entirely by the loveless practicality of their preceding generations. They were each saved by the love of one parent—Mama, by her gentle father, and Daddy, by his sweet mother.

Mama's daddy was a drinker; toward the end he was a drunk. He wasn't ambitious, but he was a dreamer. His dreams, Mama once said, were not about money, but about beauty. And for him, beauty was the sea—more to the point, Santa Rosa Sound. He didn't have a big enough boat to venture far into the Gulf, but he knew every inch of the splendor that lapped at his family's doorstep. He made sure his beloved little girl grew to appreciate this beauty. The countless afternoons spent rowing and puttering around the bay by her daddy's side was nature's educational classroom for my mama.

If Anna Lee learned from her daddy the beauty and artistry offered by the bay's lovely setting, she learned from her mother to fear this body of water and the world beyond.

Martha Miller was cold, some say, because she came from cold— Bismarck, North Dakota. Her parents had departed South Carolina in 1893 with ambitions to reach the West Coast, where land was free and the fishing a vast, untapped dream. Her dad, Jon Miller, took an alternate route northward from the Overland Trail, for reasons still not clear. Their dream ended a thousand miles short, as they settled in Bismarck, slowed by the early onslaught of winter and my great grandmother's pregnancy. My grandma was born two months later. Plans were made to catch the railroad westward that spring, but tragedy intervened. Great-grandpa died in a farming accident, leaving Martha fatherless.

My grandma spent her early years in the bitter cold of Bismarck, before her mom met and married a textile worker from Seattle. He moved the family, which included Martha and three older brothers, to the panhandle region of Florida.

The marriage soon broke up, and Martha saw her mom break apart not long after, the threads of her dreams split apart and blowing listlessly in the coastal winds. She died suddenly from an unknown illness. Grandma Martha felt she knew the reason.

"Too much dreamin'," she told Mama once. "My mother just thought there was more to life than there really was."

My grandmother learned well from all the broken dreams splintered around her. She built a fortress of cold steel to keep her dreams from growing "too big," and to repel the dreams of others. She relished her role as mom, not to expand the minds of Anna Lee and her three brothers, but to show them the frigid, hard practicalities about life.

Having seen all vestiges of love disappear from her parents' lives, Martha looked reluctantly for a husband. She hoped to control her marriage, not with love, but with barriers to keep out all emotional attachment. And children fit into these same borders—love would be kept at arm's length, with emotions and dreams limited to what could ensure practical rewards of material success.

But she couldn't secure her fort enough to keep out Johnson Tyler.

Johnson was nothing like the ambitious, upwardly mobile man she had envisioned for herself. His limited ambitions did not extend past the horizon of Santa Rosa Sound. He was a fisherman, but only a passable one. He loved the beauty and grace of fish too much to hunt them with the ferocity needed to flourish in the profession.

Grandpa Tyler loved where the fish lived. He was entranced by the water, even when its saltiness burned his eyes as the wind whipped spray over the bow. He savored the briny taste of the Gulf, claiming it opened some inner yearning he could not describe. He described the colors as "enchanting," the first time my mama had heard that word. He was taken with the different hues, especially how they changed with their depth and how they moved in shades with the sun. He called them the "jewels of the sea."

"I told Mama about all the beautiful colors Daddy showed me one day," my mother related to me. "She let me go on and on describing the water in the new words Daddy had taught me—turquoise on top, cobalt deeper down, and shades of sapphire in between.

"My mama just shook her head when I was done talking. 'Girl, what you been seeing is fool's gold. Water is water. It ain't got no color, no matter how you look at it, no matter what fancy jewels your daddy attaches to it.'

"I wanted to cry right then and there, but I was careful not to. Your Grandma didn't take to cryin' and I didn't take to gettin' whipped for it. I went to my room, shut the door and cried into my pillow. Daddy came in a little while later, after putting his fishing gear away in the shed and washing up the best he could with volcano soap. He still smelled a bit like mullet and cut bait when he slipped into my room to give me a kiss and thank me for spending the day with him on the water. He noticed the wetness on my pillow, and saw my red-stained eyes as I turned to accept his kiss on the cheek.

"I told him, in halting words, what Mama had told me, that there was no color in the water and I should just accept the world the way it is. Daddy sighed, as he always did when forced to answer to something my mama said without sounding like he disagreed.

"'Your mama's right, I guess,' he started, searchin' for the right words. 'Water is clear; it ain't got no color. But color, the color of anything, is just a reflection of the sun on somethin'. Maybe it's our eyes playin' tricks on our heads, but we see colors everywhere there is light. I don't question the why of this. I just know what I see. And in the water, I see the most beautiful, shimmering jewels, finer than all the stuff kings and queens wear. The water—that's what they're really talkin' bout when they say 'the riches of the sea.'

"My eyes were dry now, a bit red, but wide open in wonderment, looking with love at my daddy. I hugged him, saying, 'I will always see the colors, Daddy. I will always see jewels in the water.' I felt like a princess in the arms of my daddy, the king of my world."

Like my mama, Daddy had a drunk for a father. But whereas drinking had a soothing, almost sedative effect on Mama's daddy, alcohol turned Grandpa Lyon into a brutal tyrant who terrorized his family.

"Whiskey simply brought out the monster already living inside Grandpa Lyon," noted Mama. "His past was a mystery, beyond the fact he was orphaned at a young age and taken in by a family who gave him their name but not much else. But there were clues about what started the monster growing inside him."

Locals suggested he was a decent enough guy before he went off to serve in World War I. He survived fighting in the trenches of Belleau Wood and Chateau Thierry in northern France with only a limp, but some say he carried deeper scars back to Panama City. The war that was supposed to end all wars never ended in the head of Grandpa Lyon.

Little Grandma, Mildred "Millie" Battle, met Big Grandpa a few months after he returned stateside. They both worked at the same seafood processing plant—Millie as a can packer and Grandpa as a fisherman. Millie had heard the rumors that the war wounds he brought back were more severe than a gimpy leg. However, she was drawn to the quiet way he carried his pain, feeling it indicated he possessed a caring and sensitive nature. Little Grandma felt he would respond to the tenderness she could offer.

For a while, Millie probably thought she had succeeded. He was a hard worker and a decent, if distant husband, and though they struggled for money, their early years of marriage seemed happy. They had two sons and a daughter in the first five years of their marriage. After a fourth child—a daughter who died at birth—two more sons were born, including Daddy in 1927. The sixth and last child—a son, Ronnie—was born in 1930.

Grandpa might have become the loving husband and father his wife hoped for, had he not been such a violent man when he had whiskey on his breath.

Mama said Grandpa was always a drinker, but his taste for liquor deepened after his daughter died. "By the time Shell came along," Mama recalled, "Grandpa was a full-fledged drunk, spendin' most evenings in the local shanty bar after returning from sea."

He started hitting his wife shortly after Daddy was born, and added the boys to his list soon afterward. To my mama's knowledge, he never laid a hand on his surviving girl.

Daddy never spoke of these things to his kids, but Mama told us some of the details. "His daddy's drunkenness was only surpassed by his meanness. At times, he would throw what money he had left from drinking into their burning fireplace. When he wasn't doing darn fool things like that, he was beatin' the kids or drownin' their pets out of spite."

Grandpa rarely got his hands on my daddy. Mama said Shell Sr. started working a morning paper route by age seven, partly to help his mama out and partly to avoid his daddy's wrath. In his teens, he added an after-school job at a hardware store. Daddy was small and quick, and used both attributes when his daddy arrived home drunk. The few blows he suffered occurred when he stepped in to move his mother out of harm's way.

Mama says when he was drunk, Grandpa Lyon liked to announce he was a "Frenchman," even speaking words that sounded French. "He claimed he was in France during the war, and had recuperated after the battles in a town called Lyon. 'I must be related to one of those Frenchies over there,' he would tell anyone who would listen. His drinking made him forget that he was an orphan who didn't even know his real last name."

I remember hearing these stories as I got older, and thinking that maybe his problem was he couldn't forget those sad things when he was sober.

"Grandma Lyon always said she thought he left his heart somewhere back in 'France land.' I don't know about that, but I sure think he lost his mind there."

If it was Grandpa Lyon's brutal ways that made Daddy into a stoic, workaholic kid, then it was the kindness and stubborn resolve of his tiny mother that calmed his fears and forged him into a gentle man and memorable father.

"She was like bamboo growing in the sand," Mama once told me. "She was bent and almost blown over by all that happened to her, but like bamboo swaying in the hardest hurricanes, she never broke. Sometimes, she was knocked clear to the ground, but she always popped up. And the times Grandpa dug deep to hurt her, he could never sever her roots. The painful things that would twist most others to the ground could not budge her. She was firmly anchored and passed this strength to her kids, especially your daddy."

"She was not even five foot, but she was tough and stubborn as hell," added Mama, shaking her head. "To look at her, cheerful as all get-up while doing a million things at her husband's beck and call, you would think she was the happiest woman around. That frustrated the old man, because he wanted her to be as miserable as he was."

I still recall my sister crying when we heard Grandpa had died back in Panama City. Though I was only seven and didn't know Grandpa well—he was nearly eighty when I was born—I cried too. Peter, on the other hand, had no such sentiment. "I can't bring myself to cry for a man who threw good money away and treated Grandma so badly, not to mention scaring the bejesus out of us all the time. He was just a mean old man."

Christine, who was about ten at the time but seemed much older when it came to discussing family ties, could not understand my brother's anger toward Grandpa. "Why are you saying those things? Don't you care he was Daddy's—"

"No," Peter interrupted, with finality. "I don't. He was mean to Little Grandma and Daddy, and to all of us. Why should I care if he died?"

My sister looked at him like he had just killed somebody. "Do you know what you are saying? Do you really understand?"

"Nobody liked him, not even you."

"This doesn't have to do with liking or disliking. This has to do with family." She paused to let her words leave an impression. "You know, Grandpa helped make Daddy who he is today."

"Yeah, a better man than he was."

"Well, actually, you're right. For all his bad stuff, Grandpa left a mark on Daddy that helped him become a great man and father. We cannot forget that."

My sister taught me there are few, if any sins within family beyond forgiveness.

Over the years, I had my own recollections of Grandpa Lyon. He seemed like a giant when I was little, though I was told later he was only a shade taller than Daddy. Maybe he seemed so tall because he usually wore a tall, rounded hat. When he drank, though, he often put on a fedora and spoke in a language I didn't understand.

I remember, more than anything, the musty smell of his room in the back of the house, where he slept alone on a narrow wrought iron bed resembling an army cot. He had his own cubicle-sized bathroom with a simple sink, shower, and toilet off to the side, in which I never saw anything but a straight razor, Old Spice aftershave, a small washcloth, and toilet paper. The room seemed huge when he was alive, and I always thought it was neat how Grandpa had such a big place all to himself.

When I returned on family vacations after he died, the room seemed half the size I remembered. On my last trip, when I was sixteen, I sat on his tiny bed and looked around the room. The bed's spongy springs made their familiar squeaking noises, but the tone seemed more melancholy. The only personal item I had ever seen in the room, a model of a clipper ship, was gone. For the first time, I realized there were no windows in the bedroom or bath. The room, which once seemed big enough for a king, felt more like a prison cell. As I walked toward the door and heard the creaking of the warped floorboards echoing off the bare walls, I recalled feeling like an adult for the first time. And as I looked back at the room in which Grandpa died, it was the first time I understood the definition of loneliness.

Chapter 5

DADDY'S CALIFORNIA DREAM

*W*hen I was eight, Daddy packed all of us, including our cocker spaniel, Lucky Lady, into a Ford Fairlane station wagon and moved our Southern way of life three thousand miles to his version of the Mother Lode—a Gold Country suburb in Northern California.

Daddy chose California because of what he discovered during a charity service trip with his Fraternal Order of Masons. "Your daddy fell in love with the state even before his plane landed in Sacramento," said Mama. As he gazed down through the clouds, I bet he was attracted to the bigness of it all—the small towns and large metropolitan centers, and the incredible mountains, foothills, rivers, lakes, and ocean waters stretching in all directions. He likely felt akin to a pioneer leading his family to a more fulfilling life.

Daddy's decision to uproot our family was a bold move. He took us from a South whose exquisite, lush surface visage was imploding from its long history of social evil, and transported us kicking and screaming to the Golden Land of Opportunity.

Or so my daddy thought.

This simple Southern family might as well have been moving to Istanbul or Peking, so foreign was this new land. Heck, it could have been Mars or Pluto for that matter. My brothers and sisters felt they were the ones from another planet, as the curious reactions to their accents and simple clothes suggested to our new neighbors we weren't from any parts nearby. Eventually, they adjusted in their own way, except Christine, who felt each and every injustice toward her Southern heritage.

My short time in the South left its mark, but the ink had not yet dried and the impressions were somewhat smeared. I only knew I was leaving behind the Circle, along with the gutters leading to The Ditch, and the fireflies lighting up all of my crackling hot summer nights.

The South's enduring legacy was inked indelibly into the soul and psyche of the rest of my family. They were Southerners way beyond the accents and drawls they couldn't shake. Something was inside them that had escaped me or never developed.

The salt water of the Gulf of Mexico still flowed through their veins. Daddy and Mama had a mixture of oyster and lemon juice transfusing their blood, while Christine had watermelon seeds growing within her. For Hank, every day would forever be crisp, Alabama autumn afternoons smelling of freshly cut Bermuda grass and newly laid white lime, signaling another football kickoff; or breezeless, humid Mobile summer evenings punctuated with the staccato infield chattering and hard balls snapping against soft leather, defining another timeless game of baseball. My big brother's dreams appeared to begin and end on the finely coiffed, lush green playfields of his Southern youth.

Peter's appetite for adventure was universal, one his Southern heritage neither helped nor hindered. But the forced education and insight into the injustice and evil of man he learned as a Southern child propelled his search for a higher power and eternal truth.

My parents, brothers, and sister could taste the South in their hungry dreams. I could only picture my birthplace in a dizzying prism of colorful images, from the vividly green Bermuda grass soaked by spring showers to the wedding cake white beaches along Gulf Shores. Whereas the warm Alabama spring rains had soaked deep into my family's inner being and the white sands had melded with their skin, I soon dried myself and kicked loose the sand of my Southern youth.

Sometimes, I felt I missed out on the feeling that goes with being a Southerner, with all of its breathtaking beauty, flavored history, and flawed social lessons. However, my detachment from the South allowed me to adapt to my California surroundings better than the rest of my family.

I was not locked into a Southern way of life, allowing me to avoid the cultural shock that affected the rest of my family, especially Christine.

A shy and stubborn youngster, I dodged the pitfalls of this evocative, psychedelic new world that tripped and nearly crippled my sister and brothers. Later, though, as I moved from my safe and secure childhood, I would receive an education in the light and dark faces of love every bit as forceful as the cultural shock felt by my family.

After initial adjustments to the pace, Daddy figured his family would flourish in a land offering everything necessary for the good life. However, "everything" proved too much for us. It was as if the tornado from "Wizard of Oz" took a detour from Kansas, lifting our family from its Alabama roots and dropping us woozy and disoriented to the Northern California ground.

In Christine, we had our very own Dorothy. The tornado of change and confusion blowing our family slightly off-kilter was not so kind to the delicate sensitivities of my sister. The culture jolt shook her sense of self-worth and cast her adrift, a scared Southern girl lost in a foreign Yankee land.

Christine showed subtle signs of an acutely sensitive nature even before our move west. She sucked on her thumb and pinkie until an advanced age, past when I stopped doing so. She started twisting her hair into her mouth, eventually tearing so much out of her noggin Mama had to shave her head bald. Mama and Daddy had little chance of deciphering her signals. Kid psychology then was little more than what Dr. Spock offered in his writings—and Mama and Daddy didn't read his books.

Mama, who developed in a household divided and ultimately split completely, never had the security of a mother and father who loved each other and passed this love to their children. My mama grew to fear each day, because she thought separation loomed just ahead. She passed this fear of the unknown to her children.

Most of us would learn to separate real fear from imagined. Christine, though, inherited her mother's wariness, and it manifested itself in budding low self-esteem that blossomed into an ugly flower of self-hate later in her life.

Christine turned to Daddy early for the reassurance Mama could not provide. Possibly because of his own tortured upbringing, Daddy was ill-equipped to deal with the subtle emotions of his children, especially one as sensitive as Christine.

Daddy did his best, though, to be a reassuring presence to Christine, especially during the early stages of our move from Alabama. He didn't understand Christine's pervasive need to be loved and comforted, and he didn't know how to guide her through it. He was a wait-and-see type of guy, and in this case, he hoped things worked themselves out on their own. His patient approach seemed to work, as his quiet, gentle nature soothed Christine through her early years and she flourished under his attention.

All aspects changed when Daddy's job schedule moved to the three to eleven evening swing shift, rendering him unavailable during the crucial "kid's primetime" at night. Most children could adjust to such changes, as was the case in our household—except for Christine, who treated the separation as punishment. "I must've done something wrong," she told Mama once, "'cause Daddy don't come home no more."

Failing to find the reinforcement at home her tender heart needed, Christine sought her own fairytale solution. Daddy's little Dorothy would cling to the first scarecrow she met. He would have an advanced brain, but prove to have the Tin Man's heart defect, and her tale would take a dark turn. There would appear to be no yellow brick road for her to follow, no tapping her heals in the hope that magic would bring an end to her sorrow.

∽

Daddy's determination to move his family westward, with all the inherent risks and complications, ran counter to everything we knew about him. His gutsy move was that of a bold adventurer; it wasn't just a move from his static, quiescent nature, it was an epiphany.

Despite the chauvinistic times, Daddy wasn't a macho man—except, maybe, in the way he smoked a cigarette. I was secretly enthralled by how he managed to do everything with a Raleigh no-filter jutting from the side of his mouth. He rarely handled the cigarette—he would stick one in his mouth and it stayed there almost the entire time it was lit, perched precariously on the edge of his mouth while he talked or worked with his hands, until it burned down to nearly nothing. Occasionally, he shook his head slightly or twitched the side of his lip to loosen burned ashes, but most often, the cigarette stayed glued to his lips, looking like an extension of his face.

Most memories of my daddy centered around our week-long camping trips to Far Away Lake, nestled not so far away in the foothills east of Sacramento.

I loved the entire process of camping at Far Away, especially the bustle of activity at the heart of its preparation. There was Mama's insistence on bringing every scrap of food in the house and almost every piece of furniture, and Daddy's last-second tinkering on the motor for our twelve-foot aluminum skiff. There was the sullen, scowling face of my sister, who was not into memory making at this time in her life. She would skulk around the house, making sure everyone knew the torment she was experiencing. She was the only one left, besides me, who was forced to go on our family trips. I went willingly and gladly. I enjoyed needling Christine about being separated from all her snaggletoothed boyfriends.

Then there was Mama's meticulous packing process, in which every object had its appointed place, down to where each of us sat for the ride out of Sacramento.

My daddy wheeled us eastward through the rustic towns and green-and-gold foothills of the California Gold Country, over Miwok tribal lands, and finally, up a narrow, rocky one-lane road leading to Far Away Lake, the Holy Grail of my childhood.

Spread across a watery canvass of azure blue, framed on all sides by golden slopes and crooked oaks, the panoramic view greeting me each spring never disappointed my wild anticipation. I felt a rebirth of my senses and an affirmation by God and nature that all was right with the world.

I wanted to do everything at once and right away—swim, fish, and play. So, I was always perturbed by the work and time needed to prepare the camp—the hour or so of unpacking, organizing, and pitching the tent always seemed like an eternity. Inevitably, I would get lost and absorbed by each minute detail—collecting fallen oak branches for the fire; smelling the canvass from the tent as it was first unfurled; hearing the familiar, comforting sound of the tent zipper each time it was pulled; studying Daddy in his meticulous outfitting of our fishing gear, and carrying our boat into the water.

Our camping world grew more exciting with each passing minute. On the first evening, my anticipation was nearly unbearable as Daddy and I skimmed across the lake to the first fishing hole. Then came the first tug, the first disappearing bobber, the first battle between boy and monster fish, the first six-inch bluegill held proudly by me as my father looked on quietly, a cigarette in his mouth covering the slight smile that had formed.

Then there was the walk up the hill that first night, showing off our stringer of panfish to Mama and an uncaring Christine. I held the lantern by the faucet, as Daddy cleaned the fish in the methodical, no-nonsense manner honed from his hard early life, when fishing was work and his speed with a knife meant survival for him and his family.

Later, curling up in the warmth of my cotton Coleman sleeping bag, I squinted in the dim glow of my flashlight to follow the thrilling cartoon exploits of Sergeant Fury and his Howling Commandos, eventually falling asleep dreaming of flashing red-and-white bobbers.

I looked forward to the morning camping ritual most of all. Awakened in the still, dull early light of dawn by my own anticipation or a gentle nudge from Daddy, I would emerge from the tent to see his darkened form, hatless even on the coolest morn, leaning over his Coleman stove, waiting for the hot water to boil for his coffee or already sipping the first of countless cups of the muddy brew.

Throughout my childhood, coffee and cigarettes were an inseparable part of Daddy's existence—a cigarette was a natural extension of the tips of his right thumb and forefinger, and a coffee cup seemed permanently hooked to his left hand.

After Daddy's thermos was filled with black coffee and our foam ice chest stocked with red worms, nightcrawlers, grubs, and Canada Dry Cactus Coolers (pineapple-orange sodas I treasure to this day), we would slide our boat into the water and putter through the early morning mist still hovering over the lake. The sun would reveal itself slowly, before bursting over the low-lying ridge of foothills to the east in an explosion of color and infusing the morning clouds with layers of red and orange hues.

What my daddy got out of our camping experiences or any other activity we did together, was hard to decipher. He often simply leaned back and watched silently, as I struggled against the fish and other forces of nature. He offered an occasional half-smile at my animated antics. Sometimes though, I wished he let me know what was going on behind the stillness, behind the part of him he concealed from all of us except his wife.

If anything frustrated him, it was probably his inability to relay his passion for machines to his boys. Stone and mortar were his work, and the bit-by-bit process he brought to his masonry was as much a reflection of his personality and character as anything he did in his life. But his first love, his consuming passion beyond everything else besides his wife and kids, was working with the intricacies of machines.

"If'n he was interested in doctoring people, he'd probably been great at it 'cause he could fix anything mechanical," my mom told us more than once. "He could put any type of broken-down engine back together and make it run like new. The way he could get an old motor back to running, I bet he'd been a really good heart doctor."

When Daddy wasn't working on one of the old Oldsmobiles or Chevrolets he usually had parked on the grass next to our driveway, he was tinkering with a lawn mower or a boat motor. He worked on each of his sons to interest us in the mysteries of mechanics. Hank was too into sports to buy into Daddy's mechanical dream, and I had a similar disinterest, daydreaming of playing fields and fishing holes while Daddy tried to educate me in the science of machines. I always managed to disappear when he wanted to school me in the art of changing the oil or rotating the tires on our imitation-wood-paneled Chevy station wagon or candy red Comet sedan.

His one hope was Peter, whose early spiritual bent was matched by his desire and ability to work with his hands. But Peter's first car was a Volkswagen, which Daddy balked at even letting him park at our house. "That's not a car, that's a wind-up toy," Daddy told him.

My daddy probably felt he failed as a man and a father because he was unable to pass on the two talents he had developed over a lifetime.

Chapter 6

HANK

*H*ank was not meant to be the oldest son, though his early years suggested he was born for the role. He was a natural leader in the athletic arena, playing quarterback in football, catcher in baseball, and point guard in basketball throughout his childhood. However, unlike his boyhood idol Joe Namath, he wasn't flamboyant. He was good in a workmanlike manner.

Although his dark, thick hair was always nicely groomed and framed an earnest, good-looking face, his smile made him Hollywood handsome—without the phony pretense. And it was this smile that drew the girls from an early age. They were further drawn by his eyes—dark green and set back into his head, they were dreamy bedroom invitations.

Hank initially chose to stay behind when our family moved, so he could finish his high school football career in Mobile and enroll at Namath's alma mater, The University of Alabama. As the oldest, his stakes were more firmly planted and thus harder to uproot. He eventually decided to travel west later that summer. I think he missed his family.

Hank arrived in time to wow the football coaches at Bella Sierra High with his passing skills—and the girls with his good looks. He didn't have much enthusiasm for either at first, as his heart still resided in Mobile. Though his passion was lacking, his skill was enough to earn the starting nod at quarterback. Then, at a pep rally two days before the opening game, he saw Ingrid Johansson for the first time.

From that day on, Alabama was a distant memory.

Ingrid was Head Cheerleader and Hank, upon first glance, noticed her commanding presence. Hank noted her leadership went well beyond her elected capacity—she was the focal point of the squad, for sure, but an aura of spiritual energy radiated from her.

"Though we were both leaders, I soon understood we were nothing alike," Hank told my brother later.

Hank, who was reserved, almost shy outside of the athletic arena, realized Ingrid was, in many ways, everything he was not—blonde, bubbly, and vivacious. She carried her glow wherever she went and was as comfortable in front of screaming crowds as she was in the classroom or talking with classmates, especially boys. Hank surmised Ingrid's goddess aura with his first look; he received substantiating facts about her all-around perfection from Jeff Hilburn, his wide receiver and the first friend he made at Bella Sierra.

"Pick your jaw up off the floor and stand in line, buddy," shrugged Jeff. "She not only looks perfect, she *is* perfect. She's an A student, a member of a shitload of clubs, a volunteer at the hospital—and a nice girl, to boot. Not to mention her daddy's loaded."

Hank never completely picked up his jaw as he watched the rest of her routine. "I still don't remember walking onto that gym floor with the rest of the guys or hearing the band playing our fight song," he related. "Jeff said the crowd went crazy when I was introduced and that I waved to them. Don't recall any of that. All I remember is falling for her."

Hank kept his feelings to himself, but they smoldered as the season wore on, igniting a heretofore unknown level of passion in his game and his heart. After a slow start, as he sorted out his new teammates, Hank lit a fire underneath the Mustangs that lifted them from the mediocrity of their recent seasons. Winners of seven straight games after opening with two losses, they entered their last game against Camino Real with a chance at the league title and a berth in the Sacramento County playoffs—their first such trip in two decades.

I started the game where I usually sat, wedged between my parents. They were not the rah-rah types, given to wild vocal ranting and raving. Each had their own quiet way of supporting our athletic endeavors. Daddy sat like a statue, feeling his physical presence was the ultimate show of support—even though he stood five-foot-seven and weighed 140 pounds.

My mama also had a silent approach—but one relying on an intense spiritual power she sent telepathically to us on the field. Often during my brother's games, I would see her eyes closed, her face scrunched and hands balled into tight fists. I was sure other people thought she was praying, but I knew she was willing her energy to intervene and support us.

Though I'm sure my brother appreciated my parents' support on this evening, I can say without too much doubt it wasn't their presence inspiring him.

The divining rod for him that night was the incandescent smile and curvaceous figure of Ingrid Johansson, who danced on the sideline cheering him on.

Throughout the season, when Hank made a mistake or his self-doubts started clouding his mind, he simply turned to the sideline to where Ingrid was leading her troops. Her composed, self-assured stature invariably gave him a shot of confidence, and the sight of her never failed to light his fire and fuel his effort.

Although he held this same flame for her off the field, his fire burned deep inside. He could not bring himself to approach her, managing only a mumbled "hello" while walking past her after practice or in the halls. He was usually with friends at those times. When he was alone, Hank— the hot-shot quarterback and most popular player in school—could do nothing but lower his head after meeting her gaze, then keep walking without uttering a word.

He had one class with her—American Government—and it was this fifty-minute block of time he anticipated more than anything in his day. He positioned himself in the back of the class, directly diagonal to where she sat in the front row. He rarely took his eyes off her; only when she turned in his direction did he turn away. Sometimes he wondered if she were looking at him, but quickly dismissed those thoughts as a joke.

The biggest game of his high school career started ominously—a ninety-yard kickoff return for a touchdown by Camino Real—and became worse soon afterward. Hank, sensing that his teammates' emotions were frazzled by the huge crowd and the immenseness of the game, tried to settle into the game with two running plays. On the second run, though, his sophomore halfback coughed up the ball and the fumble was run in for another touchdown. Less than a minute into the game, the Mustangs trailed fourteen to zero.

Hank made one mistake—a pass into the flat picked off by Camino's all-league safety Ronnie Wilson. But Hank fought through a block and managed a touchdown-saving tackle. Camino settled for a field goal and led twenty-four to seven at halftime.

Despite the tackle, Hank was disconsolate as he walked to the locker room. I had weaseled my way to the sideline and was about to say something, anything, to raise my brother's spirits. Someone else beat me to the inspirational punch.

"Great tackle, Hank," said a voice behind him, one he recognized as an angel come to life. "You just saved the game."

He turned to see Ingrid standing an arm's length away. He felt the cobwebs forming like cotton in his mouth, but Ingrid bridged the silence. "I can tell that you haven't given up, and the rest of the guys see it too," she said. "You're a real leader."

"But the interception..." he stammered. "Phooey," she laughed. "Hank, you showed Ronnie Wilson and the rest of them you still have heart."

Hearing Ingrid use his name and the word "heart" in the same sentence was like a dream and made Hank's head feel woozy. He was snapped to attention by two teammates who clapped him on opposite sides of his helmet and pushed him toward the locker room. He turned to say, "Thank you," as he was pulled away, but his words were drowned by the cleats clattering on the concrete. He noticed, as he turned the corner into the locker room, Ingrid was still looking in his direction.

Hank's last-ditch tackling effort lit a fire in his teammates. They stopped Camino on their first drive, and then their hulking defensive end, Tommy "Tiny" Gallagher, broke through the line and put his 310-pound bulk in front of the punt. Tiny almost flattened the ball when he fell on it in the end zone for a touchdown.

Hank took over from there, mixing short passes to his wide receivers and tight ends with runs by his running back Benny Johns. Benny, the sophomore who had fumbled in the first quarter, finished the drive with a ten-yard catch from Hank for a touchdown cutting the Bella Sierra deficit to twenty-four to twenty-one.

The teams played evenly through the rest of the third quarter and most of the final frame. The Mustangs took over on their own seven-yard line with just over a minute remaining. Hank moved them up to midfield with three precise, medium-length passes, and then called the Mustangs' last timeout.

Hank went to the sideline to discuss the last play with his coach, Vernon "Red" Watson, who played at Bella Sierra on the last team making it to the county playoffs. He had returned triumphantly a few years later to coach his alma mater. Only an adequate coach, he was a better man—thoughtful, diligent, and open-minded.

There was time for one play—a desperation pass toward the end zone some fifty-five yards away. Watson outlined a play calling for Hank to throw a high-arching ball toward the end zone, hoping for a fortunate deflection. Hank knew his strengths and accurately throwing a ball more than half the length of the field was not one of them. He thought of another idea, and outlined the play in the dirt on the sideline, like he remembered doing as a kid playing on the Circle field in Mobile. His coach was dubious, but nevertheless gave his confident quarterback the green light.

Designed to go straight at his nemesis Ronnie Wilson, the play at first appeared to be the same one Wilson disrupted with his interception at the end of the first half. Hank took the snap, rolled to the right and looked for his friend Jeff in the flat, about fifteen yards up the field. Hank knew Wilson would not be in position to intercept this one, because he was playing back for the desperation pass. But he was certain Wilson would close in fast as soon as Jeff caught the ball. In fact, Hank was counting on this certainty.

Sure enough, Wilson broke on the ball early and was on Jeff just after he caught the ball. The crowd gasped in unison as Wilson hit the receiver with a bone-rattling, game-ending tackle. But their gasp wasn't for Wilson's savage tackle ending the game. It was in response to the ball, which feathered up from Jeff's hands the split-second before he was crunched by Wilson and landed in the arms of Benny Johns, who had flared out of the backfield and trailed, unmarked, closely behind Jeff.

Wilson had also seen the ball flying sideways, but he was a train hurtling down a one-way track—in the wrong direction. He completed the tackle on Jeff, but watched hopelessly from his seat on the ground as Benny flowed past, ball tucked under his left arm.

The BS receivers formed a blocking wall along the sideline and Benny and his jets did the rest, taking off and not coming to a stop until he landed in the end zone.

As Benny outraced the last stunned Camino player and crossed the goal line, I turned to see what my brother was doing. He was standing in the middle of the field with his head down, like he always did whether he had won the game with a great play or lost it with a bad one. Then I saw him look to the sideline toward the cheerleading squad, locking his gaze on one blonde in particular. He shook his fist toward the prettiest one, who rushed on the field to embrace him before the players and fans swallowed him in a sea of red, white, and black.

Hank later called that particular moment the greatest of his life. "Geez, big brother," I said, when he told me. "That touchdown was the biggest moment of my life too, except maybe when the Jets and Joe Willie won the Super Bowl."

"Not the TD, little bro," Hank corrected. "The hug. The hug by Ingrid was it."

I was only eight at the time and hadn't been in love yet. Somehow, though, I knew exactly what he meant.

My dad smiled wide and actually stood and clapped. My mom had her eyes open and they were filled with tears of self-satisfaction, as she was sure my brother had felt her vibes and been empowered by them.

Hank and Ingrid started dating soon after and graduated side-by-side later that year. Hank did, indeed, earn a scholarship to The University of Alabama, but this time he reluctantly returned to his Southern birthplace. It didn't matter he would be learning football, the game he loved, under the tutelage of legendary Crimson Tide coach Paul "Bear" Bryant, or that he would be following in the white shoes of his hero, Joe Willie Namath.

He didn't want to leave Ingrid and she had to talk him into doing so. She convinced him by pledging to keep in touch with letters and calls—if he agreed to do the same. He had no problem with that promise and headed off with renewed excitement. Who cared if he was only fifth on the quarterback depth chart at Alabama? He had the love of the girl of his dreams to keep him going.

He returned for short periods during Christmas, Easter, and summertime breaks, quickly settling into a routine of seeing Ingrid as often as he could. She introduced him to cocktail parties and golf at her father's country club. He was uneasy, at first, in moving toward her world, afraid of not fitting in. But he observed her confidence as she moved through all worlds easily, and her strength of self rubbed off on him. He loved the way she held his hand and made him look into her eyes. The shadows had completely lifted and he could see clearly where he was going.

Ingrid begged him to try horseback riding. "Our love can withstand anything except me falling onto my head from one of your dang horses," he laughed. "Might knock some sense into you," she countered. She won, as she always did, and he learned to ride on the grassy acres surrounding her family's ranch in the foothills overlooking Sacramento.

Hank never felt fully comfortable on a horse, but he loved to watch Ingrid ride her second love Diamond. "She can do anything and everything," he mused. "And she makes it all look so easy." When she made even loving him appear effortless, he began to visualize and believe in a world with them together.

During spring break of his junior year, he decided to share with her his vision of their world together. He would tell her under "their" tree, a stately oak standing atop Diamond Ridge and overlooking two different counties. Beneath this tree, they had months before grown from boy and girl into man and woman. On this day, secure in her wrapped arms, he planned to bare secrets behind the shadows covering his eyes.

There was a vague unsettling feel in the air. "I don't know what it was," he recalled. "Maybe the grayness outlining the clouds overhead or the breeze picking up." Or maybe it was his fear of exposing Ingrid to his doubts and dreams.

He pushed aside his self-doubts, buoyed by the feeling it was a spectacular day to be in love. The rains had been plentiful that year and the green grassy fields had not yet turned a golden brown. Wildflowers were still in bloom and the air was filled with the sweet aroma of their nectar, thanks to the industrious bees. "Before meeting her, I picked a bouquet of lilacs, purple lupine, and honeysuckle, and packed it into a small knapsack."

He rode with purpose that day, racing Ingrid to the top and winning for once. Exhausted from the exertion, they both collapsed on the ground in the shade of their tree. Hank remembered her smiling face, flushed from her ride, as perhaps more beautiful than he had ever seen it. "I knew I could not wait long, or I would lose my nerve," he recalled. "If I kept looking at such perfection, I would start doubting my worthiness."

His hands shaking, he thrust the flowers toward her, and then gave her his heart. "I don't know if you would be willing, but please marry me."

Ingrid accepted the flowers and his heart, shaking her head. "Silly, silly man," she laughed, through tears rolling down her cheeks. "You know I will marry you."

"Ingrid!"

Hank's yell of pure exultation resounded down both sides of the ridge, echoing into both El Dorado and Sacramento counties.

My brother and Ingrid made love underneath their comforting tree. They did not feel the rain at first, but Ingrid mentioned she had heard thunder sometime earlier. By the time they felt the first raindrops filtering through the branches of the big oak, the trails were already muddy from water running downhill. They rode down steadily together, showing respect for the sloppy footing. But their giddiness eventually got the better of them and the ecstatic lovers took turns racing ahead of each other down the trail.

"I'll beat you again, slow poke," shouted Hank.

"No way, silly boy…not twice in your life," Ingrid yelled.

In their rush to reach the bottom to share their news, they forgot about the wet path.

Riding hard enough to lead again, Hank sped around a slight turn. He saw the limb too late, swerving hard to miss a ten-foot long oak tree branch lying jagged across the bend in the trail. As he pulled off, he saw Ingrid flash by.

Seeing Hank on one side of the trail, Ingrid twisted Diamond in the other direction. The diligent horse tried to jump the lower end of the branch, but seemed to struggle lifting from the muddy terrain. Still he almost made it, clipping the branch with his trailing hoof. Diamond pitched forward and to the right, lurching toward a large, jutting rock. Ingrid pulled back on the reins, but Hank could see her maneuver would not be sufficient to stop Diamond's momentum. Diamond's right shoulder hit the rock at a ninety-degree angle, jerking Ingrid out of her stirrups and over the horse's right side. Hank saw her still battling, as she shortened the reins just before she slid completely over to Diamond's other side, and out of sight. Horse and woman disappeared over the edge in a splattering of mud and water.

As the debris settled, Hank rushed across the trail and peered down the hill. A short distance away, he saw Diamond standing, alone, in chest-deep brush. His heart started beating again and he blew out a big gush of repressed air when he saw Ingrid's hand, her arm, and then her head as she pulled herself back onto the saddle. She had managed to hang on to Diamond's neck with one arm and avoid crashing into the massive boulder on her right. She was breathing heavily and rubbing Diamond's head.

"I saw her smile light up her face and I knew she was OK," Hank recalled. "I patted Dixie on the side of her mane to calm her, then walked her toward Ingrid and Diamond."

He then saw Ingrid turn around and pull hard on Diamond's reins. It appeared to Hank she was still trying to assess any damage to her second love. Hank saw Diamond shuffle his front two legs, then raise them a foot off the ground.

"I heard Ingrid use a tone I didn't recognize, because of its sharpness. I looked underneath Diamond, and then I saw it, framed between his two front legs."

"It" was a Diamondback rattlesnake, coiled up against the rock face. Diamondbacks, though plentiful in these foothills, normally do not pose a problem because they skitter off when humans or horses come their way. But this one had been surprised by the awkward swerve of Diamond into its sunning spot. And Diamond had been equally surprised he had fallen into the snake's den. He rose again, but his jerky, abrupt movement caused his right rear hoof to slip on the wet trail.

Hank watched as Ingrid fought to stay in control, saw her lean back and to her left to keep Diamond from falling right. He saw her momentarily level Diamond out, but then his right leg slipped and Diamond's right shoulder dipped forward, carrying Ingrid with him as he crashed forward. He fell against the rock, pinning her at the base of the boulder.

"I knew it was bad," he said. "I rushed forward and tried to move Diamond aside." But the big horse was stunned from the impact against the boulder and did not respond to Hank's initial coaxing. Remembering his athletic background and the lessons in poise he learned from his girlfriend, Hank breathed deeply to compose himself.

"I took a couple of steps back, lowered my left shoulder and took a running start at Diamond's flank."

Hank had amazed his coaches and teammates with his impressive strength in blocking drills. His coach told him he had never seen a quarterback push a blocking sled as far as Hank could. My brother's prowess paid off. Hank hit Diamond's hind end with explosive force, then kept churning his legs as he heard the coaches in his head, yelling at him to finish his block. He was brought back to reality by a moan beneath him. He was standing over Ingrid now, with Diamond, still unmoving, pushed five feet away.

Ingrid was wedged under the rock, her head tilted tellingly forward and her eyes closed. Hank knew she needed help and he shouldn't move her. He had trouble finding a pulse and was in the process of trying again when her eyes flickered open.

He was startled at the dullness in her eyes, which had always sparkled like stars on a cloudless night and pointed him toward hope. She moved her lips, but he told her to save her strength. She smiled slightly, grimacing from the effort. "Always trying to save the world, trying to make things easier for everybody else," she said, her words coming out in struggling, raspy whispers.

"Quiet," my brother ordered softly, trying to stop the shaking he thought Ingrid would feel in him. "I'll go get help." She closed her eyes briefly before reopening them. She tried to shake her head "no," but her neck wouldn't move. "No, stay here," she whispered.

"But I…" he started, but Ingrid raised her voice slightly. "Stay here. And hold me. Please." There was urgency, but no desperation, in her tone.

Hank stopped fighting her. "I sat next to her, putting one hand around the back of her neck and the other around her waist." He felt like he was holding a broken porcelain doll. "I was afraid to pull her closer, for fear of breaking her further."

Reading his mind as she usually could, Ingrid smiled and whispered in a voice clear but growing fainter, "I'm broken already. You can't hurt me. So hold me. Hold me close."

Hank pulled her close before she could see the tears rolling down his face. She didn't say another word, as the life blew out of her and she died in his arms.

My brother, who would later save Mama and others, could not save his true love. And for the second time that day, he yelled "Ingrid" at the top of his range. This time it was not exultation, but a moaning, mournful wail that shook the surrounding mountains.

The Johanssons buried their daughter beside her horse in a field of wild flowers through which she loved to ride.

My brother vowed never to ride a horse again, though his friends and the Johanssons tried to help him with his guilt. But he could not be consoled. Too heartbroken to focus on football or school, he never returned to The Crimson Tide of Alabama.

He drifted through his twenties with the bitterness of an old man looking back on a lifetime of failure. Although our family saw his gradual bend toward drinking, then total fall into alcoholism and despair, we did little to intervene. As was the Lyon trademark, we talked amongst ourselves about his unraveling, but figured he would come to his senses or someone would step in and lead him toward the right path. It would not be until much later that we would understand and use the power of love and healing existing between us. We would not learn to be a family until fate and failure taught us more tragic lessons.

Chapter 7

CHRISTINE THE MEMORY MAKER

I have often been told I live too much in the past, and that I cannot move forward because I'm always looking behind me. It's true, but I'm not sure why. Perhaps I'm afraid of what the future might bring because of my proven ability to make stupid decisions.

My sister Christine held a different take on the importance of history, even as a kid. She used to pull me aside when we were doing something special, and excitedly whisper, "We're making memories, Stone. We're making *forever* memories!"

For my sister, there wasn't an event too small or a moment too short to "make a memory." Everything mattered, everything left an impression. She recalled the days we walked home after school, kicking rocks in the drain and talking to all of the dogs behind the fences. She remembered the nights we joined the neighborhood kids to play hide and seek, hiding behind garbage cans and bushes, or ducking in the shadows created by the shine of the moon or the flickering light from the street lamp on one end of the Circle field.

Whenever I wanted to relive growing up in the South, I merely brought up a tidbit I barely remembered. Christine would then weave a tapestry of vivid, colorful memories, a kaleidoscope of descriptive imagery touching all of my senses.

I could say "ice cream," and her words returned us to our huge back yard in Mobile. "Our family is gathered around Hank, as he grunts through the last turns of the steel crank in our faded, but perfectly wonderful wooden ice cream maker. Mama hurries about, getting everything ready, and Daddy just sits back, coring an apple with his pen knife, watching the whole scene with a quiet smile. Stone, everybody laughs at how big your eyes grow as the crank becomes harder for Hank to turn, and how you can barely sit still while waiting that extra hour for the ice cream to ripen. After the time finally passes, your fingers turn blue from shoveling the salted ice aside as Hank detaches the cranking mechanism."

Christine knows to say just enough to prompt me to recall my own stories. "Don't stop," I scream, my hands shaking. "Don't you remember how cold the ice cream was? How Daddy would take turns giving us the churning blade, pulling it from the middle of the metal tank so we could lick off the sweetest part of the ice cream? Or how we ate our ice cream so fast our temples throbbed to the point we felt our heads would fall off? And how, five minutes later, we ate our second bowl just as fast and our heads froze *again*!"

At this point, Christine taps her head. "It's all up here," she says. "Just close your eyes and think back, and you will see everything clearly. You made these memories too."

Growing up, I rarely thought of Christine as my "big" sister. Her tiny physical stature (peaking at five feet tall at age thirteen) and our slim two-year age difference, coupled with her struggles involving self-esteem, made me often think she was my younger sister. But when she spun stories and painted pictures so vivid I could see them in living color, I felt like a little kid in the midst of a wise sage.

Her favorite memories focus on watermelons—specifically, the elongated ones she remembered from the South. At the mere mention or sight of this fruit, her eyes glaze over and she launches into her melon mantra. This recollection is uniquely hers—she didn't just pique my memory base with small details, she painted a permanent mosaic.

"Watermelons were the essence of my youth," she likes to say. "I can still hear Daddy's first cut into the melon and the hollow cracking noise moments later when its own weight split itself open." As her story gathers steam, she acquires a distant, faraway look. I can almost see her shrink in front of my eyes, to the tiny freckle-faced girl covered in red curls, her gap-toothed smile making her rounded cheeks even rounder, and her aqua-green eyes widening like two over-flowing mountain pools.

"In my mind," she says, "spring and summer will always be built around watermelons, with all of us leaning forward in our white wooden chairs, so the melon juice drips between our legs and we can spit the seeds into the grass."

Watermelons were the connection to her Southern past, her link to family togetherness. Later, she tried to pass these memories to her own family. Her house became a shrine to the beloved watermelon, with every conceivable knickknack or kitchen item having a melon connection: decanters, bowls, salt and pepper shakers, cookie jars, place mats, shower and kitchen curtains, kitchen wallpaper—even her pajamas, which she made herself.

There were no honeydews in her collection, I pointed out to her one day. "Those are *California* melons," she explained, emphasizing "California" like it was a bad smell. "They are yellow, bland, and boring." I knew, then, her love for watermelons had nothing to do with the fruit, and everything to do with her fondness for the South, the final resting place for all memories worth remembering. To her, "making memories" was a way of preserving the good times when the present wasn't so good.

But she found that not all memories are of our own making. Some are thrust upon us and become ones we would just as soon forget. These unwelcome memories, forged for her as a tenuous teen bride and a battle-hardened housewife, ultimately led to consequences testing the furthest boundaries of love in our family.

⎯⎯⎯⎯

I have heard from several female acquaintances that a woman hopes to marry a man in the image of her father, while hoping she does not end up acting like her mother. There seems to be a crooked, self-defeating flaw in this logic.

My sister did not see the bend in this line of thinking. Attributing much of her unfulfilled childhood to an indifferent mother, Christine searched for a man resembling her loving daddy to fill the void of what she lost growing up. In her haste to leave a memorable, but painful childhood, she set her sights on the first man who reminded her of Daddy. She found him in a shy, darkly handsome boy one grade ahead of her at Bella Sierra.

On first appearance, Jonathan was as different from Daddy as darkness is to light. At an even six feet, Jonathan stood five inches above Daddy. Whereas there was a lightness about Daddy's pale skin, slight features and wavy, blondish-red hair intertwined with gray, Jonathan countered with olive skin, a thick, dark mane of black hair and long, lustrous eyelashes brushing against eyes of polished, darkened jade. Daddy's cobalt blue eyes were no less mysterious, but seemed to be a doorway to openness. Jonathan's brooding eyes seemed an impenetrable wall that did not invite questions or portend answers.

If Jonathan's tall, dark, and mysterious differences weren't enough to attract Christine, his similarities to Daddy sealed the deal. Descending from large families with mothers who were both sweet and forgiving, each man emerged with a quiet, serious-minded disposition and a strong, dedicated work ethic.

One of my sister's fondest memories was being held in Daddy's outstretched arms at Gulf Shores, feeling his focused, solid strength as she laughed and playfully kicked the waves. She felt this same strength and security from Jonathan's embrace.

As she grew to know her first love, Christine discovered that his quiet nature was shielding pent-up pain from a harrowing childhood. While Daddy somehow overcame his troubled upbringing, Jonathan had not healed so thoroughly from the wounds of his past. Christine would soon feel the brunt of his childhood damage, and find her belief in the wonderment of memories challenged to its very core.

Chapter 8

PETER THE PREACHER

$\mathcal{P}$eter didn't start out with the goal of becoming one of the chosen messiahs of the North American continent, with the spiritual responsibility to lead his followers to the highest ground when the world imploded under the weight of its own evil and flood waters covered most of the land. His quest began in a more conventional vein—as a youth leader in the small interdenominational church we attended in Folsom.

Christine believed Peter was a natural-born spiritual leader. "His magnetism was evident from the start, as he quickly organized intense, unorthodox bible study classes that emphasized questioning, then reaffirming the words of God. But his music classes proved the biggest hit with me and the rest of the other kids in our church."

Peter introduced new, faster-tempo songs focusing on spiritual energy and interaction. "But his 'look' was what really excited the kids," related Christine. "His black hair flowing to the middle of his back, along with his jeans-and-t-shirt wardrobe, were instant attractions to the straight-laced teens in the congregation. They had missed the Psychedelic Sixties and weren't getting any history lessons from their uptight parents. They were eager for my brother's hip approach to Christianity.

After some initial suspicion and hesitancy, church officials and parents looked past Peter's appearance and gave their whole-hearted approval to his efforts. Youth attendance was higher than ever during the services, and his bible study and music groups were so packed Peter had to take on two assistants. Christine was one of them.

My parents, who were once-a-week churchgoers and low-key when it came to spiritual matters, were taken aback by their middle son's fervent church involvement. He had allowed his hair to flow freely and been espousing radical rhetoric since his first year of high school. They weren't sure what to think during the following year when he started channeling his energies toward church activities and his youth ministry.

The acme of their disbelief came when Peter mentioned that he was thinking of attending a bible college, with hopes of becoming a minister. "We didn't know how to answer him," Mama recalled. "He was never real thrilled with school, though he loved to learn new things. We never thought he would be interested in any kind of college or school past Bella Sierra. And to think he wanted to be a preacher, even if it was probably going to be a weird sort of one—well, that was almost too much to hope for."

"We started believin' Peter had the smarts to become a minister," added Mama. "He knew that Bible inside and out. Sometimes, I think he knew more than the preacher."

On occasion, my brother did indeed think he knew more than Pastor Anson Garner. Peter and Pastor Garner often had fervent discussions through the night and into early morning, with the tenor and tone sometimes rising loud enough to wake the pastor's wife. "Pastor Garner liked Peter's outspokenness and refreshing nature, "Mama continued. "He said Peter was an able challenger who kept him on his spiritual toes."

Pastor Garner's support notwithstanding, my brother's success with the kids soon made some church officials and parents uneasy. The church was wary of his unorthodox approach during bible studies, wherein he had the kids question the text and teachings of Christ. Peter answered these queries with a shrug. "Jesus taught his disciples the most by having them question the meaning of his words. The truth is still in his words and the Bible. I ask the kids to question the truth, and then I show them where they can find it."

Peter pushed self-expression in his music classes, and the resulting Christian rock band he formed was one of the first of its kind anywhere. As with anything ahead of its time, his youth band and program ran into opposition from the establishment. Church officials didn't like the rancor and unconventional nature of the music, and the parents of the young Christian rockers grew suspicious of the long hair and ragged clothes they had adopted as part of their reverence for their teacher.

My brother appeared calm in his response to the concern and criticism, but he was bristling inside. He tired of the constant judging based on his appearance. "Jesus addressed this same issue countless times in his teachings, that a person is much more than his appearance and should be judged on his heart and not his looks."

The criticism escalated when a rock band member was caught smoking pot by his parents. Hoping to avoid being sent to an out-of-state prep school, the boy told his parents that Peter had confided to the group he tried marijuana and was not against its use. The youth failed to tell his parents that he himself had been smoking pot long before Peter arrived at the church, and didn't mention Peter's advice to the youth group to wait until becoming adults before considering trying the drug.

Other parents began pulling their kids from his bible studies and music classes. Though still supporting the content of Peter's message, Pastor Garner felt the heat and quietly suggested Peter modify his teaching methods and even cut his hair.

The smiles and handshakes Peter received from even his staunchest doubters were replaced by disapproving looks and indifference by some of his closest supporters. Christine related, "My brother had gone from messiah to pariah in just a few months."

Peter possessed the charisma and wherewithal to change the thoughts of even the narrowest of minds and survive the controversy. He could not, however, overcome his anger and pride enough to make these concessions.

Pastor Garner recognized this dark side of Peter, the part of him unable to avoid judging those who judged him. He tried to convince Peter to turn his cheek a bit. "Peter is a natural born leader of men, one who has the power of the spirit in his touch," Pastor Garner told my parents. "But he is still a young man in many ways, and as such is marred by the curses of youth—impatience and lack of perspective."

Peter could not turn aside his cheek. Instead, he thrust his jaw defiantly into a wall of generational intolerance. The pastor worked to restore Peter's status, and may have succeeded had my brother not given in to the human failing of frustration. Peter excommunicated himself from our tiny church, and as he did when touched by evil in the barbershop, he walked away without looking back. Peter left our church when he was eighteen years old and to my knowledge has never set foot in another one.

My brother's long and tragic battle with the establishment had begun.

Chapter 9

WALKING TO THE OTHER SIDE

I was drawn to defending the underdog in my childhood years, when I first noticed which direction the scales of justice swayed. My development happened on the grassy fields and asphalt courts of competition forming the first remnants of a young man's honor.

I maintained a low profile when I first arrived from Alabama. A shy kid by nature, I rarely spoke and merely watched the other boys play during recess and lunchtime. I looked forward, however, to "physical play time," a structured class that forced me to participate in sports activities. I surprised myself and others with my specialized athletic talents.

I was the essence of quickness, not blessed so much with the wings of Mercury but gifted instead with feet of the artful dodger. Though fairly fast on a straightaway, I was never comfortable running between the lines. But my reactions when I was thrown into a crowd convinced me I had spent a former life as a hyper tomcat. I became king of tag, eraser football, and dodge ball. No one could lay a hand on me. I had the ability while running at full speed to contort my body into shapes that would make Harry Houdini gasp in amazement. My feints, twists, and turns left my pursuers grasping futilely at the wind.

Although my lack of size and straight-line speed would limit my athletic accomplishments in later years, as a nine-year-old third-grader I was dynamite.

In the classroom, I wore my shyness as a veil of protection. I tossed aside this shield when I stepped on a playing field, and my tenuous steps became punctuated with leaps and bounds. I became a dynamo of energy and passion, a powder keg of spirit and emotion.

My transformation from a shy, meek "brain" in the classroom to a wild child on the field amazed the other kids and made me popular with the popular boys—the fledgling fraternity of athletic studs who had ignored me until then. When teams were being determined, I was always chosen early. And when less democratic methods were used (which was most of the time), I always ended up with the "studs."

These stacked teams were the mythological playground champions of our kid-dom, the unassailable armies of third-grade "might" who routinely crushed the weaklings by scores as lopsided as eighty-three to two in kickball and ninety-eight to six in football. These lunchtime mismatches became part of Northdale lore, and as conquering victors, we walked the schoolyard with our heads held high and our regard for the losers somewhere far below.

We were the poster boys for Darwinism.

This natural evolution followed course for me until the day I met Alexander Hamilton Ashe, the least athletic, but toughest kid I ever knew.

The only kid in class shorter than me, Alex was *real* tiny. Bullies didn't bother stuffing him in the outside garbage cans; he fit quite nicely in smaller containers like cardboard boxes and hallway lockers. Once, my teacher glanced around at the start of class and noticed Alex missing from her inventory. It wasn't long before rustling came from the coatroom. Miss Picture investigated and found Alex wedged upside down in a wastebasket.

Alex never said who put him there.

Alex may have been the smartest kid I knew growing up. He read more books than our librarian, and I marveled at his ability to do math problems with a ballpoint pen. I always used a pencil with a huge eraser, which I had to replace at least once a week.

He even looked smart. His glasses were thicker than the bottom of coke bottles, and when he peered at you his eyes appeared gigantic. He made *you* feel tiny, like you were a bug he was examining through a magnifying glass.

He wasn't athletic, though. Besides being the smallest kid in class, he was also one of the slowest. He looked the part of an egghead, with his black horn-rimmed glasses and thin, scrawny body. He always ended up with the have-nots and on the other end of many legendary blowouts.

But there was a reason Alex's glasses had a crack in one lens and black electrician's tape holding his frames together in two places. He had toughness belying his slight build and lack of coordination. He never flinched when stuffed in a wastebasket or tackled by kids two or three times bigger than him. His silence when in these situations was out of pride, not fear. He wasn't scared of anybody or anything.

And he hated losing, even if the results were pre-determined by the mismatched teams. He played every game as if the score was tied. Down by fifty runs in kickball, he would still dive onto the hard red clay for pop flies. He usually missed them. He would dust himself off and do it again. It was the same in football. Losing by ten touchdowns, he would still throw his frail body around the field, trying to catch a pass or make a tackle.

During one lunchtime gridiron drubbing, I went to make a two-hand touch tackle on one of his hapless crew. Out of nowhere, Alex flew at me, his body horizontal with the ground. Though I wasn't much bigger, I deflected most of his blow and flicked him aside. I tackled his teammate while Alex rolled like a log across the field. He repeated his actions on the next play, with nearly the same outcome.

"You're supposed to be a math whiz, Alex," I pointed out to him. "Can't you figure out you're losing by seventy-seven points? Why the heck are you killing yourself?"

Alex, who didn't say much to anybody, rubbed his stiff jaw and straightened his perpetually crooked glasses before looking up at me. "Josie Milmington," he said in a matter-of-fact manner.

Until that moment, I had never really thought about Josie Milmington—or any other girl—as athletic inspiration. Not for me, Alex, or anyone else. Girls were, well, just girls. Then I turned and saw Josie, sitting alone on the small green bench next to the field, and I realized she was always there, every single day, when we played our games. It never dawned on me girls would be interested in watching a bunch of guys play ball. When I realized this, my entire athletic world changed. I started playing like a wild boy—like Alex—with one eye always looking over at the benches, hoping a girl would be there watching.

The same day Alex opened my eyes to the female world, he taught me another lesson. After sharing his motivational secret, he demonstrated its power by shellacking some of my teammates. Jimmy Farnsworth and "Big Mike" Johnson, the fastest, toughest, and meanest guys in third grade, took umbrage at Alex's unbridled effort.

"Don't you get it, pipsqueak?" Jimmy growled, rubbing Alex's head in the mud after two-hand "touching" him face-first into the ground. "You and your wimpy friends are just here to be buried by us. And we *are* stomping you. Why the hell are you still trying?"

Alex spit mud from his mouth as he turned over. His face and glasses were covered with a single sheet of brown ooze, except for his forehead, where a large dirt clod with grass still attached was stuck. He resembled an onion sticking out of the ground. Alex removed his mud-splattered glasses and looked calmly up at Jimmy, who was straddling his chest.

Alex's revelation to me about his secret admirer must have also freed his voice to speak out against a lifetime of tiny-kid oppression. His first verbal blast was a doozy. "Well, if these 'pipsqueaks' weren't here, you guys would be stuck playing with yourselves, like you usually do when we aren't around."

I didn't fully understood the joke then—Alex's wit always seemed to be a bit ahead of my understanding—but I knew it was good one, based on Jimmy's reaction. He grabbed Alex under the armpits and lifted him, yelling, "You little shit. Now you're gonna die." While I didn't think Jimmy was gonna kill Alex, I knew it was gonna be a long flight to the ground. Alex tried one futile kick below Jimmy's waist as he was lifted skyward.

Alex never made it past Jimmy's shoulders. I took three running steps and threw my body sideways into Jimmy, hitting him just below the waist on one side. At first, it looked as if my body had no impact on the much taller and bigger Jimmy, as I bounced off him like a ping pong ball hitting a brick wall. But I must have hit him at just the right time and place, as he started to teeter, then began swaying like a sapling in a rising storm. He dropped Alex to waist level, and then tipped over like a redwood falling in a forest. On his way to earth, Alex connected with the kick to the groin he had missed earlier.

The only thing missing from the scene was the lumberjack's chant, until someone yelled "Timber!" as Jimmy hit the ground.

There was brief silence, and before anything else could happen— namely, getting the heck beat out of us—Mr. Dean, the teacher on duty, came over to see what was brewing. Order was soon restored, with Jimmy flexing his bruised ego (and swollen balls) before re-joining his side. Standing between the two teams as they lined up for the next play, I turned my back to the haves and walked over to the have-nots.

Nothing really changed; the score ended ninety-six to twelve that day. But I had crossed the line and wouldn't be going back. Although we lost every game we played against those guys in grade school, that's not what I remember most. I recall looking sideways to my buddy Alex and seeing the same gleam in his eyes he must have been seeing in mine, the gleam indicating nothing could stop us—not those faster, bigger guys on the other side, not our own lack of size or talent, not even the certainty of losing every game. We thought nothing could stop our superman hearts, as we glanced at the girls on the benches for our motivation, not knowing we were looking at kryptonite in a linen and lace disguise.

I followed Alex's example into high school, where I would learn further lessons in love and life from my unlikely guru.

At Bella Sierra High, we played Indian dodge ball in the gym during P.E. when it rained. No one knew why "Indian" was the chosen name. A few years before, coaches had received flack because this form of rainy-day dodge ball was aptly called "Slaughter Ball." A couple of broken noses and countless bruises and abrasions caused a furor by outraged parents, prompting the coaches to remodel our grand game into a more humane version.

The facelift was in name only. The kinder, gentler "Indian Dodge Ball" was still little more than organized mayhem.

And we loved it. Well, maybe the seniors loved it, and some of the tenth and eleventh grade jocks, too, because it was another chance to solidify their hold over the hopeless minions—mostly us freshmen, especially the diminutive ones, such as myself and Alex.

School rules required students with glasses to wear a wire contraption around their head for protection during dodge ball. Though he could see barely ten feet without his glasses, Alex would have none of the "face cage." Maybe it was vanity or maybe it was just another challenge—I never found out for sure why he chose not to wear the protective gear.

He adopted a unique style to compensate for his blindness. We called him the "Kamikaze Kid," because he would spend virtually the entire game at the mid-court line separating the two teams. This area was not a safe place. He was a prime target of the jocks, who would prey on anyone, especially a tiny ninth-grader, venturing near the mid-court line. Usually, it was jocks against jocks up front, firing at each other while the rest of us hovered near the back, waiting for the occasional loose ball to roll our way.

Alex explained his bravery as being a practical matter. "Before, when I stood in the back, I could never see a ball coming, especially when someone would duck in front of me. *Pow!* I got tired of getting blindsided. I went up front so I could see. No big deal."

He rarely lasted long before some jock nailed him. He got in his licks a few times, though. One memorable day, he accomplished more, tipping the scales of justice toward the have-nots with an incident that became known as the "Freshman Rebellion."

This particular game started out much the same as any other slaughter of the innocents, with us freshmen cowering in the back and Alex up front, getting thrown at from every angle. But unlike other days, Alex wasn't getting hit. He weaved, dodged, and dipped, and try as they might, the jocks couldn't get him. Resembling a weird Fellini-style ballet, the scene defied explanation.

Richard Orhouse, the biggest, baddest—and ugliest—senior, was particularly frustrated with Alex's evasiveness. At six-foot-four and more than 240 pounds, Richard was nearly three times bigger than Alex's eighty-five pound frame. Richard's claim to fame, aside from his all-league status in football, basketball, and track, was his girlfriend, Penny Shalloway. She was the only girl in school with a bigger chest than Richard's, prompting one clueless freshman to suggest he needed a better "boob" job to match hers. Richard reacted with a two-fisted implant on the guy's head.

Richard was called "Big Dick" by friends and foes alike, and he reveled in the moniker, thinking it had something to do with his anatomy. No one had the guts or stupidity to explain the name referred only to his nasty disposition.

No jolly giant, Big Dick hated most everybody. He reserved special hatred for small, smart guys like Alex. "They got no business being out here with us athletes," Big Dick once said in his own eloquent style, turning "athletes" into three syllables (ath-o-letes). "They got brains but no nuts. They should stay in the library where they belong."

Most kids avoided hitting Big Dick, even when they had a clear shot, because his revenge was one hundred percent, immediate, and extremely painful. Alex, though, never avoided breaking this rule. On this day, he would step even further across this line.

Toward the end of the first game, mostly everyone was out on both sides. Big Dick and his jock teammates, tired of missing Alex, had turned their attention to destroying the rest of the ninth grade class. I was the last to go, smacked on the thigh shortly after all my human shields were demolished. I limped to the first row of bleachers.

I turned to watch the end of the devastation. Instead, I witnessed a most peculiar thing. Alex was standing at his customary off-to-one-side midcourt position, about ten feet away from where I was sitting. Already carrying one ball, he grabbed another as it rolled by. This act wasn't novel in itself—many a sly player collected a couple of balls when they were plentiful near the end of a game and threw them at the same guy. While treacherous against an unarmed opponent, the double-throw was rarely effective against a player who held a ball—the opponent simply used his ball as blocker, then dealt evenly with the thrower.

I noticed Alex was honing in on Big Dick, and I was shocked—because it was Big Dick and he was armed.

But nothing was a bigger surprise than what Alex did next. Straddling one ball on the floor, he turned toward me and bounced the other ball hard and at about a forty five-degree angle. Appearing to come directly at me, the ball flew over my head and kept rising. Higher and higher it climbed, kissing the last row of bleachers and glancing toward the ceiling.

I was struck by the feeling I had seen this strange scene before. I was thinking of where it was, when I was jerked around by Alex's shrill, unmistakable voice.

Alex's voice wasn't what caught my attention—and everybody else's in the gym—it was what he said. "Hey, *Little* Dick! Stick this in your mouth!"

The air went out of the gym as if sucked out by one collective gasp. Winding and throwing as he yelled, Alex let loose a throw toward Big Dick, who stood just ten feet away. On target at head level, the throw looked to be going only half-speed and was easily parried by Big Dick. I saw indignant shock in Big Dick's eye quickly turn to an evil gleam, and his right arm brought the executioner's ball backward. He wasn't in a hurry—he wanted to relish this killing. But something in the back of my mind told me to look up.

I followed the last few feet of the falling ball as it cleared Alex's right shoulder and landed in his hands. The "deja view" came back to me, and I knew what would come next.

Over Alex's left shoulder, perfectly framed as if on a platter, was Big Dick's pig-like face. The devilish gleam was gone, replaced by a blank look of impending doom. Big Dick now knew what was coming, but was powerless to stop it. His arm twitched forward slightly, freezing in full wind-up, and his blank, ashen-like face completed his statuesque stance.

In the split second it took for Alex's right arm to whip forward in complete follow-through, I remembered why this scene seemed so familiar. A couple of times the previous week, I saw Alex in a nearby park horsing around with two balls. I didn't pay much attention the first day, but the second time, I stopped and watched for a while. Over and over, he would toss one ball against the handball wall, grab another ball on the ground near him and make a quick half-hearted throw, then, almost simultaneously, catch the other ball and make another quick, but harder throw.

I recall muttering, "Why the heck is he doing that?" as I continued on my way home.

Now I knew. Alex had elevated revenge to an athletic art form.

As the ball hit Little Dick's face, smashing his nose sideways and entertaining the stunned crowd with a colorful blood shower, I knew the meaning of justice served.

I always marveled at the fearless attitude Alex displayed in attempting to balance the scales of injustice existing in the inhumane hierarchy of school. His relentless, fierce desire for self-respect caused me to consider him my best friend throughout high school and someone I would count on for inspiration the rest of my life.

And just before our graduation, he introduced me to the first love of my life.

Chapter *10*

STONE DREAMS

*T*hough scared to death around girls through my teen years, I was not without my fantasies.

The girls in my initial dreams were faceless, but real ones began to take shape. Elissa Cavelli was the first, and I watched her from afar until I graduated from high school. Others bloomed—Tani Morris, a goddess whose beauty went beyond her golden tresses coifed in a Farrah Fawcett-style, and Inga Thor-Jenssen, a Norwegian foreign exchange student whose hedonistic passion lit up every boy on campus. Each time I was swept away by these teen sirens, I thought I had found the last love of my life.

These loves, though, were tightly held secrets known only by me. I poured my feelings into letters, poems, and drawings, signing them in my alter ego, "The Phantom of Love," and taping them to their lockers. I left flowers, mostly home-grown roses from my back yard that Daddy crafted for Mama. None of the girls guessed that this shy, diminutive nerd was their secretive suitor. I sat at a back row desk diagonally from the front door, so I could witness the reaction of the objects of my attention as they entered the classroom shortly after receiving my mystery gifts.

I realize it must have been creepy to them to have some unseen guy lurking around and leaving notes. I was a stalker before the word or crime had even been identified. Why did I practice my craft in such an anonymous, hopeless manner? Maybe it was fear, the one element that would transcend all stages of my life.

I was so much the silent pursuer of illusory love I did not notice when the real thing crept up and tapped me on the shoulder.

I was eighteen years old and in my last semester of high school when I began an odd (many would say crazy) personal fitness program. Stuck in the jocks' PE class because I had played on the soccer team, I was supposed to do weight lifting with the other athletes for the entire second half of the year. I was self-conscious about my sapling-like limbs amidst a class full of hulking redwoods with tree trunks for arms, and I hated weight lifting because it confirmed my wimpy strength. I weaseled out of this requirement by promising the football coach I would embark on my own fitness regimen.

Cursed with a Pillsbury Doughboy tummy despite my slight frame, I decided to do something about it. I started doing sit-ups during class, huffing and puffing through a couple of hundred each day. I tried to stay as inconspicuous as possible, doing them in the corner of the gym out of sight from the PE teachers. Not wanting them to change their minds and make me return to lifting weights, I added repetitions each day. I kept a low profile while methodically pumping out 500 to 600 sit-ups a day.

I would have made it through the rest of the semester without incident, if not for some fatheaded football players who didn't want to be outdone by a skinny soccer player. Johnny Gentry and Daniel "Grunt" Grafton wandered over one day and started hassling me for evading weightlifting. Their beef was only a ruse; they had a consuming hate for soccer and felt any kid who played it was a loser.

"Hey, ya skinny pipsqueak," growled Johnny. "I don't care how many Goddamn goals you kick or shitty sit-ups you squeeze out of your ass, you're still not an athlete."

Even in my youth, I had figured out that discretion was better than a big mouth. At the same time, I knew keeping my clap shut at this moment wouldn't necessarily save it from being punched in after school. Once targeted by these slobs, you were in big trouble.

A soft, but firm voice broke the difficult silence that had settled around me as I weighed my limited options. "That was some fucking fancy assonance and alliteration you delivered there, Johnny Shitface Shakespeare."

Johnny spun around, looking for the source of the insult. Alex, all of four-feet eleven-inches, and the only guy in class with smaller arms than mine, sat calmly on a workout bench doing curls in a steady, rhythmic motion. As was his custom, Alex was comfortable in the face of domineering intolerance. An instant legend after his face-shattering slaughter-ball incident as a freshman, he had drifted from the limelight back into the shadows of the unpopular. He didn't care he was no longer part of the in-crowd.

What he did care about, though, was love.

I never told him that, while I was in the halls at all hours taping my love messages to the lockers of my dream girls, I had seen him doing the same thing. I was not the only bird on campus caged by a captured heart.

At this moment, Alex was bent on saving this doomed duck from becoming a dead one. At first, I didn't like his approach. He challenged the fat footballers' athletic talent, which wasn't usually a good idea.

"If this little runt is such a weakling, how come he can kick your ass in sit-ups?" he said, nodding in my direction.

I looked behind me, hoping he was pointing toward some other unfortunate target. But it was me to whom he had firmly attached a bull's-eye. True, I had been doing sit-ups consistently for a few days, but I had been doing them at my own leisurely pace. I wasn't sure how I would react when pushed by these behemoths.

I found out. After briefly thinking Johnny and Grunt were going to make Alex's challenge moot by crushing both of us with their hands, I was only slightly relieved to see Johnny signal for someone to drag two more mats over.

"He'll beat both of you, hands down," Alex said, in a matter-of-fact way, doing nothing to ease my tension.

"Little boy, care to put some cash where your big mouth is?" countered Johnny.

Alex, whose eyes were sparkling with excitement like a cat ready to pounce on an unsuspecting mouse, replied in the same nonchalant manner as before. "Sure. But not cash. I wouldn't want you guys losing your chimp change for the bus ride back to the zoo. How about something simple you guys can handle, like grunt work?"

Grunt, who had seemed only mildly interested until this point, suddenly stiffened his size-nineteen neck and grunted, "Whattaya mean by grunt work?"

"Physical, sweaty, mind-numbing labor, something you guys will need practice in, since you will be doing it the rest of your life."

Grunt seemed dazed, but satisfied by Alex's answer, emitting only a low guttural sound. Johnny, though, was not amused. "Okay, smart ass. It don't matter what ya have in mind, 'cause we're gonna whip his ass, then we're gonna stomp you for good measure."

Nonplussed, Alex stated his conditions. "Simply, if either of you do more sit-ups than Stone, we will load and unload weights on your bars during PE for the rest of the year."

"I have a better idea," countered Johnny. "When you lose, you will load all our weights onto the bars and wipe down our sweat from the weight benches after each rep. And after class, you will hand-wash our gym clothes, including our jock straps. Basically, you will be our Chinese laundry bitches."

Again, I saw a flash come over Alex's eyes, but this time it was anger at the racial slur directed at his maternal Taiwanese heritage. But his tone never changed as he noted calmly, "So, what I have heard *is* true. You two like it when other guys handle your jocks."

Geez, I thought if Alex doesn't keep his mouth shut, they're going to kill us even before they bury me in sit-ups.

He wasn't done though. "Maybe I've been too hard on you two sensitive beacons of Bella Sierra pride. I'll make it easy for you. Not only will Stone do more sit-ups than one of you, he will do more than both of you put together. And don't worry about the grunt work. When Stone kicks your asses, both of you will bow down on your knees whenever you see us anywhere on campus, whether it is in the hallways or the locker room, or here in the gym. This will last until the last day of school."

"Yeah, yeah," mumbled Johnny, flipping a middle finger in our direction. "It doesn't matter what you want us to do, 'cause it ain't gonna happen anyway."

Turning to the small crowd that had encircled us, Alex shrugged and said, "You are all witnesses. They agreed to these conditions, so if they don't follow through afterward, we know what kind of piss-ants they really are."

As Johnny and Grunt gave each other high-fives and flexed and stretched themselves in preparation for the challenge, I pulled Alex aside.

"What the heck are you doing?" I whispered, my voice reduced to a rasping cackle by my impending humiliation. "These guys *are* athletes, you know—pro prospects, thoroughbreds, gosh darn *studs*. And I've only been doing sit-ups for two weeks."

"Yeah, but those guys have been doing bench presses the entire period," he shrugged. "They're not going to be able to put their arms behind their heads, much less be able to use them to pull their bodies up." After pausing, he added, "Even if they are faster than I think, you'll win anyway. I've watched you every day, so I know about your secret weapon." He nodded at me knowingly, but I had no clue about what he meant.

What he meant hit me a little while later, like it always did when my mind was trying to keep up with Alex's computer brain. Alex was not only the smartest kid I knew in school, he was a genius about human nature. He knew me better than I knew myself. He had watched me do sit-ups for two weeks and noticed my routine never varied. I started with a lot of energy, so if the coaches looked at me they wouldn't get on my case the rest of the period. I eased up when they stopped walking around, essentially loafing until about ten minutes remained. At that point, my energy level invariably shot up and I finished on a tear.

If he had truly watched me every day, he knew the reason why I cranked out the sit-ups beginning at about ten minutes to two. That's when the gym door opened and the girl's cross-country team would peer in before heading out to practice. And that's when Inga Thor-Jenssen would walk in and take a seat on the first row of bleachers.

Though I realized she barely knew I existed and that she came every day to see Sir Studly Sean O'Grady work out, I still busted a gut trying to impress her. She was blonde, buxom, and brazenly sexy enough to swim naked in the school pool late at night—I had seen her during one of my late evening sojourns to the halls. This uninhibited Norwegian beauty queen was the ruler of my young, lustful dreams.

I didn't know if Alex knew the extent of my lust, but he believed it was powerful enough to risk both our shame and circumstance.

A larger crowd had gathered by now and formed two very different, very physically uneven factions. There were the jocks, made up mostly of football and basketball players, and the neo-jocks, made up of soccer and badminton players. Some of the badminton players, probably fearing for their lives, joined the jocks; I knew they were secretly rooting for me. Still we were outnumbered about ten for every one and outweighed by several tons.

Coach Jensen sauntered over and looked on approvingly, though he normally frowned on unofficial athletic contests not under his strict control. But as he stood stone-faced and rigid like a statue of Patton, who he fancied himself to be, I knew he relished the opportunity for the jocks to squash the soccer contingent. He hated soccer, despising its simplicity and foreign roots. "Hell, any kid can play that game," I overheard him say once. "There's no strategy, no adjustments needed, no direction given by the coaches. It's just a bunch of short, skinny kids running around willy-nilly. It's damn un-American, I tell you!"

Despite their fan support, the jocks could not match my motivation—the first girl I had ever seen naked was sitting twenty feet away. I could not, I would not lose. At least, I hoped not.

With Alex holding my feet, I ripped off a hundred sit-ups in the first two minutes, taking a slight lead over Johnny and leaving Grunt rolling on the mat, gasping for air. Johnny seemed to be gaining confidence and stamina, as we both pumped out 110 or so repetitions in the next two minutes. At the four-minute mark, I signaled Alex to let go of my legs. I saw his puzzled look, but then he understood he himself might have underestimated the power of teenage hormones. He let go and sat back, a knowing, satisfied look on his face.

I looked over at Johnny and saw my move had the desired effect—his eyes grew bigger and the air seemed to go out of him when he saw I had actually quickened my pace without my legs being held down. He sped up, but his pace soon slowed, and then he simply stopped and lay there, unable to lift his arms, with his head on the mat and his eyes staring dully at the ceiling.

With the crowd now chanting my name over and over, I increased my pace to more than sixty sit-ups per minute. I leaned over to him and said, "Oh, done so early?"

"I've just lost to a ninety-eight pound soccer weakling," he said out loud, though I think he meant to say it only to himself.

"By the way Johnny Boy, I'm 110 pounds, and baby, soccer rules!"

I did 650 sit-ups in ten minutes—more than doubling the combined output of the football duo, who now lay nearly comatose on the floor. I was warmed up and would have continued had the crowd not surged onto the mat. My soccer buddies and the entire badminton squad gathered around, and I noticed Coach Jensen had turned and walked out of the gym, shown up by a silly soccer player.

After the cheering and backslapping subsided, I looked toward the bleachers where Inga was sitting—on Sean's lap, of course. In the midst of my greatest triumph, there I was, cloaked in defeat, deflated and beaten down by the vicissitudes of mercurial teenage love.

Alex tugged on my arm, trying to get my attention. I didn't look. "Inga is talking to Sean. She doesn't even know I exist."

"Well, somebody else does," said Alex, as he pointed me toward another girl in the bleachers. "She's been trying to get your attention."

In my downcast state, I had not seen the face smiling back at me when I looked in Inga's direction. I hadn't noticed the hand waving or my name being called, both by the same smiling girl.

I didn't recognize the girl, a brown-haired, dark-skinned cutie who stood between two giggling blondes. "I don't know who she is," I said, squinting in her direction.

"She seems to want to get to know you," continued Alex. "Go over and talk to her."

I usually watched the objects of my affection, not the other way around. And I was used to writing down my feelings, not vocalizing them. Alex had to shove me toward her.

I was struck by her eyes—the color and consistency of melting milk chocolate, they appeared to look straight through my wide eyes of blue and down to the depths of my soul. I saw within them the same look of breathless anticipation and tremulous hope I had in my own eyes when I sneaked glances at the girls of my dreams.

This girl with the breathtaking, silky brown eyes sensed my awkwardness and opened the conversation leading to the first unimagined romance of my young life.

Chapter *11*

CHANDNI

$\mathcal{H}$er name was Chandni (Chawn-duh-nee, as she told me it should be said) and she had indeed followed my path in much the same way I had trailed after the objects of my affection.

"That was fantastic, Stone," she gushed, jumping from between her two girlfriends and greeting me with a hug that seemed to melt and mold to my body. "You blew those jocks away. But I knew they didn't have a chance. I knew you would beat 'em."

Her words came in rapid-fire succession, like water bursting from a twisted hose after the kink is taken out. I was so startled by her gushing approach that I couldn't say anything. She erased any chance for an awkward silence.

"I was telling my friend Shari you were gonna win, you were gonna wipe 'em out."

"How did you know?" I said, my voice trailing off.

"For the past two weeks, I've been coming into the gym to wait for my sister Missy. I have an open period and she gives me a ride home after school. I've been watching you do sit-ups every day. I knew those fat jocks couldn't keep up with you."

Every day that I had been showing off for Inga, I had been turning on Chandni. I did this without even knowing she existed.

A girl hadn't shown any noticeable interest in me since the sixth grade (when a not-so-reverent Mormon lass gave me my first kiss). Hunched over in acute shyness as I shuffled through the hallways, I was used to admiring my targets of affection in controlled secrecy. I was taken aback by Chandni's unabashed interest in me, which continued over the next few weeks. We began doing things together—walking from school to the nearby donut shop, driving over Folsom Dam to view drought-depleted Folsom Lake, and going out for ice cream after my high school graduation ceremony. As the freedom of summer beckoned, I realized had acquired my first teen girlfriend.

I was drawn to Chandni's dark, ethereal beauty. Born to a handsome blonde American businessman and a stunning Sikh school teacher, Chandni's melded beauty was striking—wavy, dark chocolate hair flowing to her waist, set against skin of silken caramel matching her dreamy eyes. She stood out anywhere, especially at snow-white Bella Sierra.

Chandni's Punjabi name means "moonlight" and when she smiled it was as if the entire nighttime sky was flooded with her shining brightness. In addition to her sweet nature and exquisite beauty, I appreciated that, at barely four-foot-ten, she was one of the few kids—boy or girl—shorter than me at BSH.

Overwhelmed by admiration I was not used to, I gave my heart slowly to the darkly enchanting Chandni. Though my heart trailed behind her mad love, my body's attraction to hers was already in high gear. However, my sensual knowledge and experience lagged even farther behind my understanding of love. The same sexual naiveté applied to Chandni, whose wild, outspoken nature belied a sweet innocence when it came to her body. I could tell by the way she looked at me though that the same sexual hunger was within her.

We had little idea how to consummate the carnal desires growing within us, but we didn't let that stop us from trying. Our resulting efforts were the definition of trial and error.

We tried to do it everywhere, using the few techniques we knew. I parked my parents' big Chrysler wagon in the darkness behind a local middle school, put the back seat down and laid open a sleeping bag to make our bed of lust. Unfortunately, nothing we tried seemed to work, and afterward we stared at each other's bodies as if they were foreign objects.

We returned a few days later, but a man walking his dog spooked us before we could culminate our amorous efforts. We tried it in several outdoor areas, but our coitus was interrupted by, in order: an angry collection of bees (in a foothills meadow), a bather (as we lay by a lake), and a nun (at a nearby parochial school). Our carnal knowledge, it seemed, was being thwarted by both God and nature.

Ultimately, even the forces of Heaven and Earth could not stem our prurient growth. We made love under the shade of an oak not far from the gentle waters of Far Away Lake, my family's favorite camping destination.

Having found ecstasy for the first time—and liking it a bunch—we were not about to stop. Anytime and anywhere we could intertwine our lustful young bodies, we did.

While our bodies were fumbling their way along sensual advancement, we understood little about the consequences of these actions. We didn't realize we were playing teen-lust roulette. One broken condom after another led to one broken condom too many. So on the day I turned nineteen, I found out I was to be a daddy.

I had gone a lifetime without a tangible mistake. Though not blessed with great intellect, diligence and hard work earned me straight-A's through high school. I was a quiet, shy kid who never gave my parents worry, except for that brief disappearance after dark when I was seven. I had stolen once, but had been caught by my mother, who marched me to our neighbor's house and made me hand the toy back to the kid. I never stole again as a child. I rarely cussed and didn't smoke or drink.

Unlike my fearless friend Alex, I often avoided situations where I might fail. Strong in most academic subjects, I evaded hands-on challenges such as woodworking, auto shop, and typing. I loved soccer and played it with passion, but I loved baseball even more. I chose not to play organized baseball because I couldn't bear to fail in such a spotlighted arena.

These were all auditions for my serious fear of failing later. When confronted by fatherhood, I didn't flee from Chandni, though ultimately that may have been the braver thing to do. I ran from responsibility. I didn't feel ready to handle being a father and a husband to someone I was just learning to love. Heck, I was just learning what love was.

The real truth about my fear had nothing to do with the responsibility of being a husband or a father. I was driven by pride and narcissism to hide from all those around me the knowledge I was not perfect. Until then, I had fooled everyone—including myself. I couldn't stand to let anyone know the smallness living inside me. I couldn't handle the sad, disapproving looks surely to come from Chandni's parents and mine.

I needed someone to talk to and tell me the way. I was too afraid of God to pray and too embarrassed to talk to grown-ups, least of all my parents. My best friend Alex—the tiny guy whom I looked up to—was having his own problems.

During our senior year, Alex and I had talked about moving away to attend the same college, with hopes of learning together about life, as roommates and best friends. Just before graduation, I met Chandni and Alex met Wendy, who became his first real love after countless schoolboy crushes. While I stayed in Sacramento, he followed his girlfriend to UCLA. His joy resonated loudly in letters he sent me during his first semester.

His excitement did not last past the first school year. She found older college men to her liking and dropped him for the football team's third-string quarterback.

On the day I learned of my pending fatherhood, I received his letter relating he was dropping out of college and returning home. Absorbed by my own turmoil, I didn't contact him for several days. After feeling we could benefit from talking to each other, I drove to his house. His mom, tiny like her son, said he left just before my arrival. "He looked sad," she said. "But lately, he always looks sad. He hugged me and said he was gonna make a call before going home. I didn't get what he meant, because he was already at home."

I knew what Alex meant by "going home." It related to his granddaddy.

Alex told me many stories about his Grandpa Ying, who he considered a second father (as his Marine dad was often away on military missions while Alex was a kid). Waifish himself, Grandpa Ying taught Alex how to stand tall against intolerance—especially from bone-headed jocks. Along with arming Alex with many of the witticisms that formed his offensive and defensive verbal warfare repertoire, Grandpa taught him judo moves in their basement, a la David "Caine" Carradine and Keye "Master Po" Luke from "Kung Fu," the greatest David-versus-Old West Goliath TV series of our kid-dom.

He also left the biggest scar on his grandson, dying in his arms just before he left for UCLA. "When Grandpa looked up at me," Alex said, in describing the old man's heart attack, "he told me not to worry. He was going home, where there would be no more pain."

I hoped I was wrong about what I though his last words to his mama meant—that he did not care to live anymore. I hoped I was right about where I thought he had gone—a phone booth near Temple Park in the quaint Old Town section of Fair Oaks. When he first met Wendy, this phone was his go-to place to call her (to avoid the active ears of his mama).

I found him sitting on the floor of the booth, his head slumped on his chest and his right hand grasping the phone that stretched the length of its cord. His olive skin was bleached white and his lips were dyed purple. I grabbed his shoulders and shook him, hoping to see the old fire flash in his eyes. Only a cold dullness stared back. I knew it was bad when I looked down at his arms. His wrists bore jagged red lines, the result of deep, vertical cuts. His shirt was ripped across his chest, exposing a large "X" he had sliced over his heart. The guilty hunting knife—a gift from his granddad—lay between his legs.

A glint of recognition shined in his eyes, but I thought he hadn't the strength to manage a word. As usual, I underestimated him.

"Damn you, Stone," he gasped. "Can't you just let this broken boy go. I got no moves left. This world is just too tough. Just too…"

"No, you little asshole, you ain't getting off that easy," I managed, through gritted teeth and tearing eyes. "Breathe. Just breathe."

"Why?" he replied.

And then he died, sprawled in the arms of this boyhood friend who had no clue how to answer his question.

My speechless manner continued through his funeral and for many months afterward. His last word still haunts me, and I have never been fully able to answer that damn question.

Without Alex's heart and voice to guide me, and afraid to seek help from the adults in my life, I struggled with what to do regarding Chandni.

I coaxed Chandni to buy into my fears, convincing her that an abortion was best for both of us. I didn't realize until later she didn't care what other people would think about her having a baby out of wedlock. But she knew I was afraid of what others would think and say. Seeing the fear in my eyes, she loved me too much to tell me what she really wanted.

I don't think I would have listened anyway.

Getting an abortion was easier than I thought. Of course, I didn't have to go through it the same way Chandni did. I waited outside while the procedure was performed. I bought a tiny stuffed Golden Retriever, like the real one Chandni's family had, and a single red rose. I forgot to put the flower in water, and by the time the nurse signaled me to come into her room, it had wilted. I dropped it into a wastebasket before I entered the room.

The moment I saw her face, I knew I made a mistake, one likely to change our lives forever. Her reddened, tear-strained eyes were empty, as if all the life had been drained from them. She had seen far too much to ever see things the same way again.

"I saw him," she said. "They didn't think I was awake, but I watched as they put him in a bucket. They didn't take the bucket when they left. He had reddish hair and tiny, tiny fingers, like a little doll. He was curled up with his eyes closed, as if he were sleeping. I touched his little fingers and they were cold. *So* cold."

I wasn't sure if what she described was true or an illusion of hers. But I was sure she believed it. And I could see it was killing her. I had murdered the spirit of this beautiful girl.

In a note of irony laughable if not so sad, our secret was discovered within a couple of days. Mama figured it out by watching me walk around like a zombie. Daddy wasn't there when I fessed up, but she told him when he came home from work. "You have the rest of your life to work this out in your mind," he told me the next day. "Try not to let it happen again." He turned away, and I thought he was done. As I turned to leave, he said, "But above all else, don't let your guilt about what you have done affect all of your decisions in life."

He never said another word to me about the incident.

Chandni's parents found out pretty much the same way, with Chandni breaking down and telling them the same night I told my mother.

Worse, yet, were their reactions. No one killed us or even yelled. They were mad, but not at our carelessness. They were upset because we didn't believe in them, didn't have faith they would still love and support us no matter what our choice. As Mama said, "It hurts you didn't trust us. We would have stood by you and tried to help the best we could. But you didn't even give us a chance."

I wanted them to yell at me, to validate my fear of them finding out I wasn't such a good guy. I ended hope and crippled love for no reason, except I was selfish and scared.

Maybe the loss of one hopeful life could lead to a lifelong lesson. But my fear was not done with shaping both my destiny and that of my broken-spirited teen lover.

In the end, I would hurt all those around me simply because I could not handle the shame of being human. This failing would trail me like a ghost and haunt the rest of my life.

Chapter 12

BUTCH

$\mathcal{G}$rowing up, I usually ran from situations holding potential to be dangerous. But at one point, I had no choice but to face real fear.

During the summer I began dating Chandni, I landed my first job. I worked in a gas station around the corner from my house, where I still lived with my parents. Not much responsibility was involved—it was a self-serve station, so I didn't even pump the gas. It paid just a buck-sixty-five an hour, but I liked having my own money to spend on Chandni.

The time was the late Seventies, during the last stages of the gas shortage. Situations sometimes got hairy, with cars lined long and customers' tempers flaring. Chandni often visited, bringing snacks from her deli job and helping keep track of customers. When I was particularly swamped, I enlisted my daddy to provide relief while I relieved myself in the restroom. Never hesitating to come, he always shrugged off my thanks.

No major problems happened in the daytime—though, once, a customer who had a stuck gas cap nearly lifted me off the ground because I asked him to pull briefly out of line so others could get to the pumps. Another customer intervened and cooled off the idiot.

The evenings were different and far more dangerous. There weren't many good Samaritans around, but there were plenty of bad characters, especially on the weekends. I had my share of quick-change artists and scammers, drunks and dope-heads, along with some downright scary and creepy types.

On one occasion, a guy pumps his gas and then starts talking to me about buying tires. As I am telling him we don't sell tires, the girl in his car he arrived in revs the engine and tears out of the station. "Fucking bitch," the guy yells. "My fucking wallet is in the car. The bitch is always playing games." I see her turn the car around and park in the road on top of a hill above the station. I have misgivings about when or if she will come back. I turn to phone my daddy to have him come by while I sort out the situation, but I don't make the call. The sound of the guy's boots hitting the asphalt makes me turn around. He is running up the hill, where his girlfriend anticipates his arrival by gunning the engine.

He has a twenty-yard head start, and though I am wearing thick, calf-high rubber rain boots, I chase after him.

I don't know what motivates me more—my pride, or the thought of having to pay back the ten bucks—but I run like I'm wearing four-ounce track shoes. I cut the gap to ten feet by the time he reaches his car. He dives through the passenger window and his legs are still dangling out of the car when I arrive. The girlfriend could jet off, leaving me standing there with nothing but my gasping breaths offering a retort. But she appears in no hurry, as her Grinch-like smile suggests she is enjoying my panting helplessness. As I double over and try to find the air I lost in the fifty-yard dash uphill, I hear her laugh and say, "This asshole just wasted all of that effort for nothing."

As the oxygen spreads through my body and I find my strength returning, I become aware of something in my hand—the station keys. The wad of twenty or so keys attached to a chain weighs close to three pounds. I hated carrying the keys all day clipped to my belt, so I kept them in my pocket most of the time. On this occasion, I had used them to open a storage door just before the guy arrived. They were still in my hand when I started running.

In a flash, I decide not to turn the other cheek. And the girl who laughed at my futility doesn't have time to turn hers either as I reach back and throw my three-pound cluster of keys at her face with all the pride and pissed off fury I can muster.

As the keys leave my hand, I realize I haven't thought through my course of action. I am throwing my complete set of gas station keys through the window of a car that will soon be driving away. Loss of the keys will lead to loss of employment for me.

Divine—or devilish—intervention intervenes. The keys fly through the open window and crash flush against the girl's jaw, before bouncing back out the open window and landing, amazingly, at my feet.

She raises a hand to her face, and the whiteness of her hand and wrist starkly contrasts with the deep red blood splayed across her forehead.

"Thanks," I say calmly, though my eyes dance wildly at the revenge I have wrought. "That was worth the ten bucks you cost me."

As the little Chevy Chevette takes off down the hill and disappears into the darkness of night, I think there can be nothing as joyous as revenge.

Even with my occasional run-ins with ne'er-do-wells, I felt safe. I left my office door open, though keeping a wary eye out for what was going on outside. Some nights were so slow I paid little attention to the pumps. I kept myself busy and awake by doing homework or other personal tasks I didn't have time for during the day.

One particular night, though, was much different than the others.

On this evening, I am pouring over college class schedules in preparation for my upcoming spring semester, while listening to "America," "Seals and Crofts," and other Seventies radio rock while keeping an occasional eye out for the infrequent early morning customer.

I haven't had a customer for at least an hour, when I think I see a flash of a car stopping at the first row of pumps. Glancing out my window, I don't see anyone at the pump. As I'm lowering my gaze, I catch something else flash past the bottom of the window. The hair on my arms and back of my neck tell me of the reality that I am about to have visitors and they are not the paying or invited kind.

I am seated in a cubicle that is part of a larger office. On my right is a five-foot high counter separating my area from the foyer and bathrooms. The glass door to the foyer is locked, but not the door to the large garage area to my left. A few feet from the unlocked garage door is the open sliding door of my cubicle.

As I hear a footstep come through the garage door, I reach to close and lock my sliding cubicle panel. I glimpse the wrinkled black leather of my visitor's glove curl round the inside of the door before I can grab the handle. I briefly think this might be my friend Mort playing a joke. This hope soon becomes folly after the door slides slowly open.

I catch my startled, open-eyed face in the mirrored blade of a huge knife as it pokes through the opened door. My image blurs as my gaze slides up the twelve inches of the Bowie blade, stops briefly, then jumps to the hooded head.

The intruder is tall and his width fills the doorway, and he is dressed as the darkness of night from which he appeared—black army boots and jeans, charcoal jacket zipped to his throat, and a black Oakland Raiders hat. Two dark brown eyes, set so deep they appear black, peer sullenly from holes in his black ski mask, which camouflage his purplish lips.

I feel a jolt from my racing pulse that literally lifts me from my seat. I jump halfway up the counter to my right, catapulting to a standing position in the lobby. As I step toward the lobby door, another figure, smaller than the first, emerges from the shadows and blocks the entrance. He too is draped in total blackness, including a bandana covering his face.

When I see the first robber enter the cubicle, I circle around to sprint out a side garage door. The other robber stands calmly at the exit door when I enter the garage, so I start circling my parents' station wagon parked inside. The second robber enters the garage and they move in unison, taking slow, unrushed routes around the car's sides. As they close in from both sides, I feel like a zoo animal facing attendants coming in from all directions.

Neither of the robbers say a word as they close in. I throw my hands up in resignation and they motion with their knives for me to head toward the lobby. The smaller robber precedes me into the waiting area, presumably to dissuade any thought I have of dashing out the lobby door. As I back into the lobby, I notice a third hooded intruder, bigger and wider than the other two, enter my cubicle. I assume he is searching for the money in the till.

"Go that way," orders the first robber, who seems in charge of the smaller one. He points his knife toward the restroom in the small hallway in back of the lobby.

As I am guided into the bathroom, I realize I have run out of places to run. I will be OK, I figure, as long as they keep their masks on so I cannot identify them. Still, I'm not sure of their intentions, even when the bigger of the two announces in a gruff voice, "We're not going to hurt you. We're just gonna tie you up."

The smaller one produces bright yellow twine, thicker than kite string but thinner than typical rope. It looks like binding used to tie up a boat or a dog. Or, in this case, a human. I don't understand how they intend to tie me up. Am I supposed to let them tie my hands behind my back? The bigger one seems perturbed by my hesitation.

"Get on the floor. Lie on the fucking floor now!"

Jesus Christ! I finally figure out where I'm headed and it's face down on the restroom floor, still wet from my mopping ten minutes before they arrived.

I never really understood the term "hog-tie" until this moment. The two of them work quickly, with the bigger one focusing on binding my feet while the smaller one struggles to tie my hands. Soon, I'm trussed up like a hog ready for slaughter. I'm not sure the same fate doesn't await me.

As I lay on my right cheek in the thin film of filthy mop water smelling strongly of ammonia, urine and rotting twine, I struggle to establish relations with the masked men who hold my life in their hands.

"Hey guys, keep your masks on. I don't have any good reason to see your faces. And I have good reason to keep on living. I got a girlfriend I want a life with. I got brothers and sisters I wanna see. I got parents—"

"You got parents…that makes one of us," snapped the smaller one, in a high-pitched voice much younger than I first thought. "Shut-up, asshole," snaps the larger man, whose voice also sounds younger than I originally believed. These two were teenagers like me.

"That's OK, guys," I say, trying to extinguish the smoldering feelings between them. "My parents don't understand me anyway."

I talk as fast as I can, trying to foster rapport while dissuading either of them from saying anything self-identifying. But I also have to watch what I say. I can't let any of the three masked boys know that I know the identity of one of them.

I had an inkling of the third robber's identity when I looked briefly at him in the cubicle before I was backed into the lobby. There was something about his gait, a subtle dragging of his left foot that struck me as familiar. But it was the tuft of bright red hair sticking ever so slightly out the back of his ski mask that clinched my ID.

Bradley "Butch" Williams is my age and grew up around the corner from my house. He's the meanest kid I've ever known, and has more than once threatened to kill me.

When I first moved into our California home, I didn't pay much attention to Butch. Even at my sheltered age, I figured all neighborhoods had a kid like Butch who didn't want to play baseball, football, or "army," or who were just plain mean and liked to fight. I learned to avoid this type of kid, and I hung around friends who felt the same way.

But there was a different kind of meanness to Butch, a dangerous and pervasive brutality not be easily avoided in our small neighborhood. Nearly six-feet and 200 pounds by age thirteen, Butch was bigger and brawnier than any other kid around. Heck, he was bigger than any two kids put together, and larger than most of our dads. Though he limped on a bad leg, he carried himself with an imposing swagger he didn't need.

There were instances I glimpsed a humane, tender side to Butch, and these invariably involved his dog, Lex Luther. Butch worshiped his pugnacious bulldog, and the feeling from Lex Luther was mutual. They were inseparable. When Butch was cutting a swath through the neighborhood, punching and pillaging the scared and frightened, Lex was at his side, growling and baring his teeth in perfect imitation of his master.

All the kids knew it was only a matter of time before Butch appeared in their paths. I figured my time would come someday. I remained vigilant, swiveling my head whenever I strolled my neighborhood alone, or when I hung out with my friends in open places. I figured there was safety in numbers—not that we could take him on, but that he might get distracted and go after one of the other unfortunate kids in the group. Our Darwinistic survival code of sacrificing the smallest and skinniest knew no shame.

My diligence paid off with months of Butch-free interactions. But I let my guard down as spring approached and my attention focused on the other great fear of my teen years—girls.

While walking home from school, I was distracted by my day-lusting of Elissa Cavelli. I had just taped to her locker a poem written on parchment paper and bathed in Jovan cologne. Instead of taking my normal way home through a grassy field with visibility in all directions, I took a shorter route cutting through the hundred-yard fence-enclosed concrete path connecting the school grounds to my neighborhood. Maybe the ecstasy I felt at expressing my Romeo feelings to my oblivious Juliet had left me feeling immortal.

As with Shakespeare's fable, my Romeo thoughts nearly killed me. A familiar whistling brought me out of my black-and-white dreamlike embrace of Elissa and back to grim black-and-blue reality. Butch was thirty or so yards away at the end of the pathway, leaning against one of the five waist-high metal poles erected to block cars from entering the path. I wasn't concerned until I saw his growling sidekick was not by his side. As the hairs on the back of my neck started twitching, I knew which animal threat my ancient instinct was signaling. I turned and spotted Lex Luther about seventy yards away, standing behind the poles at the other end of the path. The two things I had over Butch—speed and deftness of foot—appeared useless at this moment.

Faced with Butch's massive frame of menacing fury, I decided to take my chances with the dog. I started jogging toward Lex, continuing even after I heard Butch's trademark attack call. I had one slim chance to avoid Lex's jaws, and it was contingent on reaching as far up the path as I could. I picked up speed and the space between Lex and me rapidly fell away. I stole a look back and saw what I hoped—Butch was lumbering up the path, feeling no need to hurry as he felt Lex would adequately slow me down.

As the distance between us closed, I made my move. Lex was fast for a muscle-bound dog and his jaws could crack bone, but he wasn't much of a jumper. At least I hoped not. As he closed in, I saw his head twist slightly and his eyes roll back shark-like as he prepared to clamp his jaws into my leg. I took one long stride, nearly into his biting range, then pushed off and leapt toward the fence.

I could feel the pointed imperfections of the metal links tear into the palms of my hands as I grabbed hard onto the fence, hoping my weight would not bend it back onto the pathway and into the waiting jaws of my worst nightmare. As luck and my skinny body would have it, the fence was secured to a side of a wooden shed next to the path and did not collapse under my weight. But I still had to scramble along the fence for twenty-five yards without falling, then likely have to deal with both Lex and Butch when I jumped off.

I felt Lex throwing himself against the fence just below my feet as I struggled in my sideways crabwalk. My hands were torn and bleeding and my crushed velvet shirt was nicked and stretched from repeatedly catching on the silver metal. In a testament to the fear of mothers everywhere, I briefly pushed the imminent danger out of my mind and thought instead about how mad Mama was going to be because of my ruined shirt.

I turned to see Butch had quickened his pace to a run and it was clear he would beat me to the end of the path. I was about to give up and take my biting or my beating, or both, when something divine—and sad—occurred.

On Lex's last leap, a cross attached to his collar became entangled in the fence and he was left hanging inches below me. I continued crawling a short distance, then jumped off the fence and turned to face Butch's onslaught. I was prepared to fend off the first blows I would ever receive in my life.

Butch lunged in my direction and I flinched. But he was reaching for his dog, not me. As he struggled to free Lex from his inadvertent noose, I took a couple of steps backward toward the end of the pathway and freedom. I didn't know whether to accept my good fortune and get the heck out of there, or watch and see how this surreal situation played out.

I chose to get away from the imminent danger. However, my tendency to run from trouble had not fully ingrained itself in my character. I slowed my sprint at the end of the pathway and surveyed the scene of my once-certain death. I was amazed.

Butch never turned in my direction. The biggest, meanest guy in the neighborhood, the same one who once laughed when a kid we knew almost drowned in his own bathtub, was cradling the world's ugliest, meanest dog like it was the most precious thing in his life. He was crying so hard that large pear-shaped droplets fell onto his massive forearms.

I wondered what could make a kid bully every boy he knew and then cry like a baby over a dog. I didn't know the answers, didn't understand the twisted lives of Butch and other kids like him, where love was held back to be earned like a carnival prize but was never awarded. I didn't know this world existed, where praise was withheld but blame was given freely and without discretion, and administered with fists and belts.

I wish I knew then what I came to know later—that when Butch was chasing me or hitting the others, he was running a race and fighting a battle he could never win until he knew the true objects of his wrath. Maybe then, I could have told him it would work out someday. I doubt I would've said it, because I hadn't yet learned how to lie.

The best I could do was to tell Butch the location of the nearest veterinarian. Then I ran from the scene. I found out later Lex had survived his near hanging. I heard, too, that Butch got slapped around pretty good for taking his dog to the vet.

Under the normal bully code, this litany of pain and embarrassment I had cast upon Butch would mean a lingering death sentence. But springtime also had a strange effect on Butch, for it had opened the first blooms of love within his heart.

On the day Butch tried to destroy me, he lost his heart to Linda, an assistant at the veterinarian's office where Lex was treated. They hit it off immediately. Butch and Lex Luther's reign of terror disappeared abruptly as spring turned into summer. Butch had found a girl who tolerated his personality. Or maybe she simply found a way to reach the goodness inside Butch none of us knew about.

Linda was everything Butch was not. Small, petite, and soft-spoken, she excelled in school and came from a family of modest wealth and high achievers. Stories filtered in from Linda's friends suggesting Butch had changed, that he was becoming kinder and showing flashes of compassion and generosity. Linda told them she was seeing this troubled boy developing into a gentle man.

But such change was not coming to his brutish father. As Butch became more sensitive and caring around Linda, he started bringing these values into his home, hopeful a transition could be accomplished there too. But he didn't realize he was dealing with countless generations of Williams males and a cycle of father-son abuse, the hate and pain growing uglier with each twisted relationship, worse than inbreeding because it deformed the hearts and souls of the sons and their futures as fathers.

Linda recognized what Butch could not, that the blackness surrounding him in a stifling, heartless shroud might still exist in their future, whether in the form of a turned back or a raised hand, or in a sharp word or a brooding silence. She tried hard to get through his cover of darkness. Open to change, Butch worked hard to remove the cloak of doubt and despair. His rage against others all but disappeared, replaced by the glow of hope and love.

And the day Linda accepted his invite to the Valentine's Day Dance, the light shined in. He had already hopped and pranced around at school, expressing his joy like Scrooge the morning after his enlightenment. We laughed (to ourselves) at his excitement, not out of ridicule but because we no longer feared for our lives. He rushed home to tell his mother.

I was sitting under the cherry tree in my back yard writing a poem to Tricia, my latest Love Phantom target, when I heard the first wave of sirens. Normally foreign sounds to my neighborhood, the sirens had been heard in connection with one family on many occasions over the years. I rushed out our gate to the edge of my front yard in time to see the ambulance and fire truck roll to a stop in front of Butch's house, behind the police car already parked there.

The sirens and flashing lights had drawn the neighbors to the street like a brilliant Fourth of July show, but the fireworks were already over inside the Williams residence. We watched as the police led Butch, his head bowed and his hands cuffed behind him, to the patrol car. He was limping worse than normal and his face was bleeding from a gash on his forehead and mouth. When he glanced briefly in the direction of his neighbors who were ringing the court in which he had been trapped his entire life, his face was the color of sheetrock. He had the blank look of a boy who had just turned into a man without a future.

His mother and father were dead, and Butch had killed one or both.

I looked at my neighbors and wondered where they had been during the years of screaming and yelling coming from the Williams home. My mother was standing next to me, and I saw she too had her head bowed, hoping, I think, to hide her own complicity. I looked at my own hands to see if they were clean.

We all had a part in the disintegration of this family, either by not raising a hand to stop the violence or closing our ears to the cries for help. Details soon trickled in regarding the only violent deaths our neighborhood had suffered since anyone could remember.

When Butch reached home to deliver his ecstatic Dance news, he was met by his mom's wild eyes and blanched face. When she tried to push him back and close the door, he shoved it open and demanded she explain the scratches on her face. Head down, she told him his father had arrived home from work drunk, slapped her around and kicked Lex when he started growling. Butch didn't wait for his mom to finish. Ignoring her pleas to stop, he sprinted out the back door and into the back yard. What he saw stopped him in his tracks.

The scene before him explained the rest of his mom's story. When Jerry Williams had continued his wife's "education," as he called his physical and mental abuse, Lex lunged and sank his jaws into the man's left calf. A hammer was nearby and Mr. Williams used it to crush the skull of his boy's best friend. As Mrs. Williams looked on in horror, her husband, a butcher by trade and by nature, gutted and skinned Lex Luther and hung him by his hind legs on the back porch.

No one knows what went through Butch's mind when he first saw Lex's hanging carcass dripping blood slowly onto the patio concrete.

Jerry Williams sat in a metal lawn chair at the end of the patio, his face obscured in shadows. "I was gonna throw the bastard in the trash where he belonged, but I thought you would like to pay your last respects and all, you know," Mr. Williams said, according to the police report. "I'm plum tuckered out by my overtime work. Before you get to your chores, I want you to clean this blood and other shit off the patio."

The evidence suggests that Butch exploded into a rage, dashed across the patio and grabbed his dad around the neck. As the two struggled on their tiny back lawn, his mom stepped in between the two. She died after being thrown like a ragdoll against a stone wall.

I attended his trial, watching Butch bow his head each day as he entered the courtroom. He wasn't ashamed; rather, I think he just didn't care about anything anymore, including the girl of his brief dreams. Saying nothing in his defense, he stared blankly throughout the proceedings, barely listening or showing interest, even when a merciful involuntary manslaughter verdict was rendered and he was given a three-year sentence.

I was haunted by details I heard related in the courtroom, and I hoped to never again see in the eyes of another the hopelessness engulfing Butch when he was led away.

Linda wrote to Butch and tried to visit him during his incarceration, but he ignored her efforts. She eventually gave in to his despair and moved with her family out of state. Released after two years, Butch moved in with two guys he met while in Folsom Prison.

⸺⁂⸺

And now, as I lay face down on the restroom floor in a pool of mop water smelling of rotting mildew, I realize I haven't thought about Butch in the two years since his trial. Maybe I too shared in the complicity that allowed a family to disintegrate—my neighbors' indifference to the screams late at night, the teachers who turned a blind eye to his bruises, and the social workers who shuffled the story of his broken life to the bottom of the stack.

Still I cannot let him know that I understand his pain. No matter the guilt I feel for his history, he and the others have masks on for a reason. I cannot let on that I recognize his red hair and limp. Keep your cool and you'll get out of this, I tell myself.

As the bigger one of the two makes one last cinch to tighten the binding holding my legs and hands together, the smaller one sits on the restroom sink idly twirling his knife. He suddenly stops the knife's spin, and says casually, "Ya ready to do it?"

The bigger one steps back to admire his handiwork and answers offhandedly, "Yeah, it's about time to end this."

I havn't been overly concerned about my welfare until this point, but their interchange has a chilling effect. "Hold on guys," I manage, though trying to talk is now a struggle. "I haven't seen your faces and I don't know your names. Take the money and go."

The younger-acting one leans down close enough that I can feel his breath on my cheek. "Ya know, I just might want to make damn sure you don't remember nothing." I feel something cold and hard rub against the bottom of my ear.

"Knock it off," barks the bigger one.

I release the breath I thought would be my last, as the knife is lowered from my neck. My relief is tempered by the bigger one's next statement.

"Our friend outside will deal with you," he says. "He has something special in mind."

The bigger one's chilling statement has just registered in my brain when Butch opens the door and squeezes into the room. "What's taking you guys so long?" Butch barks at the two boys. "The money's out of the till. And where are the keys to the safe? You were supposed to get them out of his pocket and bring them to me."

"Okay. Okay," says the bigger one. "I got 'em. Here they are."

"Keep 'em," says Butch. "I got something to finish in here."

"How much was in the till?" asks the younger one.

"Fifty-eight and some change," notes Butch, as he turns his attention to me hog-tied on the floor.

"Fifty-eight bucks," says the bigger one, who I realize now is no savior. "Dude," he says, turning toward me, "that's not a lot of money to die for, is it?"

The two masked boys laugh as they edge past Butch and out the door.

I notice Butch push the button on the door, locking it.

"I came here to kill you tonight," he says, removing his mask and shaking his long reddish mane like a wild horse, then pushing it backward. "I thought about killing a bunch of people while I was sitting in jail. I blamed a lot of people for not helping my mom and me, and I wanted them all to pay. And I hated you, hated all the fucking kids in the neighborhood for having decent parents."

It takes me a moment to realize that he has exposed his identity in a swift and shocking manner. I want to close my eyes and ignore what I am seeing, because acknowledging it means certain death. Mine.

"My parents aren't perfect and I bet the rest of the parents we know are messed up too," I say in a firm voice, though I still feel light-headed by the deadly significance of Butch's unmasking. "Having good parents hasn't stopped me from screwing up."

"I couldn't think, couldn't feel when all the shit happened," he says, talking more to himself than to me. "I wanted to fucking die too. I couldn't see no hope, couldn't see no love, even from Linda. And locked up, without anything, my hate came back. Everybody was right—I am just like my fucking father."

"You became what you saw every day," I say. "But inside, you are nothing like your daddy. Your heart was turned once; it can be again."

"No, it's too fucking late for me. I had a girl once, but I don't got her no more."

As he is speaking, I realize this is the first real conversation I have ever had with the bane of my youthful existence. He doesn't seem to be a monster and probably never was one.

Still, he has a knife firmly gripped in his hand.

He senses what I'm thinking. "Those guys out there are expecting me to kill you, 'cause I told them how much I hate you and 'cause I told them I would. Where we've been, you ain't nothin' if you don't back up your shit."

He crouches down beside me and I know my life is over. I feel the knife next to my throat. I think about my mama and daddy and the pain they will be in when I die. I hope someone else will identify my body. And then I feel a tug, and the tension releases in waves from my body.

Butch hasn't cut my throat. Instead, he's slashed the rope looped around my neck and tied to my wrists and ankles.

"I can't kill you, and I don't rightly know why," he sighs, as he cuts the rope where my hands and ankles are bound together. "Maybe it's 'cause I never heard you say anything bad about me. Maybe 'cause it was you who told me where the vet was for Lex, so it was you who helped me find Linda. Ya might be just like the others, but I'm not killing you."

He drags me toward the sink basin and props me up in a sitting position against the counter. I feel stinging sensations in my hands and feet as blood rushes back in their direction. I rub my neck, which feels like it's on fire from the rope burns.

I watch as Butch slices the underside of his forearm without so much as a wince, and wipes the blood onto the blade and his sleeve. "This will do the trick, at least for a while. I'll tell 'em you went down hard, put up a good fight. Don't come out for a half hour."

He turns and walks out, disappearing into the night, leaving me alive and wondering why.

Maybe having the hate and power to kill me, but choosing not to, is his way of vindicating himself for not saving his mother's life.

After Butch and the two men leave my station, they try to rob a convenience store across town. The store owner's twelve-gauge is too much for the trio's Bowie knives. While his two cohorts flee in a beat-up Firebird, Butch stays near the scene. Dodging the owner's buckshot, he runs next door to the County Animal Shelter. Brandishing his knife, he orders the staff to release the animals. Police arrive just after the last ones—two violent, aggressive bulldogs—have scattered from the premises.

One bulldog stays with Butch. Shelter staff marvel at the instant rapport he has with the old dog—a brutal veteran of numerous prizefights who had been removed from its owner. Butch holds the dog as if it is his own and the dog licks his face like an old friend.

Butch calmly puts it on the ground when ordered by the officers. He has his hands up ready to surrender, when the protective pit bull rushes toward the officers. The dog is shot twice by a rookie cop.

Seeing this, Butch grabs the knife at his feet and lumbers toward the officers. He ignores their order to stop and is hit by a hail of bullets, dying instantly.

In his pockets, police find Lex Luther's dog tags, a silver locket with Linda's picture, and a thick card, folded and unfolded so many times it is worn to the consistency of silk, announcing the location and time of the 1978 Bella Sierra Valentine's Dance.

Butch had decided it was time to stop running.

Chapter *13*

LOSS

I was barely twenty when I found out my daddy had cancer.

He had reluctantly visited the doctor after Mama became worried about his recurring dizziness and the shakiness in his hands. The doctors found he had a brain tumor, which they later determined spread from his pancreas.

Mama gave me the news as I was sitting with Chandni in her father's auto shop, where she worked part-time as a "gopher." When my mother walked in, Chandni and I were arguing. It was barely a month after the abortion, and things were unraveling between us.

I don't recall why Chandni and I were fighting, but I remember the look on my mama's face. It was the look of despair universal to women with dying children and lovers.

I had seen this pain, fear, and desperation in a woman's face only once before, when I was nine. I heard several loud knocks on our front door that startled me out of my snail's pace preparation for school. When I opened the door, there stood a woman I didn't immediately recognize. She had her fist pulled back, ready to pound on the door again. I glanced again at her face, which seemed to be drained of all its color, and noticed the wild, frantic look in her eyes. I realized it was a neighbor, Mrs. Dawson. She shrieked something about her son being sick and needing help. Stunned by the fear dominating her face, I didn't immediately notice Hank sprint past me until he was ten feet out the door. Hank revived her fifteen-year-old son, who had suffered a heart attack brought on by a congenital heart defect.

There would be no such hero to erase our mama's pain.

A week after finding the tumor, the doctors operated to remove as much of it as possible. I was in the waiting room with the rest of my family, except Peter, who had not yet returned from whatever distant place he was at the time.

I tried to remain calm for Mama, but couldn't help pacing the room. Finally, as our wait approached its fifth hour, the chief surgeon emerged. He beckoned Mama and Hank, and upon hearing his news they started crying.

I couldn't believe what I was seeing. It had all happened so fast. Daddy was dead, and I hadn't said any of the things I wanted to tell him.

While everybody approached my mama and brother to get the news of his death, I was frozen in place. I lost my breath. I felt chilled, then flushed with heat. The room began spinning. As I began to fall, hands grabbed both of my shoulders to keep me upright. After I was given some water, the room slowed its rotation.

I heard Christine ask, "Should we tell him now? He doesn't look so good." I was about to say I knew Daddy was dead, but I didn't have the strength to voice the words. I heard Mama say it was best I know sooner than later. Her voice sounded more composed than I thought it would, and when she leaned over, her face showed more concern than grief.

"The operation didn't come out so good," she said, patting the back of my neck.

"I know," I said. I closed my eyes, hoping to block out the finality of her next words.

She didn't say what I expected to hear.

"The tumor is malignant, just as the doctors feared. While they were inside, they took out as much as they could, but they think it has spread to other parts of his body."

Mama thought she had delivered Daddy's death sentence to me, not knowing she had handed me back the ultimate gift—his life. As I look back, that moment may have been the single happiest of my life. How often does somebody get his daddy back from the dead?

I realized it would look odd to start smiling after hearing Mama's news, so I hugged her to hide the glee on my face. I felt like George Bailey in "It's a Wonderful Life" after he found Zuzu's petals in his pocket while standing on the bridge. I wanted to jump and shout and hug and kiss everybody in the room! When I looked at the faces filled with pending death, I knew no one would understand my joy.

I didn't understand what I was feeling, but I knew I had to get out of there, had to leave the place where my father had just died and been resurrected in a matter of minutes. I mumbled something to Mama about not feeling well as I stumbled to my feet and wobbled toward the stairs. Still shaky from the news. I took the steps two and three at a time, and when I reached the lobby my lungs were on fire and the muscles in my legs were burning. My dizziness was almost gone, though, and I sprinted the last steps to the door and burst through with my arms upraised as if I had won an Olympic gold medal.

Daddy was alive!

I began to feel guilty later in the day. I recalled everyone's faces—the stunned, heartbroken looks brought on by the news of cancer's death grip on my daddy. While my confusion turned my loss into another life with Daddy, their worst fears had been confirmed. I didn't tell anyone about my second-chance secret, including Chandni. I didn't want people to know I was happy even though Daddy was dying

In the coming weeks, I sat by his bedside almost every day, holding his rough mason's hands during times he cried out in delirium. I struggled to understand his slurred, fragmented words. I was able to make out names, including his little brother, Ronnie, and a friend, J.J., here in California. Others I couldn't quite place, like Emory Wilson and Jackson White, and one that scared me, "The Grand Wizard." One name I didn't recognize, DeeDee, intrigued me more than all the others.

When I asked Mama about the names, she said there were things in everybody's life too painful to talk about. I didn't press her for more information. I held on to the names and fragments of details, though, and pledged to someday learn my father's secrets.

My elation at his resurrection notwithstanding, Daddy's decline after surgery was as inevitable as it was rapid. After a short remission provided a vestige of hope, he started slipping and was taken to the hospital.

He didn't die directly from the pancreatic cancer or even the tumor that had spread to his brain. The doctors said the complications from the cancer spreading through his body and the recent brain surgery caused his heart to give out.

I was in the room when he died. Mama was holding his hand, and my brothers were holding her. No one was holding me.

Christine was the only one of our family not gathered in his room at the end. She was on her way by bus, not knowing the gravity of his condition. She made the trip alone and arrived an hour after Daddy died. My brothers and I met her at the bus station. None of us wanted to face telling her. None of us wanted to say the words.

Hank was supposed to tell her, but he could do nothing more than turn away from her eyes when she walked off the bus. Peter delivered the news as delicately as he could.

I'll never forget the look of surprise and loss on Christine's face. It was as if she were a five-year-old girl again, her hair sucked into her mouth and her favorite dolly out of reach.

"But I didn't know I had to be here so soon," she moaned, over and over until it almost became a mantra. "I could've, I should've been here," she said, as she sagged into the arms of her two oldest brothers.

We told her it was OK, that it would have been harder for her to see him at the end anyway. But she remained inconsolable, staggering through the wobbly days that followed. I'm not sure she ever forgave herself.

I'm not sure I've forgiven myself, either, for failing to take advantage of my father's "second" life. I had four months to bridge the distance between my father and me. There was time to say all the things a son should say when he knows his daddy's time is near. The bridge wasn't crossed and I didn't say thanks or anything else.

I didn't even say I loved him.

I thought about speaking at his funeral, but couldn't do it—I don't know why. I wrote my feelings in a note and slipped it into his casket as I walked past during the viewing.

I told him I loved him. The other stuff I wrote, that's between him and me. I'll take those words to my own grave.

Daddy had a quiet way of bringing everyone around him closer. In death, he held the same subtle power. In the painful days following his heart attack, our family came together for the first time in several years.

After the funeral, we pledged to stay in touch, to meet as a family more often and not lose touch as before. But the semi-taut binding barely holding us together was loosened further in the months after our daddy's passing.

Peter and Hank floated back to their far-away lives, attached tenuously to the rest of us like spacemen connected to the mother ship by the thinnest of life-lines. Peter returned to his flock in Northeastern Washington near the Canadian border, to continue preparations for the end of the world, and Hank fled even further north, to Alaska.

Hank took Daddy's death harder than even the most sensitive among us, Christine. Losing his daddy before he felt he made him proud left a heavy burden. Hank lost his heart when his true love Ingrid died, then lost his spirit when Daddy passed away.

Unlike his brother, Hank had not embarked on a search for God and eternal truth. Death had intervened in his life twice, coldly and inexplicably, and he had nothing left in his heart to battle the fates. Where bright, shimmering light once shone, blackness now ruled. There was no God or truth to find, only eternal memories of the futility and falseness of love and his failure as a son. He had to leave the scene of love's crimes.

He left shortly after Daddy died, and our family would not see him for fifteen years.

Christine, buoyed briefly by the strength of our family coming back together and the memories evoked from her childhood, returned reluctantly to a husband who reminded her of nothing of the past except her failure to fit in.

In the midst of my first failure in love, I had little time to seek answers from my daddy's legacy. Over the years, though, I would struggle to understand his subtle messages.

I imagine Daddy spent many nights wondering what made us splinter as a family, and he probably died feeling he had failed as a father. But the maturation of a family, as much as any child, is a gradual, ripening process and we Lyons—a motley clan ridden with evolving phobias—were as much an example of this as ever existed.

We, his four children, thought he would always be around, calm and supportive, guiding us through all of life's storms. We lost this seminal belief when he died. His death left a void, an emptiness we tried to fill in different ways. One of us ran, a second searched the heavens and a third hid from reality. The fourth continued a futile search for a fairytale.

It would be a while before we realized our daddy never really left, that his gentle, helpful legacy was still with us, connecting and binding us into the family we once were.

Chapter 14

DYING LOVE

*A*dulthood sucks.

I had ample evidence of this before turning twenty one. In the three-year period after I became old enough to vote, I lost my best friend, my daddy, my unborn son and my enemy-turned-savior. The only thing I had left, my relationship with Chandni, was crumbling.

I tried to get our life together, tried to make it work, tried to find the spark that had once fueled my love for her. At one point, I asked Chandni to marry me and she accepted both my proposal and the eighty-five dollar promise ring I extended to her from my knees.

The sweetest girl I had ever known, I still found her dark eyes and exotic beauty breathtaking. I loved the way she moved; even her walking was an exquisite dance. I cared for her with all my flawed heart and was still stirred that she loved me despite my doubts.

But even being engaged, with its pledge of lasting love, was not saving us. Guilt hung over me like a soaked blanket, smothering the fire between us. Though my family and friends supported me, I felt they could see the weakness within me. Worse yet, I believed I would always see my failure reflected in Chandni's eyes. I could not accept this smallness of self I felt in her presence.

I was afraid to let her know my feelings, scared to admit to myself and our families I had failed to love her enough, even after all I had put her through. With my listless manner and distant ways, I thought I had made it clear to Chandni our relationship was ending. I figured it was as evident to her as it was to me—our mismatched natures would not work and first loves were destined to fail. Especially one riddled with overbearing guilt on one side and irreparable emotional damage on the other.

Chandni did not believe in failed destiny. To her, our love and the ring on her finger sealed our fates. She was half right. Her love would battle my fear to determine our future.

So we both let it drag on—I feeling afraid to say the truth and she being afraid to hear it. I allowed my unsaid words to turn into avoidance and deceit, lies and indifference. I could not admit to anyone, especially myself, that I had messed up my first attempt at love. I kept my feelings quiet, hoping Chandni would sense my change of heart and confront me, or better yet, dump me. Chandni, though, held on tighter the more she felt me slipping away.

I had moved on to the witty, sophisticated and intellectually gifted Janina Holden. A blue-eyed, auburn-haired beauty whose precocious, spirited nature drew me to her, Janina was the youngest member of the college newspaper staff. (I was the second youngest.) She was into reporting news, I was into sports reporting; soon, we were into each other. Her erudite worldliness belied her farm girl roots from the rural flatlands of Davis, fifteen miles west of Sacramento.

I felt love stirring for a second time, but I had not yet escaped the web spun by the heart of my first love. Extricating oneself from the broken dreams of another is a sticky matter. I didn't have the heart to be honest.

I spent as much time away from Chandni as I could, working on the school newspaper, doing homework and seeing Janina. The time spent with Chandni was usually taut, strained, and punctuated by angry words and dramatic departures. There was no formal statement we had broken up, but I thought it was clear what we once had was over, buried with a dream in a bucket in that hospital room. I didn't think cold, final words were needed.

On a Saturday in late autumn, when the orange and brown leaves of the elm tree in my front yard were fighting against the wind to keep from falling to the ground, Chandni arrived unannounced at my house. I had not seen her for more than two weeks and figured she understood the unspoken end to our relationship. Like the elm leaves, she was not yet ready to give into the winds of change.

Tragic how life is laid out, how much is fate and how much is decided by the decisions of others. A persistent fault of mine is I wait until the last minute to make choices, preferring to let the actions and circumstances of others force my direction.

Chandni burst through my front door without knocking and I could tell she was not surprised to see Janina sitting in my living room. She must have been watching the house when we drove up. She paused for a moment, to size up my new girlfriend and to steady herself. She seemed drunk or high, which surprised me as she pursued neither of these vices.

The pause was all she needed to regain her anger. She let loose with an obscenity-laced tirade directed at both of us. I don't remember much of what she said, but the gist suggested I was "a dirty, rotten asshole" and Janina was "a dirty, rotten bitch." I let her rant for a while, hoping she would lose steam. I didn't stop her more forcefully because I believed most of what she said about me. I only cut her off when she started in on Janina.

Her ravings escalated when I defended Janina and might have gone on forever or led to some blows, had my mama not come in from tending the backyard garden.

Mama had not been thrilled with my lack of closure with Chandni and told me so in the past week. "You're just like your daddy with your wishy-washy ways," she said. "You better make it clear to that girl or there's gonna be trouble."

I could practically hear "I told you so" coming from Mama's mind as she came into the living room. Chandni adored my mama, so her entrance was enough to calm her down.

Chandni left soon after the confrontation, yelling, "You really don't understand a damn thing about love," and slamming the door behind her. I took Janina and Mama to lunch to let them get to know each other and to quiet everyone's frayed nerves. I sensed Chandni was still somewhere close and I didn't want more trouble. My mama said no at first, but saw my harried face and changed her mind. "I'll drive, Stone," she said. "You look plum beat."

When we returned home an hour or so later, I still felt an uneasy feeling, not as if someone was watching me but from another kind of presence I couldn't comprehend. I looked down the street, searching for Chandni's familiar black VW. Relieved it was nowhere in sight, I walked over to my own car to make sure it was locked.

I noticed the lock button was up, and as I reached to open the door I was startled to discover Chandni had indeed not gone far. She was curled up fetal-like in the front seat. Two "empties" lay beside her—a pint of Jack Daniels and a bottle of sleeping pills.

Amazingly, she was still semi-conscious, though her eyes were glazed and rolling back in her head. I yelled for Mama to call an ambulance. Holding the empty pill bottle, I knew time was precious and I had little knowledge of even basic first aid. My brothers were the Boy Scouts, not me.

All I could do was try to keep her awake and wait. I went to hold her left hand, discovering it already held a lavender rose. Her palm was bleeding from squeezing the thorny stem. Her right hand clutched a pair of blue baby booties.

Just before she slipped into unconsciousness, her eyes became lucid one last time and she used them to look into mine. "I only wish you still loved me, Stone," she said, her voice slurred to a hollow whisper.

"I do, Chandni. I do," I said, but I did not look into her eyes because I was afraid she would see what was missing from my heart.

She didn't have to see it in my eyes to understand the truth. "You never were much good at lying, at least not out loud," she gasped weakly. Though she hadn't said them to hurt me, her words stung because they were the truth.

She seemed to be laboring to stay awake. I sensed her fading, slipping away. "Hold on, the ambulance will be here soon." Then I realized what Chandni already knew, that no ambulance crew, no team of doctors in the world could repair her broken heart.

She opened her eyes once more, and her last words rolled slowly out. "Love someone like I loved you."

All of human tragedy was left lying in my arms as the life faded out of her.

As I held her lifeless body, I lamented the ill-fated love lives of the Lyons. Hank had lost the love of his youth, Mama had lost the love of her lifetime, and now I had lost the love of my innocence.

Not only did she die due to my selfishness, Chandni looked last into the eyes of a man who no longer reflected her love. She left this life knowing she was unloved by the one who mattered most, and for that I have never forgiven myself.

I thought then that my life would be entwined with hers in pain and sorrow forever.

Part **2**

ALL STORIES OF LOVE
ARE TALES OF HEARTBREAK

Chapter *15*

SILENT HEROES AND FADING DREAMS

$\mathcal{A}$s long as I can recall, I wanted to be a hero. This goal emanated from my early desire to score the winning touchdown in the closing seconds or score the clinching goal with a diving header. My savior goal exploded into manic passion when Chandni died in my arms.

I didn't want to become a fireman or paramedic, where being a hero was a daily expectation. I couldn't handle the constant pressure. I was hoping for a situation to suddenly occur, in which I would be called upon to pull someone from a burning house or to perform the Heimlich maneuver in a crowded eatery.

Driven by regret, I worked hard at becoming an instant hero. I took CPR and First Aid courses with religious fervor and looked for opportunities use my life-saving skills. I hung out around swimming areas waiting for someone to cry out, and I circled the mean streets looking for trouble whenever I could.

I thought my prayers were answered one day when I saw a guy pummeling a woman on a sidewalk. I spun my car around and pulled within shouting distance. He called me names not my own and told me to mind my own business. "You've made this my business, buster," I yelled, opening my door. "Why don't you pick on someone your own size?"

When he lifted off the woman and turned his attention fully toward me, I noticed he *was* picking on someone his own size. Actually, she was bigger—*much* bigger. I quickly realized my intervention might have saved *him* from a savage beating.

This spindly, toothpick-of-a-guy probably figured I was an easier foe than the daunting behemoth he had momentarily out-wrestled. He left her lying on the asphalt and approached me, putting his hand in his pants as if he had something inside boasting real ammunition. I figured whatever he had down his pants would shoot blanks, but I didn't feel like taking a chance. I jumped into the car and gunned it to where the fallen woman was kneeling on the pavement. I lifted the lady to her feet and half-walked, half-dragged her to my car.

For some reason, I couldn't open the passenger door, a problem growing in importance when I noticed the man walking shakily toward us. As I fumbled to let her in, he stumbled toward the driver's side of my car. When he saw I didn't leave the keys in the ignition, he pounded the roof with his fists and gave the door a couple of swift kicks. I circled the car toward him with no plan other than to somehow stop his progress. I didn't have to solidify my intention because he seemed to lose interest in us and stumbled away.

As we sat in my car afterward, I noticed the heroine of this tale wasn't exactly a lady. She smelled like a mixture of urine, whiskey, and BO. "Why the hell did you butt in, Mister?" she slurred. "I was about to kick his skinny little ass."

I really couldn't argue, so I ignored her lack of appreciation and asked where she needed to go. "To O'Malley's around the corner," she shrugged. "Just drop me off there. I wanna git a few more drinks in me before I git home. Then I can whip the bastard's sorry ass and no one'll be there to save 'im."

My hero interest waning, I obliged her request to drop her at the Irish hangout. As I drove away, I saw her flip off two customers leaving the bar as she entered.

Although my fair damsel turned out to be a sweaty fireplug with a sailor's mouth and tattooed anchors on each bicep, she was still a woman who didn't deserve to be pummeled by anyone. I cherished the dent left in my door as the first real evidence I had hero potential. I refused to fix the damage and left it as a testament to my pseudo bravery.

Guilt spurred my superhero mindset into adulthood, to make up for the lives and loves I let slip away, starting with my ill-fated first lover and our doomed child. I first ran from commitment when I was twenty-one years old and I have been on the run ever since.

Strangely, when set free from commitment, I became hesitant in my next move, wandering if I had, indeed, missed an opportunity for true love. Such is the fate of the heart, which is often fondest of what it fails to choose or cannot have.

Many years and a trail of broken hearts convinced me this pattern started with Chandni. She was the first girl I made love to and the beginning of many who would love me more than I loved them. She would be the first of many whom I could not leave cleanly, and the one against whom I would measure the levels of pain I could induce on my lovers.

I cheated on almost every woman I dated, moving on to another lover before the relationship was over because I could not figure out any of Paul Simon's fifty ways to leave. I started drifting away, until my girlfriend felt provoked enough to confront and leave me. I usually sided with her assessment of my frailties, and we invariably agreed to call it quits.

I got karmic payback, but good. The women I adored, the women who turned my world upside down emotionally and sexually, were the ones who turned the tables and dumped me first. I fell apart a few times, after wallowing in self-pitiful, woe-is-me doldrums. I usually concluded I got exactly what I deserved because of past indiscretions.

My goal to be a hero molded my career pursuits. I majored in journalism, with the hope to one day tell the stories of those lacking voices to speak for themselves. After toiling on several small-town papers, writing obits, wedding previews, and crime blotter reports, I found my niche writing for a little known magazine, *The Eternal Flame*.

Specializing in inspirational stories, this monthly publication was my salvation. After years fighting guilt regarding Chandni and other discarded lovers, I relished the chance to recognize insignificant people who did significant things for others. I wrote about fathers and mothers, bosses and mentors, and teachers and coaches. These individuals overcame obstacles to help others, as in the spinal cord injury survivor who founded an organization to help similar survivors, and the former homeless man who pioneered "Parks of Hope" respite centers for displaced families in Sacramento, which spurred a nationwide movement. I championed unknowns who were, in reality, the true champions of the world.

I often thought about Willie-Mays, my guardian angel in Mobile, and Alex, my passionate booster growing up, and Butch, my arch nemesis and tragic savior, and how much I learned from their examples of heroism in both life and death.

Most people would not view these guys as heroes, but I did. Silent heroes are the hardest to spot. You have to know what to listen for and where to look. Often, they are right in front of you most of your life. My daddy, the eternal teacher whose lessons outlasted his life, and my mama, the ultimate survivor of both love and death, were two of my quiet heroes who remained invisible through much of my life.

Early on, I did not recognize my daddy as anything other than a pleasant, kindly man. He never told me what to do or how to live my life. He led in ways so subtle I didn't understand his messages until much later.

When I was eight or nine, one of our zillions of kitties started choking on a piece of ham in the living room, leaving Christine and me bawlin' on the floor and wondering what to do. Daddy strolled past unnoticed, in the casual, invisible manner that was his way. We didn't see his attention turn to the scene, but suddenly he was next to us. Not overly fond of cats, he tolerated them because they were loved by his two youngest children.

Without a word, he bent down, swooped up the kitten, and cradled it on his knee. He slowly slid two fingers into its mouth, and just as the kitten's eyes were beginning to roll back and disappear, he plucked the ham out. He set the dazed kitty on the floor and gave it a slight tap from behind, like the nudge the Grinch gave Suzie Who before sending her back to her room with milk and cookies. The kitty wobbled a bit before gaining its balance, then returned to playing with its other kitten friends. Daddy straightened up and turned away without saying a word. He continued his walk through the house on his way to the back yard to tend to his beloved garden, disappearing out the back door as if nothing had happened.

When I was twelve, I planned to go with a neighbor kid to the opening game of the 1973 World Series. I mean *the* World Series, with my favorite team, the Oakland A's, hosting Willie Mays and the New York Mets. At the last minute, my friend came up with a lame-ass excuse to un-invite me. As I walked in the front door crying my head off, Daddy asked what the problem was—repeating the question when blubbering made my answer nonsensical. Finally, he deciphered the depths of my despair. He said, simply, "Let's go."

I stood there dumbstruck, and he repeated his suggestion. He didn't need to repeat it a third time. We drove the hundred or so miles, bought tickets in the third deck of the Oakland Coliseum, and settled into our seats just as Kenny Holtzman's first pitch whistled toward Felix Milan. The greatest single moment of my childhood!

Mama says she didn't know why Daddy appeared drawn to helping those who seemed determined not to help themselves. He had protected his little brother Ronnie throughout their growing up in Panama City, pulling him from fights and dragging him out of bars on almost every weekend. Daddy could not save his brother, though, when in a drunken stupor he fell out of his fishing boat on Santa Rosa Bay, drowning at age nineteen.

John "J.J." Jenkins was another he tried to rescue from the depths of human failing.

Father to four darkly handsome kids who drew their beauty largely from their exotic Sioux mother, J.J. worked alongside Daddy in the masonry. Daddy said he never saw a man work better with his hands. "He can shape brick and stone into anything," he once told Mama. "But he just can't seem to get a grip on his own life."

One thing he could grasp was a beer glass. Though my daddy worked with him to curb his drinking, J.J.'s life became ruled by alcohol. Daddy did what he thought was right to help him. He covered for J.J. at work, handling his workstation when he was too hung over to function or still too drunk to care. He drove him home from work, partly because J.J. had lost his license, but mostly because he wanted to keep others safe and him out of the bars.

"Some nights," Mama recalled, "Shell would drop him off, only to circle the block and find him walking to his local bar. He'd escort him to the door and hand him to his wife."

Daddy didn't give up. He showed John the family life he was endangering by inviting him and his family on camping trips. He even started attending church again, coaxing his friend to come along. His persistence seemed to be the tonic for the troubled father, who curbed his drinking and began attending AA meetings.

Then, one early morning, the phone rings, startling me from my late-night homework. I walk into the living room just as Mama is hanging up. She tells me it was Daddy and he is coming home late because there has been some trouble with a friend.

I stay up to see what is going on. Daddy comes in sometime after three in the morning. I wander toward the kitchen, where I hear my parents talking in hushed tones. They stop when I enter. "What's going on?" I begin, halting when I see my dad's reddened eyes. They look sadder and wearier than I have ever seen them.

"Nothing, son," he says, and from the tone of his voice, I know immediately my dad has lied to me for the first time. "Now go back to bed."

Intrigued, I stop half way to my bedroom. Crouching in the darkness, I can see and hear my parents. I am struck by my daddy's voice—raspy and halting, it sounds foreign compared to the soft-spoken, reassuring tone with which I am familiar.

After work, Jenkins slipped away while Daddy was talking to his boss, took a cab home and "stole" his own car. When Daddy realized Jenkins skipped out, he checked all his usual drinking haunts, but could not find him. He swung by their home to wait for him to return. As he arrived, his stomach dropped when he noticed the police were there.

With almost two pints of whiskey in his system, Jenkins had run a red light and smashed into a car full of teenagers, killing two of them instantly and seriously injuring three more. Jenkins, who was not wearing his seat belt, flew sideways over the steering wheel and halfway through the windshield. His throat slashed, he bled to death on the hood of his car.

"I let my guard down one time, just once, and now three people, including my best friend, are dead," Daddy says, in a high-pitched tone I have never heard in his voice.

"You did everything you could possibly do but hold the man's hand," Mama says, taking hold of my father's hand.

"There is always something more you can do," my daddy sighs.

"At some point, it comes down to his choice and the decision of God," Mama replies.

"I'm starting to think there is no God," he mutters. "Or, if there is, he doesn't listen so good or talk loud enough."

The weary, defeated words coming from my Daddy's mouth hit me like a hammer, forcing me to gasp. He glares in my direction, and I search his face for recognition of my presence. His eyes are devoid of any comprehension, except despair.

I have seen this look of desperation on his face once before, on that night when I was lost in the woods. This time, though, his eyes do not hold the vision of fear I had seen so clearly in the moonlight. They register the blankness of someone lost and utterly defeated.

They are the eyes of a man who has lost his faith.

I had my own struggle with faith, starting in my early twenties. That's when I stopped dreaming.

I had been a heavy dreamer growing up. Three to four times a week, I had dreams that were typical fare—running and falling scenes, and scary monsters under the bed after watching Frankenstein, the Wolf Man or Kolchak the Nightstalker. An overriding theme developed in my teenage years. In my running dreams, I was no longer being chased by a mystery stalker; instead, I sprinted after people who needed help to escape some sort of peril. I didn't fall out of trees or tumble off cliffs—I caught people who jumped out of burning buildings and I pulled persons from raging rapids.

In the occasional dreams where I faced life-threatening peril, like tumbling off a cliff or being swept out to sea, no one was there to save me.

My dream life took on a new dimension after Daddy died. I dreamed every night, with my night stories no longer limited to short, heroic vignettes. These visions were vivid, memorable journeys into another world. So striking and vibrant and real were they that for years it seemed I lived a parallel existence. Everything in this alternate dream world was occurring in present tense—friends, family, work, vacations, sports. Each dream was uplifting and seemed to last for years. There was one difference in my parallel universe—Daddy was alive and cancer-free.

In these dreams, Daddy never smiled or talked. His stoic, pale blue eyes simply watched all that was going on. His silence didn't bother me. I was elated to once again be in his presence, seeing his forehead wrinkle and his eyes turn to pinpoints of concentration as he tied a fishhook with calloused hands resembling gnarled garlands of oak. Nothing had changed from my childhood, as I watched him sip black coffee, his sad, dreamy eyes staring off past the end of his pole, through the early morning mist swirling around Far Away Lake, toward the hills and beyond, lost in thoughts I could not fathom even in my clearest dreams.

The dreams became so profound I often did not know which world I was in—the real or the imagined. I often woke with a start, thinking I was camping with my family or eating a one-pound T-bone beside my parents in our favorite steakhouse. I often laughed at myself when I realized I was home in bed, but there was always a tinge of regret that my other life wasn't the real one. In that life, I knew I would be comforted by my daddy's silent presence.

After these vivid dreams stopped, I could not recall the sound of my daddy's voice. I would awaken, choking and gasping for air, straining to hear his words from a dream I could not remember. The resonance, the timbre, the deep, reassuring bass of his voice, and the soft, rare occurrence of his laugh were gone from my memory.

My dreams had slipped away. I hadn't stopped dreaming, as my lovers testified to my unsettled slumber, my fitful tossing and turning, my talking and gesturing. I never recalled any of this. Whatever visions I had were hidden deep inside. I had buried my dreams.

Theorists have maintained dreams play compelling roles in our waking lives. Freud felt dreams helped preserve sleep, while Jung believed they compensated for the underdeveloped parts of our waking psyche. Others viewed dreams as extensions of our everyday lives, imbued with problem-solving functions. Recent theorists purport dreams serve no viable purpose in our lives, not even as an adaptive role in the maintenance of either our physical or bodily health. Dreams are, in a word, worthless.

I came to the same conclusion at various times in my life that dreams are indeed meaningless. They lead you to hope, and hope is a path wending toward false expectations and bitter disappointment.

As my dreams faded, I seemed to lose focus in the real world. I began forgetting dates and times, misplacing keys and wallets, and losing important papers and bills. I reached the low-point when I found my car missing from my apartment parking lot and reported it stolen, only to recall I had allowed a friend to borrow it for the day. He did not appreciate being approached at gunpoint later by two policemen who recognized the car as stolen.

I discovered the source of my shaky memory retention while researching a story on learning disorders in kids. I recognized my attention deficit started in early childhood. I finally understood why I fidgeted so much in the classroom and church. I managed A's through my school years but it was a constant struggle. I had to read a page twice to comprehend it, and study twice as hard as others to remember what I learned.

My impressive grades usually landed me in the accelerated classes, where I felt inadequate compared to the brilliant kids surrounding me. I envied Alex and another brainy friend, James Fairchild, for their ability to do their math work with a ballpoint pen, or Kevin Mott, who never seemed to open a book but sailed through classes with perfect grades, while playing three sports and dating the prettiest girls in school.

I won the battle back then by following the well-ordered routine that comes with a secure childhood. My emotional listing would begin later, during the vagaries of young adulthood, and escalate through my twenties when the hearts of my family began to break apart in sections.

As one after another relationship ended, it became harder for me to handle the pain of love's loss. As I entered my thirties, I thought I hit bottom when I broke up with a beautiful, strong-willed Italian woman, Elaina, my editor at *The Eternal Flame*. The resulting fallout sent me into a tailspin that caused me to quit my job and ultimately my writing career.

I didn't quite know what to do with my mediocre life. I finally decided if I couldn't help myself, I would try to help others by working with troubled kids. Maybe I was trying to recapture the dreams I once had of changing the world around me.

Or maybe I hoped to rediscover the sound and comfort of my daddy's voice, the one that had given me so much faith and hope for the future of my world.

Chapter *16*

HOPE HOUSE

$\mathcal{I}$ was ready to change the world, or at least the worlds of the unfortunate kids in my charge, as I began my career as a counselor at Hope House, a group home for troubled teenage boys.

My boss cautioned me to check my idealism at the door and approach these kids with realistic goals in mind. "If you can reach most of the kids in a positive way, even if it is just helping them survive until they are eighteen, then you've succeeded," explained "Big John" Mahoney, a hulking former collegiate shot-putter who supervised Hope House and two other group homes run by a non-profit agency, Believe in Miracles.

"With only six kids in the house, that would seem pretty manageable," I replied.

"Yeah to a point," he agreed. "Our goal is for them to thrive, not just survive. Sometimes, reaching eighteen alive is more than they could have ever hoped for."

"Geez, that sounds frustrating for the counselors."

"This can be a fulfilling job, but the kids are really challenging at times and the pay is low," noted Big John. "The counselors who stay past a year or two usually are the ones who love what they do. But even the dedicated ones can burn out after another year or two."

My first day did not start auspiciously.

Five sets of dulled eyes looked lazily up at me from inside the dim, almost completely darkened living room. Another kid, dressed in all black and hunched on the couch with his arms around his knees, never looked up. No one greeted me, though I heard a muddled "asshole" come from the darkest area of the room.

I hadn't noticed that three sets of the eyes were severely bloodshot. The counselor training me, Omar, hadn't missed the tell-tale signs. Omar, a muscular black man in his mid-twenties with a bald head so shiny it looked freshly polished, pointed out their bloodshot eyes were probably from some stashed Wild Turkey or rolled Cannabis. "I've called their probation officers, who are coming in the morning to bottle them."

"Bottle them?"

"Take a urine sample to see what they've been taking. If they've been using, their P.O. can decide if they should spend a couple of days in the Hall."

Later at the dinner table, five kids introduced themselves in a lackluster manner. I struggled to keep their names straight. I asked the sixth kid, who had remained silent, his name. "Christian," he replied, not looking at me as he walked to the other end of the table to retrieve a pitcher of juice. The other guys had ignored his request to pass the container.

"They are all full of bullshit," Christian said in a nonchalant manner. "Those aren't their names. They don't know their last names because they're all bastards." I noticed he was much bigger standing up than he looked hunched over on the couch. He appeared close to six feet tall and two-hundred-eighty pounds.

He glanced up at me briefly, flipping aside the mane of black hair hanging down into his plate. "Satan Rules!" was tattooed on one side of his neck. I was struck by the paleness of his face, made starker by his dark brown, almost black eyes that were surrounded by layers of black mascara. His skin had a dull, lifeless hue resembling the grim pallor of death.

Though I figured he was searching for a reaction, his dark eyes remained blank even after I met his gaze with a nervous smile. Without another word, he resumed eating.

Intent on studying this kid's peculiar traits, I hadn't noticed the ruckus erupting at the table. I tuned back in to a cacophony of combat words, including "fuck you," "asshole," and "shithead" used in many creative combinations. A stern voice cut through the din.

"Well, with all that caked-on black shit and those big tits of yours, I would say your name must be Elvira," said a wiry, but solidly built kid sitting at the other end of the table. He seemed to boast stature among the other boys, as their voices drifted away at the sound of his. "Either that, or you are the big, fat Lord Jesus Christian himself, in drag, no doubt."

"Well, at least my mother wasn't a crack whore who left me bleeding on the front steps while she partied with a bunch of tweakers," shrugged Christian.

The thin kid was out of his chair and at the other end of the table before I knew he had moved. Fortunately, Omar saw it coming and slid smoothly between the two. In a calm, but firm voice, Omar told the thin kid to slow down. "Take it easy, Sean. You know one fight, even one more punch could get you on probation and kicked out of this program."

"But you heard what that fucker said about my mother," Sean said, leaning around Omar and pointing his finger at the kid in black, who had not moved during the altercation.

"I know what Christian said," Omar countered. "I also heard what you said first. You both need to learn to keep your mouths shut. I suggest you go in the back yard and take your aggression out on the punching bag. We'll talk about this more when you calm down."

Sean continued to scowl at Christian as he passed him and stalked out the back door.

"And no cussing while you're out there," said Omar, slightly raising his voice. "The neighbors are looking for any reason to get us kicked out of the neighborhood."

Omar turned to Christian, who had finished his mashed potatoes and was on his third chicken leg. "Okay, Mr. Darth Vader, rinse your plate and let's go to my office to talk this over." Christian's only answer was a grunt as he stood up, walked to the kitchen, and held his plate over the sink. He dropped the plate to make a loud clatter but not to break it, then lumbered to the end of the hall and waited in front of the locked office door.

"Okay, the rest of you guys can stop showing off for the new counselor," Omar said in a brisk, business-like yet personable voice. "There's a ton of stuff needs doing around here, so if the cussing and name-calling continue, there'll be a lot of work details handed out. Get started on your chores if you want TV privileges tonight."

After the boys completed their chores and went to bed, I poured over their case files. I had considered heeding advice from some of the counselors who felt it was better to get to know the kids before scrolling through their pasts. "It's easy to judge these kids based on what they've done or been through," said Big John, who appeared to be a man of almost delicate sensitivity despite his massive size. Omar was more pragmatic, advising it was best to know the worst that could be expected from each of the boys.

After what I witnessed at the dinner table that first night, I decided I needed to know about the stuff going on inside these kids before I went too much further. What I found opened my eyes to childhood worlds I never knew existed. Their stories read like horror movie scripts, only the monsters and their victims in these tales were painfully real.

Donnie was a solidly built, handsome black kid from the streets of North Sacramento. His father left home when he was two, spent time in jail, and later was shot dead while robbing a convenience store. His mother, struggling with severe diabetes, put him in foster care when he was three, then drifted out of his life. He was adopted at age five, then "un-adopted" at age seven and returned to the local children's home. His mother tried to get him back, but died before the process was completed. After enduring more foster placement failures, he became "unplaceable," as one social worker wrote in his file. This social worker also noted: "It's tough placing a fifteen-year-old diagnosed with severe depression and prone to violence." Donnie appeared stuck at Hope House until his eighteenth birthday.

Freddie, a black teen from a depressed neighborhood in South Sacramento, never knew his father, but came to know his stepfather all too well. When his stepfather was drunk (which happened frequently, according to Freddie's social worker), he enjoyed terrorizing his son. His favorite pastime was dragging Freddie from the house, ordering him to straddle the center line in the street, and then driving his car 80 miles per hour toward him. He would see how close he could come before stopping. If Freddie moved or even flinched, he beat him senseless. If he didn't jump out of the way, he called him stupid and beat him anyway.

The stepfather, who was white, liked to ridicule Freddie when his mother wasn't around. He called him "nigger baby," "bubble lips," and "ape bastard," among other things. Freddie's mother was oblivious to much of what was happening to her son. She had a crack habit and was more interested in scoring drugs than protecting her kid.

Sean was an Irish teen with a shock of black hair perpetually hanging over one eye. At age 16, he was caught in the middle of a fight between rival gangs in Oak Park and shot three times. He stumbled four blocks to his apartment home and managed to make it upstairs, where he found his mother in the middle of a cocaine party with her boyfriend and others. The boyfriend persuaded her to clear the place of drugs before calling an ambulance. His mom never visited him in the hospital and was gone when he was released six days later.

His social worker's report noted: *Sean still clings to the hope of finding his mother; expect him to go AWOL every once in a while to try to track her down. He has capable survival instincts, as evidenced by his ability to make it basically alone on the streets of Oak Park after his mother's abandonment. Given the name "Sean-Sean" by both the Crips and Bloods, he gained a reputation with the local cops as "a smart-ass kid with a quick wit and even quicker fists." Part con man, part chameleon, he has avoided major brushes with the cops while fitting in seamlessly with the disparate groups of gangs, pimps, pushers, prostitutes, and working-class families in his neighborhood.*

I asked Omar how Sean ended up at Hope House.

"He got too smart for the streets," Omar shrugged. "He wanted to go back to school, but needed a legitimate address to get enrolled. He knocked on our door one day and asked to live here. Most of the guys hate this place. Not too many volunteer to come here."

Jesus' file contained several Polaroids of his father Jesus Sr. showing off his tattoos. Senior wore his life on his body, a pictorial record of love and loss. Over his heart, the name of his mother was written in red-and-black Old English Gothic script. On his right bicep, "Alexia" was snaked around a red rose. His brown skin was blanched white around this elaborate work—the result of a tattoo removal of a similar snake entwined with "Gabriela."

Everything else on his body was related to his Norteno gang affiliation. A hollow star circled his navel, surrounding a large "IV." One shoulder blade was covered with a sombrero lying atop a machete dripping blood; the other shoulder blade bore a sad-faced mask drawn beside "RIP Jorge." On one side of his lower back, script letters spelled "Sacramento County-Folsom," with a tiny star above the "u" in county signifying he had done time in Folsom Prison. On the other side, a five-pointed royal crown circled the Gothic letters "NF," which stood for Nuestra Familia. Under his left eye there dripped a tear, signaling not the loss of a love but the vanquishing of an enemy.

Stenciled on the back of his neck was PBSP921347, standing for his time behind the bars of Pelican Bay State Prison, located on the beautiful California north coast but one of the toughest maximum security prisons in the country. He carved this same number—his prison inmate ID—on the chest of a Pelican Bay prison guard shortly after he had taken this guard's revolver, jammed it down his throat, and pulled the trigger. He targeted the guard for protecting a rival Sureno gang member inmate during a fight in the prison yard. Shortly after the killing, he was clubbed to death by a half-dozen of the guard's comrades.

According to Omar, Jesus had one other photo he was allowed to keep in a bedroom drawer—a picture of his dad in a pinewood box. An inmate friend of his father had gotten hold of the prison morgue photo and smuggled it to Jesus' mother. Jesus landed on probation and was nearly sent to the California Youth Authority, the state's criminal institution for young adults, for nearly beating to death a kid who teased him about his father's photo.

For all his swagger and boasting, Jesus was considered at most an entry-level gang member. A prolific tagger, his trademark graffiti could be seen on freeway overpasses, office buildings, and school walls throughout Sacramento. He was sent to a group home instead of CYA because the judge believed he was still be on the fringe of gang activity and had a shot at being straightened out in a place like Hope House.

Jake and Omar agreed sending Jesus to CYA would have cemented his future in the gang life. They also thought his tagging skill suggested he might have a talent to take him off the streets. "Still," cautioned Jake, "with a father and numerous uncles and cousins involved in gangs and his footsteps already firmly planted behind theirs, it won't take much more to keep him going in that direction."

Charlie had been removed from his house because his parents could not control him. He had threatened his mother and continually harassed his little brother. A Child Protective Services report was filed on his father after a school counselor noticed bruises on Charlie's face and arms. Charlie first said his dad hit him for "picking on his little brother," but later changed his story to say he had fallen off his bike. Police went to the home and interviewed Charlie and his parents, but no charges were filed.

Prior to the CPS incident, Charlie had been a steady student with near-perfect attendance. Charlie's school performance nose-dived and he began skipping school two or three times a week. According to his parents, he became increasingly defiant and oppositional at home. After he stole a kid's bike and threatened his mother when she confronted him, his parents asked to have him removed from the home. The social worker agreed, but her report noted she suspected ongoing child abuse. He was being removed "as much to protect him from the family, as the family from him."

Christian's father had left home on the day his son turned five. There had been allegations his father molested him, but Christian refused to discuss the matter with social workers and psychologists. At age nine, he was molested by a counselor at a camp for troubled kids. The counselor pleaded to a lesser charge, which allowed Christian to avoid testifying. He refused to discuss the incident with anyone. One psychologist wrote: *"Testifying might have helped Christian release some of his feelings, and allow him to see his statements directly impact the perpetrator's culpability. Instead, Christian's voice was not heard, legitimizing the act as a minimal incident. Because of his background and lack of opportunity to discuss his feelings, I am worried he could perpetrate with smaller kids."*

Christian then took a route similar to many kids rebelling against their surroundings—he sought refuge in drugs. He started with pot and alcohol at age eleven, experimented with glue, whiteout, and other inhalants two years later, added speed at fifteen, then discovered LSD and other hallucinogens a year later. He adopted his gothic look about the time his LSD trips began, and had been calling himself a Satanist for the past year.

Not surprisingly, he struggled in school, rarely going to classes and arguing with teachers when he did. But before being bounced out of his latest school, he had flourished in his English class and was called an "outstanding and truly unique poet" by his teacher. He was waiting to be admitted to a continuation school.

Each kid at Hope House had his own set of problems, but all had been neglected, abused, and abandoned. The six boys represented a melting pot of disintegrating childhoods.

The counselors around me came from troubled childhoods and shaky early adult years each of them had somehow straightened out. This probably explained why none of them appeared to have major problems relating to the kids.

Joaquin "Jake" Arias, a Filipino ex-gang member, was built like one of those inflatable bop bags I had as a kid. He had a small head and narrow shoulders, but his body broadened the rest of the way down. His biceps and forearms were the size of my thighs, and each of his thighs was as thick as my waist. With his expansive middle and short, massive legs giving him a low, powerful center of gravity, he resembled a human paperweight.

I made the mistake of running into Jake coming out of a door the first day we worked together. The blow knocked the breath from me and sent me sprawling into a wall. As I slid to the floor, I noticed the collision hadn't budged him. He scowled down at me, with eyes looking as if they had witnessed murder at some point and wanted to see one more.

Then he broke into a broad grin crinkling the corners of his almond-shaped eyes. "Let me help you up, little buddy," he said. "It wouldn't look good for the kids to see me knock you out on your first day."

He had a roughness about him suggesting he wasn't too far removed from his days running with both Asian and Black gangs in south San Jose. The murder in his eyes was real. Though he told me later he had never killed anyone (to my great relief), he had seen plenty of death. His best friend died in his arms. "It could have been me. I had been shot in the leg and knifed in the back, and pretty soon, I knew my time would come. So I got out. Most of the guys understood. I still keep in contact with some of them."

"I'll keep that in mind if I ever need some guys to help me move—or someone to help me move a body," I laughed, albeit uneasily as I checked to determine if he got the joke.

Jimbo was another staff with whom I quickly bonded. We had two things in common—watching sports and chasing foreign au pairs in the coffee houses and nightclubs.

I was drawn to his upbeat way of relating to the kids. He saw the upside to every situation, which was extraordinary considering the downer of a childhood he had experienced. The product of a well-to-do but broken family, Jimbo was the oldest of four children. His father was a hard-driving, philandering lawyer who wanted Jimbo to follow him into his law firm. Though Jimbo had the aptitude to become a lawyer, he had no desire to follow his father's Type-A model. When he told his father of his interest in becoming a coach and teacher, his father yanked his college financial support.

"No one fucked with my father," noted Jimbo, "except, of course, his secretaries."

The rift between dad and son led to his parents divorcing. Jimbo's mom had accepted her husband's abusive, cheating ways but could not handle his mistreatment of the children. Without his dad's support, Jimbo struggled to put himself through college. A string of odd jobs helped and finally, after six years, he attained a teaching degree. "If my fight with my dad helped Mom stand up to him and walk out, then it was all worth it," he said.

Planning to become a college baseball coach, he began working toward an advanced degree in physical education. He had a high school teaching position lined up, but instead took a job at Hope House. Having worked as a group home counselor to help pay his college bills, and finding that it gave him the most rewarding feeling of his life, he was drawn back to the kids. "I wanted to do hands-on work right away with kids to get that feeling again."

He had been back at Hope House for just over a year when I arrived.

Omar (who I discovered didn't actually polish his head but used lotion to give it its sheen) grew up in Sacramento's troubled Oak Park district. He never ran with gangs, using sports as an outlet. "I got called out a couple of times and jumped a few more times," he said, showing me several scars on his upper body, including one on his neck from a knife wound. "But my momma told me she would whup my butt if I ever even thought about joining a gang. She was tougher than all my thug friends put together."

He had several friends who didn't listen to their mommas. They were swallowed up in the gangs or the drug scene. "One by one, they got knocked off," he said, "either by getting shot or ending up in prison, or by taking the drugs instead of selling them."

He wasn't a great basketball player, but his participation led him to college, where he realized he liked helping kids. After earning a four-year degree in child development, he was working toward his Master's in social work when we met.

I knew I was hired because of my "life experience," but I felt like a rookie next to my savvy colleagues. Though older than everyone except Big John, I had little education or background in helping kids. I soon realized I had misjudged my ability to transform the worlds of these boys. Heck, I felt lucky to influence these guys to do anything as simple as passing the salt without them saying "fuck you."

While I felt like a kid at heart in many ways, I thought I had little in common with these kids. With my affinity for James Taylor, Dan Fogelberg, Chris Isaak, and the like, I had little knowledge or understanding of the rap or death metal these kids favored. I couldn't figure out their video games or grasp the slang in which they conversed. They might as well have been speaking a foreign language.

I was just as big a mystery to them, as they spent a lot of time those first few weeks shaking their heads and laughing at my differences or ignorance. While I tried to fathom why most of them wore their pants drooped halfway down their butts, they laughed at my "butt-hugger" jeans. When a staff let it slip I didn't cuss, smoke, or take drugs, they started calling me "White Mr. Clean." (Omar was already dubbed "Black Mr. Clean," for his shaved head and similar clean-living habits.) It was clear to me they thought I didn't know anything.

If they cared to, the boys could have run me out of the house in those first weeks. They were tough and unrelenting with each other, as I had witnessed at dinner that first night and many times afterward. Just before I arrived, according to Big John, they had banded against two rookie counselors fresh out of college and did enough to convince them to quit. If they did the same to me before I got my feet on the ground, I would be out the door too.

"Well, we *were* a little desperate when we hired you," Big John admitted. "I saw a spark, though, telling me you could do this, that there is a reason you are here."

I didn't tell him I took the job because I was lost and needed something significant to do beyond writing about other people's lives. Big John sensed what I was keeping inside. "Everybody tells me what a great guy I am, giving so much of myself and sacrificing my life to help these kids," he said. "Most of that is a load of crap. Part or maybe most of the reason any of us does this job is to feel better about ourselves. There's nothing wrong with this reasoning, as long as the kids' best interests aren't forgotten."

"How do I get that feeling if I don't know how to help these kids? I didn't have a troubled childhood. No one beat me. I was good in school."

"So you don't think you can relate to these kids?"

"I don't know their slang. I don't understand their cultures—even the white kids are a mystery. And I don't know their pain."

"Did you ever lose anybody close to you? Your father or mother? A good friend? Did you ever break-up with a girl? Did you ever move into a new neighborhood? A new *state*? Did you ever feel like you didn't fit in?"

"Yeah, most of that has happened to me in one way or another," I said.

"Then you've hurt like they have, even if it is in a slightly different way."

"Well, most of the bad stuff has happened after I became an adult, and a lot of it, truthfully, has been caused by my own mistakes."

"Then you can teach them how to overcome screw-ups. Most of these kids, despite their outward blaming of everyone else for their problems, live under the presumption *they* are the main reason their lives—and all the lives around them—suck."

"But I had good parents and a stable home life. We never hurt for anything."

"A stable childhood and family support can give you a good start, but it doesn't ensure you can handle the ups and downs that come with living and dying. You've had your share of pain and struggle, but you seem stable. That's what you can teach the kids."

"How do I do that?"

"By being yourself. These guys see through phonies better than anyone. They may not always like or understand you, but they'll know if you're honest and will give you a shot if you care enough to hang in there."

After the initial few weeks sizing me up, they began throwing out challenges. They brought up areas in which I obviously had very little knowledge or experience. John and Freddie said I couldn't possibly understand what it was like to be black. Sean said I couldn't relate because I had never lived on the streets. Jesus said I knew nothing about gangs. Charlie said I was just too old "like my dad" to know anything about being a kid.

I became defensive and tried explaining my reasons for not being able to relate to them. I recalled Big John's advice and decided that either defending or hiding my ignorance would turn me into a phony in their eyes. So I let them know what I didn't know.

"Why the Fu—, uh, I mean, hell, uh I mean heck, are you even here?" said Sean.

"Obviously, I must be here to learn, considering what an idiot you guys think I am."

Befuddled by my honesty, they couldn't believe an adult would admit to not knowing everything. Then they started feeling sorry for me. I overheard Freddie telling Donnie, "Man, that White Mr. Clean, he don't know nothin'. He don't know what way to dress or even how to clean his shoes (they kept their tennis shoes in pristine shape with a tooth brush and Comet cleanser). That guy is just plain goofy. Damn, he needs *us* to help *him*."

It didn't bother me that I made it past the first few months because of their pity. They had taught me their most important canon—that survival is the only imperative in life.

Chapter 17

LIFE AT HOPE HOUSE

$\mathcal{B}$efore I arrived at Hope House, I had no idea of the fragility of a child's life. In nature, I knew the mother usually stays with their young until they are old enough to face danger alone. This period of protection in the animal kingdom is relatively short. In the human world, at least in most societies, I thought a kid had at least eighteen protected years to learn life's dangers. Darwin's survival of the fittest doctrine is supposed to kick in during adulthood, after the world's dangers have been revealed slowly and safely.

The kids I dealt with at Hope House had faced Darwin's survival law way too early, and most emerged with deep emotional wounds before reaching adulthood. Over the years, I learned that evil has a voracious appetite for youth who have been damaged, left behind or pushed off the path. Left exposed and vulnerable, these kids become easy prey for pimps, pushers, pedophiles, and other predatory humans. These creatures of opportunity attack the weak and wounded like cheetahs stalking the lost and lame young on the African plains.

These grim reapers are not the creators of this evil, just its ruthless beneficiaries. The wickedness maiming our youth happens before these heartless human hyenas pick over the remains. Sinister strangers do not pose the foremost danger—kids are invariably crippled by the hate and anger, abandonment and neglect of those closest to them.

This power to destroy is not limited to malevolent monsters and the truly depraved; it exists in all of us to some degree. It is passed to us from our parents and their parents, our sisters and brothers, our teachers and coaches, friends and neighbors. Like an heirloom, hate and anger can be handed down to the child, and the results are often life-long and deadly.

I learned a lot from watching and listening to Big John. "The iniquity of character destruction is within us all," he once told me, "but the capacity to help a kid grow into a caring, capable adult is there too. Counteracting the emotional violence done to a child isn't easy. Many child psychology experts believe damage done to kids in their first five years cannot be undone. I don't agree. If I did, this place would be called 'Hopeless House.'"

I, too, believed in transcendence. My aim was to use the calm, reassuring presence instilled by my daddy to guide these kids. Sometimes I was close to the mark. Other times it felt like I was shooting in the dark. About six months after I started at Hope House, an incident challenged whether I had the guile or guts to work with these kids.

Freddie was scheduled to attend a week-long summer camp, and in the week leading up to the trip he had been the most excited Big John had seen him during his two years at the house. He had never gone to a camp or even ventured outside the Sacramento area.

So I was surprised he was avoiding packing or doing his chores. I let him know what was expected of him to be allowed to go to camp. He ignored me, so I calmly reminded him.

"Fuck you," he said firmly, without making eye contact. "I'll do it when I'm ready."

I had been called everything in the book in the short time I had been at the house, but the venom in his words caught me off guard. I was a little hurt too. I had related with Freddie better than any kid in the house since I arrived.

I raised my voice and hardened my tone, informing him he would be receiving consequences for verbal abuse.

"Get out of my room, you fucking cracker."

As mad as I was, I should have done what I had always told him and other kids to do—walk away and readdress the situation when tempers cooled.

Instead, I took a step toward where he lay in his bed. He rose to a standing position, and soon we were red-face to red-face, six inches apart.

Neither of us was ready to back down, adult and young adult both acting like kids.

"You aren't going to camp or anywhere else, for a long time, after what you just said," I barked, looking straight into his cocoa-colored eyes.

Before I knew it, he hocked in his throat a wad of saliva and spat it into my face.

A *huge* wad of spit. His gooey lugie hit dead center across my forehead and oozed onto the bridge of my nose and down my cheeks.

I was stunned. I had never been punched or hit in my life, but I believed this type of assault was infinitely worse. It felt degrading and disgusting.

Furious, I balled my fists and felt ready to explode. But somewhere—maybe in the echo of my daddy's calm voice—I found the self-restraint that had momentarily eluded me. I wiped my face with a sleeve, spun on my heels, and stomped out.

It was the closest I had ever come to hitting anybody, let alone a kid.

I was still shaking with anger when I called Big John. He listened patiently as I let my emotions explode. At the end, I told him I didn't think Freddie deserved to go to camp.

He complimented me for taking a timeout. "Boy, that's a tough one," he said. "There's nothing worse than getting a face full of spit."

"Tell me about it. I wanted to smack him in the face."

"You passed a big test," he said. "A lot of guys would have lost it."

"Yeah, but my thin skin caused a lot of the problem in the first place."

"You'll learn from that misstep. But you showed that you could handle just about anything. You were the perfect model for Freddie." He paused, and I sensed another lesson was coming, one more important than how I handled my pride.

"Though he says he's excited, we all know Freddie is anxious about this trip," he said. "And we know he's a mixed up and depressed kid. He's been holed up in his room the entire summer—well, actually his entire life. This is his best chance, maybe his only chance, to get out and relieve some of his depression. Even after what he did to you, going to camp could be the best thing for him. But it's your call. Do what you think is right."

I understood what Big John was saying. This was definitely a severely depressed kid in need of a healthy escape, and despite his behavior to the contrary I believed he wanted to go. But I was still pissed off. I waited a few more minutes, so both our heart rates could fully return to normal. After a few more deep breaths, I returned to his room.

His head was in his hands and he didn't look up when I came in. "I didn't like the way you spoke to me—and I still don't," I began. "But I overreacted. I should have respected your space and I'm sorry I didn't." I paused for a moment, then added, "But Freddie, spitting in my face was uncalled for. There's no excuse for that kind of stuff."

He kept his head down. I braced for a possible explosive comeback. Instead, I was nearly bowled over by the tone and content of what he said next.

"You spit on me first," he said so quietly I wasn't sure if I heard him clearly.

"What?"

"When you were close to my face and yelled at me, you spit on me. On my face."

"What—," I started, before stopping. I sighed. I forgot about my habit of practically foaming at the mouth when I spoke in an excited manner. I probably *did* spit on him.

"Oh," I said. "I didn't realize I did that. If it's any help, you got me back real good."

Freddie looked up for the first time and gave me a sheepish grin. "I'm sorry about spitting on ya. I kinda lost it there for a little bit."

"So did I."

"Yeah, but you walked away. A lot of counselors would have called me names or even popped me."

"I felt like losing it."

"But you didn't."

"Well, we were already even, right?"

"Yeah," he said, smiling again.

"But there's the matter of consequences."

"I know. I don't get to go on the trip, do I?"

"Let's talk about it."

And we did. In order to go on the trip, he agreed to complete three hours of work around the house (for the verbal abuse before being spat on), clean his room and finish his chores. He would serve his two-day house restriction upon his returned from camp.

We talked about why he was anxious about the trip. He confirmed what Big John and I had surmised—his fear of trying new things, meeting new people, leaving the security of his room. As he released his feelings, he seemed to brighten and relax. By the end, he was beaming and expressing excitement about the camp. "All of this could have been avoided," I thought to myself, "if we discussed these issues *before* I confronted him on his laziness."

"The next time I think you are worried or anxious about something, we can talk about what's going on, right?"

"Maybe," he replied, "now that I know I can talk to you, and you will listen."

As I was walking out of his room, I heard him say, "Thanks."

"For what?"

"For saying you were sorry. No one has ever said that to me."

"You're welcome. And thank you."

"For what?"

"For teaching me a lesson," I said. "And cleaning my face. It was really dirty from cleaning the fireplace."

Freddie's booming laughter was tonic to my ears. It was the first time I ever heard him laugh.

In an ironic twist, Freddie paid me back for giving him a second chance at attending camp. He did so a couple of days after returning from camp, and in a manner that would teach me another lesson in humility and the value of second chances.

I had taken Freddie with me to run an errand, and was talking non-stop about my own first trip to summer camp, when I started to cross a street in downtown Sacramento. Ever so gently, I felt his hand on my shoulder as I stepped from the curb. I stopped, wondering why he had interrupted my progress. A split second later, a large Ford truck rumbled past me, missing me by six inches.

"Jesus, Freddie that truck would have destroyed me!" I gasped, looking back at him in wonderment. "You know what you just did? You saved my life!"

"No, no I didn't," he shrugged. "It's really no big deal. Please don't tell the guys at the house what I did."

"Why not?"

"Cause they would never let me live it down. Saving a counselor and all. That just wouldn't be cool. That would ruin my rep before I even have one."

This time, it was my booming laughter that ended our conversation.

I learned more about patience from Donnie than anybody except my sister.

Near the end of one of my particularly tiring shifts—which included two fights and the police being called by a neighbor because somebody had thrown a rock through his window—Donnie gave me a dose of perspective.

"Don't worry," he laughed, patting me on the shoulder and flashing a radiant smile that seemed to make his Popeye eyes even rounder. "You get to go home tomorrow." At that point, I knew the meaning of time, home, and hopelessness.

Donnie had experienced more than his share of lost hope, losing both his mom and dad before his eighth birthday, and missing out on anything resembling a stable home.

Nevertheless, he maintained an amazingly upbeat attitude, even when he was continually passed over for foster placements. Gone were his mood swings as a child that left him labeled "dangerously violent." He stopped asking to be placed and rarely brought up the subject of living outside of Hope House. I would bet his reticence to move had more to do with his dread of the unknown and fear of rejection than affection for our group home.

I never understood how differently kids could face similar adversity. Some struggled mightily, while others like Donnie showed amazing resiliency.

Still, I worried about Donnie. Survival and little else appeared to be his main goal. He was satisfied with his life at Hope House, even with its constantly changing cast of characters and varying levels of comfort. I suppose it provided the stability he had been missing throughout his life. He didn't feel the need to look beyond his day-to-day existence.

As with many people who had spent much of their lives in institutional settings, Donnie's biggest enemy was hope.

We all fought the urge to be complacent in our approach to Donnie, because he was so pleasant to be around. His comforting presence was something I looked forward to every shift. It was tough to move him from the nest, even if I knew doing so would do him good.

Though Big John and I continually pushed for a foster placement, the social worker's admonition had proven true—no one seemed interested in a "physically imposing teenager with a history of severe emotional problems."

Then, when Donnie was a just a little more than six months away from turning eighteen and facing the world without any family support, I stumbled upon a possible match. It came from a memory close to my heart.

I had kept reasonable contact with the parents of my young friend Alex—Mai-lee and Henry Ashe. During the almost fifteen years since their son had killed himself, the Ashes had buried some of their sorrow by becoming active in several programs dealing with teen depression and suicide. They had recently decided to become foster parents.

I immediately thought of Donnie. Though I wondered about the mix of a white dad and a Chinese mom with the complicated sensibilities of this young black man, I felt the personalities and histories on both sides would be an appropriate meld.

I encountered the expected doubts and resistance from his social worker. "This is a tough kid, probably not a good match for a first-time foster family," she cautioned.

"His toughness and their newness won't be much of a problem," I assured her. "I know all about their passion and conviction when it comes to caring about kids. I know all about their hearts. They won't be deterred or overwhelmed."

Donnie's attitude presented a more formidable barrier. "I ain't going to live with no honky or chink," he snapped, when I began to describe the Ashes. "There ain't no way."

I had never heard Donnie speak with such anger and racial venom. I suspected his words emanated more from fear than hate. I had the Ashe's permission to tell him the entire story of their lives, including their son's death.

Donnie was quiet throughout the story of Alex. He had gone somewhere deep inside, possibly contemplating their loss as it compared to his own. When he spoke again, his harsh tone was gone. His words, though, weren't soft.

"Why didn't they stop him? How come they didn't know what he was going to do?"

"He didn't tell them much over the phone or during his short visits home from college. I don't think they will ever stop asking the question of why he did it or what they could have done to stop him. I ask myself what I could have done differently to help him. But their pain and sorrow have not stopped them from wanting to try again, to take another chance, to find hope from having someone around like you."

"Someone like me?" he asked. "How the hell could I help them?"

"Probably because you are a survivor," I said. "Just like them."

Donnie didn't reply and returned to his room. He approached me the next day to say he would check them out. "I guess everybody deserves a second chance," he said.

He spent the weekend with the parents of my childhood best friend, and came back beaming with excitement. "I'm scared, but I want to try it. I want to give them a chance."

As Donnie was walking out of Hope House, I wondered if I had pointed him in the right direction. As if to reassure me, he turned and smiled. "I hope this dang family thing works out," he laughed, "or I'm gonna kick your ugly white ass. Uh, I mean butt."

I had never heard him use the word "hope," and when he said it, I realized he had already taken the most important step into the world.

Charlie was a small wisp of a lad who almost disappeared when he turned sideways. He was a goofy attention seeker who wanted to be liked by hip Sean and Donnie. He wore the same baggy clothes and bright white tennis shoes as them, and tried to walk and talk their way. He shaved his head when they announced plans to shave theirs. He didn't get mad when they rubbed his bald head and told him they were only joking about cutting their hair.

He liked to know what was going on throughout the house and often wandered aimlessly back and forth from one room to another, like a fish in an aquarium. He had problems sitting still and focusing on activities for any length of time

His inability to focus on tasks at school and at home had placed him squarely in the path of his railroad train of a father. If his condition could be improved by taking medication, as was suggested by his social worker, maybe he could co-exist with his family.

Omar thought I was blaming Charlie rather than the real culprit. "You're asking the kid to change, when the real problem is his father."

"We both know it's harder to change the adults," I countered. "Charlie, and kids like him, stand a better chance if they have a more tools with which to work through things."

I asked Charlie why his father hit him.

"He hits me when I do something bad, like when I leave my bike in the front yard or don't pick up my clothes. Sometimes he whacks me for looking at him the wrong way."

"Does he hit you hard?"

"Most of the time he slaps or backhands me. Sometimes he hits with his fists closed, and that hurts. When he really gets mad, he whips me across my back with his belt. Sometimes his belt buckle leaves marks on me for days."

"Is that why you started skipping school?"

"Yeah. I was tired of the teachers making a big deal out of it. When they did, Dad would just beat me harder."

"Why did you threaten your mom?"

"I don't know. She pissed me off by saying I stole a bike. Mostly, I guess I did it 'cause I ain't afraid of her. But she told Dad and *he* beat the crap out of me."

"Why did you steal your friend's bike?"

"My dad tossed mine in the trash after I parked it on the lawn too much."

"He threw your bike away for leaving it in the wrong place?"

"Well, he beat me first. Then he drove me to the dump and made me throw it away."

"Do you think that was fair?"

"I done bad. My dad says I'm lucky. He says he got a lot worse from his old man."

"Do you think if you could concentrate better, things at home would improve?"

"Naw. My dad would still hit me, cause I'm a bad kid."

"Do you think you're going to treat your kids the same way?"

"If they do bad, I'm gonna hit 'em. That's how you gotta be with a bad kid."

I struggled for words to break the cycle. "We all make mistakes, kids and adults. But that doesn't make us bad people."

"But my dad says I make mistakes *all* the time," he said. "That's why I'm in here. I don't belong at home."

I realized Omar was right. Getting Charlie to focus more wouldn't go very far in solving a problem fueled by hate and anger stretching back generations.

Some days I felt small and weak, like I was battling an invisible army I had no chance to stop because it hid behind the impenetrable shield of the past.

Some kids, particularly the ones involved in gangs, were tougher for me to reach. Whether it was a cultural or language gap, or my total inexperience with the gang culture, I struggled reaching these kids. They sensed I understood little about them and tuned me out.

I was especially frustrated with my inability to connect with Jesus. His arrests for tagging and fighting with rival gangs, along with the shrine he had erected in memory of his gangland father, suggested he was deep into the gang culture. Though his Mongolian-style ponytail had been lopped off at Juvenile Hall, and our dress code prohibited the baggy khaki pants, Pendleton flannels and bandannas promoting his gang image, he seemed possessed by his gang persona. "IV," "NS," stars and crowns, and several other symbols and initials representing his Norteno affiliation were drawn everywhere on his belongings. Despite receiving repeated consequences, he showed little inclination to change.

"Most of your family is getting killed or sent off to prison," I told him one day. "Don't you see this kind of life as a dead end?"

He never answered my question.

Though I had little clue to the inner workings of the gang mentality, I knew about a kid's need to fit in and be accepted. I examined Jesus' tagging exploits to learn clues on how to reach him. We had photos of some of his tags in our files and they indicated remarkable talent. Samples of his work were also showing up everywhere—on walls, tables, doors, and appliances. Though repetitious and hastily drawn, his work nevertheless showed amazing preciseness and attention to detail. Jesus was an artist.

He took more satisfaction from his identification as a Norteno than praise for his artistry. Maybe there was some way to adjust his priorities. Instead of trying to change his gang ties, I worked on turning his artistic talent toward a more constructive direction.

I added weekly art nights to the poetry-writing evenings I had started for Christian's benefit. I hoped to open similar communication with Jesus. My chicanery seemed to work, as Jesus appeared at the first meeting with pens, pencils, and a stack of paper. Forgetting with whom I was dealing, I didn't specify any guidelines about what was acceptable and what wasn't. I was disappointed but not surprised that he chose only to draw his various tags. I sensed he had a lot more creativity he was aching to display to the world. I encouraged him to draw anything except his tags and the old world script he favored.

Nothing worked to alter his subject matter, so I curtailed the activity. He begged me to continue having art nights, even making rare eye contact with me while pleading his case. I thought his desperate tone odd, considering he had plenty of time to draw in private. I realized recognition and feedback might be the driving force behind his art interest.

Armed with this notion, I tried a different approach. I told him he could draw anything—his tags, the script, whatever he wanted. The only catch was he couldn't show anybody what he had created and he had to destroy it immediately afterward.

"He's only gonna spend his time practicing and perfecting his tags," Omar predicted.

I was hoping something else might occur. "I think he really cares about what people think about his work. Let's see what happens."

His excitement heightened and he set about drawing with renewed fervor. Then he tried to show the other kids what he had drawn. I reminded him of the rules. A few more times he tried to show his work to me and the others. On each occasion, I told him to keep the work to himself and to destroy it, as we agreed.

He reluctantly followed the rules. He started handing me the work and asking me to crumple it. I made sure I did so without looking at it.

This went on for a while, until one night he spent an extra hour on a project. Excitement illuminated his face as he handed it to me. I noticed he did not fold it as he usually did, though it was turned away from me. I was about to scrunch it up when he said, "Look at it." As if catching himself, he said, "Look at it. *Please.*"

I was startled even more by the desperation in his voice than his firm request. I also noticed his dark brown eyes were aimed directly at my blue ones.

"But you know the rules," I said.

"Please," he repeated, and I saw in his eyes it was a necessity more than a request.

I flipped it over and was greeted by one of the most stunning renderings of a female face I had ever seen. The portrait had the crisp detail of a sharp photo, but it was his deft shading and delicate attention to the curves and nuances of the woman's face that made the drawing purely and simply a work of art.

"Now that wouldn't have been nice of me to crumple up your mother, right?"

"No," he smiled. "She wouldn't have liked that. She gets bruises on her easy."

"Good job. Go ahead and keep this one."

He did. From then on, he showed me everything he did. Cats and dogs. Cars and trucks and motorcycles. His mother, over and over again, and his two sisters. A girl he met at school. Soon, the wall beside his bed was covered with his art and none of it bore any tags.

At school, he begged the principal to let him join an art class. His tagging reputation had precluded him from taking art. After checking in with us, the principle relented. A few weeks after Jesus joined the class, his art teacher approached him about painting a huge mural celebrating Cinco de Mayo.

"Wow," he exclaimed upon telling me of the teacher's request. "They used to check my backpack every day to make sure I wouldn't paint on the walls. Now they are *asking* me to paint on their walls."

A photo of the finished mural with Jesus smiling next to it appeared in the *Sacramento Bee.*

He didn't draw any more tags, either in his pictures or on anything in the house. His artwork no longer appeared around town unless he was commissioned to do it. He also stopped wearing colors and throwing down signs. He kept the photos of his father, but he no longer displayed them on his dresser. In their place were hand-drawn pictures of his father. His tattoos and threatening scowl were gone, replaced by a look of peace and contentment.

Jesus had found acceptance and recognition in the world around him simply by drawing it the way he wanted it to be.

After six months of startling progress, Jesus was let off probation and allowed to live with his aunt and uncle. As he was leaving, he handed me one last drawing.

"It's not folded, so I assume you don't want me to wrinkle it up," I said.

"Naw, you can keep this one," he said.

It was a portrait of me drawn in pencil, except for the eyes. He had used watercolors to paint them in three shades of blue—a light turquoise on the outer ring drifting into a slightly darker violet that melted into a dramatic indigo in the center. My eyes looked like twin pools of translucent spring water gradually darkening as their depth deepened. "That's pretty cool, with the three-layered blue eyes thrown in and all," I told him. "This isn't your best work though. The art is great, but the subject is just plain awful, a throw-away."

I didn't throw it away. I hung it in my cottage next to one of my other prized possessions, an autographed photo of Jimmy Stewart in a scene from "It's a Wonderful Life." Some days I gazed into Jesus' drawing as if it was a mirror, dreaming that the depth of character I saw in those deep blue watercolors was true to life. Other days, I looked a little to the right at George Bailey and fantasized I had a wonderful life.

<hr />

One morning, I was scheduled to take Christian to his interview at a continuation school for kids with severe attendance and behavioral issues. I knew something was up, when he took more than an hour to put on his "face."

I had grown accustomed to Christian's black fingernail polish and the thin layer of eye mascara. When he emerged from the bathroom this time, I was startled. He resembled a cross between a 280-pound Alice Cooper and a medieval executioner.

He was wearing a full-length black trench coat with a hood pulled over his head. Underneath, he had on a black leather motorcycle jacket dappled with silver studs and adorned with several chains of varying sizes and thickness. Skulls and pentagrams, painted by graffiti artist Jesus, covered a large area of the jacket. A road sign of "Route 666" dripping blood adorned the front of his black t-shirt, and he was wearing numerous necklaces and rings with devilish symbols on them. His left ear held a silver earring of a grim reaper holding a scythe.

His face was blanched whiter than usual and he had black raccoon-like circles around his eyes. His lips were also painted black, with the corners turned down into a frown.

Was I transporting a seventeen-year-old kid or Phantom of the Rock Opera?

This was the mask Christian put on to face the world. I called Big John to clarify if his non-traditional look fit the school scene. He laughed, saying it was not only acceptable, but probably on the mellower side at this school. "Just have him give you the heavier chains and pointed necklace. The school doesn't allow them, as they can be used as weapons."

The kids in the house had evidently seen Christian's dress-up act before, as they barely made notice of him. Freddie, though, saw my startled look. "Christian must be startin' at a new school or counseling group," he said. "He likes to impress the other kids."

"Or scare them to death," I laughed weakly.

"No, he aims to do that to the principal and teachers."

Christian adhered to his dark and dangerous persona throughout the morning, but I did get a laugh during the drive when I mentioned the "Satan Rules" tattoo on his neck. "At least you are a coordinated dresser. Not many people can match their shirt to their neck."

Despite his striking appearance and sullen, dark demeanor, Christian was one kid I thought I could reach. It took several weeks of asking before he let me read his poetry. He showed me his stuff a few weeks after I stopped showing interest in it.

Offering glimpses into his conflicting, complex emotions, Christian's writing was at times dark and brooding, filled with angry, violent imagery, and references to demons and death. Other passages exposed a lyrical, heart-felt voice of tender, delicate beauty and seemed a tentative reaching toward faith in love and hope. I surmised that underneath the cloak of leather, piercings, and black mascara, there beat the heart of a romantic.

A battle raged between the opposing voices within him, a fight to the death between his snarling growls of hate and gentle whispers of hope. He had little control over these diverse and divisive voices and no way to find middle ground. His control weakened further when he acquired a girlfriend. After a period of compliant, upbeat behavior during the "honeymoon" portion of the relationship, he started to fall apart when their relations were hit by the typical teen maladies (immaturity, jealousy, and separation anxiety).

His poetry, after blossoming with hope for a few weeks, became darker and more depressing than ever. Talk of suicide drifted into his conversation, veiled at first, but becoming more concrete as relationship problems monopolized his mind. I spoke to him about developing perspective. But he was as passionate as I once remembered myself, so getting him to think beyond the minute was hard. I tried to help him balance his emotions by reminding him to take his medication, maintain school attendance, and continue journaling.

He came home from school one day and headed to the bathroom without his customary "Hey, Stoney." Finally emerging a half hour later, he was in full "Clown Prince of Darkness" mode. He was also dazed and speaking in a slow, slurred manner. He mumbled something about having to "fulfill a blood pact with Darla," his girlfriend, and started to leave. I delayed him with small talk about school. After a bit, he seemed more lucid and angry, which I welcomed. I looked for signs of fight in him, an indication of a will to live.

Almost sure I had him distracted enough to stay until emergency backup arrived, I was drawn away by an altercation between two other residents. When I returned a few minutes later, Christian was gone. I saw he had taken his journal, and I hoped he was considering my advice to write his feelings down instead of acting them out.

Then I noticed a drawing he left on the table. It was a picture of a black valentine heart pierced with a red pitchfork. At first it looked as if the burgundy-colored blood dripping from the heart was made with a colored pencil like the rest of the drawing. When I peered closer, I realized it was real blood.

Underneath, scrawled in more blood, he had written: "In death, our blood will run together as one."

I felt a chill pass through me that belied the sun-filled sky outside.

When I called Big John, even his normally unflappable demeanor was shaken. We mobilized forces, calling in the police and several of our off-duty counselors. We called his girlfriend's parents, who said she had left to meet with Christian despite their orders forbidding her to see him anymore. We checked his normal hangouts, and even called his mother, who lived more than a hundred miles away in San Jose.

We waited for something to break. Then a week later, I received a call from Christian, who said he was OK but wasn't coming back. "I'm glad you're alive," I said. Before hanging up, he said, "Well, if I'm still kicking, I guess there's still hope."

He had remembered. I had told him many times, almost like a mantra, "It is hard to handle the mistakes of others, but even harder to live with your own. If you have the strength to survive your own mistakes, there is still hope."

Over the years, I often thought about him and his tortured heart, and hoped he remained hopeful.

In my early years at Hope House, my stormiest relationship was with Sean. It was mostly my doing. Sean was the leader in the house, with the potential to be a leader in anything he chose to do in the future. Because I expected more out of him, I pushed and challenged him more than the rest.

He challenged me in much the same way, though I think it was more a course in street smarts to determine if I had what it took to hang with the job. Initially he interpreted my easy-going nature as weakness. He didn't feel sorry for me like the rest of the guys. He led mini-rebellions to disrupt study hour and outing preparations, and he defied my authority to discipline him. When neither my resolve nor reasonable nature was ruffled, he backed off.

On one occasion though, he became particularly enraged at me. His girlfriend called to check his status for a weekend pass and I informed her he wasn't eligible. She called him on the residents' phone to discuss the matter. Hearing him slam down the phone, I made the mistake of shaking my finger at him when I went into the living room. I had forgotten that on the streets, pointing your finger is the ultimate sign of disrespect. Moments later, an incensed Sean charged into my office. I remained seated, as he stood over me, his fists balled up and his arms shaking. With his face flushed crimson red and a nerve in his neck convulsing, he accused me of making his girlfriend cry and challenged me to fight.

I was one move of aggression or one twitch of fear from prompting something ugly to happen. I wasn't scared of him, though he could probably pound me pretty good. He had calluses on his knuckles to indicate how he had survived on the streets of Oak Park, not to mention scars from three bullets. Instead, I was scared *for* him. He was a punch away from the Hall and probably CYA. I knew any kind of prison would be a death knell for him.

I didn't move, but I kept my eyes focused on him to indicate two things—I wasn't intimidated and I didn't want to provoke him. When I didn't react in a confrontational manner, he exhausted his verbal energy before turning and punching the wall. His fist carved a clean hole, like a knife slicing through cardboard, and the force of the blow made his arm disappear into the wall up to the elbow. He stalked down the hall, kicking the walls and pounding the washing machine in route to his room. He slammed his door in a final, defiant act of anger, like a musician clashing a cymbal at the end of a particularly rousing rendition.

He never apologized for what he said or for nearly hitting me, but he did approach me a few days later and extended what appeared to be grudging respect.

"You know I could have taken you apart, counselor or no counselor," he said. I didn't take the bait, sensing he might be looking for another confrontation. I noticed though he didn't have anger in his eyes, only puzzlement. "I knew you didn't want to fight me, but I didn't see any fear in you. And even after I cussed you, you didn't seem pissed. You just sat there, doing nothin', like you were waitin' for something. I didn't know what to do then."

"You're right," I said. "I didn't want you to hit me. But mostly it was because of what would happen to you, not me. If anything positive came out of that situation, it was you chose to hit the wall instead of me. Something kept you from doing it, even though every ounce of you wanted to pulverize me. That shows some growth in your maturity toward authority. Now all you have to work on is your mature approach toward walls."

Sean seemed to turn the corner after that incident. He went to school and did his chores regularly, and he helped other kids follow the program. He even backed off on Christian, asking to read some of his poetry and complimenting him on it. ("That's some dark and scary shit, but it's good shit, Dude.") He continued to try my patience over the next several months, but the incidents involved relatively minor issues. Then, just a few weeks before his eighteenth birthday and the end of his probation, his world caved in.

The telling incident started innocently enough, with a small bottle of pills falling from Sean's pocket.

There had been rumors Sean was holding drugs for his girlfriend, who had a speed habit. We had barred contact between the two, after she twice showed up at the house strung out. It was unrealistic though to believe he wasn't seeing her on his free time. The pills he dropped indicated he might be supporting her drug habit.

I didn't know whether to be direct or discreet after I saw him pick up the bottle of pills and stuff it into his jeans. Part of me didn't want to respond because I knew his P.O. was still pissed about the punching incident. One more serious incident would likely prompt the P.O. to send him to the Hall and extend his probation past his eighteenth birthday.

I had no choice. Maybe his P.O. would make an exception because he was approaching program graduation. "I need to know what you have in your pockets," I said.

"You can't make me," he challenged. "And you can't put your hands on me."

"C'mon, Sean. If you don't show me, you will be considered automatically guilty in your P.O.'s eyes and he's the one with the hammer.

But if we sit down and talk, maybe we can figure a way to convince him you're only doing this to help your girlfriend."

He didn't agree. He turned and ran out the door. Though I couldn't keep up with Sean's pace, I didn't have to. I knew where he was going.

I found him sitting in the corner of an enclosed playground not far from the house. As he sat smoldering, unaware of my arrival, I checked the gate locks on the fifteen-foot high roofless chain-link "cage" enclosing the playground. The scene didn't remind me of any playground I knew as a kid. It was more like a prison yard.

Sean loved the playground, even on the days he had to climb its fences to get in. He spent a lot of his free time there, sometimes hanging outside the gates watching the kids play inside, and other times sitting inside on a bench or a swing, reading a book. It must have reminded him of something pleasant from his childhood. In his mind, *anything* positive from the past, even this jail-like play area, was worth clinging to.

The four gate locks appeared to be secured; I was checking the last one, when Sean heard the door handle rattling and noticed my presence for the first time. He became agitated, striding from locked gate to locked gate, shaking each one with increasing vigor, the resentment of eighteen years of pain and anger building with each barred gate. He passed up the gate in front of me and paced the yard with escalating fury, like a wild animal confronting confinement for the first time. I wasn't sure he wanted to get out or wanted me to come in, just that he wanted to get at me one way or another.

So I let him.

I clicked the handle of the fourth gate and pushed open the door. "It was never locked," I shrugged, but he showed little reaction beyond a faint glint of recognition in his eyes. "You assumed it was locked, but it was open the entire time. Lots of gates—to get in or to get out—are open to you, if you're willing to work with those willing to work with you."

"You guys can't help me," he said, walking tentatively through the gate. He stood next to me, his face close enough to see the weariness in his eyes. "Nobody understands what I been through. I got two bullets still in me, stuck where the docs can't get to them. On some days they hurt like hell. And my ma...well, you recall what Christian said on that first day you got here. He was right. She *is* a motherfuckin' crack whore."

He paused for a moment, biting his lip. "Nobody can help me because no one can bring my ma back. And no one can change what my girl is becoming."

I remembered something my daddy told me when I was thirteen or so, after I complained about being one of the smallest kids in my class.

"Sean, my daddy once told me every person has two lives—one he is given and one he makes. Some people get saddled with a raw deal from the start, and they can choose to wallow in their misery or do their best to change the situation. Maybe things won't change even if you try; but one thing is for certain, nothin' is gonna change if you don't try at all.

"There isn't any doubt you've had it hard, even tougher than most. And you're surrounded by people who have had it tough too. Some of these people haven't made the best choices to change their situations. Some of them don't appear to be trying anymore. You have to save yourself before you can try to save others."

He appeared to be listening intently to what I was saying, but he didn't respond. I thought I saw tears at the corners of his eyes, but I wasn't sure.

Without another word, he started walking, stretched his stride into a jog, and broke into a full sprint toward the looming darkness. I watched him go for as long as I could, until the ruddy-colored skyline just above the horizon surrendered to the gloom, and his shrinking silhouette vanished into the blackened background of night.

Two months from his eighteenth birthday and the end of his probation, he was gone. He could not face even one more day locked up. I knew he would not be back.

Somehow, I hoped the lessons we showed him and the insight I had passed on from my daddy would guide him down the right road. I often wandered about the path he had chosen and his fate in the world.

Chapter *18*

HOPE AND HOPELESSNESS: LESSONS LEARNED

$\mathcal{B}$ig John was right. Over the years, I realized I had more in common with the boys than I first thought. It was more than pain and loss we shared, as fear was also our companion.

As with me, their fear reflected how they each moved through the world. Many of them were inner city kids imprisoned by their boundaries and afraid to leave their 'hood or barrio; in much the same way I was attached to the static, enclosed nature of lakes and mountain valleys and fearful of the vast oceans, fast-running rivers, and wide-open spaces.

We were all crippled in some way by our fear and mistrust, a condition keeping us from moving beyond our self-imposed borders. The kids feared abandonment while I dreaded the turbulent waters of a deep relationship. We each had a similar way of coping—neither of us would reach out often to others. We had long since realized we could not fail or be abandoned if we didn't attach to anyone or anything for very long.

Maybe we could learn as one to explore the world, to reach beyond self-imposed limits, to seek freedom beyond the unknown of our borders.

One of my continuing challenges was adjusting to the ever-changing faces of both the kids and the counselors. I really felt it when my friends began leaving. Jimbo and Omar attained their master's degrees and moved on to jobs better fitting their interests and careers. Jimbo, as a coach and physical education teacher, and Omar, as an activist working to refurbish Oak Park. Jake lasted the longest, almost five years, before leaving to manage his family's restaurant after his father died.

With the flux of counselor transitions and the occasional flurry of changing residents, some new kids fell through the cracks. One such kid was Mitch, a fifteen-year-old who within the first week he arrived taught me a valuable lesson about listening

Mitch didn't want to go on our outing to a haunted house, one of those barely scary productions thrown together in a temporary warehouse. He remained adamant even with my gentle urging and the kids' brutal peer pressure. Finally, either their razzing or my promise to walk him through the house convinced him to go—albeit with extreme reluctance.

He freaked out just a few steps inside when the hallway suddenly went pitch black and howling music played. He grabbed my hand with both of his and began gnawing on his arm. He totally lost it shortly after someone brandishing a knife and dressed as *Halloween*'s Michael Meyers brushed past us in the darkened hallway. He grabbed my arm so hard the knuckles and tips of his fingers turned white. I could feel his entire body trembling as if he was shivering with hypothermia. I tried to calm him but he had tuned me out. He slid to the floor and curled up with his arms and head tucked into his knees

I asked a ghoul who was wandering through the hallway if there was a way out, and he led me to a side door. I half-carried, half-pulled the catatonic kid through the door and into a lighted area of the warehouse. Mitch rebounded immediately, as if the light and open space had infused life back into him. His color and breathing returned to normal. I slipped him into the lobby where the other boys were milling about. They hadn't seen his meltdown and seemed surprised he had made it without incident. Mitch himself seemed surprised I didn't blow his cover and kept looking at me to see if I was going to mention his freak-out.

I looked in his file later that evening and discovered his mother had been known to routinely punish Mitch by locking him in a closet for hours at a time. Counselors and psychologists at previous placements had reported he often became agitated and even violent when forced into dark, closed spaces.

I admonished myself for not checking his past beforehand. After that, I went back to scouring each arriving kid's file for triggers, and made sure the rest of our team did the same.

At first sight, some kids didn't seem to match the info in their files. Devin appeared to be one of our toughest challenges, if reports could be believed. He had a history of attacking both his mother and little sister, and abusing, torturing, and killing animals. Sent to live with an aunt, he set fire to her apartment and a nearby school. He had bounced from one placement to another, from shelters and group homes to juvenile hall and the county ranch.

During his travels, he left behind an equal number of enraged peers and mental health workers. Several kids had attacked him and been sent to stricter placements, and a few counselors had been suspended or fired because they could not hold back their frustrations with him. He was placed with us because his estranged mother was back in the picture and a judge wanted him to have a last chance at a stable family life. If he didn't make it at Hope House, his next step was the California Youth Authority or a high-level psychiatric facility.

Expecting the demon seed of Charles Manson to walk in, we got a freckle-faced, cherub-cheeked "Opie" twin instead. Struck speechless by the sight of the curly-headed, frail-looking thirteen-year-old, I turned to Omar, who just shook his head and laughed.

Within fifteen minutes of his arrival, we had sufficient understanding of why "Opie" had been booted from Aunt Bee's place and was considered one of the most dangerous kids in our county mental health system. After eating a late lunch I had specifically prepared for him upon his late morning arrival, he started foraging in the refrigerator for more. I told him to hold off until snack time, when the other kids arrived from school. I wasn't surprised he became agitated at my redirection. Kids were often jumpy when they first arrived.

I just didn't think he would threaten to kill both Omar and me over a delayed snack.

"You're an asshole, you fucking four-eyed geek," he said, without looking up from the refrigerator.

The suddenness and directness of his words caught me off guard. I had been called names before certainly, but few had come from so far out of left field—or been delivered by a kid who just arrived and looked like the neighborhood paperboy.

"What did you say?" I asked, trying to hide my surprise.

"You know what I said, you fucking old man," he replied in the same cool, measured tone. He slowly closed the refrigerator door and turned toward me.

I noticed his eyes for the first time. They were dark, almost black, with no noticeable reflection or emotion in them. They resembled the glazed, empty look in many of the "Most Wanted" posters adorning post office walls. They were eyes that trapped what they saw and dragged it deep into the hellhole of darkness within them.

His next words were like long stabs.

"It is simple, Mr. Fucked Up Counselor. I could kill you and that stupid nigger back there in the office if I wanted to. I could slit both of your throats in the ten minutes it would take the police to get here."

Several kids had said much the same things to me over the years. This was the first kid I believed. The words were all bluster and bluff, but I was concerned by the lack of provocation involved and the cool resolve I saw deep in those dark eyes. I prided myself on believing everyone has a chance to succeed if given the chance, so I was surprised my mind flashed that this kid was going to kill somebody someday.

Stevie, who arrived at the house a few weeks after Devin, seemed another hapless case. He shut down the moment his social worker dropped him off. He was upset that the court had ruled his mother wasn't able to take him back from the shelter. He had been removed because chronic depression had left her unable to care for him. He refused to make eye contact or talk, except to repeat over and over in a crying, but firm voice that he wanted to go home. I tried everything in my smooth counseling arsenal, from a straight outline of the rules and regulations to a friendly, chatty approach extolling our program perks. Nothing worked. He simply stared back with the dull, expressionless eyes of a dead fish.

After hours spent encouraging, convincing, and cajoling, I called Big John and told him I thought it was a lost cause. He said to forget the persuasive tactics and stand firm. "Tell him mom's not an option—he either stays here or goes to the children's home."

It worked. Once he realized we weren't backing down, he shrugged and accepted the situation. But I never got more than a grunt or shrug from him over the next few months.

Then one day, as if some great shadow had lifted and allowed the sun to slant in, he smiled and thanked me for what I had made for dinner. Although I realized his sudden graciousness was likely prompted by his first home pass to his mother's house, I was still giddy inside about his mere acknowledgement of my existence. I felt even better the next day when he asked me to drive him to his mom's place.

When she didn't answer the door or her phone, I had a sinking feeling she had stood her son up. The door was unlocked, so we went in. I cautioned him we could only wait a short while if she wasn't there. He took a step down the hallway toward her bedroom. "She sleeps a lot during the day after she gets home from work," he said, though I knew she hadn't worked for almost a year because of her mental disability.

For some reason, I felt uneasy with him walking so far ahead of me. A sudden sensation made my stomach turn and the hair on my neck stand on end. I was about to call to him to wait for me, when I noticed he had already made it to the last doorway down the hall. He stood silent and frozen in position as I made my way toward him.

Then I noticed an odd smell. It was sweet and ripe, like decaying fruit. But there was something sharp in this odor, like it was laced with vinegar or rubbing alcohol, and it burned the inside lining of my nostrils as I moved closer to where Stevie was standing. The odor seemed vaguely similar to the rank, tart smell of spoiled garbage at the dump, and as I reached the doorway and peered over Stevie's rigid shoulder, I hoped the smell was caused by the shoddy housekeeping of a preoccupied woman.

It was the smell of death—a mother's death.

She was hanging from a wooden beam, the life choked out of her by the noose she fashioned from a green canvass sash—the taekwondo belt Stevie had earned a year before.

Amazingly, Stevie did not fall apart in the weeks following his mother's death. Maybe he was relieved her suffering was over, or that he didn't have to look out for her anymore. Either way, he began flourishing in the program and at school. There was talk of placing him in a foster home and he was open to the idea.

Not even persistent antagonizing from Devin could throw Stevie off track.

I believed in giving guys second, even third chances. But we neared our limit with Devin when he hung a doll over Stevie's bed with an attached note: "What do you do to get rid of a bitchy nigger mother? Nothing. Just let her hang herself." This came after he made other threats to kids and counselors, and his boasting that he knew the locations of the gas mains and could blow up the house with one match. When we found a detailed map to these gas mains, it was time for him to go somewhere else, somewhere more secure.

He was the first kid taken away from our house in handcuffs.

On the other hand, Stevie walked away of his own accord. He moved in with a foster family who eventually adopted him. Sometimes, it felt right to be proven wrong.

Chapter *19*

MY SISTER,
SAVIOR OF HEARTS

*C*ompassion may be the deepest virtue associated with the Lyon clan. Unfortunately our well-meaning hearts have often been misdirected in the exercise of loving. The result has been pain and hurt in some cases, loss and disillusionment in others. In the worst instances, hearts have been broken forever and lives lost.

My sister embodied the best and the most perilous sides of the Lyon penchant for unconditional loving. Christine made the rest of our family seem like novices in the art of caring. The scope of her love knew no bounds or restrictions. She was the only Lyon who regularly called and mailed birthday and Christmas cards. She made sure Mama and the rest of us received cards signed by all her kids.

Christine sought a fairytale version of love in her marriage, fighting mightily to maintain this vision over the years as it crumbled around her. I could not understand the steadfast, stubborn manner she clung to a love seemingly not being returned.

Jonathan inherited his father's cruel methods of breaking down the wills of those in his dominion. There was not the smallest mental or physical foible by his three sons that went unnoticed or unpunished by Jonathan. His retribution was swift and harsh. A cereal bowl left on the table meant no cereal for a month; a toy left out meant no more of that toy.

Christine put her foot down when he threatened to take the boys' German Shepard puppy Dario to the pound after the boys left the gate open and the dog wandered out. Jonathan countered by assuming training duties over the young dog, turning it into a vicious, volatile sentry responding solely to his commands. Out of fear, Christine and the boys didn't venture into their own back yard for more than a year. After a couple of near-attacks, neighbors started a petition to have the dog removed, and finally succeeded after Dario broke through a fence board and charged a woman who was pushing a baby carriage.

Jonathan responded by barring neighboring parents and kids from visiting the Jolson home. He had extended his war to a second front, isolating himself and his family from the outside world while maintaining a stranglehold on his wife and children inside their home.

Christine countered to prevent her sons from having the humanity choked from them. This familial war was played out against a placid suburban background, punctuated by Jonathan's ranting and raving and Christine's constant rearranging and redecoration of the battlefield. This family tug-of war may have seemed comical at times, had the stakes not involved the hearts and souls of three young men and their mother.

My sister still felt that despite the damage done to her kids by their father's cruelty and her own tacit acceptance, hope remained for their hearts to emerge intact.

Her plan was as methodically upbeat as Jonathan's was dictatorially negative. She matched every belittling remark or harsh invective directed to her sons with a soothing word or positive rejoinder. She filled their world with color and art, painting their rooms in vivid hues and prompting them to cover the walls with posters and pictures. She made sure they "made memories" by joining sports teams and clubs, keeping them involved even after their father restricted access to playing by throwing away their equipment. She ensured they learned the joys of camping, even if it was with other families.

She helped them hold on to memories by capturing everything on film. She photographed every social event and family gathering, no matter how big or small. Picnics, barbecues, miniature golf outings, camping trips, and birthday parties—even at other kids' houses. (Christine would volunteer to take photos for the birthday kid, then include one of her sons in almost every picture.) She embarrassed each son equally, accompanying them on school outings ostensibly to shoot photos for school purposes.

Though Jonathan chastised her efforts as being "unprofessional," Christine was determined to document and retain every moment of her kids' childhoods. She displayed school projects, papers, and report cards alongside the art and handmade cards they made for her on "special days." Her house became an artistic and photographic shrine to her three sons, a temple dedicated to their accomplishments and filled with framed pictures, sports trophies, school awards, and other mementos marking the memories they had made in life.

The boys grudgingly accepted the comprehensive testament to their lives, even as it was spread through the house for all their friends to see. They shook their heads and sighed each time their mother framed a new group of school pictures and added them to the overcrowded fireplace mantle and surrounding walls, or when she stuck evidence of their latest school success on the refrigerator underneath a watermelon magnet.

They drew the line when one of Jon's friends stumbled out of the bathroom and collapsed on their couch, laughing so hard his face had turned red and tears rolled down his cheeks. "Cute baby pictures," was all Jon could discern from his friend's delirium.

Jon and his two brothers rushed into the bathroom and were greeted by a triptych of newly posted pictures of them on the wall. They weren't surprised to see themselves frolicking nude in the bathtub, as their mom always had her camera ready. But they let out a collective "Shit" when they realized these weren't baby pictures.

"Geez," gasped Mitchell. "We're at least four or five years old in these photos."

"Six," corrected Jon. "I'm six fucking years old!"

Though she was free in exposing her sons' private parts, my sister was much more protective of their hearts. She wasn't sure if she had shielded them enough from the hate and resentment surrounding them.

Jon Jr. was the oldest and felt his father's wrath to the greatest extent. He struggled with stuttering throughout childhood, but his problem stopped when he went away to college. His stutter stopped all together when he moved out permanently. The next two boys suffered as well, with Drew developing an eye tick and stomach aches, and Mitchell struggling with bed-wetting. Their problems also cleared up when they left for college

My Sister's steadfast support had helped them leave their phobias and fears behind.

Jonathan became furious as his control over his sons flickered and then flamed out. Eventually, he hoisted the white flag and abandoned his fight for their souls. He refocused all his venom on Christine. "The boys were leaving the nest," she recalled. "He had done all he could to twist and mangle their lives. He was left with just me to attack."

My sister persevered in her marriage, because she remembered the little boy who had once cried out from within the man she loved. She held onto the memories they had made together early in their relationship, clutching them close even as the fabric of their love continued to unravel. As with many women whose tragic hearts love tortured souls, she felt she held the power within to help her man overcome the demons of his troubled childhood.

But in Jonathan's case, his fate had been formed into a final ugly and twisted shape well beyond the healing power of my sister's loving hands.

"We all start out as babies, son," Daddy told me once, as he was giving me a half-hearted whipping after that memorable time I didn't come home from The Ditch until well after dark. "It is up to the mamas and daddies to make sure we live and learn the right way."

Jonathan never had this chance. My gentle sister suffered most from his missing opportunity.

Jon, Joseph, and Mitchell found women with giving, sensitive hearts like their mother. But these women quickly proved scholars of the Jolson family history, and they endeavored to ensure their relationships did not mirror the one that produced three caring, but angry sons. Christine marveled as she watched them accomplish what she could not—establish ground rules of respect and kindness—from the beginning of their relationships.

"They are able to see the good in my sons, but they also understand the bad dwelling just below the surface," she said. "They don't put up with any of the garbage, like I did."

"Your sons picked women who had independent spirits and strong backbones, and commanded respect," I replied. "Yes, they learned from your mistakes, but they discerned far more from all the things you did right."

She shook her head. "What do you mean? Did they learn to roll over, to not fight back? Because that's about all I taught them."

"No, you were the buffer, the soft spot between your sons and their father. You taught them love and forgiveness. You ensured they didn't inherit his brutality by cushioning their lives with love and care. This allowed them to develop into sensitive, giving men. You saved their childhoods by helping them "make memories" to pass on to their own kids. You taught them there are no sins committed within families that cannot be forgiven."

The last statement was barely out of my mouth when I saw my sister's body stiffen.

Christine turned away from me and faced the window, looking past the lawn and trees outside, across the street and through the fields stretching beyond, her eyes searching for something further away, deep in the past but just around the corner in her memory.

"Almost no sins" she said softly, and I knew my pep talk was over. Maybe one day we would talk openly about the secret we shared about the true brutality of her husband.

Chapter *20*

THE PERILS OF PETER

My brother was an idealist in the spiritual realm very much like I was a dreamer in the romantic world. We both sought true love, though Peter set his sights a little higher.

I knew him first as my brother and second as Mama's favorite son. Mama liked his spunk from an early age. A favorite story of hers centered on when she came to realize Peter might have a future in the religious world or would, at least, be a major pain in the neck.

"I was fussin' one day about having too many kids and not enough time to get everything done, when Peter, who was near six or seven, looks up at me and says, 'I thought our preacher said God don't give no one more'n they can handle.' I didn't have to think too hard to come up with an answer for that one. 'Well, last I checked, God never had no four kids to take care of, including two of 'em still near babies, on a hot day when both the washing machine and ice box done broke down. Let *Him* spend a couple of days with you four hardheads, and He would learn a thing or two about what someone can handle.'"

"Your brother pauses a bit, seeming to think real hard, then asks, 'Aren't we all God's children? If'n that's so, that's a lot of tending to for one person, even if He *is* god, and even if all the washing machines and ice boxes are working.'"

"I didn't know whether to laugh or give him a good swat on his fanny. I just shook my head and watched him run outside and climb a tree. He

171

said he liked climbing, 'cause he could 'see the whole big world.' I could already tell he could see more of it than most of us."

Though enlightened at a young age, he sometimes carried his insight like an entitlement. Maybe he had some kind of God complex. But he was no wacko or cult fanatic trying to shape young minds to feed a warped power trip. He was, simply and sincerely, trying to help others make sense of a chaotic, senseless world.

My brother did not take the easiest path to spiritual enlightenment. During every step of his journey he met human failing, including in a few of his spiritual teachers. One such encounter cost most of his material belongings and very nearly his life.

One summer in the early Nineties, Peter moved his family and their belongings—including their twenty-five-foot converted school bus that served as their "Home on Wheels"—to the "Spiritual Insight Institute," a ranch sitting on 400 acres just outside Coeur d'Alene, Idaho.

"I thought the dude running this place was cool," Peter related in a letter. "He was helping a lot of people, including several of my friends, by letting them bring their families to live at the ranch. The people would help him run his medical supply business, which was dedicated to collecting and delivering medical supplies throughout the world.

Peter mentioned that the guy, Dr. William Seymore, had access to one of the world's largest supplies of an underground drug used to treat AIDS—a successful drug, according to Peter, that the FDA refused to approve. "I liked the way the guy went around the government to help people who were being held back by the system," he wrote at the time.

Soon after he arrived at the ranch, Peter realized something very different and dark was happening. "People were complaining that Dr. Seymore was pressuring some families to leave, telling them it was becoming overcrowded and they could return later to pick up their possessions. But then they weren't allowed to come back on the ranch, which was patrolled. I realized this guy was a sinister, wicked force. He was in it for the money and wanted everything these families had."

Peter quietly helped several families gather their belongings and move off the ranch. He was a day away from moving his own family when Dr. Seymore confronted him.

"I was in a barn where our stuff was stored, getting it ready to move, when he came in," recalled Peter. "I could tell by his jerky, twitching movements that he was lit up, probably on cocaine. I told him I was gettin' my family's belongings organized so we could leave. He didn't like it, saying I was stirrin' up trouble and messin' up his ministry."

I knew from experience what came next out of my brother's mouth. He reserved special distain for phonies, especially false prophets.

"You sick, phony bastard," Peter began, in a measured tone quickly moving up the scale. "You're the worst kind of liar, one who hides behind a spiritual cloak and uses the hopes and hearts of others to line your greedy pockets. You've taken the trust of these people and their families and twisted it into something grotesque."

My brother recalled the bad doctor's reaction. "His face clouded over, his eyes closed to half-slits, and a smile slowly formed. I remember that smile all too well. It was slimy, like the cartoon Grinch, but without any redemptive quality. Even though it was twenty degrees outside the guy was sweating from the drugs. I felt coldness like a chill of death coming from him. He didn't say anything while I talked, but never took his eyes off mine."

My brother knew he might have already said too much. He decided to get his family as far away as possible in the shortest amount of time. "I turned to pick up a box of my gardening tools, then turned back toward the barn door to leave. I saw the shadow of the shovel before it came toward my head in a swooping half-arc."

Raising his right arm to shield himself, Peter felt the flat side of the blade thud against his wrist before deflecting off the top of his head. Stunned, he fell to the dirt floor, where he was brought back to consciousness by throbbing in his arm and a stinging sensation above his right eye. As he collected himself, he felt blood running down his cheek.

Snapping back to the danger at hand, he saw Seymore raising himself from the ground. The force of the swing and resulting follow-through had pulled him to the ground. Doubting he could withstand another blow, Peter took action.

"I thought of rushing him, but he got up fast and came at me again."

Though my brother worked with his hands and battled with nature for survival on a day-to-day basis, he was not by nature an aggressive or violent man. He had rolled through his adult years without physical confrontation, except for some occasional pushing and shoving from cops or pushy vendors at crafts fairs. He preferred to handle situations with loquacious oration, using it "to bore my enemies into submission."

But as a kid, his fists did most of his talking. At first, he fought for the typical neighborhood reasons—pride and turf issues. He later narrowed it to philosophical disagreements, only doing battle with "idiots and jerks" who disagreed with his views. He stopped his fisticuffs when he became youth director at our church.

My brother was able to roll away from Dr. Seymore's next shovel thrust, but found himself wedged against a feeding trough. With no more room to roll, he knew he had to find something, anything with which to fight back. Nothing was at hand.

As Seymore raised the shovel behind his head for a final, fatal blow, he paused, looking past Peter who was down on one knee. Peter shot a glance back, and saw his daughter, Josia, standing in the barn doorway. Spurred by Josia's arrival, Peter lowered his shoulder and charged, slamming full force into the man's exposed middle. The force knocked the shovel loose and the two tumbled over a haystack.

Though fighting with a left wrist that later proved to be broken, Peter was oblivious to the pain. He let loose with a series of hooks and haymakers, and Seymore seemed to come apart in sections before crumbling to the dirt floor. He considered finishing him off with the shovel. He knew Seymore was the type of evil that would only answer with revenge to the beating. Jesus wouldn't kill him, my brother sighed, so he wouldn't do it either.

He scooped up his daughter in his good arm and hurried back to his family's barrack-like quarters. Finding that his RV had been disabled, he took a battered delivery truck belonging to the institute. He gathered his family and drove away, leaving behind the mobile home, a trailer, a tractor, and most everything else of material substance they owned.

During the trip back to Eastern Washington, my brother asked his daughter what caused her to venture into the barn. During a dream she saw a vision of Christ and another man on a cross. "I felt really sad for Jesus, and then I saw that the other man was you, Daddy," she said. "You were crying and bleeding from your head. I started crying too. That's when I woke up. I heard noises outside, so I ran—"

"Into the barn and saw Mr. Seymore with the shovel," concluded Peter, finishing his daughter's sentence so she would not have to relive the terrifying moment. "You saved my life, honey," he said, patting her on the head as she started to cry. He didn't tell her she had also saved her own life and the lives of her mother and two siblings. He shuddered at the thought of his family being destroyed, which would have confirmed a frightening vision he had seen many times in his sleep over the past months.

Compassion was a trademark we Lyons wore proudly through the years, but this penchant for caring about others would also become a brand seared into our breasts, leaving us wounded and broken-hearted. My brother had helped these families stay safe and keep their possessions, but his good deeds cost him everything he had except his family.

After barely surviving Dr. Seymore's "dark forces," my brother sought to rebuild his family's world. However, the traits making my brother a charismatic, passionate spiritual scholar and leader did not serve him as well in his married life. His devotion and desire to understand God's message did not leave him much time or energy to understand the love directly in front of him. Carma suffered through his many battles with the dark forces. Her patience wavered under the weight of Peter's obsessive spiritual involvement.

The battle with Seymore and subsequent loss of most everything they owned prompted Carma to demand a shift in Peter's priorities. In one of his infrequent letters from up north he wrote: "She's becoming more insistent that we slow down our mission and focus on family priorities. She doesn't quite understand this mission *is* our family's priority, and we are running out of time to get God's message across before the end comes."

The fact he was acknowledging Carma had demanded *anything* led me to believe his family priorities had indeed gotten out of whack. Carma had the face of an angel and the disposition to match. I had never heard her voice rise above a whisper, and she moved so softly she appeared to be floating. I often wondered if Carma was merely an extension of my brother, the soft part allowing him to have compassion for the lost and dejected sons and daughters who drifted his way, hungry for spiritual help.

Looking back, I think she was a life force of her own that my brother did not yet recognize.

My brother, for all of his spiritual enlightenment and visionary compassion, was a chauvinist at heart. He would dispute this label, claiming he was merely interpreting the Bible as it related to the necessity for a wife to be obedient to her husband. "For the past few years it seems many of my undertakings have failed as a result of Carma's inability to truly commit to our mission," he wrote. "Though she's listening, she is still very strong-willed and independent. It's important she dedicate these energies toward our goals."

My brother was the most spiritually enlightened person I knew, so I felt funny sending a reply saying, in essence, "Wake up brother and smell the incense." I suggested he was becoming the worst kind of social and spiritual activist, the type working so hard to save the world he forgets the smaller, but greater entity surrounding him—his own family.

His response was what I expected. "Jesus' followers and his own family did not understand him and tried to deter him from his mission. Mama is probably disappointed in me and maybe so are the rest of you. I'm torn between settling down and enjoying life with my family, or following the path laid out for me by the Spirit. An intense, undeniable force is leading me to organize a circle of spirit teachers. People are telling me I'm supposed to be one of the thirteen 'new' messiahs. I don't know about that, but the fact I am on a spiritual mission is becoming evident and undeniable.

"There are dark forces controlling much of the world. I have seen the evil running throughout the legal system, how it is destroying people. The system is powerful, dangerous, and merciless. I want to do something about this evil before it destroys all of us."

Armageddon came earlier than even my brother expected, and it was accompanied by considerably less fanfare and scope than he envisioned. The skies were not filled with mushroom clouds and radioactive rainbows, and the polar ice caps had not melted. People were not yet scurrying for higher ground in the world's tallest mountaintops or seeking out Peter as one of the chosen leaders of the beleaguered survivors.

The end of the world, at least in my brother's eyes, was limited to his own singular pain. All of his spiritual awareness and Godly faith could not save him from the atomic bomb leveling his heart when Carma walked out.

Peter related the news in a letter of lament, beginning, simply, "Carma left me today." She was gone, and so were Josia and Rachel.

He blamed "dark forces" for ending his marriage, but hinted that much of the darkness working against him was in the black hole of his own heart. "Maybe there is something within preventing me from using God's light to see what is right in front of me."

When it came to women, the most spiritual man I knew was as blind as the next guy.

Chapter *21*

RUNNING INTO PERFECT BEAUTY

*L*ove sometimes starts with something as simple as a turn not taken or a twist of one face toward another. It can begin with the slightest touch of skin on linen or a chance word spoken. You can look for it in all manner of places, or you can just stand around and hope that it comes your way.

Or you can just barrel into love, like I did while jogging through McKinley Park in downtown Sacramento on a spring morning in my thirty-third year.

I had taken up running in my mid-twenties and had become consistent at it by the time I entered my thirties. I didn't particularly like it, but felt my heart needed the work. I preferred running around tracks and circular loops rather than along straighter routes. I felt more at ease knowing where my path was headed.

I liked tracking my progress. Precisely timed and compared to past clockings, my runs represented the few moments in my life I actually felt control over the sands in the hourglass. Other times, a clock measured all I had wasted or lost in my life.

I enjoyed jogging through McKinley Park in East Sacramento because it was located near my office and the group home. I also liked that the running trail wended through Sacramento's Municipal Rose Garden. I had been drawn to the beauty of roses since I witnessed the magic of my daddy's handmade lavender blooms. On my days off, I often drove 45 minutes from my small cabin in the foothills above Folsom Lake to continue my running regimen through the park. I wish I could say I was motivated to witness the rows and rows of roses forming a dazzling kaleidoscope of striking hues, both as a way to remember the romance of my youth and to regenerate my withered cultural and creative side.

Alas, it was the Cro-Magnon side of my brain leading me down this path to where lust, not love, was in bloom. As the weather warmed and the new buds of spring opened from the plants and trees, I noticed something else bursting forth in the rose garden. Surrounding me, seemingly on all sides as I ran through the park, were baby carriages being pushed by well-scrubbed, well-built foreign au pairs.

I ran in the park on Mondays, before my two-day overnight shift started at the group home, and on Wednesdays, after my shift ended. Jake, who clued me to the au pair legions, lived nearby and let me shower before I went to work or headed home. I also began running in the park on Thursdays and Fridays, and occasionally on weekends when the weather was clear and sunny.

The au pair army was easily distinguishable from the housewife battalion by their hair, clothes, and "natural perkiness." The au pairs' hair was usually long, flowing and split-end free, standing out in stark contrast to the bob-cut or pulled-back styles of the harried housewives in charge of their own kids. The au pairs dressed in sexy, sophisticated style, wearing form-fitting cashmere sweaters and petite skirts or skin-tight jeans and shorts. Their bouncing walks and winsome, yet inviting smiles hinted they had little worries beyond taking care of someone else's children and finding a way to stay in America.

But the moment I ran into love, time stood still for the first time in my life.

I hold close the memory of that particular morning. Here it is, just as it occurred:

As I glide through the heart of the park at my usual turtle-like pace with my head telescoping like a submarine periscope, I catch the eye of not one, but two spectacularly beautiful au pairs looking my way. As I focus, I think the two look a lot alike, almost as if they could be sisters. Slowing my run to a near walk, I realize the two look so similar because they're more than just sisters, they're twins. They're taking care of what appear to be two sets of twin toddlers.

I return their smiles and give them a little wave while calculating the double entendre circling my mind. When a duck waddles past me, I realize I'm practically running in place. I shift gears, making a mental note to take one more loop through the park. Increasing my speed as I head up a small hill, my mind is still focused on the miracle of genetics and the two pairs of tight jeans I have just seen.

I throw one more glance over my shoulder to make sure what I saw was not merely an exotic dream, and then turn my head forward.

Pow! Something hits me hard in the face and knocks me off balance. A woman tumbles backward onto the grass, her arms outstretched toward a double baby carriage. My momentum carries me a few steps sideways and I hit the handle of the carriage, spinning it toward where I have just come. Stumbling, I touch my hand to the ground, but avoid falling. To my left, the woman yells, "Oh, no!"

I turn just in time to see the wheels of the carriage inch their way onto the asphalt path and begin rolling slowly down the slope. Not a steep hill, it's still big enough to create sufficient speed to cause a problem if the carriage turns over.

I take a quick step, but my running shoes are soaked with the morning dew and can't find a grip in the grass. I lurch forward, landing hard on my hands and knees. Refocusing and taking a steadier approach, I find traction with my first step onto the pavement and catch up to the rolling carriage in four long strides. Reaching out for the handle, I am startled by someone else's hand as it flashes past and grabs hold of the carriage at the same time. The woman, who was sprawled on the ground the last time I looked, has somehow caught up to me near the bottom of the hill.

Her momentum, however, threatens to carry her past the carriage. I wrap my free arm around her lower waist and turn my body and feet sideways in an attempt to stop the force of our combined forward motion. We come to a skidding stop at the bottom of the hill, but our momentum throws me off balance. Falling backward, I realize I will tip over the carriage if I keep holding it.

I release the carriage, which comes to a sideways stop on the path. I continue my fall, dragging the surprised woman toward me. We land in a heap on the grass, with her on top. Collecting ourselves, we glance into each other's eyes. My world is filled with pools of green, and I feel woozy as I descend deep into the dark emerald waters.

A sudden movement resuscitates me from the dizzying depths. The woman is pushing off me and scrambling to her feet. Upright, she peers into the carriage and starts speaking in a foreign dialect I recognize as French from my three years of placid high school study of the ultimate romance language.

Feeling cold clamminess creep over my body, I sit up and check my situation. I have fallen onto a lawn flooded into a virtual swampland by a broken sprinkler head. Water drips from my arms and my t-shirt clings like plastic wrap. Lucky me.

My show is a big hit with the au pairs and housewives, who paused from their duties to watch the spectacle and are now clapping and laughing loudly. The twin bombshells laugh the loudest, apparently quite satisfied with the havoc they have wrought.

Somewhere in the back of my head, though, I hear the last verse from the Jimmy Buffett song, *Margaritaville*: "There ain't anyone else to blame/ It's my own damn fault." Adopted long ago as my personal anthem, it seems quite appropriate in this situation.

Shaking my arms to loosen the water, I survey the scene. Meeting my eyes is a steely gaze quite different from the languid pools washing over me moments before.

"Why do you not look where you are going?" she barks firmly.

"Maybe I wasn't looking, but what were you doing in the middle of the path?" I manage weakly, sounding like a man on trial who is unsure of his own innocence.

"I was on one side of the path," she responds in a frigid tone, emphasizing "side" with the hardness of an ice block. "I saw your head pointed in one direction and your mind aimed somewhere else. I tried to stay out of your way, but you veered directly into us."

"If it's any satisfaction, your elbow caught me square on the jaw," I say, trying to rub feeling into both sides of my face. She doesn't answer, but her unaffected look tells me that she wishes she clocked me about two feet lower. "Well, at least I stopped those munch-kids from rolling down the hill," I offer, though I suspect my gallantry won't be appreciated.

"We both stopped them," she corrects. "But it was your carelessness that made them start rolling down the hill in the first place." She says "carelessness" so slowly it seems ten times longer than its three syllables.

My head clears so that I can take a good look at the lady I just trampled.

When I size up a woman, I start in the most important area of the body—the ring finger on her left hand. What I see determines the extent of further inspection. As a practical rule more than a moral one, I don't date married women. But a ring means I can gaze at their physical beauty without fear of either commitment or rejection. I am more relaxed, witty, and articulate in these situations because I harbor no hope worth spoiling.

So, when I spot a modest silver wedding band on her left hand, I'm surprised it brings only momentary relief. The detached calmness usually present when I discover a woman is married leaves me the moment my gaze finds this lady's face. Her lips are round and full and naturally crimson. Her skin is smooth and flawless, with its olive tinge taking on an incandescent glow from the brightness emitting from her large, mesmerizing eyes.

Oh, her eyes! They are the color of fused opal and jade, with small, rust-colored veins adding texture. When I came face-to-face with her anger moments before, they were fiery, green marbles. Now as I catch them in a calmer moment, they are languid and full and dreamy like a watercolor painting still moist and beginning to run ever so slightly.

I have seen several women who at first look rendered me speechless, prompting me to spontaneously buy a rose or grab a handful of daisies growing alongside the road and present them as gratitude for their striking good looks. I have scrawled poems to memorable waitresses and handed notes of fierce passion to delicious women in grocery stores.

Until this moment, I have never met a woman whose exquisite beauty locked my heart and threw away the key, all in one look

Maybe the blow to my jaw knocked something loose. I shake my head crazily, trying to rearrange the insane thoughts and feelings already swirling in my head. I try to right my swooning ship with a practical question or two.

The ring indicates she might not be an au pair as I had initially figured based on her cultured looks and double baby carriage. "Are these your kids?" I ask, as I watch her check how well they survived their wild ride. I peer over her shoulder and see that the little boy, who appears to be two or so, and the infant girl are both smiling and laughing. When she fails to acknowledge me and continues to comfort them, I answer my own question. "They must be yours, after you pulled that Jessie Owens act to catch up to them."

"What did you say?" she replies, turning toward me in an absent-minded manner. She recalls the gist of my words before I repeat them. "Oh, they are not mine," she sighs in a tone clearly indicating she wishes they were. "They belong to this couple who are both incredibly busy lawyers. I guess I am not unlike the many other young ladies in this park you seem to admire so much."

I'm stung again by her uncanny knowledge of my lustful eye toward the foreign nannies, though I'm not sure if she has confirmed proof of my wolfishness or is merely fishing. I avert my eyes, fearful of showing my guilt, and am drawn again to her ring.

When reminded of the thin, almost invisible wedding band, my heart skips a beat for a reason I cannot explain. Not only had I just met this woman, I had flattened her while eyeing other women. She is married and probably already despises me—and I'm still having heart palpitations like a smitten school boy.

Realizing that she sees my gaze locked on her ring, I feel sure she can hear the pounding in my chest as well. "I hate to disappoint you," she says, "but I am not a wild and free young thing from Estonia or the Ukraine searching for an overly excited American to be my ticket to stay in this country. I do not need a husband—I already have one."

Chagrined that she can so easily discern my inner nature, I play it off in a comical manner. I feign a punch follow-through to my face, throwing my head over my shoulder. "Pow! You really tagged me with that one." Turning my face, I offer my other cheek. "Here's the one you clocked once before. Finish me off."

She laughs in a way that surprises me—knowing, comfortable mirth intimating we have been friends or something more for years.

Instead of saying her name, she hands me her business card. "Madame Merchant," I read aloud, "Muh-Dhom" and her last name, "Mare-shont."

"I am impressed," she nods, and her tone tells me she genuinely is. "Most Americans see my name in print and pronounce it 'Mad-em Murchent.' How did you get it right?"

"Ah, three years of French in high school," I respond. "Most guys took Spanish or German, but I heard French was the language of love. I kind of liked that part. I also liked the odds—I was one of only three boys in the class, compared to twenty or so girls. I didn't learn much, except how to guess well at pronunciations."

The first name on the card confuses me. "Madame? No offense, but that seems rather formal for an au pere."

Her response is sharp as a French sabre. "My name is Elise, but I put 'Madame' on my cards because I want to be taken seriously, to be respected in this country," she retorts, emphasizing "respected" like three short sword jabs. "I want parents and their kids to address me with respect."

I fend her off by saying, "My name is Stone and I feel like rolling away."

Fortunately, my name slowed her thrusts. "Stone—a usual name in America, yes?"

"Not really. I was named after my daddy, Shell Stone Lyon Sr.," I say.

"Lion? Your last name, how is it spelled?"

"L-y-o-n. Pronounced just like the king of the beasts. I think it had an 's' at the end once upon a time, 'Lyons,' but the tail got bit off some time or another."

"That is so funny," she said. "L-y-o-n, pronounced 'Lee-own' in French, is the town I am from in France."

"There you go," I laugh. "We might be 'kissin' cousins.'"

"Kissing cousins?" she says, puzzled. "Cousins kiss each other here in America?"

"Only back where I come from, in Alabama."

She still seems confused, so I wave a dismissive hand and let her return to putting her baby world back in order.

While she fusses over her young charges, I take a second, surreptitious look at her. She indeed bears resemblance to many of the European au pairs I have seen in the park and the local coffee houses. I dated two foreign nannies, one from Italy and the other from the Ukraine, and hung out on occasion with their friends, most of them also au pairs. This lady has the European look common to her au pair counterparts, with the bangs of her dark brown, almost black hair cut short across her forehead. Her hair runs long and straight to the midlevel of her back, where it is cut with precise evenness.

I guess it's true that most, if not all, men look at women in much the same way a butcher sizes up meat. We have our favorite parts like a butcher has selected cuts. There are breast men and leg men, butt guys and shoulder guys. There are thin men and fat fetishes, piercing lovers and foot freaks. I admit a decided interest in full lips and dark, flowing tresses. But down deep, I find luminous, exotic eyes my lustful weakness.

Elise's translucent pools of green leave me trembling below my waist.

I spy attributes indicating Elise is different from other au pairs—and almost any other woman I know. Though her cute hairstyle and large, rounded eyes suggest a false naiveté common to au pairs (and often used to their benefit to woo gullible, lustful American males), Elise has a seriousness and maturity level belying her relative youth, which I guess to be twenty-six or twenty-seven years old.

I search for some sort of smooth line to use as a ruse to meet again. I don't want to come across as a come-on artist, but glibness under pressure, especially when it comes to women I have just met, is not my specialty. Then, just before pushing off to leave, she turns her head slightly, locking one eye on me. She holds the look almost as if she expects me to say something.

Under the pressure of her gaze, though, my thumping heart drowns the thoughts I try to gather. When the words finally form, they're like cotton in my dry mouth and roll forth like tangled tumbleweeds. "Ah, uh, I thought that, maybe, you or me, I mean both of us, could get something, sometime near the future, together, I mean, uh…"

"Well, if somewhere in that muddled speech you are asking to get together for coffee or lunch, then I think we can do that. How about noon tomorrow, right here?"

"Sure," I say slowly, sure she can hear the noise my heart is making.

"But you have to promise me one thing," she adds.

"Uh, what?"

"That you will not knock me down when you see me."

"I won't." Emboldened, I say, "But is it OK if I pull you on top of me in the grass?"

"I do not let anyone do that to me until the third date."

And then she marches off without looking back, leaving me with my mouth wide open and my heart exposed.

She and I met for lunch the following day, and I remember this meeting almost as vividly as our first.

She arrives alone, with no baby carriage or kids in tow.

"Who are you—the absent-minded au pair?" I say, rising from my sitting position on a bench near where we had met yesterday in a heap on the ground.

"Oh, and how are you, too?" she chastises, startling me with a kiss on each cheek. I quickly dismiss it as a European custom, but the softness of her lips stays with me and I fight the urge to touch my face to see if I can feel the moistness from her kisses.

"Uh, I'm sorry," I say, trying to regain composure from both her pointed rejoinder and soft kisses. "I thought you might have forgotten something."

"Oh, the kids," she says, shrugging. "It is one of my days off."

"Days off? I thought au pairs worked every day. At least the ones—"

"You dated? Slept with?"

Her directness again jolts me. I manage a vague comeback, complete with proper grammar. "With whom I have been acquainted."

"Well, I hate to burst your red-blooded American male balloon, but I am not a full-time au pair. Actually, I am more like a part-time nanny. I do not live with the family and I only work a few days a week on an as-needed basis."

"You seemed to take great joy in making me believe you were a full-fledged au pair."

"I have been in the park enough times to see how you look at those young au pairs," she shrugs. "And I never told you I was an au pair. That was all in your little head. Just for fun, I wanted you to think wild, exotic thoughts about me before you found out I was just a boring married woman."

I flinch at her "little head" remark but brighten at her reference to noticing me and being a "boring married woman." I steer our talk toward practical subjects, mostly because I fear the wild, exotic thoughts growing in me for a woman who is out of reach.

"What do you do with the rest of your time?"

"I teach and play music. The flute, more specifically."

"So that's how you lure men to your side. You are the Madame Pied Piper of Lyon."

By her puzzled face, I quickly determine this is one of the fairytale colloquialisms she doesn't recognize. Then again, it may be my abridged French version throwing her off. I move to another subject, one I surprise myself for broaching.

"What about your husband? What does he do?"

I really want to ask her why he has to exist at all, but instead I listen to her tell me about the man I already envy beyond all others.

Though she has thus far given little hint of feeling self-conscious or guilty about meeting me for lunch, she seems relieved to have an opening to discuss her husband Albert. Talking about him probably insulates her from any self-judgment issues.

A budding young executive for an international trading firm, he was sent from the company's headquarters in Lyon to the Sacramento area to assist in establishing the company's West Coast operations. Married for two years, Elise accompanied him willingly to the States, though she left behind a successful teaching post and a promising career in France's leading symphony orchestra.

Both twenty-three, they have been together for eight years. They started as friends, with him supporting her through tumultuous teenage rebellions against her parents. Friendship evolved into a tenuous first love and his gentle nature helped them avoid the pitfalls often derailing teen relationships. Married at age twenty-one, they were considered by friends and family to be a perfect match in interests and temperament.

"Somehow, even from the little I know of you, the match in temperament would be translated into 'opposites attract.'"

"Yes, he is the quiet, steadying force, while I am the volatile, emotional one. But our different natures make for a pleasant contrast. And we both have a similar love and talent for music. When we dated, people said we were the missing pieces from each other's puzzle."

She says about his love and passion for her has grown even stronger after the newlywed stage. "He is still in that blissful and blind romantic stage, where he just cannot get enough sex. He must do it two or three times a day, even when I'm tired at night and just want to go to sleep."

Despite her glowing words about Albert's passion, I can't help but notice a hint of detachment in her words and tone.

She discusses her passion for music, which started under the watchful eye of her forceful mother and continued under the guidance of several of France's leading music teachers. I figure it is her mother's stern hand and will, and the years of musical training fueling Elise's air of sophistication and composure.

She admits frustration with her limited involvement in music since arriving in California. "Teaching opportunities initially looked promising," she says, "because of all the young families streaming from the San Francisco Bay Area to the more affordable Sacramento region. For some reason, however, few kids are taking private lessons. I only have a few students."

Her performing opportunities have also been limited. "My credentials seem to work against me getting work locally, where I am seen as overqualified. I have considered auditioning for the San Francisco Symphony, but I am not yet ready to make the drive."

For now, Elise says she finds most of her joy in taking care of the two children in her charge—Mathew, age two, and Sylvie, age one. Her nanny duties are clearly a training path toward her own coveted goal of becoming a mother, which she seems every bit as passionate about as her music.

As I listen to her, I realize she talks with no hint of a French accent. Her words roll from her mouth in crisp, confident syllables, and I notice she never uses contractions. She speaks English more fluently than anyone I know—American or otherwise.

So when we stroll to a small French café and she talks to the owner in her native tongue, I'm jarred by her transformation. She speaks in a thick, flowing accent, sounding neither typical or clichéd but every bit as romantic and sensual as books and movies portray the French language. Hearing her voice and watching her lips form the French words make the hair on my arms and neck stand up, not to mention other parts of my body. When she speaks the different languages, I feel in the presence of two completely different women. Fortunately—or unfortunately—they are both sexy as hell.

I find myself drawn more and more to her other enchanting contradictions. She carries herself with dignified, almost royal grace, but there is a restless nature about her suggesting she cannot wait to get where she is going. And her well-aligned figure, constructed with lines and angles and curves of symmetrical perfection, contrasts with the imperfect—yet perfect—contour of her face. Her ears are a little large and rounded and her nose is tilted ever so gently off-center, like a chess piece slightly askew from its square.

At once exquisite and enigmatic, unique and unmatched, Elise is, in a word, unforgettable.

"I do not know why I am telling you all this," she says, sounding sincerely surprised with herself. "I have not talked about these subjects with anybody here in the States, and now I am telling you, a perfect stranger, about my entire life."

"Well, let me correct you on a couple of points, Miss Chatterbox. First, we're not exactly strangers. You've eye-balled me daily for a while and we've already rolled around in the grass together. Second, I find a lot of people feel comfortable opening up to me. Maybe it's because I work with troubled kids and I used to be a journalist. I've had to be a good listener. Or maybe I'm just a dull guy with little to contribute beyond a comforting ear."

I had thrown her a self-effacing bone and she took off running with it. "I do not know you well, but one thing I am sure of is that there is lot bubbling inside of you," she relates. "You are anything but dull, if evidenced only by your work with children."

"Ah, that's only a cover job to get chicks. This is the Nineties—ladies are taken with men who have a sensitive side. Take the guy who shows up at a coffee shop with a baby or a dog. Women flock to him. I know guys who borrow babies and dogs just to attract the ladies."

"Do you have babies or dogs you borrow?"

"Naw. I just work with a kid who has "Satan Rules" tattooed on his neck and one who held his classmate out a school window until he coughed up his lunch money. They're a big hit with women at the coffee cafes. I just have to remember to keep them on a leash."

At one point, she glances at her watch and realizes we have been talking on the park bench for almost two hours. We have completely forgotten about lunch.

"Oh, gosh," she says. "We have been here awhile. We never did get anything to eat. Maybe we can still grab a bite."

"Ah, that's alright. I'm not big on food. I'm partial to young, delicious au pairs."

"I am glad I do not qualify as one of your entrees. But I have been told I am quite a tasty dessert."

"What are you—a cream puff or chocolate mousse?"

"Neither. I used to be a cherries jubilee. Now I am a French tart."

Wow! Dazzled again! She has thrown the bone back into my lap, but all I can reply is a weak "I bet you are" as we trade kisses on the cheeks and say our goodbyes.

As she walks away, I realize we did not set another time to meet. I'm not sure she even wants to meet again, but I ask anyway. "Hey, how about lunch again soon?"

"Cool. Next Tuesday, same time right here. Is that good?"

"Yeah."

"And do not forget what I like to do on my third date."

"A roll in the grass," I murmur to myself as my jaw sags. Though I have no doubt she is just teasing me, she again succeeds in leaving my mouth agape as she leaves the scene.

I watch as she walks across the park lawn without once looking back. She carries herself in an almost regal manner but her perfect posture is neither stiff nor wooden. She moves with an ease and confidence in her surroundings suggesting she has lived her entire life in America, not just the past three months.

I wonder if the reason she feels so comfortable has something to do with me.

During our lunch, I thought that underneath her self-assured, polished veneer there seemed to be something lost or misplaced. At times, her wondrous eyes looked empty and her confident voice trembled. At other moments, I detected a hint of desire in the inviting nature of her eyes when they looked into mine.

At least I hope I did.

Or am I just dreaming?

Either way, I have run smack into perfect beauty and there will be no turning back.

Chapter **22**

MUSIC OF THE HEART

$\mathcal{E}$lise and I met regularly once or twice a week for lunch or to just sit in the park and talk. We both had the time—my two-day shift at the group home didn't start until Thursday morning, and she only took care of Mathew and Sylvie in the mornings and did not begin teaching until the late afternoon. Soon, we branched to other activities that included browsing local art museums and hole-in-the-wall bookstores, and hiking nearby trails. We even visited a small planetarium to check out a laser show set to Mozart's symphonies.

I was curious as to why she always left it to me to choose our afternoon agenda. I attributed this deference to her busy schedule or an element of her French nature. But as I saw her more, I realized passivity was not a normal part of her personality, nor was she following a cultural edict. I wondered when I would come to understand the reasons for her acquiescence.

We talked about everything—our families, beliefs, triumphs, losses, and past love interests. I related the pain of losing my daddy and the emptiness I still felt. She had never suffered a major loss of a loved one and was sure she couldn't survive the death of her dad.

She related her first sexual encounter, occurring when she was fifteen. "He was an older dancer, nineteen I think, with a finely chiseled physique. It was totally forgettable, as he was more into his perfect body than he was into me. Pfft! It was over in five minutes."

She related Albert was the only other man with whom she had slept.

Though I didn't feel comfortable talking about other women, I told her about my first sexual experience—with Chandni—including our initial farcical attempts. She thought our bumbling efforts were hilarious and sweet.

I didn't tell her of the fate of my unborn son and my first love. Maybe one day I would take a chance and tell her.

I needn't have worried about discussing sex with Elise. She was not the least bit self-conscious about the subject. Instead she seemed stimulated, imploring me to talk about my sexual background. I figured her sexual frankness and interest might be a cultural thing.

"Our whole family, we walk around naked in our house," she said one day, confirming a cultural link to her openness. "Well, except for my mother. With my father, my brother and my sisters, that is the way it has always been since I was a little girl. Sex and the body, it is not such a big deal in France like it is here. Everybody here, they are so uptight. Especially the American women. They need to relax and explore their bodies more."

She was equally frank in her assessment of my recent misadventures in love, which had included short-lived relationships with the aforementioned au pairs, and a waitress and bartender at my favorite Sacramento sports bar hangout Triple D's. I admitted losing interest before they did, but waiting until they figured it out or I had met someone else.

"It is OK to have a relationship just for the sex, if both of you know that is the reason," she said. "But you have been acting very stupid, keeping things going even after you know your feelings are gone. If it is not meant to be, it is better to cut things short right away, before hopes get raised and hearts get broken."

Making cutting motions with her fingers, she added, "Snip! Snip! Just cut it off!"

I learned more about her parents and her family's unique lineage—generation after generation of her relatives had perfect health and even healthier marriages. She reiterated, however, that her marriage to Albert was considered to be the one by which all others in the family, past and present, were measured.

I couldn't tell if she was trying to reinforce my impression of the marriage—or hers.

"We do have a great marriage—I mean, he has always been there for me, and we are best friends," she said, but she didn't look me in the eyes. She looked somewhere in the distance, maybe all the way back to France.

"Sometimes, though, Albert and I are not on the same wavelength," she said. "He thinks we should be as passionate as when we were dating. But I do not think love can sustain that level of heat. The feeling does not lessen; it merely spreads out over time."

"I have to agree with your husband on this one," I said. "I've never been married, but I couldn't accept the passion lessening until it became a homogenized mixture."

"What is this word 'homogenized?' I do not know this word."

"It means making everything mixed to an acceptable, agreeable level."

"What is wrong with that?"

"Nothing, it you don't want your life to have flavor, or if having everything safely mixed and matched isn't contrary to your very being and nature."

"There is a place for comfort in life."

"But there is no room for complacency," I said. "As *you* well know, passion fuels creativity, and creativity is what gives meaning to life."

"Stone, are you saying my life is meaningless because I am missing a little passion?"

"No," I said, a bit surprised by the sudden venom lacing her words.

"Well, you do not seem to have gone far enough with a woman to have your own passion tested."

"My problem's been a matter of commitment, not passion," I countered, leaning toward my car door to avoid the next verbal haymaker I expected to be thrown my way. I had just pulled into her apartment complex after sharing lunch at a small Italian café.

"My husband and I, we make love all the time—morning, noon, and night," she said, pinning me against my car door as much with her forceful voice as her leaning body. "If you want, I can tell you of the many positions we do it."

"No, that won't be necessary," I said. "I've been developing a pretty good picture in my head of the passion that goes on between you two."

Leaning over the steering wheel and practically on top of my lap when she fired her sexy salvo, Elise froze at my semi-quick-witted comeback. I tried not to look down her white blouse fringed by embroidered flowers, but my eyes and my body could not ignore the fact she wasn't wearing a bra. I looked away quickly, but the twinkle in my eye probably let her know I had seen both of her small, perfectly proportioned and delicately upturned breasts.

When she leaned back to collect herself, I could see the outline of her hardened nipples clearly through her white blouse. Her nipples were large and pointed, and resembled chocolate kisses pressed against waxed paper.

"Whew! Now that's the passion I've been talking about!" I said, not sure if she was buying my ruse that I was talking about her words rather than her breasts.

She didn't let on either way, but I noticed her eyes slide from my face down to below my waist to where my hardness had made its presence known unbeknownst to me.

"I see your passion comes out in public every once in a while, too," she said smiling as she stepped out of my car. For once, she turned toward me as she walked away. I don't think it was for any other reason than to let me know her breasts were still excited, and would likely remain that way until her husband spotted them as she walked through their front door and took her right then and there, on the living room floor.

At least, that was what I thought she was saying to me without using words, as I looked at her once again with my mouth open and my lust exposed.

The next time we got together, I asked how her husband felt about her having a male friend. "What do you tell your husband about our lunches and the other things we do?"

"I tell him most everything—where we go, what we do. I even tell him you are a handsome American with big blue eyes. He just shrugs and goes back to what he is doing."

"He doesn't sound like the jealous type."

"In his mind, there is nothing to be jealous about. He is used to men showing interest in me. He knows I like the attention, but feels I would never do anything beyond an occasional wink and a wave. 'They can look all they want, but it is me you come home to.'"

I didn't remind her we were doing much more than just winking and waving. I also didn't tell her the hopes growing inside my chest and the visions I had while awake. I didn't tell her that she was at the center of all of these hopes and dreams, however foolish or farfetched they were. I didn't tell her I wanted much more than a wink and a wave in return.

Instead, I kept my passion hidden and my heart rolled into my sleeve, as I focused on developing my first friendship with a woman whom I wasn't dating.

As our days and weeks of meeting turned into months, Elise opened my world to the subtleties of music, the nuances of the tones and notes of the classical compositions I had previously avoided out of fear and ignorance. My parents had neither the money nor the inclination to expose me to music lessons as a child, and I grew up educated only in the pop music of the Beatles, Rolling Stones, Monkees, and the like favored by my brothers and sisters. Over the years, I developed my own musical tastes, focusing on lyrics and not the music. I agreed with lovesick crooner Chris Isaak's belief that "the only good song is a love song." I didn't understand classical music and I was intimidated by those who did.

Elise understood my preference for lyrics, but felt I was missing a major part of the picture. "Many of the most beautiful love songs in the world have no words. They create a feeling right here," she said, grabbing my hand and placing it on her breast just over her heart. "They paint a picture of love as beautiful as anything Monet or van Gogh created."

As I slowly removed my hand from her chest, I realized my appreciation for classical music was expanding—and growing larger—by the second.

Surprisingly, her favorite composer was an American, Samuel Barber. She called him the "Romantic Composer," which I didn't understand. Used to music with words, I couldn't close my eyes and imagine that instrumental music alone could pull my heartstrings.

Elise was patient. She never belittled my lack of music sophistication or my inability to play an instrument. Many of her adult students had tackled music later in life, and she respected their effort. She saw I was eager to learn, no matter what she was teaching.

"You may not know how to play or understand much about instruments, but you can learn how to listen to music. Music has a message all its own, especially for those who understand romance. I can tell by your way with words, the rhythms and cadences you use, you feel the romance of music. You just need to know how to listen."

She didn't go too much in-depth with me, but emphasized I should always listen to the secondary instruments playing behind the music. "The main instrument is the heart of the piece, but the layered tones and notes underneath are its soul."

She lost me with discussions of pitch and tonal scales, but I seemed to catch on fairly well when she discussed the differences between minor and major key. She played various examples and was amazed I seemed to have a natural ear for this one aspect of music. She also noticed most of the music I liked was played or sung in minor key. I shrugged when she pointed this out. "I don't know why. I have always liked sad, melancholy songs. Maybe I hit my head when I was little and my brain got stuck in minor key."

"You cannot hear the difference in your head, you feel it right here," she said, placing her hand over her heart."

"That explains it," I said. "My heart has been broken enough times it probably can only feel in minor key."

She walked me through all the great composers and explained their individual drawing points. She introduced me to the technical mastery of Beethoven, the passionate appeal of Mozart, the delicate artistry of Chopin.

But her discussion of music, especially music of the heart, always made its way back to Barber. Her favorite love song was his composition, "Adagio for Strings."

"This is the music of love," she explained in describing the adagio. "It depicts the act of making love better than any photograph or painting. It starts slow and deliberate, like two lovers intimately exploring each other with their lips and fingers and tongues. It builds with tension as the impatience of each lover grows, until their bodies almost whine with intense inner longing for each other. With the music building toward a shattering crescendo, there is a wavering of rhythms, as if the bodies are on fire from the friction and their sweat is dripping, stinging their eyes as they near a shuttering climax.

"But instead of an explosion of cymbals and drums expected from such an awe-inspiring, breathless buildup, there is only an ethereal siren of exclamation, like a primal scream coming from deep inside each of them. Then, as if this perfect act of love has taken from them their very last breaths, a great silence is all that is heard."

"You make it sound so dramatic, like some kind of Greek tragedy," I said.

"It is in a way," she shrugged. "The silence not only signifies their breathlessness at the height of their sexual ecstasy, but also their death. For these two lovers, there is nothing worth living for after such perfection."

"When can I listen to this epic tragedy?" I asked, in a manner bordering on flippant. Though I was mesmerized by her description of this wordless love song, I tried not to let her know the full extent of my growing desire to hear this song with her in my arms.

"When the time is right," she replied, only elevating my desire.

Using my portable boombox, we spent many afternoons listening to each other's music, from Beethoven and Barber to Simon and Garfunkel, from Mahler and Vivaldi to Taylor and Springsteen, and much more.

I watched in wonder as she listened to the music. Any type of music made her come alive. The change was a physical transformation, marked by a flushed face turning her cheeks almost translucent and making her rounded eyes more animated than usual. She often struggled to express these feelings, her near-perfect English becoming mixed-up and choppy, as she searched for the right words. "Some music, it makes my insides come outside of me, like I am exposed, open. I know those words do not sound right in your language." In desperation, she would grab my hand and make me feel her flushed face. "It is like I am burning up," she would say. "Look, I have goose pimples," she would add, pointing to the small bumps covering her arms and forcing my hand to touch them.

I didn't let her know a similar fire engulfed me whenever she touched me, and that I got "goose pimples" all over just by watching her listen to music.

She told me more than once that I had to let the music inside to truly enjoy and understand it. I wondered if she could see the music already playing in my heart.

While Elise revealed the passion existing within music, I showed her the magic of lyrics. Impressed I knew so many love songs, she asked how I developed my love of words.

"I was scared of girls," I shrugged. "Talking to them was out of the question. So I wrote them notes, silly things of course, the musings of a love-struck kid."

"Nonsense," she said. "I bet they were not silly, and I bet you were a big hit with those lucky girls."

"I don't know about that," I said. I proceeded to tell her of my anonymous love affairs with the girls of my dreams.

"And you never told them?"

"Well, I did tell one of them at my last high school reunion. Vaguely remembering the cards and flowers and other stuff, she admitted to being freaked out about them at the time. She had even called the cops to report someone was following her. I didn't know it at the time, but I was probably the first stalker on record."

I told her about how I was inspired to write about heroes—not movie stars or great athletes in the limelight, but simple people who toiled in the shadows of society to achieve great things. Elise implored me to show her some of my work. Reluctantly, I agreed. She loved everything she read, though I passed off her praise as being from a biased friend. She cared less about the substance of my stories than the tone and feeling they conveyed.

"It is not so much what or whom you are writing about, but how you do it that moves me," she explained. "Your words, they are so full of flavor, like a well-seasoned meal or a robust wine. They are so descriptive, stimulating all of my senses to come alive. You write as if you are making music with your words."

She asked if I had saved any of the love notes I had written. I lied, telling her I didn't have them anymore. "Love notes don't do much good unless the object of your affection reads them," I shrugged. She wasn't buying it. "There are such things as copy machines. And I bet you wrote to other girls besides your high school puppy-love crushes. I bet there were a lot of not-so-secret notes to girls over the years."

"There were a few," I admitted. "And you're right about them not being secret anymore. I'm too vain now not to identify myself."

"I bet you kept copies of your poems, if only to hold on to the memories of how you felt about these women. Your poems are to you like photos are to other people. They hold captive deep feelings you have, in the same way a picture imprisons a face for someone else. The past has much meaning for you. I cannot see you discarding evidence of it."

I tried not to show how precisely she had pegged me. I hoped I was not such an open book in other areas, like how much I wanted her.

She hounded me for several weeks, until I admitted I had saved a couple of poems "for prosperity," or something along those lines. She begged to see them, but I said I didn't feel comfortable sharing something as intimate as my feelings for another woman.

"I think we have become close enough friends for you to share your feelings about other women," she said. "Besides, you know all about my sex life. And for goodness sake, you *have* seen my nipples!"

I laughed self-consciously about her last statement. She had obviously divined my puppy-love interest and played along with it, occasionally giving me angled glimpses of her bare breasts or the tops of the lacy thongs she was wearing. Though I fantasized about her, I had no illusions her bold talk was anything more than mere teasing. I was just the latest of many silly men who had looked upon her with the eyes of a lust-struck teenager.

Elise said she was "overwhelmed" by my poems, actually crying while reading several of them. I didn't tell her I had written most of these poems in the last six months, and they were all about her. Maybe I didn't have to.

<hr />

I felt the freedom to flirt with her, because I believed the ring on her finger would protect both of us.

Occasionally, I carried this freedom too far. We had taken to meeting three or four times a week for lunch in local cafes or grabbing a sandwich to eat in the park where we met. It seemed simple and safe—two friends munching and talking in a park. One day, I surprised her by packing a picnic basket.

Yes, it was one of the many stupid things I did without knowing why. She was married, happily from most appearances, and I was bringing her grapes and brie cheese, and fresh watermelon juice and chocolate truffle ice cream softened in the sun. And because she complained on the phone earlier about being exhausted from standing on her feet teaching all day,

I brought a jug of warm water and cotton washcloths, and offered to rub her feet.

"There are some things so sensitive only my husband is free to touch," she said, pulling her feet away in a startled manner and quickly putting her shoes back on. "When my feet are touched, I lose all control."

I tried to tone down my approach on future outings. When we met the next week, I had pared our picnic offerings to simple items—bread, soft cheese, and lemon-flavored carbonated water—packed in a grocery store shopping bag. The only extravagance was the butter cookies covered in hazelnut-flavored chocolate that I brought for dessert.

I noticed she removed her shoes soon after sitting down on the blanket I had spread on the ground. The location, a small patch of grass under a weeping willow well off the path at the farthest end of the park, had become our favorite meeting place. The willow's distant location and low-hanging branches kept us out of sight from most park visitors. Still we were only a few feet away from the edge of the park's sprawling rose garden.

I fantasized this was our "rendezvous" spot, though I knew Elise favored it for a more practical reason—its isolated nature allowed us long, uninterrupted conversations.

And boy, this girl loved to talk!

I sometimes wondered when we would run out of things to discuss. Music, movies, poetry, her two "kids," my six "kids"—we never struggled for topics.

But on this day, she seemed to be preoccupied from the moment she arrived, as if something was on her mind. She said little, so I took the lead in talking about the latest shenanigans my boys were up to. She seemed to be distracted and barely listening to what I was saying. This surprised me, because she normally hung on every word of mine. (I didn't believe her interest had so much to do with me, as it did her intense desire to learn more about the American way of living, talking, and thinking.)

She had a couple of sips of the lemon water and a bit of bread, but touched nothing else. I thought she might still be upset about my feet groping from the week before—though if that were the case, I didn't understand why she had so freely taken her shoes off the moment she arrived. I hesitated in bringing out the last item in the grocery bag, a yellow rose I had snipped from the bushes nearest us just before she arrived. Thinking she might get the wrong idea, I gave a hasty explanation.

"This rose is appropriate for us. Its yellow color is symbolic of friendship, which I feel is clearly evident between us. Its name Graceland is what I feel we are surrounded by when we meet here."

I cringed, expecting some sort of rebuke or sarcastic remark about my risking the fifty-dollar fine the park officials charged for anybody caught pilfering a rose from the municipal garden. But Elise didn't say anything; she simply took the rose from the vase and held it to her nose while closing her eyes.

"It smells like the perfume of spring," she said. "It is beautiful."

She seemed a bit overwhelmed by my gesture and could not bring her eyes to meet mine. Her reaction moved me, though I didn't want her to know. I turned my attention to the picnic lunch. I hadn't eaten all day, so I made quick work of most of the food, though slowing periodically to see if she had regained her appetite—and her composure.

Overtaken by the volume of food I consumed, I leaned back and closed my eyes for a brief rest. Just coming off a two-day shift at the group home, I felt myself winding down.

I figured she would fill the void in our conversation as she always did, but she said nothing for what seemed like a long while. As I was about to drift off for a bit, I felt a shadow come across my face. I opened my eyes and was startled to see Elise's face had filled my world. I was about to rise to a sitting position to determine if anything was wrong, but I stopped when I felt her hand on my shoulder. It was a slight touch, more symbolic than practical, but I interpreted it to mean she wanted me to remain lying down.

Elise appeared to hold onto the words as if to say them might mean death, and I thought I knew what she was holding inside. Attracted to me in some slight way, she was embarrassed about it. She probably wanted to get these mixed-up feelings into the open, to get them out of her system. I was already thinking of some cute comeback to put her at ease, something like, "school-girl crushes on older studs like me are common, so don't feel bad."

"I love you! I love you! I love you!"

Her words gushed forth in a torrent of emotion, as if a gaping hole had opened in the world's largest dam.

"I am shaking when I am with you, so much is my excitement," she exclaimed. "When I do not look back as I walk away, it is because I am sure you will see the depression in my eyes because I am leaving you. And when we are apart, we are not apart. You are there with my music and I am playing for you. You are there when I am making love with Albert, for I am making love to you. I am possessed, wholly and completely, by wanting to see you, talk to you, to hear your voice, your laugh, to feel your touch, your mouth on mine. Every minute without you is like death. My words, they lose so much in English. If I could tell you how I feel in French, you would melt from the heat."

There was sweat on my forehead and in patches all over the rest of my body. "I'm melting already," I said.

I looked at her hands and they were indeed shaking.

"I understand how painful these words are to say."

"No, no," she exclaimed. "Not saying them for so long has been the real pain. Holding them inside was like holding my breath. I had to get them out, to let the truth free, or I would have surely died."

My head was swooning, like it did after she clocked me in the jaw on the day we met. This time the dizziness was born not of pain, but of joy. Deep, eternal, surrealistic joy.

This feeling seemingly could get no better, but it did. Elise's face, floating just above mine, moved closer. I kept my eyes open to enjoy her flushed beauty until the last possible moment, then closed them as her hair covered my face and the darkness swallowed me.

As I felt her mouth on mine, I pulled her down onto me. I found the small of her back and in one motion, with her lips still caressing mine, turned her beneath me. Smooth and devoid of hesitation, it was my greatest moment of grace.

The kiss of kisses! Deep in my enchanted heart, I knew all of history's kisses had failed miserably to match this one.

Chapter 23

THE CRYING TRAIL

*W*hen I loved a woman, I didn't hold anything back. She received everything I had to give, at least for as long as I could hold onto the feeling. Women liked the way I loved them, not because I was well endowed or blessed with yeoman-like stamina. I had patience and appreciation, a willing mouth and creative hands.

Learning mostly through trial and error during my early education into the female body, I benefited from many years of in-depth research. I slowly, but surely, became a scholar of the female figure—the ellipses and natural curves, the soft twists and subtle turns making this exploration a geographer's dream. Creating female pleasure was one area in which fear did not hold me back.

But the first time I knew Elise and I were going to make love, I was shaking like a scared teenager.

The details of this day are imprinted into my heart and seared into my brain.

She had told her husband she was visiting a friend in the Bay Area and would return two days later. She drove the wending road up to my cottage in the hills above Folsom. A small place with a tiny kitchen and a one large room, the rectangular brick cottage had two notable attributes—a "sky light" ceiling window directly above the bed, and a floor-to-ceiling window running the entire 15-foot length of one side, affording a breathtaking view below of Folsom Lake and the sprawling Sacramento Valley.

"Oh, I love this!" Elise burst out, describing the panoramic scene greeting her first look outside my cottage window. "All the world seems spread out below me!"

And now she wanted to spread out on my bed, which looked directly out the window.

My window to the world also afforded a view of the sun setting below the Western horizon. Neither of us said a word as the sun made its descent, spreading its shades of orange, yellow, and red in layers as far as our eyes could see.

"Oh, I almost forgot," she said, uncurling from my arms and rising from the bed. She walked to her purse and removed a CD and put it in my stereo. "This will complete the mood," she said, as the first low notes began to float from my speakers and fill the room. I had never heard the song, I was sure, but as the notes played on they became familiar, like an echo of someone else's words. I knew it was Barber's "Adagio for Strings" before the music in minor key had played thirty seconds.

She returned to my bed and slid on top of me, but I had something different planned. I turned her over, like I did just before I kissed her for the first time under the weeping willow. My mouth followed the contour of her figure. Wet and moist, my tongue wended around every curve and turn of her body, flowing over her like a slow-moving river current. My desire could not be damned. I washed over her in waves of untamed fury.

Elise could not take my tongue for very long. She pulled me on top and moved her hips until I slid into her. She shuddered with orgasmic pleasure before I even started moving inside her. She seemed possessed with a hunger for repeated pleasure, and she expressed this need by arching her back and thrusting her hips forward in an almost attacking motion while digging her fingernails deep in my back. Over and over she came, with each successive orgasm seeming to increase her appetite for more.

Later, as I lay exhausted on my soaked cotton sheets, I noticed Elise sitting on the side of the bed. I pulled her close. She seemed on the verge of tears, and I figured it had something to do with guilt. Elise never turned around, but I felt her tears drop onto my arms encircling her. I asked her what was wrong, and all she replied was, "perfection."

She never said another word, telling me later she didn't like anyone seeing her cry. We fell asleep together, and I awoke the next morning with her naked body lying warm against mine, her arms around my neck.

I felt rested, which surprised me. I rarely slept calmly with a woman next to me, as lovers would testify to my fitful tossing and turning. But this time my sleep was dark and soft and warm, broken only by the mid-morning light slanting through the half-opened wooden shutters. Maybe I was just exhausted by our whirlwind lovemaking, which had lasted into the early morning.

As my head cleared from its peaceful slumber, I eased myself from her arms without waking her and made a pot of coffee. I took a sip from my cup while the liquid was still black, as my daddy preferred. But as I cannot drink an entire cup prepared this way, I added half-and-half and two sugar cubes.

I turned to see if the scene I had awakened to was merely the first dream I had recalled in years. If it was a dream, then it had not yet ended. In her sleep, Elise had kicked off the quilt and was lying slightly on her side, facing me. Black, curved lashes, long and lustrous like those on a baby doll, covered her eyes. Her long black hair, its straightness slightly ruffled from sleep, swayed across the front of her body like an Oriental fan, covering half of a breast and leaving the nipple exposed like an unwrapped chocolate kiss.

In the early morning shadows, the light drifting through the ceiling and side windows revealed her naked beauty in delicate streams, creating a visage I knew would haunt my dreams should they ever return. As I watched her sleeping, I knew I was looking at God's ultimate piece of art, a work of subtle curves and inviting turns that was perfection defined, delicately formed by divine hands and presented to me on the condition I give it back one day.

Everything about her made my senses come alive—looking into her eyes, touching her cheek, holding her hand, smelling her subtle, delicate scent, both natural and store-bought, feeling her breath on my neck, and tasting her mouth and her wetness.

For all of the sensual curves, languid eyes, and pouting lips suggesting her body was a mold for beauty unequaled in perfection, the soul of her attraction lay not exposed before me but hidden somewhere deep within.

As I watched her lying naked on my bed, there was nothing tangible about her—not the shape of her face, curvature of her body, or softness of her olive skin—making me in that moment fall in love with her.

I fell in love with how she made my heart feel, and even then I knew it was a feeling not easily to pass.

When she awoke, I did not tell her of my decision to love her for the rest of eternity. We made love until noon, and then washed each other's hair in the shower. We spent the day hiking in the foothills and woods nearby.

In the evening, I started a fire in the small wood stove fireplace for warmth and lit several candles to "set the mood." I needn't have done either. The heat emanating between our bodies and the firelight in her eyes provided more than enough.

I prepared my specialty (girlfriends would say it was the only thing I could cook)—curry chicken with potatoes and carrots over coconut milk-soaked jasmine rice. Elise said she loved it, but I noticed she left part of everything on her plate. I didn't say anything as I cleared our plates, but she read my mind.

"In France, it is custom to leave something on the plate, especially bread. It goes back to the times when famine left little food on the table. I guess you would call it a good luck gesture, no?"

"I call it foolish," I said, using the large serving spoon to scoop the last bit of her curry chicken and rice into my mouth. "Food is not wasted in my house!"

"You have much to learn, then, about the strange, mysterious ways of Europeans," she said, spinning me around and giving me a look indicating she was ready to give me a crash course in foreign etiquette not taught in any charm school, French or American.

"But I have "Scent of the Papaya," a sexy foreign film for us to watch," I protested.

She had already unzipped her jeans and was pulling them off before I could say another word. "I have something better," she said, slowly sliding her cream-colored panties down her legs. "You can taste my wet and juicy papaya."

"Well, if you insist, teacher."

She insisted, pulling me on top of her in the middle of my floor. With Barber's Adagio playing in the background, we made love throughout the night and into the early morning. She continued to teach elements not previously on my love-making study board.

⚮

As Elise lay curled in my arms later that evening, her sleeping face illuminated by the white light of the perfectly rounded moon shining through the skylight, I thought of the words coming together in my head as the result of her challenge during our earlier hike.

The words had first started forming as we sat resting near a branch of the American River we followed through most of the trek. We had stopped to eat lunch next to a pool in the creek, which was fed by a thin sliver of a waterfall. The low rumbling of the stream bouncing off the canyon walls, mixed with the sound of the water falling into the slow-moving flow from the granite overhang fifty feet above, made for an interesting cacophony.

"Oh, what a beautiful, almost mournful sound the water makes," said Elise, who seemed keyed into even the subtlest tones of her surroundings. "There is a whining coming from somewhere, and it sounds like something, I do not know, like something sad, like—"

"The whole canyon is crying," I said, completing *her* thought, for once. "The Hopis named the path that wends through this canyon, "The Crying Trail," after the wailing sound the heavy winds make when they blow through the rocks and the trees, and because the waterfall looks like tears falling from the sky."

"Wow, this canyon is like a giant natural wind instrument," she said. We ate the rest of our lunch of French bread, soft ripened cheese, and fresh fruit in silence, listening as the wind played its haunting concerto for the two of us. I spent most of this time looking at Elise and marveling at her sensuality in performing even the simplest movements, as when she slowly licks her fingers after eating an apple to taste every last bit of its juicy nectar.

She looked across the river, seemingly fascinated by the waterfall. Finally, as if some great truth or Hopi revelation hit her, she began talking in a low, measured tone. "When the waterfall joins the river, it appears to be dancing on the surface. The falling water does not seem like tears or

208

anything sad; it looks excited when it lands, skimming over the river as if tap dancing on the surface. For a moment, the waterfall appears it can dance all the way down the river. But then it realizes where it is, believes it cannot hold itself up, and sinks beneath the river and drowns."

"So, you think it drowns in its own doubt?"

"Fear, doubt, they both have something to do with it," she shrugged, still looking toward where the waterfall was disappearing into the river. "Mostly, though, the waterfall drowns because it opens its eyes and sees reality."

Turning toward me, she continued her explanation, though it soon appeared she wasn't discussing the waterfall any longer. "I guess if the waterfall kept its eyes closed, it would not have to accept reality. It could go on dancing."

"Wouldn't it sink anyway?"

"Maybe. Maybe not."

I thought I detected a hint of sad realization in her eyes, or maybe it was the reflection of my own sad eyes I saw. I turned away and blinked to remove the reflection, but a ghostly image remained in the back of my mind. I turned back toward her and tried to say something to lighten the moment. "Ah, Dances with Waterfalls," I grinned. "And you say *I'm* the creative one. The Hopis and Kevin Costner would be proud of you."

"That is just a tiny story," she shrugged. "You take words, simple words, and wrap them with your feelings, and turn them into grand love stories as no one else can."

"You're the one who just brought life to a waterfall. I merely write what is real and what I can see."

"No, you write about how what you see makes you feel. There is a big difference."

"I don't really think about it."

"I know. You feel it."

"I guess, if you say so, teacher."

"Well, as my pet—" she began, before I interrupted her.

"I prefer Number One Student, if you don't mind."

"OK," she continued. "As my number one student, I have a couple of lessons for you today. Your first lesson is to write me a poem about this waterfall."

"Let me think about that one. What about my second lesson?"

"Make love to me—*Now!*"

I followed the second lesson as instructed, taking Elise on the pine needle-covered ground while the water fell from the granite sky and danced and died on the river next to us.

Later, as I lay next to her in the earliest moments of morning, I was amazed at how soft and supple her skin looked, even in the harsh glow of the new moon slanting through the sky window and lighting her body like a stage spotlight. I was reminded of the soft fill close-ups of Grace Kelly in "Rear Window" and Donna Reed in "It's a Wonderful Life." It was as if God was controlling the lens filters.

I thought about her first assignment and the words I had penned in my head. I hadn't written them down and was surprised they remained aligned and coherent in my mind. I had never been good at recalling words to songs, passages from books, or lines of poetry. But something was different with Elise. My thoughts about her did not come and go, as they had with others before; they remained imprinted in my mind and readily accessible to my lips. As if she felt my urgency to reveal these feelings, she opened her eyes and kissed me softly on the lips. The words poured out of me with unerring fluency, like a waterfall:

"You swept over me the moment you flowed into my life. Closer to the edge I rolled, as your current rushed through me. Over the deep end I flew, as your beauty covered me. And I was falling, falling in love, falling in love with you.

"Out of breath and out of control, but afraid no more, I tumbled downward in a spiral of ecstasy, calling your sweet name as your warm wetness washed my cares away. And I was falling, falling in love, falling in love with you.

"Closing both my eyes, I smiled as you came over me in waves. Twisting and turning, I found myself swimming in your stream. Then you led me to the quiet waters and stilled my nervous heart. And still, I was falling, falling in love, falling in love with you."

When my words stopped flowing, I noticed her eyes were more rounded than usual. "Are you saying what I think you are saying?" she asked.

"I think you just heard me say it over and over again."

"You said you were 'falling in love,'" she said, emphasizing "falling."

I wanted to yell, to shout out the words, exclaim to the world this feeling that was deeper than any I had ever felt.

Instead, I pulled her close and whispered in a voice only the angels and she could hear: "I love you."

The passion I felt for her came gushing out in uncontrolled fury, like a person speaking in tongues:

"You have filled my life with a colorful, almost indescribable glow. The part of my life once black and white is now a rainbow of shades. One look from you, and I lose all sense of reason. I forget the hour, the day, the month, even the season. My mind is lost and my heart is taken, leaving my existence one of wonderful confusion.

"Since our eyes first met and my heart felt yours, I have not been moderate in my desires. Your presence has stirred feelings I had long since buried. Now my love cannot be obscured. It is dauntless, spirited, and unworried. I am thunder and lightning, hurricane and gale, driven by winds of change. I am smoke and wildfire, pouring rain and hail, unleashed upon the open range.

"Because of you, there can be no rest."

"Make love to me," she said, pulling me closer. "Make love to me until I die in your arms." I noticed a craving in her eyes, born not of lust, but of desperation.

I pulled her toward me until there was nothing between us but my breath on her neck. For some reason, I felt her same desperation. "Let us make love with burning desire," I whispered into her ear, "until our ashes are all that remain."

As we lay exhausted in each other's arms later that morning, I knew I had found perfection, if only for one perfect weekend. "I pity all those who have not felt this love," I whispered in her ear.

"Pity then all the world," she whispered back.

I thought, then, I would pity only more the man who might lose this love. I thought this with an understanding nod to my past, where I had too often found promises exchanged under moonlight betrayed their fate in daylight.

As the weeks stretched into months and the months into the first year and then the second, I enjoyed what fortune had shone upon me. Yet, I couldn't help but look over my shoulder, expecting any day to see reality closing in on my dream world. In my lucid times, I saw the incredulity of what I expected to happen, that Elise would leave her perfect marriage and perfect man and ride off with me into the Northern California countryside. In the dark places deep within me, where doubt and fear ruled, I believed no chance for happiness could come from such folly.

Elise had her own doubts. Her struggle did not so much center on her feelings for me but on the ramifications of leaving her "perfect marriage." There had not been a single divorce in the history of her parents' families, and her union with Albert was looked upon as the crown jewel of all the marriages.

My doubts were closer to the surface and sometimes slipped above to where she could discern them. She always knew when I was upset, by the tone of my voice when she called to inform me we couldn't meet because something had come up at home, or in the irritation on my face when she mentioned Albert's prowess in his profession, sports, or dancing (the jerk was great at just about everything).

Too often, though, when I believed my dream world was not heading fast enough toward reality, my impatience gushed forth in angry words and loud recriminations. Afterward, I always regretted my outbursts. After one particularly testy moment, I slipped this note under the windshield wipers of her car:

Despite all the jealousy and strife, you have captured my heart. You are the essence of my life, the necessary part. You give me my rhyme and my reason. I know a love now I have never known before. I realize some day, honey, all of this time waiting will seem like a momentary thing. So, please be patient with my impatience.

At times, the pressure got to both of us. She broke up with me three times in the first couple of years. They were relatively short separations of a week or two, marked by angry confrontations, plaintive appeals for another chance on my part, tentative reaching out on hers, and then tearful and passionate reunions.

After one of these sexually charged make-up make-out sessions in a park near her home, I discovered a note stuffed into my jacket pocket. She had written to me before, but never in her native French. She penned a small bit of a poem by French surrealist Jacques Prevert, and only provided a translation of the title, "Cet Amour" (This Love) and a note explaining the excerpt "laid out the warfare of emotions battling within us":

«*...donne nous signe de vie, beaucoup plus tard, au coin d'un bois, dans la forêt de mémoires, surgis soudain, tends-nous là main, et sauve-nous."*

Calling upon three years of high school French and my tattered fifteen-year-old *Dictionaire au Francaise*, I translated her words the best I could.

THIS LOVE...

"*...give us a sign, a sign of life. And then later, deep in the forest of memories, appear surreptitiously, give us your hand, and save us."*

In the past, I would have listened to the suspicious whispers at my core, heeded the dark voices telling me what a fool I was, and followed the commands always directing me to run away. But there was something different this time, something I had never felt before, stopping me from breaking into a run and taking full flight. I had felt it begin somewhere in the depths of my gut, a deep, almost mournful pledge of resolve after that first night and morning together with Elise and the realization I had fallen in love with a married woman.

On that first morning, as I watched her sleeping naked on the crushed linen, her soft curves and incomparable beauty silhouetted in the shadows of dawn's earliest light, my newfound love for her strengthened my will to fight. Lying beside her in the stillness of the coming day, my fear and cautiousness slipped away.

With this hidden heartfelt resolve, I felt it unnecessary to be overly demanding or inquisitive about when a change was coming. I simply waited.

We filled the waiting with wild, almost ravenous lovemaking. We explored each other's bodies every place we could and anytime there was an opportunity. In a movie theater, she whispered she had removed her panties in the restroom. I touched her discreetly, until she shuddered in the darkness. In the park where we met, I lifted her against an oak and eased her down on top of me, an act in the midnight twilight both undeniably illegal and incredibly intoxicating.

We made love in lakes, rivers, and oceans, and on the clay, rocks, and sand lying beside them. We made love on muddy hillsides amidst driving rainstorms and in canyon meadows surrounded by fuchsia lupine, golden poppies, and fluttering Monarch butterflies. We even made love on a frozen mountain slope. Afterward, as the snow fell on us and we could see our breaths turn to smoke rings in the cold air, we watched the steam rise from our entwined bodies like retreating souls.

But beyond that first weekend, we only slept together overnight a few times. After a wonderful afternoon holding each other or an evening making love, she invariably returned home to her husband and I returned to my restless state of waiting. On the dark days, when doubts permeated my thoughts, it felt as if our relationship was without substance, like a wonderful cream puff without the filling.

Still, I believed.

Chapter 24

MAMA'S LESSONS ON LOVE

*D*espite long odds facing our star-struck love, I persevered with tenacity that would make my sister proud. I wrote these words to Elise shortly after I professed my love to her:

"My entire life, I have waited for someone to hear my voice. My silence, though, has been by choice. No one has stopped me, no one has used force. You came along and opened my vault. Now I cannot be silenced, not by doubt, not by fear, not by anything."

From kings to fools, it is said that love makes the rules. Not the case with this particular imbecile. Doubt and fear have ruled every one of my adult days, and this would not change even when I was faced with losing the greatest love of my life.

I had my sweet mama to thank for my expertise in the use of self-doubt to sabotage hopes and dreams. She was both an expert practitioner and highly skilled teacher of this deleterious art form. Mama was a paradox I was always trying to figure out. She was both the giver of my life and the bane of my existence, for she introduced and constantly reinforced the two forces—love and fear—directing my path through life.

The way she lived her life and loved her husband showed me how a person should feel for a soul mate. Love wasn't displayed with showy affection or grand gifts of jewels. It was demonstrated in the little things shared—a touch on the arm, a soft kiss "goodbye" on the lips, morning coffee and cigarettes on the back patio together. Her love could be discerned in other ways—how she waited past midnight for him to come home from work, even though she was exhausted from being awake since early morning, just so she could see him come through the door.

Not until much later did I realize the passion that had existed between my parents. Mama's guidance in the ways of love was subtler still, and her messages often eluded even my overtly sensitive nature. They took most of my adult life to leave their mark.

My mother's methods of teaching the merits of fear and doubt were more direct, and I became a devoted disciple in these areas from an early age. She instilled her fear of the ocean into each of us, starting early enough to ensure it lasted our entire lifetimes. She had a "healthy" reason for hating the sea—Daddy's brother drowned in Florida's Santa Rosa Bay and she had at an early age (eight) been dragged a mile by a rip tide off Panama City Beach. She was saved by "a strong, handsome young man who risked his life" for her.

She had a ritual each time our family ventured to Gulf Shores State Beach or any other stretch of sand on the Gulf Coast. Before we ventured into the warm, blue-green Gulf, she lined all of us up, from smallest to tallest, including Hank when he was almost an adult. She paced back and forth in front of us, her head hunched over in deep thought and her arms wrapped as if she was holding an imaginary clipboard to her chest. She resembled the world's smallest football coach.

Her tone may have been pure Knute Rockne, but her message was not inspirational in nature—unless fear could be considered a motivational tool. She preached fear and respect. "Don't trust the sea 'cause there ain't no end to it," she would always begin, drilling each one of us with stern looks. "The Gulf's got sneaky undercurrents that will lead you sideways along the shore when you ain't payin' attention, then drag you out to sea."

About this time, Peter would start fidgeting, standing on one foot and then the other, digging his toes into the sand and flicking the white grains on Christine's feet. Christine ignored him as she paid rapt attention to Mama's monologue. Peter invariably turned his nervous energy to me. When Mama wasn't watching—and sometimes even when she was—he would pick up stones, shells, or anything else he could get his toes around and flick it in my direction. He had the amazing ability to control his toes as easily as someone else could maneuver their fingers. When he attracted my attention with a well-placed foot flick, he would stick out his tongue and make any number of goofy faces.

Mama ignored Peter's antics, knowing Hank would eventually still his brother's youthful impertinence with a withering glance or a firm hand to his shoulder.

"I don't know which side of the family that boy got it from, but I swear he's half-monkey," Mama said many times, usually while looking up at Peter standing on our roof or halfway to the top of our massive pecan tree. "He must spend half his life off the ground."

Standing there on the beach, watching him making those funny faces and flipping shells and stones at my head with dead-on accuracy, I had to agree with Mama that my middle brother hadn't developed much past the primate stage.

I must have inherited some of those monkey genes, because I was also a notorious fidgeter. But not on the beach when Mama was disseminating the rules of life and fear.

"The ocean, it's a lot like life," she continued. "The waves, even the big ones, come in nicely and act like they're goin' to keep you safe and close to shore. But those waves are a lot like a lot of people—they got hidden secrets that can pull you down and hurt you."

Believing her esoteric warnings might be above our heads, she threw in the ultimate fear factor in easily understood terms. "All kinds of sharks are in this water, not to mention jelly fish that sting like scorpions and barracuda with teeth like piranhas."

I didn't know much then about either scorpions or piranhas, but the darkness barely visible in the slits of Mama's narrowed eyes suggested I have a healthy fear of them anyway.

Before she could complete her signature ending line, "be careful and don't go out too far, but have fun," Peter usually broke ranks and sprinted to the water, throwing himself into the first set of waves welcoming him. Hank waited until Mama had finished before emitting a low sigh only my sister and I could hear. He then turned and slowly trotted toward the water, shaking his head but saying nothing. Christine and I would stand half-tilted toward the water like Easter Island statues, poised to sprint into the blue-green waves but frozen in place by Mama's words of warning. We eventually made our way into the water, but it was always with a wary eye and tenuous heart.

Mama was much more comfortable around lakes, with their placid waters and finite horizons. She made us boycott even these languid bodies of water for a while, when my big brother was chased through Gulf Shores Lake by a twelve-foot gator. My daddy's patient plodding and our natural curiosity and love of the water eventually overrode her stop sign, but not without her constant dialogue on the dangers of this water zone.

Most of my mama's teachings on fear were subtle and nearly invisible, yet they were the ones having the most telling and detrimental effects on her children.

In her mind, the world was a threatening place, a minefield of unavoidable obstacles and formidable challenges. She never told us things in life would be hard; she said they would be impossible. She was trying to protect us, to prevent us from being hurt from our failures or from hurting ourselves with false hopes. For her, lowering one's expectations was the only way to ensure an enjoyable life.

"If you don't think things will work out, you'll never be disappointed," she was fond of saying. "If for some strange reason they do, well, that becomes a pleasant surprise."

Over the years, her lowest expectations centered on her children. She was often heard to say to her friends or to any one of us something like this: "While I don't receive many if any pleasant surprises from my kids, at least I'm rarely disappointed by anything they do, no matter how big a failure it might be, because I don't expect much from them to begin with."

Though she didn't show it, I believe Peter disappointed Mama more so than the rest of us. His actions cut closest to her heart and soul, probably because the truest bond of Lyon love existed between these two. The connection between mom and middle son began when Peter almost died at birth and wasn't expected to live past infancy. His rambunctious sense of adventure as a child linked him to Mama's untamed, adventurous Santa Rosa Bay childhood. She claimed later to have something akin to a telepathic kinship with him.

"There has always been something there with him, and him alone," she often told the rest of us. "It's some kind of mental connection. I can always sense when he is going to call, or some news will arrive from him. It's just a feeling I get."

We often told her she "had a feeling" he was going to call almost every day, but after a while we stopped saying anything. There *was* something between them, at least regarding Mama's feeling for Peter, which was probably stronger than any real or imagined ESP link.

For whatever reason, his trials and tribulations were hers, though she hid more of her suffering than she showed.

While she reserved her deepest feelings for Peter, she seemed most often to live and die on the mistakes of her daughter. She reserved her outward display of contempt and disappointment for Christine and her dubious attempts at maintaining a stable home life. Peter could be off living in a teepee, Hank could be holed up in Alaska and I could be bouncing from one "eternal" love to another, but she would still express her loudest recriminations in the direction of her "silly, headstrong girl."

"Christine married too young" seemed to be the opening statement of every conversation Mama had about her daughter. She dismissed all suggestions regarding Christine's upbringing having any impact on her rush into an unsuccessful marriage.

If Mama had she shown Christine a bit more attention, her daughter's fragile sensitivities might have developed into stronger self-confidence and personal resolve.

"Ah, parents get blamed for everything these days," she said when I mildly broached the subject one day. "*My* mama never said boo about anything I did good, and she gave me a good whippin' plenty of times when I did bad—and I ain't blaming her for nothin'. I didn't like her much back then, but now I understand what she was doing."

Christine mostly bit her tongue and quietly shook her head at Mama's reasoning. Inside, she would be screaming at the irony of her statements. "Doesn't Mama know she raised me like her mama raised her? She doesn't know I kick myself. Not because we failed to be like her, but because we failed to be different."

In adopting my mama's doctrines on fear and self-doubt, I had also failed to be different from her. So the woman who taught me the most about life and love was the last one I could talk to regarding my worries about losing my true love.

After the initial short-term breakups during our first couple of years, Elise and I moved into a smoother period of our relationship. We both realized fear was guiding our steady path. We knew lasting decisions made at this point would likely point us in lifelong directions. We were afraid to take this risk.

My worst fear was that her love for me wasn't strong enough to withstand even a short separation. As such, I couldn't force her decision by walking away. I couldn't take the chance of losing her. Any expression of doubt or any hint of movement away from her on my part was met with tearful, angry charges I was abandoning her. My choice to remain in limbo had more to do with my lack of faith in myself than it did my love for Elise.

Besides, every moment with her was spectacular, precious bliss. Even if the total picture was incomplete, I could not conceive of leaving the only perfection I had ever found.

My fears appeared unfounded. Though she rarely used the term "divorce" or even "separation," she related her plan to move out, and even began looking for a place to live on her own. She went so far as to show me some of her choices, including a charming cottage in the hills that backed into a small creek.

And she wrote me a note leading me further to believe, to hope…

Because…
Because of your shoulder against my shoulder
Because of your mouth on my neck and your hands in my hair
Because of you inside me, when your skin brushes my skin
Because of your cheek against my cheek
Because of the morning
Because of the night
When you said "come," I came
When you smiled, I smiled
Because of here and there
Because of your land

As long as you are here
I am there

I tried not to get my hopes up, but everything pointed toward togetherness. I had backed off applying any pressure, emphasizing it was important she make a decision regarding her marriage independent of her feelings for me. She was making the move to be on her own; after completing this step, we could discuss our future together.

Soon after, she dropped a bombshell. On their anniversary, Albert had surprised her with a candlelit dinner, tearfully restating his love for her and suggesting they move into a new house and start over. She had never seen her husband display such emotion and passion for her. His efforts moved her to give their marriage another chance. "I owe it to him and my family to give this one more shot. I am sorry, but I have to do this."

The poetry of my heart, the language of love serving me so well in the past, was stunned into muteness. I was further silenced by her announcement they had decided to christen their fresh start by moving into the house she had shown me, the one with the backyard meadow and creek. As she was telling me this, I could think only of the day we gazed into that stream and swore the reflection of us together would last forever.

I retreated to my cabin in the foothills, reflecting upon my fate. I tried to restore some sanity in my life. I focused on the relationships with family and friends that I let go fallow in my quest for Elise's love. I was hoping to give her time to reflect on the emptiness I knew was in her heart. In time, she would make a lasting decision to be with me.

I could not hold my ground. Doubt and despair took hold, and I worked passionately to change her heart. I wrote her poems and letters, and daydreamed of ways to change her heart. The first letter was full of promises I feared I could not keep:

His love is a familiar, comfortable one. Your heart needs time to grow again in its love of him. This is your time to be alone with him.

Our memories, like the daylight hours, will fade with the onset of autumn. I will seek shelter in the darkness of night. But I fear I will never escape your memory.

Because in every sunrise and every sunset, and in every moonlit starry, starry night, I will see your eyes reflected in luminous detail. I will hear your heart pound on my chest and feel your chin tremble on my shoulder. I will taste your cherry lips on mine and smell your heavenly natural scent all around me.

My only sanctuary will be to close my eyes, shut off my senses, numb my feelings. But I fear you will be there even then, a lovely visage to haunt my waking dreams.

I will pray for perspective and try to understand why I seek the dream of love that can never come true.

As for your future—you will know the merit of your choice not by your comfort, but by your happiness.

She wrote a response, describing it as a conclusion to "Because." Her words indicated she was hurting too—but gave little solace to my situation.

Because I love you, I chose to leave
It is better, much better, for me to go
While our love is so present and strong
Because I am scared
To see the seconds, the minutes, the hours
Plunge into the depths of the past
Because I know very little is needed
To come undone one night
And to be lost once the morning is here
I will not let shadows of regret lie beside our bed
I will not let you and me, nor our love, fade day after day
So our love is never caught by time
I take it with me
Where it will stay alive
Inside of me
Forever

As usual, I found myself on the fringe peering in at what I wanted but could not have. I watched from across the road on the night they celebrated their new house and new life together by throwing a party with their friends. I stayed, crouched in my car, until all the guests departed, leaving only when the light went out in their bedroom.

It was pathetic.

Women want strength in their men—if only because they get such joy from testing it. Elise would have respected me more, I suspect, if I simply turned my back and walked away.

I could not move, but I found the strength to write. The words poured from me, flowing to Elise in the form of countless cards and letters. I penned this note to her car:

Sometimes, I close my eyes just so I can see you once again. And then you are there beside me. I move toward you, my breath hot on yours. I know I should, but I cannot let go. I reach with hands unsure, to touch the only love I know.

I draw you near and feel your trembling breast against mine. Two hearts beating together as one, but his is the other one you hear. I do not care if you cannot hear the truth, for I have come undone. All I want, all I need, is your love.

My eyes still closed, I see us come together, our lips touching, tender and soft, like an angel's caress. And I know I will never forget this feeling, the scent of Graceland, and the taste of our first kiss.

I will remember the laughs and smiles, the adventure and your passionate embrace. The memories will transcend the miles, and in all my newfound dreams, I will see your lovely face.

Again, my life was ruled by fear and doubt and the inability to move on. Mama would be proud. I had learned her doctrines well.

Elise appeared to be doing her best to readjust to married life without a lover. She accepted my poems and letters, but said little or nothing to me about them. I finally gathered by her reticence she had cleared me out of her system. I wrote her one more letter, and hoped to have the strength to make it my last:

I understand now I cannot by sheer force of will—and my unrelenting, undying love—guide your heart in my direction. Your commitment will either come in time or it will not. Time is the only element on my side, because its passage is the only sure thing I know, besides my love for you. And since I will always be in love with you, the passing of time can only bring me eternal joy.

I have often thought time apart would bring us together. I no longer suffer this delusion. I feel you have already forgotten the only perfect feeling either of us ever had. The thought of this is like a black cloud hanging over me—but I am prepared for the storm.

As my dream disappears, I will not despair. It will be sad not having your physical presence in my life, not to feel your body next to mine, not to see my reflection in your green pools. But I have had a revelation, something that happens to a Tibetan monk or some other holy person. Like a monk who never loses faith in God, I will never lose sight of you in my heart. Your spirit will live on within me, whatever separate paths we travel.

I realize I can never run far enough to escape the glow surrounding me, engulfing my world and permeating my very existence. It is love in its purest form, for it is given freely in defiance of all reality. It is a fairytale love, of myth and magic, of giants and unicorns, which has somehow turned real under the spell we cast upon each other.

I do not have an explanation for these feelings, these unadulterated expressions of love. I never want these feelings for passion, or my passion for these feelings, to change. It makes me different, for better or worse. All I can do is accept them for what they are, for what they mean to me.

All I know is that you will live in my heart forever.

I did not hear from her for several weeks, and was about to break my pledge and send another letter when she called. She said little, aside for asking if we could meet at McKinley Park. I was mystified about her intentions

I was to meet her at our favorite tree. She spotted me when I was about a football field's length away, and started sprinting toward me. I froze in amazement, and was still standing in a daze when she ran full force into me. I fell backward and we tumbled to the ground. It was déjà vu of our first meeting, except this time *she* ended atop me.

She pulled me close, squeezing me so hard I felt her nails digging into my back.

The words poured out of her in uncontrolled torrents. "I tried, I tried to love him. I really did. I tried to make it like it was before. But I cannot get your face, your beautiful words out of my mind. I have missed you like I have missed nothing else ever in my life," she gasped. "Life without you has been like death. I have found myself forgetting to breathe and not caring if my life continued. You are like the air and wind and water to me.

No, you are more. Those things I need merely to keep living. I need you to *love* living."

The touch, the feeling, the ecstasy of our togetherness returned as if it had never departed. The pain and sorrow ruling my recent days melted under the heat of our restored passion. I was no longer merely surviving. I was loving living again. I could tell she had returned to life too by the look in her eyes.

Two months later, I met her on the Crying Trail to celebrate the first day of fall with a short hike, I knew something was amiss the moment her eyes would not meet mine. My alarm was confirmed by the tautness of her kiss. When she could not find words, her silence told me everything I didn't want to hear.

Her eyes again sent me the message of a change coming.

Elise's eyes and mouth were barometers of her mood and feeling. When her jade eyes welled up and spilled over in pools of aqua green, I knew a shower of emotion was on its way. And when the corners of her mouth turned downward or her lips were held tightly in a taut straight line, a different type of storm was in store.

I had dreaded this moment, the moment when my presence no longer cast its spell, the moment when I felt her heart take the turn for the final time.

She broke the silence with words direct but bringing no relief. "I think it is time I try to make things work with Albert," she said, but there was surprisingly little force behind her statement. It may have been because she said them with her head down and her body half turned from me. "It is time for both of us to direct our energies toward putting our marriage back together. Our families have been imploring us to return to France. Albert's company headquarters are there and my best teaching and playing opportunities are there as well."

I noticed her words still lacked a certain aura of conviction, but I ignored this as my anger took over. "So you're just going to up and leave me and what we have because of your jobs and your family?"

"We have the opportunity to go home now," she replied. "This gives us the best chance to make it work."

"But you *have* a home here, the home we will make together," I said. "You also have a life and a love here."

"But I have a life in France going back even further."

"So history means more than substance," I said shaking my head. "Of course you are free to drift back to France, free to do anything you please. But you have to know what it is like for me to watch you float away. I'm like a damn tree, anchored to the ground while you drift merrily away like pollen released from flowers by a carefree wind."

"I am not drifting," she sighed, and I could see by the wrinkles in the corners of her eyes that the strain in her voice was real. "I am returning to what is meant for me, what has always been my destiny."

"You're going back to what your family and everyone else wants for you," I retorted. "Maybe your family and the others have your best interests at heart. But they don't know you like I do. They have seen only the façade of Elise for all these years; they haven't truly been inside you like I have. Even your husband, who knows more about you than perhaps anybody, hasn't felt your heart or reached down into the depths of your soul like I have."

"Stone, I know what you are saying—"

"Then why are you doing this?" I said in a hard tone, trying to appear unmoved by her uncharacteristic tears. Something told me her heart really wasn't in this break-up. "Why are you doing something that is breaking both our hearts in two?"

"This is the way it is with me, always," she said, a slight moan in her voice. "I get happy, but cannot stay that way. I feel maybe I do not deserve to be happy. Either way I go, I will be miserable. If I stay with Albert, your heart will break. If I leave Albert, his world will crumble. Either way, I will feel responsible. There is no hope for happiness."

"But somehow you have come to a decision, *this* decision, precluding me from your life. How have I become the odd man out of your heart?"

Elise glanced at me, then returned to her downward gaze. "Because I am pregnant with Albert's baby."

The karmic irony of her words hit me like an unseen punch and jarred the breath from me. I long wondered if God would give me another chance at having a child after my indiscretions of the past. I doubted it, though. I had hoped God would forgive me enough to let me have the true love I had found with Elise.

In one sentence, God had wreaked revenge by taking everything I had ever hoped for—life, love, and a child with the one woman who mattered most. And he did it without fire and brimstone or pain and death. He simply let nature take its course.

"When…and how did this happen? You've been saying nothing has gone on between you two in quite some time."

"But I did tell you it happened once, when we moved into our new place. We only did it that first night, and it had to have happened then."

"Couldn't it be mine? We did it those times before and after."

"No. For one thing, I can feel when it happened. I just know. And second, the doctor pinpointed it to the time I was with Albert."

I dropped my prosecution. Even if the baby could be mine, she obviously wanted it to be his. Maybe this was what I wanted all along, a reason to have this end sharp and clean, an intervention of fate and circumstance beyond our control. Maybe this would free me to start anew without regret or backward glances. Or better yet, it could let me wallow further in the depths of self-pity, gnashing my teeth at this latest bitter turn of fate.

"I could have an abortion," she said, in a whispering voice. It was as if she didn't want the world to hear her words. "Albert does not know yet. Then I could be with you."

It was a heart-felt try on my behalf. I could tell by the lost look in her eyes, though, such a gift would likely come at the terrible cost of her soul. I had pledged to myself not to make the same decision I made as a teenager, or to let someone else agree to a similar choice because of what I wanted. I wasn't trying to save my soul—I lost that years ago when I made Chandni touch the cold, stiff fingers of our dead son. I simply couldn't let another woman lose her way in the world because of my selfishness.

I was touched by her gesture, though I didn't feel like showing it. After the one-two punch she delivered, I didn't have much emotion left to give.

"You must keep it," I said softly. "That baby is the only symbol of hope either one of us has left."

"But if it means not losing you, then I'm willing—," she began, before I cut her off.

"No. It's best this way. It'll give both of us a fresh start."

She began to speak again, but I raised my hand signaling there wasn't anything left to say. She hadn't much fight left in her anyway.

I took one more long, hard look at her exquisite face. I wanted an imprint on my brain so I would have no doubt as to the cause of the misery haunting the rest of my days. Her eyes shone wild and untamed in shimmering light from the dulling sun, which hung like an afterthought on the horizon. They were green emeralds darkened in stormy seas, and her cheeks were flushed a coral red. My own eyes were cloudy and overcast, blue violets laden with a pending downpour. I could not breathe, as my breath had been stolen by her honesty.

I then remembered this was the first day of autumn. Rain wasn't supposed to come today, but there they were, the first drops hitting my cheeks. They had arrived quietly, under a veil of sublime, formless clouds. There was no thunder in the hills or lightning in the distance, no sign of the storm sure to come.

There was only the wind rustling through Elise's silken hair as she turned and walked away, disappearing like an apparition into the mist lining the Crying Trail.

The gaping hole she left in my heart felt all too real.

I sat there the entire afternoon, until the shade crept over me and the chill crawled beneath my skin. I was waiting for something to change, waiting for her to burst through the glade across the meadow and sprint toward me, calling my name over and over until it resounded around the canyon like a call from God.

There would be no booming words from high above on this day. God had already spoken and was now silent. The lengthening shadows turned into darkness, but still I could not move from the patch of sand between the two boulders, where we had once made love on that perfect weekend now seeming so long ago. I stayed the entire night, frozen in place not by the frigid cold but by my inability to face the failure of true love.

I wanted my heart to remember our love as it once was, blessed by the stars above. But the constellations were no longer aligned and the nighttime sky had turned into a single black sheet, matching the darkness in my heart.

I didn't wake up the next morning so much as I emerged from a coma. My fingers and toes were numb, my nose and ears felt like ice cubes, and my entire body was stiff and rigid. I was literally frozen all the way through. I felt the morning sun bringing life back to my freezer-burned limbs, as a million tingles pulsed through my body like tiny electrical shocks. Reluctantly, I opened my eyes to the bright, empty world, and met a flash sending a dull stinging through my temples and sinus cavities like a case of the bends. I heard birds singing, but their music was painful to my ears as I no longer could tolerate their melodies.

I hadn't turned to ice overnight. And just as my sister told me it would no matter what, the sun had come up the next morning, the world had continued spinning, the birds were alive, and everything around me had moved forward.

Except the emptiness inside me—that had stayed the same.

I had to face the truth.

Elise was gone.

Part **3**

ALL TALES OF TRUE LOVE
ARE TALES OF TRAGEDY

Chapter 25

ACCEPTING FATE

$\mathcal{M}$any people fear what they cannot control. Airline pilots despise being passengers and racecar drivers hate to navigate civilian roads. Doctors make the worst patients and dog lovers hate cats.

But some people—maybe most of us—don't want to be in control, as that would force us to confront our deeper, darker fears of self-doubt. We don't want to figure out our own destinies. We want decisions made for us. We want excuses.

I have always found a certain comfort in letting fate—in the form of decisions made by others—rule my destiny. I find it easier to move on when dumped than when I end things. Revenge is sweet, if only because you don't have to worry if you blew it or not.

I hoped the solace coming with my forced parting from Elise would help me move on with my life. I told myself it was God's will bringing Elise and her husband back together.

The charade did not last long in my mind. I knew our relationship ended because of choices we made—and didn't make. God simply made a choice we couldn't make on our own.

Elise called a few months after our breakup. (Actually, it was seventy-three days, sixteen hours, forty-two minutes and thirteen seconds—but like I told her then, who's counting?) She wanted to wish me a happy birthday. Beyond her good wishes, her present was the announcement Albert had accepted a transfer to his company's international headquarters in Lyon. They would be moving back to France within two weeks.

Part of me wanted to rush over to her house and shake her, to tell her what a mistake she was making, baby or no baby. I would tell her I could love her baby, even if it was his. I could live with the complications of their divorce, if she could ask for one.

But I did not possess the strength in my heart to shake my own fears, let alone hers. I wished her the best of luck in a voice I did not recognize as my own.

The best I could do was to write her a letter a couple of days later:

Dearest Elise,

Your eyes led me into temptation, but it was I who followed without hesitation. I walked into your house, your life, and I wanted all you could offer. I was blessed at one time by your love. Now I am cursed, for I have known the perfection of heaven and have walked among the clouds, proud and arrogant in my ecstasy.

Though cast among the other fallen heathens who once enjoyed God's Graceland, I am not bitter. For I am among the fortunate few who have been touched and caressed by the hand of God. Radiance has pulsed through my body, giving me inspiration not of the mind, but in the only part that matters—the heart.

I have experienced all that is essential in life. I regret nothing but my indecision, my failure to believe in this true love. I am as Judas was to Jesus, as Brutus was to Caesar, unsure of the truth that should have been so evident, faithless when belief was the only hope.

My hurting is bottomless, infinite, and universal, the definition of pain. My dreams are no longer hopes, but fading memories.

We walk now down different streets, our minds and bodies separate and apart, but our hearts still joined as one. As we seek truth in opposite retreats, I hold onto the memories of our perfect love with hidden, trembling hands.

I have chosen to travel down my own path, my own personal Crying Trail, looking for the exquisite beauty once filling my life. But I still see you in my mind, and each time I picture your face, I am reminded of the folly of this search. I cannot forget all I have learned from the perfect teacher—a mentor who never really knew her craft until she met me, her grateful student in the art of love.

I must retreat toward the shadows, away from the blinding light that is your love. I still believe everything between us will enrich everything coming after. All I know of true love I owe to you. You have taught my heart all that is important and essential.

I received a response from her four months later. It was short telegram sending her love and announcing that her son Michel had been born "on a lovely day, with blue skies, soft clouds, and a bright yellow-gold sun up above."

The last line read: "His eyes are blue, like yours, except they have a yellowish ring around the edges."

The meteorologist on TV described the Northern California sky above me that day in much the same way Elise described it in France. As I turned and peered outside the window lining one side of my cabin, I could see the weatherman was wrong. The clouds hung gray against the darkened sky like tufts of dirty cotton candy and rain poured down in blurry streaks. The world outside appeared to be melting.

It seemed as if the rain was streaming down inside the glass. I rubbed my eyes and the scene outside suddenly became blue and bright and radiant, as if someone had lifted the gray woolen blanket out of the way. Soon, though, the rain returned and my view again became covered in grayness.

Dark and gray and blurry was how my world stayed the rest of the afternoon, on the birth day of the son who should have been mine.

As time ticked slowly forward, I looked back to the days before I knew her, to the time I was alone and lonely, but free from the pain of finding and losing one's true love.

When you are younger, falling in and out of love is just a stage along the path to your hopes and dreams. This ebb and flow of love lost and found is a necessary part of the search for true love, and it is sometimes comforting to wallow in the dramatic ups and downs of these early shallow relationships. When you are older and more experienced in losing, being alone and lonely is no longer simply a part of the game. It could be the final score.

Perspective that comes with age is usually a good thing, a tool to guide you through life's perplexing maze. Often, it teaches you much more than you want to know. Sometimes it shows life won't get better, that the best is not ahead of you but over your shoulder.

Try as I might, I realized I could not return to my distant past. The safe, carefree love 'em and leave 'em days of my youth no longer held appeal. I knew too much about the possibility of love's perfection.

My heart was stuck in the recent past, preventing me from moving beyond my memories of Elise.

Christine, the romanticist, always told me the merits of love are not defined by the big things in life. It's the little things, she reminded me, that leave the most lasting memories. I found this to be painfully true with Elise. I returned time and again to the small pleasures now meaning so much—the natural scent of her, the feel of her cheek against my chest, the comfort of her hand in mine while I was driving. The simple things made true love the only memory—and the ultimate misery when it left.

It saddened me to hear classical music after her melodies left my life. I turned the station or walked out of the room when Mozart or Barber or Rachmaninoff started playing. When I recognized notes rendered in minor key, their solemn reminders haunted me.

I tried to dull my senses to memories of our small talk, our knowing glances, our heated lovemaking. I succeeded on some days, recalling her only in quick, flashing images, like frames flickering from an old-style film projector. All it would take, though, was hearing a love song we shared to slice the thin shield of indifference and pierce my heart.

Looking for hope in this world after losing Elise was like listening for the answer to a silent secret or shooting an invisible gunslinger who has outdrawn you. Like my mama always told me, "It's not hard, it's impossible."

On some days, I gave in to my cravings and let the memories take over. I spent hours reliving our closeness, as in the day I stopped on the side of a winding mountain road, pulled Elise out of the car, and danced with her in the pouring rain to REM's "Everybody Hurts" playing on the radio. We swayed to the beat of our hearts as the rain soaked our bodies, cars swerved around us, and the music of heartbreak and regret played on and on.

I breathed in her raven-colored hair of delicate silken strands, laced with jasmine and lilac and the smell of autumn rain. My cheek caressed the nape of her neck—Rodin's perfect creation of sublime curvature. My hand found rest on the incline of her waist, trembling above the lush valley I yearned to explore. When our song ended, we walked into the woods, and with the rain falling on us, made love on a hillside. I became wonderfully lost in her natural glade of exotic and erotic wildflowers from which I hoped never to be found.

These memories were both my life's blood and my prison. For Elise often came to me in the night, and like a noble thief, stole the rest from my sleep. I tossed and turned in uneasy rhythm to her memories, and I could not escape the heartache and grief she had left behind. Her voice called to me in soft whispers; I heard it even as I pulled the covers over me and smothered my head under layers of pillows.

I awakened alone in the shadows, straining to see the light where her love once shone. I closed my eyes to obscure the pain of her perfect memory. But I could not vanquish the vision of her enchanting body and shimmering eyes, her liquid lips covering and swallowing me whole. The tracery of her sensuous outline lingered in the shadows of my mind. I squeezed my eyelids tighter to block the view, but I failed again and again.

She had become an impression that would never fade, a graceful shadow standing out even in the shade.

My past had turned into a single vision of her.

Soon my friends stopped giving me pep talks and told me instead to knock off the mourning and get on with my life.

I had women interested in me and consoled myself with occasional flings. Some wanted more. Jocelyn, a beautiful blonde with eyes of polished turquoise and a fierce, independent nature, was one of these women. In many ways, she was perfectly suited for me. A social worker, she was smart and attractive and loved working with children.

But in the end, she was not Elise. Nobody was.

I didn't know what was worse—when I was with Elise and couldn't have her, or after, when I could have so many other women but didn't want them.

I recalled the times when Elise was leaving on short vacations or going out of the country to visit her family in France, blowing kisses to her from behind the bushes near her house or mouthing "I love you" from behind phone booths at the airport.

The whole scene was downright pathetic.

But was it any better, three years after her departure from my life, to reread almost daily her letters or the poems I had written to her, or to constantly retrace my steps to the places we hiked or visited or made love?

I kept hoping something might happen to alter my twisted fate. Was I asking too much? In fairytales and popular love stories, couples who have lost true love invariably find it again. But what happens if it is never recovered? What if fate or God, or both, decree this love of all loves must end, and you are forced to move on knowing you will never find the same truth again? Can this one true love sustain you through all the lesser loves thereafter?

I had been searching for answers since the day Elise walked away from me. My brother Hank and my mama had been doing the same. Hank appeared to have given up, but Mama, even in her absent-minded, harried state, seemed to be at peace with where her life after love had led. "I don't need anyone else in my life," Mama commented when I broached the subject of moving forward after losing love. "I had the only love that mattered and anything else would be a bad copy. I can live on what I had before. Our love wasn't perfect, and he wasn't a perfect man, and no books or songs will be written about us. But your daddy's love is still within me and that is enough to keep me going."

"It's OK to accept your fate and not expect to discover another true love?" I asked.

"I'm guessin' everyone's a bit different," she mused. "I never tried to find another love. But if I did, I wouldn't go lookin' for the same man I had before, or expectin' to find somebody just like him. That wouldn't be fair to nobody involved. I *would* try to find the same feelin', or the next best thing making me feel good."

I couldn't get past the idea that the only feeling worth having was stuck in the past.

Unable to bear the memories hanging all around my tiny cabin, I decided to head to the coast one day. I had no plan, beyond the first place I was headed. I drove through San Jose and wended along Highway 17 into

Santa Cruz, then headed north on Highway 1 for about ten miles, until I came to the small town of Davenport. Nearby was the secluded beach where Elise and I had last made love.

I walked down the curved path to the beach, which was actually just a patch of sand no bigger than a pool table tucked beneath a rocky overhang. The sheltered oasis had served our purposes well, blocking the wind and muffling Elise's cries of ecstasy.

I reached in the pocket of my jacket and took out a sheet of binder paper creased into quarters. The paper had been folded and unfolded so many times it now had the softened consistency of a thin handkerchief. It was a copy of a poem I had written while lying next to Elise after we had made love. Though I had long since committed the passages to my memory—one of the few poems I was able to remember by heart—I read the words again, speaking them out loud:

"Diamond Girl"
You are a jewel in the sands
Glistening amidst the grains
Who alike in their sameness
Envy your sparkling countenance

Sunlight is grateful to find you
Rays dance un minuet pour deux
Across your smooth polished sides
Opening your colors in soft divides

You are a stone too precious to buy
A flawless gem to the naked eye
Reflecting a shimmering light dart
Through this simple man's heart

Silver and gold pale in value
To the brilliance imparted by you
Purity embodied by the whitest pearl
Touches not the beauty of my diamond girl

All the riches in the land
All the treasures kings command
Are worthless when compared to thee
For you alone mean everything to me

I looked down at the bed of sand and thought I could make out the impressions from our entwined bodies. For a moment, I saw a glint coming from the shaded area, reminding me of the shimmering mist in her eyes when she looked up at me after reading what I had written for her. I closed my eyes and a vision of her body formed beneath me, its nakedness glistening with a coating of sand and sweat. I reached out for her, but she vanished like all dreams must, and I grabbed nothing but the sand. As I watched the grains run through my fingers, I sighed deeply for no one's benefit but my own. I folded the poem neatly and buried it under the sand near the back end of the horseshoe-shaped beach area. I didn't think the tide reached that far, but if it did it could swallow my worthless words.

I cursed my weakness for the past and made my way back up the hill to my car.

I drove up north, detoured through San Francisco, and cut over to Highway 1 after crossing the Golden Gate Bridge. I drove through towns I had never shared with Elise, hoping to shake her memory and create new ones. I had no agenda or plan other than driving in a direction away from where I had been before.

But the beaches and coves, with their bronze sand and rugged vistas, all looked the same as the ones we had explored between Monterey and San Francisco. A string of words began forming in my head, couplets and stanzas of my memories at the ocean's edge with Elise. By the time I pulled off the main highway in Bodega Bay and took a twisting road to Bodega Head, a poem of remembrance had formed from my heart.

As I stood on a point and looked out to the distant reaches of the Pacific Ocean, the sun shone like a cinder at the height of its white-hot heat, as if defying the wind to blow it out. The breeze succeeded only in causing my eyes to burn and squint, and the wrinkles around them to crease more prominently. Having pushed the clouds away until only a pale blue sky remained, the wind turned its relentless power toward the shore. Whipping and roaring landward in thumping gasps, it slammed into my face, drying my skin and lips while numbing my cheeks and nose and turning them a rosy red. Huge waves lashed the rocks below, spraying my face with the briny, salty sea that seemed like spittle from some great sea creature.

If the world did not seem so empty to me, this might have been the most beautiful view I had ever seen.

I took a wending path down to the sheltered beach below the cliffs of the vista, finding the diminished wind and secluded solitude to my liking. I felt I had been here before. I took pen and paper from my knapsack, leaned against the cliff wall and wrote down the words springing from my heartfelt memories of our shadows in the sand:

I will always remember
Our private ocean world
Our temporary harbor
Safe from logic and reason

Where our hearts pounded
In rhythm with the waves
And we heard our souls
In the shells on shore

Like the sand receding
Into the yearning sea
I melted into your waiting arms
And we were one with nature

As surely as eternal tides
Roll one over the other
The moment is gone forever
Never to return again

But the memory remains
Pressed forever in our minds
Shadows in the sand
Where our hearts embraced

After taking a nap in the sheltered sunlight, I climbed the path back to my car and continued my aimless journey northward on Highway 1. Along the way, I noticed signs for the Skunk Train in Fort Bragg. When I drove into this small coastal town, I pulled off to check what this oddly named train was all about.

I discovered it was a train transporting passengers inward from Fort Bragg to Willits. The eighty-mile roundtrip followed the same redwood-rimmed route as when the California Western Railroad opened as a logging line in 1885. I was a bit disappointed that the line's lone steam engine, a 1924 Baldwin resembling my childhood concept of a train, was out of commission for repairs. Instead, I would ride in a motorcar running on gasoline and looking only remotely like a train. At least according to the brochure, this M-100 built in 1925 was the only remaining model of its kind in use anywhere in the world.

I barely paid in time to make the last boarding call, and had to run to make the train. As I paused to catch my breath and spy a seat, I was surprised to see the motorcar nearly filled to capacity. Who would have thought so many people would flock to a railroad named after a skunk?

I usually take a seat near the back on busses and trains (as well as movie theaters and meeting rooms), so I can survey the entire scene in front of me. This tendency started as a kid when I would routinely choose a desk in the back row of the classroom. I guess it was part of my observant nature, though some of my friends thought my habit bordered on paranoia. My pals Jimbo, Jake, and Mort knew of my mania, and whenever we boarded a train or bus they would always race ahead to secure the last seats in the back just to screw with my head.

On this occasion, though, I was content to take the last seat available, next to an older couple in the front row. I was relieved not to have to take a seat in the back, as it seemed everybody on the train was part of a couple. I had taken recently to sitting near the front everywhere, and bypassing parks or shopping malls altogether because I could not stomach looking at lovers.

Oddly, it wasn't the younger couples with their kissing and groping and other heated displays of public affection who bothered me most. The older duos, like the one I was seated next to on the train, caused me the most heartache.

At first glance, there was nothing overly romantic about the man and woman next to me. They weren't kissing or snuggling or making goo-goo eyes at each other. The husband, who was wearing a worn, but well-taken-care-of plaid hunting jacket, and a cap with a trout on the front, had his arm draped in a relaxed manner around the shoulders of his wife, who was holding his free hand with both of hers. Occasionally, he would point out the window and say something, and she would nod and smile. He wasn't handsome and she was no great shakes to look at either, but the way they looked together was perfect.

They had been married for fifty-two years, the woman told me without being asked. They had four children, eleven grandchildren, and two great-grandchildren. "Only fifty-two years?" the man said. "It seems more like forever." The woman smiled and the man laughed, and when they looked at each other, I could not deny their wrinkled faces were beautiful.

They had made the long journey together and were still smiling. I envied and hated them at the same time.

The man asked if I was married. "Only in my heart," I said, surprising even myself for blurting this to perfect strangers. I couldn't stop myself. I showed them a photo of Elise.

They thought she was a young love who had died. "She must have been something," the old man said, and his wife nodded in agreement.

"No," I said. "She was everything."

I turned away from them, ending the conversation.

To divert my self-pity, I focused on a small man standing in front of me wearing blue overalls and a denim cap. I took him to be the captain or engineer or whatever they called the head train guy. I didn't catch his name, guessing he announced it before I boarded.

I asked why the trains were called "skunks." He explained the trains received the nickname just after debuting in 1925, when their odorous gas engines prompted townspeople along the route to say, "They stink like skunks. You can smell 'em before you see 'em."

Someone asked him how long he had been at the helm of these engines. Before he answered, I guessed to myself he was a seventy-year-old retiree who took the part-time gig as a hobby after dreaming of being an engineer since he was a kid playing with Lionel trains.

I was wrong. Working this line was the only job the engineer had ever held. He had made the turn twice a day, twenty-five days a month, twelve months of the year, between what little civilization existed in the area, for the past forty-seven years of his life.

As I looked out the window at the countryside slowly passing by, I imagined what life must have been like for him all these years, trapped in a train bound by gravity and direction and the hard steel of the tracks. Peering from his metal prison, he had seen small towns build, expand, shrink, and die, their wood and tin carcasses abandoned and left under layers of redwood chips and cedar needles. He saw waterfalls gush forth with sensual flow each spring, bringing life to the hillsides with fingers of whitewater sending tingling shivers rushing downward. He watched life come to a halt in the frozen darkness of winter. Year after year, he saw the cycles of life revolve and revive themselves as his own existence played itself out in a back-and-forth straight line toward its inevitable end.

We traveled past Camp Mendocino, its campfires dormant and wooden cabins vacant in the winter solitude but poised for the inexorable hordes of kids and teenagers to come, beginning in late springtime and continuing throughout the summer. I closed my eyes and remembered my own days at camp—a one-week visit during sixth grade sponsored and paid for by my school. I managed a smile at the memory of my first dance with someone other than my sister and my first and only kiss until I met Chandni.

I closed my eyes again, and when I thought of the camp this time, it was with an older, more delicately sensitive ear. In the forest of tall, ageless redwoods, their heavy bows waving slowly in the spring breeze and cooling the thick beds of pine needles formed at their base, I began to hear something far off but slowly edging closer and more familiar. I squeezed my eyes hard to block out all noises except those within my memory, until I could make out the sounds of past campers turning over in their beds beneath the pines, and the faint echoes of young love mingling with the soft sirens of lost innocence.

I wondered how the trainman handled passing by the eternally young group of kids each year. Did their youth make him envious, or was he revitalized by their return each summer, like the wildflowers finding rebirth each spring?

Finally, I asked him if riding this train day after day, back and forth, bothered him. "I mean everything—the trees, the water, the kids at camp—seem to stay the same while you get older. Do you ever wish you took a different track in life, or one with a different route?"

The old man straightened his bent back with some effort and turned toward me with a sigh suggesting to me he didn't often turn sideways. I noticed his eyes were dark gray, the same cold, steel color of the track below but without the hardness. I saw a glint of light within them, like the twinkling of a good idea, which seemed to soften the ridges of his craggy face. The old, crumpled man with young eyes nodded toward the grove of aging redwoods lining one side of the tracks, their side-by-side trunks and gnarled, low-hanging branches silhouetted against a sullen sky making them look like old sentinels guarding one last lonely outpost. "Compared to those old soldiers, I feel pretty young."

He paused for a moment, as if deciding if I was worth the time and trouble, and then turned back toward me. "It's all in your perspective," he noted. "It's all in how you look at things. Take that same grove of trees and the ones on the other side of the tracks, except look further up ahead." He pointed to the distant horizon, where the trees came together at a point with the ending line of the tracks. "Can you see them?"

I tried to make them out, but could not focus on them even while squinting. I wasn't sure what philosophical point this transcendental trainman was trying to make, but I didn't want to expose my ignorance so I kept squinting without saying anything.

The trainman enjoyed my struggles to see both the distant trees and his obscure point, evident by the smile splitting his craggy face like a crevice on a granite mountain.

"If you look too hard when the trees are too far away, they become blurry and you will miss part of them before your eyes see them clearly again," he explained. "You don't have to look so hard and so far ahead, 'cause you're going in their direction and they are coming in your direction. Just wait a bit and you can see them without squinting."

Dazed from all the staring into the glare of the horizon, I realized he wasn't done making his point. "If you don't look too far ahead, the trees are fairly clear and will come toward you at a slow, even pace. They'll approach as if in slow motion, and you'll be able to make out everything about them, all their stories and hidden tales, from the Osprey nests in the highest limbs to the initials of some kids you once knew carved into the trunks.

"If you don't catch sight of the trees until they're passing, they'll fly right on by and become blurry again in the blink of an eye, disappearing like lost memories. If you look back too long, by the time you turn to look at the next set of trees, you'll miss them too."

I thought I understood what he was getting at, something about the need to live in the moment and the importance of not looking too far ahead or behind. I wasn't sure, though, why he thought I was worthy to hear his philosophical chat. Maybe he thought I needed it.

Unlike the trainman, I felt a certain steadiness, a grounding comfort in looking back toward what had passed. There were some memories I didn't want to forget. My friends—and several girlfriends—feel that I wallow in the past. It has also been suggested that I jump too fast to conclusions about the future.

Sitting on that train, listening to the trainman and watching the old and young lovers around me, I realized my friends and family were right on the mark. I was burdened by my guilt, worried about the future, and unsure about everything I was presently doing. I was, plain and simple, a mess.

Maybe the trainman was right. The future would come soon enough, and there wasn't anything that could be done to change what had already passed. Maybe life wouldn't be such a delicate balancing act if I focused on to what was directly in front of me.

I wondered if the trainman ever had someone like Elise in his past.

A shrill whistle brought me back to the present with a start.

"This is it," yelled the trainman. "That's all there is, folks. There ain't no more. We've run out of track. Unless, of course, y'all want to get in and do it all over again."

With his pronouncement, I stepped off the train and headed to the station. I watched as the train trembled to a start and began its slow, methodical trip down the track, toward the center of a "V" formed by two lines of redwoods converging far off on the horizon.

As I walked away, I realized I had never gotten the trainman's name. I turned and threw a thank-you wave at him, hoping he would turn my way. He never looked back.

Over time, I endeavored to heed the old man's advice. I tried to forget the death of my first love and the sons and daughters who were never born. I attempted to leave behind the baggage of my past lovers, trudge past the absence of my daddy and other loved ones—those dead and those still living—and forge ahead to a better place beyond the distant horizon.

I even tried to forget about Elise, nestled with her son and husband in a stone home with flowers on the windowsills, a million miles away across the Atlantic in a tiny hamlet on the outskirts of Lyon.

I had my own family to think about, and they were a handful.

Chapter 26

HANK RETURNS

$\mathcal{M}$ama always said Hank was the hardest one in the family to talk to. "He was just like your Daddy," she would say, and you knew it wasn't a compliment. "He didn't want to talk about things much, and he got plum mad if you tried to get anything out of him. He was darn aggravatin' sometimes, if you want to know the truth of it."

Talking with Hank was like pulling out your own teeth—the harder you tried, the more painful and aggravating was the response. Hank seemed sullen or surly most of the time. I guess he felt the world owed him the right to be dark and gloomy, and he wore his anger like a black cloud hovering over him.

He had been this way long before he left for his self-imposed exile in Alaska, the furthest stop on his odyssey of running from the past and tangible human contact. He probably felt at home in the remote north, especially during the six months of eternal blackness that was winter, when like a bear he could hibernate in his own isolation.

Fifteen years into his Alaskan stay, Christine and I had written to him about Mama's mental deterioration. Her problems began a few years before, but were relatively minor and limited to the normal trappings of advancing age: forgetting a child's birthday or failing to pay a bill. No one made much of the former, because Mama had never been terribly observant of her kids' milestones, but the latter was surprising, as she had prided herself on holding strong in all areas financial after daddy died. We even laughed when she adopted a cat and began treating it as if it were her newest child, and when she began hesitating to stay overnight anywhere else but at home because she thought her cat's feelings would be hurt.

We finally took notice when her normal orneriness escalated to nastiness. Mild conflict with any one of us was the norm, but we were surprised by her repeated snapping and short tempered rants in person and over the phone.

We became downright alarmed when her house started tilting toward disarray—dirty toilets, cigarette butts and ashes in the bathrooms, a nasty litter box by the toilet and mold everywhere. My mama cleaned houses for a living after Daddy died and had become revered for her prowess in these households. As she neared sixty-five years old, she could no longer keep her kitchen organized or the floors clean. Worse yet was her increasing ambivalence to the condition of her prized home. She didn't seem to care or notice her surroundings were sliding into squalor.

She was also beginning to lose track of time, the commodity she had always coveted most. Mama felt there was only so much one could control in a world where danger and pitfalls waited around every corner. She sought a tight handle on everything having to do with time—she scheduled her day to the minute, with everyone assigned individual allotments according to her prearranged docket. When Mama's days started slipping in and out of her mind, we knew her reasoning skills were going haywire.

Mama's mania was laid out shakily—but legally—in her will, which I inadvertently spied one afternoon as I helped her in one of her many aborted reorganization projects. These projects never seemed to get finished—the first part was successful, as bills were separated, recipes dug up, or the cabinets cleaned. Inevitably, the bills were not totaled, the recipes were left unorganized and the cabinets were never returned to form. The only movement was the growing frustration and confusion in Mama's head, as she struggled to cope with the madness robbing her memory and taking with it her peace of mind.

I was thankful to stumble upon her will, not so much for the unlikely opportunity to convince her to change it, but to sneak a preview of its contents so I could forewarn those affected. I wasn't surprised by most of its contents: her daughter had been lambasted for matrimonial misjudgment, and her sons were criticized for their distant attitudes. We had long ago agreed to split the money equitably no matter what Mama stipulated, and we also reached accord that there would be no hard feelings associated with my mom's choices.

However, we could not split money that wasn't there—more correctly, we couldn't divide money given to her cats. Mama was leaving her house—modest as it was—to her half-dozen felines, and the remaining money was to go to "caretakers" for the cats.

Christine and I chuckled at this revelation, but also knew reinforcements were needed to guide our mama through the days and nights in the house we had grown up in but had long since vacated. My sister and I didn't live close enough to provide the daily support Mama appeared to need. Peter was occupied with various issues and responsibilities, so we reached out to Hank. We weren't too hopeful, as communication from him had been sporadic in the last several years. Still we tried, knowing his first-born status had made him extremely close to Mama until his self-exile to Alaska.

When we finally reached Hank, he did not hesitate to return. The former athlete in my brother, the athletic drive and desire to be a winner, rallied him from his dormancy to return in our mama's time of need. He packed his belongings in one bag and flew home.

However, when he limped through the door looking as disheveled as Mama, we thought he had little to offer beyond the inspiration of his presence.

Hank looked much older than the forty-six years he carried, and he was far removed from the fit, confident athlete I once admired. His hunched-over shoulders were more pronounced than ever and his eyes seemed to have receded further into his skull, almost disappearing from view. Their blueness was dulled by shadows caused by his perpetually bowed head. His teeth were still straight, but had yellowed and lost their shine. They were hidden behind the taut line of his lips. His thick, dark hair had thinned on top and there were raging rivulets of gray winding through his temples.

He smoked even more than I remembered, and more and more alcohol was needed to vanquish the coldness within him. By all indications, the hero we once looked up to had no fourth-quarter comebacks, no last-second magic, no miraculous plays left in him.

He said he would take care of Mama but we wondered who was going to take care of him. Still, we left him to tend to her, partly because no one else was around to do it. We also believed that, like the rest of us, he deserved a shot at redemption.

Over the next five years, he did indeed redeem himself. He demonstrated by his quiet, unpretentious manner of dealing with Mama that he could be a hero again.

But while he had proven his worth as the dedicated oldest son, he had turned his back on any search for love or life. He barely left the premises except to shop for groceries. He spent the rest of his time lost in the loneliness of his memories. He was barely into his fifties, but he gave all the appearances his life was over.

Mama could handle his dourness because his mere presence helped her battle and at times beat loneliness. I could usually tolerate his distant behavior because I was only exposed to it in small doses. After a while even these short interactions became irritating. Finally, the day came that I could take no more of his dark gloaming. He had turned down my umpteenth invitation to go with me to watch a ball game, offering a lame excuse about needing more sleep. He never moved toward the bedroom though; he remained slumped in his chair watching a rerun of "The Rockford Files."

Hank chose a bad time to turn me down. My grand goal to leave the past behind and move on was not going well. My recent ending with Elise had left me in a deep funk. I had my job to keep me busy, but everything else in my life was empty, a vast vacuum of nothingness. I had detached myself from my friends, focusing mostly on work and stewing in self-pity. I had not made much headway in finding a relationship, beyond an occasional fling with starry-eyed women taken with my ability to espouse syrupy poetry when soused.

On many of my days off, I found myself trapped in my cabin unable to escape my memories of lost love. On this particular day, I had stirred just enough energy to loosen my chains of despair and flee my stone prison. I journeyed down the hill to my mama's house, another place love had forsaken. At least there I would get some reinforcement that I wasn't the only loser in the game of love.

After Hank denied my baseball invitation, I unloaded my pissed-off state on him.

"Jesus, Hank, you live like a darn mole or some kind of vampire," I said, shaking my head. "You come out at night, forage around for your midnight snacks and late-night TV, and then sleep all day. Why the heck are you wasting your life in perpetual darkness? What the heck are you hiding from?"

I saw his eyes flash, but he did not respond. Instead, he entrenched himself further into his uneasy chair, keeping his eyes focused on James Garner and zoning me out.

I would not be deterred by his trademark avoidance maneuver. I moved closer, so I was standing just above him. "What is wrong with you?" I said, raising my voice to my big brother for the first time ever. This was unchartered territory and I felt unsteady inside. But I forged ahead, after looking down and being reminded of the sad waste my once heroic brother had become. "You crawled into your shell thirty years ago and haven't emerged since. You carry your grief like it's some kind of charge card for forlornness. Well you've maxed out the card and it's time to come back among the living."

I didn't know what I was fishing for by antagonizing him. Maybe I was worried about his sanity. Or maybe I just wanted to push a button, any button that might spark a charge in his emotionally dead battery.

"You have no idea," he growled, "what it is to lose someone *really* close." He stared straight ahead, but I don't think he was watching Jim Rockford solve a case. His hands were gripping the chair, turning the ends of his fingers white.

"I lost Daddy, same as you," I responded. "I didn't think I would get over it, but I recovered in time."

"Recover?" he asked in an incredulous tone suggesting both disbelief and sarcasm. He turned directly toward me, and I noticed emotion in my brother's eyes for the first time in years. His eyes emerged from their sunken, receded pockets much like a turtle's head peeking out from its protective shell.

"Recover?" he repeated. "No one recovers from that kind of loss. I know I never will. And don't tell me you have. Just look at your life. You haven't been the same since Daddy died. You come across like you have it all together, with your good deeds and working with kids. But face it, Stone. You're a mess. Everybody knows it."

"A mess?" I said. "What would you know about me?"

"I know what I see, or better yet, what I don't see," he said, his eyes having a directness I had not seen since his days on a football field. "You just lost another girlfriend—what was her name? Oh yes, Barbie Barfly! Now you're alone again. Just how many women have you gone through in the past ten years anyway?"

His frontal attack caught me off-guard and I could not reply. He filled the void.

"It's been seven or eight, by my count—right?" he continued. "And that's only counting the ones you've told us about."

He was wrong…it was a dozen. Thirteen, if my latest re-involvement with Elise counted. I looked past him, not wanting to meet his gaze for I was sure he could see in my eyes that there had indeed been many others. My silence was enough of an answer to him.

"That's what I thought," he grumbled, waving his hand dismissively at me.

In the past, when things got heated with my family or anybody else, I usually turned and walked away. Something kept me there this time. I wanted to explain my commitment issues, to defend my actions and choices. I was also intrigued by his newfound passion, even if it was aimed at me.

I explained reasons my relationships didn't work out, describing some situations as "bad timing" and others as "compatibility" problems. My brother, who had returned to his reclining position in front of Rockford and his files, didn't interrupt my discourse.

But after I detailed my latest breakup with a gal from work as a "communication deal," he leaned forward, closed his eyes, and murmured something sounding like "crap."

"What did you say? Crap?"

"Why do people ask what someone said, then repeat exactly what the person said before that person has a chance to answer?" he questioned, still looking at the TV.

"You did say 'crap,'" I said, the agitation I felt inside now coming out in my voice. "I just poured out my whole love life to you, and all you have to say is 'crap'?"

"Maybe I was a bit harsh," he shrugged. I wasn't convinced by his contriteness. He soon confirmed my doubt. "Garbage," he said. "That's a nicer word, ain't it?"

I forgot about exploring my brother's pent-up feelings. Now I was just pissed off. "Where do you get off—" I started, before Hank cut me short with the wave of his hand.

"For some reason, I'm not buying your explanations," he said from behind the shield of his upraised hand. "Something about them doesn't sound right. They seem like a bunch of excuses. Either you weren't ready for these relationships or you were just plain scared. Either way it sounds like all you've been good at is running away."

I was surprised at his insight. He had more depth and sensitivity behind his gruff exterior than I imagined. But his words stung, and something inside me had gone to a hard, dark place. I wanted my brother to join me there. I wanted him to hurt too.

"Running away?" I said, adding mock laughter. "You've perfected running away like it's an art form. Ever since Ingrid died, you haven't been able to face the world."

I hadn't heard my brother speak of Ingrid since she died, and over the years people tired of trying to broach the subject to him. Actually, they were a bit scared to. His tired, sad green eyes would harden even further and questioners knew to abruptly drop the subject. I had never initiated discussion of Ingrid and I soon understood why. At the first mention of her name, Hank rose from his chair and turned slowly toward me. His hands were clenched so hard they blanched completely white. I noticed tremors in his arms and his face was flushed red. In no time, he had become a portrait of thinly controlled fury.

I sensed I was about to become the first in our immediate family to be punched by one of our own. I wasn't sure how to prepare, so I stepped back, hoping to lessen the force of whatever came my way. But my own pride had been alerted, and though I wasn't ready to throw the first blow, I was ready to fight back for the first time in my life.

"You don't know anything about love, about perfection," he stammered. "You've just played at this...this thing you call love. Love is...art. At least the love I had...Ingrid was perfect art."

I was stunned, caught off guard by his release of gut-wrenching emotion. Over the past thirty years, almost everything out of his mouth seemed a lifeless, vague monotone. I hadn't heard my brother mention Ingrid's name since the day after her accident, when he had told me their entire love story in a stunned catatonic manner. At that time, I was too inexperienced in the tides of love to understand his torment. But I remembered every word.

And now I realized the monument my brother built was not for our daddy but for someone else. "Ingrid was exquisite, maybe even pristine art," I agreed. "But you've put her on a pedestal, turned her memory into some kind of mental painting you spend all your time and energy sitting in front of and reviewing."

My thoughts drifted away from our conflict to my own memory of perfect artistry, how my mind's painting of Elise was fading, decaying, and disappearing from my mind.

My brother's voice, cold and sharp as a dagger, brought me back to reality. "There is nothing wrong with recalling the most beautiful thing that will ever be in my life, something taken without any damn reason!" he yelled, but I did not feel his anger pointed toward me. He was looking past me, at something only he could see. His words were a rail against the world as the one inexorable force robbing him of his love, hopes, and dreams.

The pain he felt was a twin to mine; only, the woman he loved was gone and mine was still alive. I hadn't figured out which was worse—loving a ghost or longing for a living memory. Was hanging on to hope any better than having none and not moving on?

"It's good Hank to recall the best thing you ever had. But you shouldn't turn that memory into a shrine you sleep with every night. You've got to get back into the game."

"What game?" he asked, but I could tell he wasn't interested in my explanation.

"Life. Love. Communication with your family, friends, other human beings. Basic human involvement. The kind of stuff you have been ignoring since you crawled into that deep, dark hole of self-pity."

"What the heck do you know about 'staying in the game?'" he sneered. "You've left every one of your relationships before the game was over."

"I may have left early, but you've given up without even playing," I replied. "You couldn't even give it the old college try—you dropped out of Alabama, remember? And you've been avoiding the game of life ever since."

Even though I had softened the tone of my words and hadn't meant them as an attack, Hank saw it differently. He took a step toward me, knocking a lamp off a side table onto the hardwood living room floor, breaking it into three pieces.

About this time, Mama shuffled into the living room. Though she tried to disguise the urgency of her entrance, concern showed in her determined gait and worried eyes. Her step was not the aimless, wandering one linked to her confused state. Nor was the look in her eye glazed or lost in some forgotten thought. Her arrival was no accident.

"I heard something break in here," she said without disclosing knowledge of any conflict. Her concern, however, showed in the deep wrinkles around her eyes. "Which one of you is the clumsy ox?" she asked in an obvious attempt to lighten the situation.

Hank didn't say anything, but his hard gaze remained locked on me. I wanted to turn and acknowledge my mama's entrance, but I wasn't thrilled by the prospect of being blindsided by my enraged brother.

"Well, if you two are tongue-tied and helpless, I guess I'll clean up this mess."

I crouched down to help Mama pick up the broken lamp. As I gathered the pieces, she stepped between us, creating a buffer between my brother and me. She sensed this was a safe time to broach the subject of our argument.

"What's going on with you two?" she asked, as if she hadn't heard our words.

"Just having a disagreement," I said, trying to sound light-hearted. "I was suggesting Hank do something other than just sit in front of the TV, wasting his life away."

I spoke so freely—and foolishly—because I figured my mother's presence would dissuade my brother from popping me. I wasn't so sure, though, when I glanced past Mama and saw him starting to shake and tremble as his anger grew.

"Knock it off, both of you," she ordered in a half-hearted tone that nevertheless meant business. "This family has enough problems without you two knocking each other over the noggin'. And besides, you might scare Pretty Girl."

My brother and I both shook our heads and sighed at the mention of her beloved cat. Everything in her life ultimately revolved around that spoiled, pampered soon-to-be-rich feline, even as two of her sons were on the verge of fisticuffs.

We watched in silence as she finished cleaning up our mess and began puttering around the room in a seemingly aimless fashion, picking up and putting down things for no particular reason until she meandered to where we were standing. Acting like we weren't there, she leaned in between us and started cleaning the candy bowl.

She dusted the dish three times, straightening up and flexing her back and neck between each effort. Apparently she was going to clean that bowl for as long as it took for us to settle our differences, or until she felt we were calm enough not to kill each other.

Before I knew it, Mama's subtle intervention had cooled our pride and anger. I no longer felt inclined to escalate matters, and a quick glance in my brother's direction confirmed he had softened his stance as well.

Maybe Mama was a crazy cat lover, but she had not lost her maternal instincts.

When Mama realized her peace efforts had taken hold, she curtailed her cleaning and sat down in the room's only chair, fanning herself. With nowhere else to sit, Hank and I sat down next to each other on the couch. He wasn't looking my way, but I could tell by his relaxed breathing that his heavy emotions had lightened. I offered the first olive branch.

"Rockford's still on? Oh, this is the one with Rob Reiner as the goofy quarterback, isn't it?" Before my brother could confirm or discount my guess about the episode, I answered my own question. "It is! That's my favorite."

I cringed when I realized he might think I was trying to irritate him again. Then I saw a slight grin slowly crease his face as he shook his head.

"I, uh, didn't mean to say goofy quarter—"

"Just shut up and make us some popcorn," he interrupted in a lighthearted manner. "And put lots of butter on it."

I knew then that everything was okay between us. He hadn't asked me to make popcorn in more than thirty years. Though we passed the rest of the evening in virtual silence, I sensed something had changed between him and me.

My intuition was confirmed when I passed by the house a few days later. Hank offered his usual grunted greeting, barely glancing upward as he continued reading a magazine. I was about to make a smart comment about the IQ required to read a sports periodical, when I noticed he was leafing through a travel magazine. "Maybe I will take a vacation," he said, without looking up. "Maybe to Lake Tahoe or Napa or Sonoma."

I was stunned, but not enough to avoid a shallow dig. "Ooh, you and mom will make a cute couple."

My brother actually smiled, a rare deep grin causing huge creases to form below his cheeks. I hadn't seen his matinee-idol dimples since before Ingrid died. "Naw. You can keep her company while I'm gone. She needs a cute guy like you to clean the litter box."

He went back to planning his get-away. This time, it appeared he wouldn't be running from the past but toward some kind of new beginning.

Every time I thought I knew everything about my family, something or someone offered a new education. Over the years following Ingrid's death, Hank showed so little emotion that I thought he was dead to the world. I should have known from my own experience—and the fact Hank was one of us—that below his frozen exterior ran a stream still dreaming of the springtime thaw. The tender, fragile emotions running deep within my brother's sensitive heart needed only a stubborn, patient person to draw them into the open.

Within him indeed beat the heart of a Lyon.

Chapter 27

CHRISTINE'S CHOICE

$\mathcal{I}$n the pursuit of romantic love, my sister was the most passionate Lyon. But when even her best efforts failed to overcome the dark memories poisoning Jonathan's heart, she divorced him. She redirected her passion toward her three sons, insulating them from the pain she had endured so they would have a chance in love.

Christine succeeded as a parent where she had failed in her mind as a wife. After her kids left to start their own families, she was content to follow the progress of their adult memory making. Though initially struggling on her own, she settled into a quiet life working as hospitality host for her small town, Sutterville, in the eastern Sierra foothills.

After years of being told by Jonathan she couldn't do anything right— "you have nothing to offer an employer except your glittering personality, and nobody cares about that kind of shit anyway"—she succeeded simply by being her shiny self. If there was ever anyone perfect for the job of representing an entire town's hospitality, it was my sister.

Christine greeted each tourist who entered her tiny office like she was accepting someone into her home, and she considered the town limits as her neighborhood. She knew what the best meals were at all the restaurants, the most romantic rooms to stay in the two motels, and even the type of playgrounds at the three parks.

She always had ice cold milk and homemade cookies ready for tourists, along with slices of watermelon (of course!). She knew how to get to any nearby destination, be it a town or city, rest area or campground, stream or river, lake or ocean. She would hand them maps, but provided her own directions using routes likeliest to carve scenic memories.

"You can always follow those main highways, the straight, boring ones in boldface type on the map. But it's the thin, winding roads you can barely see on the map that will likely lead you to the prettiest sites and leave the most lasting impressions."

"Then again," she would always say, "why would you ever want to leave our pretty little town?"

When people asked for directions in and around town, she rarely included street numbers or names. By the time she was done telling visitors how to get somewhere, whether it be a store two blocks away or the picnic area on the other side of town, they felt like they had grown up in Sutterville.

"Gettin' to the picnic area is half the fun," she would begin. "Go down this main street here—you know, the wooden sidewalks date back almost 150 years to when the town was founded during the Gold Rush—and turn at the first corner and head toward the mountains. You'll see a white wooden building in front of the First Presbyterian Church. It might be called Presbyterian, but this church accepts all comers, whatever your beliefs may be. On the far side of town, there's this one church that's got its own followin'. It's got some interesting rites, such as its members attend services in the nude—I'm told. Now I believe in each his own when it comes to worshipin' and prayin' to the good Lord, but for me personally, I would only pray naked if my toe got stuck in the faucet while I was bathing in a tub and nobody was around to get me out. Then, boy, God dressed as a plumber could see me naked all He wanted if He could get my toe unstuck!

"After the church, you'll pass by Dawson School on your right. The school's been around since the early stages of the Gold Rush, and was named after one of the town's first settlers, Erwin Patrick Dawson, who made a fortune by learnin' to extract gold from clay using a boiling process. Ain't that something? Lookin' through writings from back then, some cynical residents felt he bought his name onto the school and other buildings, and would've had the town named after himself if he could've had the original town charter revoked. Others believed his recognition was much deserved because he stayed in town after most people left during the boom-or-bust times. He bankrolled many of the town's improvements, basically keeping Sutterville from becomin' a ghost town.

"Look at the red bricks on the school when you go by—they weren't part of the original building, which was made of oak and pine before it was burned to a crisp in 1908. A kinda funny tidbit is that Mr. Dawson's grandson, Erwin III, accidentally started the blaze when he was re-enacting his grandfather's clay boiling technique in chemistry class. They rebuilt it with brick and mortar and it still serves as our town's elementary school today. My three boys went there, you know.

"The tower you see out front still has the original bell that heralded the first day of school back in 1851. The bell still welcomes students every school morning, and is also rung every day at noon to let everybody know they're hungry.

"Just before you get to the foot of the mountains where the picnic area is situated, you'll pass Graveyard Hill. Some of the first miners in this area are buried here. They had worked so hard on their claims they failed to build adequate shelters to protect themselves during the oncoming winter. They refused to leave their stakes when a bunch of blizzards hit, and many of them perished.

"The picnic area—oh, you're gonna love it here, sitting right by the river surrounded by white water lilies and purple lupine. Close your eyes and smell the honeysuckle growin' wild all around you. I'll bet you'll never want to leave!"

Though she rarely strayed from historical fact, none of my sister's directions followed the exact same storylines. She threw in something different every time someone asked to get to the Gold Rush diggings or the mining camp remnants, or anywhere else.

I listened to her spin many of her yarns and would often tease her about the variances in her story details. She would merely shrug. "A town isn't made up of street names and numbers, it's made of the people who live and die there and the memories they make and leave behind. In a town as rich in history as this one, there is no shortage of memories—and interpretations of those memories."

Many of the same people passed through time and again, if only to experience the hospitality of "Sweet Emmeline," as she came to be called by all who knew her. Word-of-mouth from tourists spread the word of the friendly hostess whose homespun storytelling and southern-style hospitality made everyone feel at home, and she even developed a regional and national reputation. "Bay Area Backroads," a television program devoted to little-known but interesting areas of California, did a segment on Sutterville after hearing about her. *Sunset* and various travel magazines also focused articles on the town, usually with her prominently featured as a main attraction.

Though my sister was thrilled by her newfound notoriety, she was worried her beloved town would be given the short shrift. She was careful to ensure Sutterville received adequate mention during interviews. She didn't worry about a letdown should her recognition dwindle. "When the fame and attention is gone, I'm still gonna have this town and all the memories it has given me. That will be more than enough."

She got more than she bargained for, though, when her flirtation with fame brought her the last thing she expected—another chance at love.

Seamus McKenna had never heard of Sutterville until he read the *Sunset* article focusing on the town's unique collection of gardens. The article included plenty of Christine's homespun insights into town lore, but she had made sure the writer concentrated on the gardens. McKenna, a gardener who oversaw the foliage in a small park on the outskirts of Aberdeen, Scotland, was initially captivated by photos of the gardens and natural flora and fauna flourishing in and around Sutterville.

Always looking for ideas to upgrade his small but accomplished garden, he was intrigued by Sutterville's series of gardens that combined a park-like setting of finely trimmed hedges and close-cropped green lawns with naturalized surroundings of twisting white oaks, climbing vines of honeysuckle, and various wild flowers and plants offering ebullient bursts of color. He was fascinated with how the stately English manor-style garden design had been intertwined with the wild naturalness of the California foothills.

But it wasn't the lure of the exotic country gardens of Sutterville that made Seamus say to himself, "Go west, Middle Age Man." He was drawn to the face and the words of the town hostess in the article, the woman who made the gardens come alive and the town seem like a home—his home. The ethereal attraction was my sister's eye color—the same deep blue-green as the North Sea greeting Seamus every day of his life. It was enough to convince him to take his first vacation in twenty years.

When he strode into the hospitality center, he didn't hesitate in telling Christine what had drawn him to cross an ocean and most of a continent. Holding up a copy of *Sunset* folded to the article about her town, he approached the counter and announced, "I have traveled 6,000 miles to look into your eyes, to see for myself if they are truly as enchanting as they appear in this magazine. They are everything I dreamed they would be."

Somewhat taken aback by his straightforward approach, my sister was nevertheless drawn to the earnestness of his tone and the accent in his words that harkened to a fairytale time and setting. She listened closely as he described his respect for the unique gardens of her town and how they reminded him of his own Scottish green. As was her manner, Christine deflected his praise and directed him to give credit to the architect of the gardens.

There had been other men interested in her over the years, men in town she had known for years—Walter, the postmaster, and Jasper, who owned a ranch in the foothills. After she started the hospitality job, there were others from out of town. There were tourists taken by her charm, even some married men who came with their wives and left falling in love with her.

Still, she balked at accepting Seamus' invitation to dinner on his first night in town. He simply shrugged, vowing to return the next day with the same request. I was visiting her at the time and spent the afternoon listening to her explanations as to why she was hesitating to go out with a perfect stranger.

"A perfect stranger?" I said, laughing. "Christine, your town's information network is more effective than the CIA. He's been here for half a day and you probably already know more about him than his parents. That makes him practically an old friend."

"But Stone, I'm afraid. I haven't exactly had a great track record with men."

"One mismatched man," I corrected. "No one says you have to marry the guy. Give the old boy a chance. It's not like you need to worry about him doing anything subversive, because the whole town will be watching. And from what I'm hearing through your CIA network, this guy is not the hit-and-run type. He's from a country billions of years old and he lives down the street from the billion-year-old stone house he was born in. He practices an honorable trade that helps things grow. Christine, give *yourself* a chance to grow."

"I don't want to get ahead of myself, but what makes you think he would want to move here? He's lived his entire life in Scotland, and this is just a small, dusty mother lode town thousands of miles away."

"Because, my dear sister, finding you would be like finding the mother lode."

"You're just plain silly, Stone."

She went on the date, and with the entire town and her little brother holding their collective breaths, they talked like they had known each other their entire lives. Seamus spoke of swearing off love after his wife died ten years before, and resigning himself to spending the rest of his life alone. His gardens were enough, he said. Christine didn't go too much into the details of her sad love life, but acknowledged she, too, had given up on chasing love. She had her children to cultivate and that was enough.

They both realized it wasn't enough. They were married six months later, on Valentine's Day. With the entire town in attendance, Christine's oldest son, Jon Jr., walked her down the aisle.

Even Mama was impressed with how happy Christine seemed. "It's about time somebody in this family figured out how to get this love thing right," she said to no one in particular. In the next breath, she threw in her usual cautionary line. "Now let's just hope she doesn't mess this one up too."

Seamus wanted to give Christine a honeymoon she would never forget. My sister had never been out of Northern California since moving from Alabama, so Seamus wanted to take her to an exotic tropical isle. Christine, though, wanted to visit the land that had shaped the strong character and gentle heart of her husband. And so they did, visiting Scotland and meeting his mum and dad, who despite their stooped, elderly bodies had the same lively twinkling in their eyes as their son.

And they loved Christine, saying they had never seen their son happier or more alive. Christine was flattered, especially after years of being put down by Jonathan.

But a memory she couldn't escape followed her even into her wedded bliss, and ultimately threatened the fairytale love she had finally found. I knew what she was carrying within her; I knew the pain under the black patch she had sewn over her heart.

The memory happened in the last year of her marriage to Jonathan.

Christine had become pregnant for the fourth time, an unplanned event producing widely divergent reactions in the Jolson household. Christine was ecstatic when tests confirmed the child would be a girl. Despite the tattered condition of her marriage and her relatively advanced age (thirty-eight) to bear a child, she was ebullient that her dream of having a daughter was being fulfilled. She quickly settled on the name Carolyn Divine and went about the task of turning Jon Jr.'s old room into a pink-filled nursery.

She didn't care when I teased her about the baby's name, saying it sounded better suited for an exotic transvestite dancer. She appeared the happiest I had ever seen her.

Jonathan was his same miserable self. When he learned of the pregnancy, he termed it "an unnecessary burden" and ordered her to get an abortion. When she refused, he withdrew even further into his dark, twisted dimensions. He badgered and ridiculed her at every turn, stopping just short of hitting her on several occasions.

Christine did not appear overly concerned about Jonathan's reaction, ignoring his verbal threats and throwing herself into preparations for her fourth child's birth. A different kind of resolve had taken hold of her. She was imbued with a sense of purpose, developing at the same frenetic pace as the baby girl growing inside her. She was no longer the timid, non-combative soul who avoided confrontation. When Jonathan began his abusive taunting, her hardened exterior bounced the negative vibes back in his face.

She had even begun to challenge him when he arrived home drunk and filled with his dark demons, which was happening often in the weeks after he found out she was pregnant. I could see the change in her, the confidence and determination blossoming, and I was happy with her newfound inner strength. At the same time, I was worried about how Jonathan would react to her evolving personality. He had been taken aback at first, but I thought it would be just a matter of time before he struck back at her independent attitude.

Though I knew she wasn't ready to get a divorce until after the baby was born, I implored her to separate from him and move out of the house—even if it meant losing the home to him. She assured me not to worry; she had learned how to handle "any situation" involving him. Disappointed she chose to stay, I warned her to stay clear of him when he was drunk. "No amount of resolve and determination will deter him," I said, "if he loses it one night when he is drunk out of his mind."

I was on a camping trip on the next night Jonathan arrived home drunk and angry, and lit into Christine. She tried to walk away, but he followed her into the newly decorated baby room. When she ignored him, he grabbed the bucket of brown paint she was using to recondition a hobbyhorse and tossed it on the freshly painted pink walls. I had told her to call the police in this type of conflict, but she decided to speak her mind first.

She didn't get too far before he slapped her. When she refused to back down, he became enraged. He hit her like never before, backhanding her face and raining numerous blows on her mid-section.

She lost the baby and very nearly her life. "I could have stopped him if I had left earlier," she told me, when I walked into her hospital room. "I could have saved my baby girl; now I just feel like killing myself. And I would, if not for my kids."

At that moment, she pledged never to search for love again.

Christine's grief and sorrow was such she could not bring herself to speak out against Jonathan, and she forbade me from informing the authorities or telling anyone else in our family what he had done. Her story was that she slipped down the basement stairs.

I was beside myself for accepting her terms, but knew her actions were part of the Lyon code of not holding legally responsible the people who wronged us. I made sure she followed through with the other part of the code—she would leave him and take her three boys with her. I shepherded her through the divorce and its sticky aftermath.

I couldn't understand why she seemed so lost and melancholy, even after Jonathan moved to the northern reaches of the state when the divorce became final. But Mama knew. "You don't know how it feels, in your mind and in your bones, to lose a baby during pregnancy," my mother said, noting that she too had lost not one, but two babies during her marriage. "The hurtin' can linger for months or years."

Or it could last a lifetime, as I understood from my own experience.

Was Christine feeling guilty for not doing everything to save her marriage? When I poised this theory to Jimbo, Jake, and Omar, who helped me "persuade" Jonathan not to fight the divorce, they thought I was crazy. "After the shit that asshole put your sister through," Jake said, "there's no way she should or could still feel anything for him."

"You don't know her devotion to the concept of family, or more importantly, the Lyon family history of allowing compassion to overwhelm our sound judgment when it comes to love," I explained. "We don't let go easily."

I didn't know it at the time, but my buddies were right—Christine's case of the blues had little to do with the end of her marriage.

But reality had finally caught up with my sister's dreams, in the form of a shining Scottish knight with a green thumb. A Lyon's fairytale vision had finally come true.

No one was sure what prompted Jonathan to return, whether it was hearing about his ex-wife's notoriety on the news shows or learning she had remarried.

Christine did not seem perturbed or alarmed he wanted to visit. The boys would be in town, so it would be a chance for them to reconnect. "Besides, I welcome the chance to clear the air," she told me over the phone. "I just want to talk to him face-to-face, to let him know how it is now, to let him know I'm OK, and that I've moved on."

"Do you think he really wants to hear you've found someone else and moved on?"

"He needs to move on—to get on with his life. I think when he sees how happy I am he will not have to worry any more about all the damage he's caused."

"After all he's done to you and the kids, and you're worried about how he feels about himself?"

"I didn't do all I could to help him—" she began.

"You did everything!" I snapped, cutting her off. "You showed more devotion and patience than could be expected from anyone. Your humaneness was practically inhuman."

"I just think, with all the pain and humiliation Jonathan carried from childhood, he needs to know he didn't waste his life, didn't cause damage to me or his kids that couldn't be fixed. He needs to know we survived, and maybe then he will realize he had a part in building some of the good that was in our lives. Maybe he can forgive himself."

"He should never be forgiven for what he did to his kids, to you and... to the baby."

I made reference to the baby hesitantly, knowing it was likely still a painful area for Christine. We had not spoken of the miscarriage since she swore me to secrecy.

"I have long ago forgiven him for what he did to me and the kids," she said, lowering her head. When she raised her head to face me, I noticed there were tears in her eyes. "He did not have to be forgiven for the baby."

"What?" I said, not understanding her meaning.

"I did."

When she told me once that there are some sins committed within families beyond forgiveness, I thought she was talking about what Jonathan had taken from her—the baby girl who would have completed the circle and allowed her to walk away from him in peace. I thought his actions had placed upon her pure heart a dark stain of hate and anger no distance of separation could cleanse.

Jonathan, though, was not the one Christine could not forgive. The person she could not absolve from blame was the one she saw every day in the mirror.

As I listened transfixed on the other end of the line, she told me of the guilt weighing upon her these past few years. Christine felt she provoked him by not backing down and walking away, as she normally did during their confrontations. Her pride and stubbornness were the reasons her little girl was dead.

I was about to tell her of my culpability in her tragic loss—by pressuring her to get a divorce—but she sidetracked me by changing the subject and telling me she had agreed to meet Jonathan at Finnegan's

Bluffs. The bluffs were a series of granite outcroppings overlooking the Mokelumne River as it wended southwest toward Sutterville. Christine informed tourists that from this vantage point one could see where gold was first discovered in the area by Cyrus Finnegan—"an ornery old coot if there ever was one!"

"No one liked the old man, and the feeling from him was mutual," she related. "So nobody much cared when Old Cyrus died, saying he was a stingy old so-and-so who probably kept every last cent he got from his gold. Some people even tore up his place, trying to find the treasure he had supposedly squirreled away. All they found were some letters he had received from his granddaughter somewhere back east thanking him for sending the money to assist her and her husband in getting a stake in some land, and help with the baby they were expecting.

"And do you know what else?" she would ask, finishing her story with a smile of triumph. "According to the bank's ledgers, the amount his granddaughter credited him for sending matched every last cent the old guy had gotten for the gold he had found. The people were right—he hadn't spent a single dime on himself!"

She always loved telling the story of Finnegan's Bluffs, if only to remember what the promise of gold once meant to her. It was on this grassy hill a lifetime ago where Jonathan had knelt on his knees and proposed marriage, sealing his promise by slipping a simple gold band around her finger.

And on this same hill, she planned to tell him his proposal had not been a mistake, if only because they had produced loving, caring children. If forgiveness was what he wanted, she would give it to him.

Jonathan had not returned seeking forgiveness.

The years away from Christine's side had not been kind to Jonathan. Left alone to confront his demons, he spiraled downward. His younger sister related to Christine that he was drinking more heavily than ever and had estranged himself from friends and family.

Christine already sensed something was amiss. In the first year after their divorce, he called the boys often but they refused to see or even talk to him. He blamed Christine and often berated her over the phone for turning the kids against him. She finally threatened to get a restraining order. He made less and less effort to connect with his kids, even after their resentment lessened and they offered to visit him where he lived in Chester, a small wooded town about 150 miles north of Sacramento.

After a while, he stopped calling. With no contact for the next four years, he seemed to have melted from their lives. No one knew what to expect upon his arrival.

I thought I knew what was coming—and it wasn't good. As I gunned my car from my cottage to Christine's meeting place with Jonathan on Finnegan's Bluffs, I was filled with a sense of foreboding similar to when I raced to find my friend Alex so many years before. To make matters worse, a spring thunderhead brooding since early morning finally burst in the late afternoon. After a treacherous drive over a winding two-lane road, I made a skidding stop in a muddied dirt lot at the foot of the bluffs and rushed up the hill.

As I broke into a clearing, I saw Jonathan with his hands on Christine's shoulders. I let out a yell, "Hey!" that bounced off the canyon wall opposite of Finnegan's Bluffs and returned to my mouth, just as I was exclaiming, "Stop!"

I was too late. He shoved hard enough for her to fall backwards. Her fall froze my ascent in mid-stride and I slipped. Positioned on my hands and knees, I watched transfixed as she hit the ground and started rolling sideways, disappearing over the edge. I scrambled up the remaining fifty or so yards, broaching the crest of the hill in time to see Jonathan lying flat on his stomach with his arms stretched over the edge of the horizon.

As I neared Jonathan, he grabbed a large exposed tree root with his left hand and swung the rest of his body over the side. My guess that Christine had somehow slowed her descent was confirmed when I heard him call out, "Grab my hand, Chrissie." I saw Jonathan's right bicep tighten and knew he had managed to secure some type of hold. I continued my shuffle in their direction, sliding to a stop at the edge of the cliff, my legs hanging over the side. I looked down in time to see Jonathan holding onto the crook of Christine's left arm. Christine slipped from Jonathan's hold but was stopped from tumbling downward by Jonathan's desperate stretch that netted her left wrist. "I just wanted to shake some sense into you," gasped Jonathan. "I won't let go."

Jonathan didn't let go, but his last grasp at making amends was short-lived. Loosened by the rain, the root gave way under the combined weight of Jonathan and Christine. I lunged for the root but could not gain a firm hold.

Jonathan held tight to my sister's hand as they tumbled like rag dolls down the muddy hillside. I knew at once that Jonathan was dead before his body came to rest on a rock ledge 150 feet below. Christine may have died then and there, too, had she not landed on Jonathan's prone figure.

She lay trapped in the hospital bed, with tubes, lines, and bandages making her resemble some kind of lab experiment, the broken bones and twisted organs inside her sapping the cherry red blush from her cheeks, until her face bore the unmistakable gray pallor of someone who had been drained of life.

My sister was dying. I didn't need the doctors to tell me.

She smiled weakly upon realizing I was the one standing at the foot of her bed, and I saw a twinkle of hope in her eye. I soon realized the hope was for me not her.

"How's my little brother doing? Are you OK?"

It was just like her, worried about everyone else but herself. I said I was doing fine, but despite the drugs and the pain she could read my eyes enough to know I was lying.

"You have to let go, little brother."

"None of this would have happened if I hadn't pressured you into getting a divorce, or if I could have talked you out of meeting him on that stupid cliff," I lamented.

"No, no, no," she said, pounding the bed with a fist. The exertion left her pale face flushed, and she paused to collect her strength. She continued in a measured tone. "I'm the one who didn't stop him in the beginning, and I'm the one who didn't walk away when I had the chance. I was the one who chose to keep the truth from you. I'm glad you made me leave. I wouldn't have seen my kids as separate from me, as strong, self-reliant men who had their own lives to live. I wouldn't have found a revived life in this town, the life with so much fun and love and hope in it. And most of all, I wouldn't have met Seamus and made these wonderful new memories. I wouldn't have found true love."

"But you have had it for such a short time," I said. "You deserve to have true love for so much longer."

"Sometimes it takes a person's whole life to find it. When you finally do, you have it for eternity. I believe some day you will find the same love I found," she whispered.

I thought about telling her I had already found the love she wished so dearly for me, but I hadn't the heart to tell her I couldn't hold on to it.

Turning to tell her this half-truth, I found her exquisite, sparkling eyes glazed and fixed, their lights turned out, and her rosy cheeks turned into pale flowers. I closed her eyes with a brush of my hand. She was gone. The best part of me had gone with her. Those who most deserved to be— Seamus, Jon Jr., Jason and Mitchell—were not by her side.

An entire town showed up for my sister's funeral, held under a cloudless sky on the first day of spring. Springtime, Christine always said, was God making good on his promise made in winter that things would get better.

This spring God lied.

I wanted to shout out against God's betrayal; I wanted to tell everybody gathered there what a travesty the Lord had perpetrated in allowing my kind, loving sister to lose her life for no damn reason. But I kept my recriminations to myself, as my sister would have wanted. She would not have me blaming God or want people making a fuss over her.

One by one, people got up to speak on the virtues of my sister. Even Mayor Erwin P. Dawson V, a lifelong Sutterville resident who often became grumpy when told of Christine's colorful characterizations of his forefathers' early namesakes, stepped up to the podium. "Christine knew how to keep alive memories and turn them into something worthwhile and interesting," he stated in an uncharacteristically halting voice. "Christine was never boring, as all the Erwin P. Dawsons before me could attest after turning in their graves at one time or another upon hearing her colorful comments about our family history. She made us known throughout the Gold Country and California, and even around the world. And while she made me shake my head at times, she never failed to make me smile. She is a sweet person that this town and the entire world will miss."

I kept my opinions to myself regarding God's fickleness with the truth about the promise of spring, but I couldn't stop from telling the people gathered there what a special gift had been taken from us all. As I stood upon the hill overlooking the town in which my sister grew into a wonderful woman and mother, I read the truest words I had ever written about the purest person I had ever known:

BENEATH AN ANGEL'S WING
You came into this world
A gift of sweet music
Born in the shadow of innocence
Beneath an angel's wing

A child of loveliness and purity
Blessed with giving heart and faithful soul
You grew into a woman of kind spirit
Rich in resonance and resolute in purpose
Searching for love you realized
The heart is a lonely hunter
A woman of loveliness and purity
Strengthened by a higher love
You are bathed in God's presence
Beneath an angel's wing

You are blessed with song
The world is privileged to hear
You are touched with compassion
The world is grateful to feel
You are loved by those fortunate
To receive your presents
Once locked in your treasure chest
Now open for all to share
Those searching for a friend can find you
Beneath an angel's wing

LEO HARRELL LYNN

You are flowers blooming
On the golden hills
Spring and summer colors
Of uncommon beauty
A meadow of rainbow hues
Vibrant and fiery and unrelenting
You are tender melody
In a world deafened by disharmony
You are striking beauty
In a world disfigured by ignorance
You are God's gift
Of sublime forgiveness
Hidden from a fool's view
Beneath an angel's wing

You felt the pain from another
Reach out from the past
Innocent now no more
Bruised, battered and betrayed
You walk down unknown paths
With uncertain steps
Yet you are not beaten
You cannot be beaten
Retreating you have found hope
Beneath an angel's wing

When the world closes in late
And casts its cruelties of fate
You find refuge in virtue
Unmatched by others
Now softly you sleep, safe
Beneath an angel's wing

Eyes closed you run like a child
Through fields of lilacs and lilies
Taking off you float above

All the hurt and pain
Free from harm you soar
To grandest heights
An Angel protecting us
With wings of your own

As I walked down the hill toward the world below and what little was left of my tattered life, I thought about how different my sister was from me.

I always felt true romantic love cut deepest, even more so than family ties. If romantic love fails, it is because someone has made a choice, someone wants something different. I always thought of family love as more of an obligation than a choice, which is probably why I struggled with my sister's excessive devotion to her children and the horrendous pain she endured because of it.

Maybe I had no idea what real love was all about because I have never experienced being a mother. Unlike the vicarious nature of romance, there is rarely a second chance when a mother's love fails. "A mother's love is not conditional, it is not temporary, it is not transitory," my sister once told me. "A mother's love has no boundaries, no limits, no expiration. It is timeless and its depth has no end. It exists, well, just because."

By the time I reached the bottom of the hill and joined my oldest brother Hank in holding up my faltering mama, I realized I learned most of what I knew about real loving from my mother and sister.

In the confusion and pain of the next few days, Hank and I did our best to comfort Mama. As I was about to go home, a surprise arrived at Mama's doorstep. Peter had returned after being away for more than ten years.

Despite the tragedy of Christine's death, Peter's reunion with Mama was among the most touching moments in our family history. The look of absolute surprise on her face followed by her welling tears and quivering mouth, coupled with the sudden realization in Peter's eyes as to the huge toll Mama's advancing age and his long absence had taken on her, was stunning. Topping even this memorable moment was the long, tender hug the two star-crossed Lyons shared, as Mama's frail, bent body melted into Peter's gaunt, stooped frame and disappeared inside his tightly wrapped arms. Maybe the pain and despair surrounding us made this reunification that much more special, if only to reaffirm the continuity of the Lyon legacy at a time when it was most needed.

The Lyon brothers discussed what had become of our lives. Peter spoke the most, describing his continuing efforts to find the truth and the light among the "lies and dark forces" all around him up north. He was less expansive, but still straightforward when broaching the state of his family life.

"I'm losing touch with my kids," he admitted. "They don't live far away, but Carma is involving them with so many other things that I am not seeing them very often. She claims I'm the one who hasn't made time to visit because I'm too wrapped up in my spiritual movement. She's asking me to choose between the kids and God."

"Maybe she's just asking you to become involved in something other than your own interests," I said. "Maybe she's asking you to choose your family over yourself."

I was surprised at my directness. Maybe the abrupt tragedy stirred feelings of urgency in me. My brother didn't respond, and I didn't pursue the subject. I guess we preferred to steer from budding strife as neither of us could not handle any more grief.

As usual, Hank had little to say but did surprise everyone (except me) by mentioning he was thinking about taking his first vacation in years. "But I don't know if I'm going, because I'm not really feeling right about leaving."

Peter and I bombarded him with reasons why he should go, and in the end he bowed to the roar of the Lyons. We talked about possible locations, with Alaska being the only place ruled out from the beginning. "You could pay my way there and I wouldn't go," said Hank, a brief smile forging deep dimples into his cheeks.

Surprisingly, he decided on a dude ranch in the middle of Montana. We wondered about his choice—he had sworn off horses and everything to do with ranches and pastoral pastures ever since he had lost Ingrid more than three decades before. He wasn't giving any reasons though he did say,

"I recently saw 'City Slickers' all the way through for the first time and thought it might be fun to get out in the open air for a while."

I didn't say much about my life, except that I was having breakthroughs with a few of the kids at work. Mama had her own opinions about the kids with whom I dealt. "You better keep your eye on them boys. One of them crazy ones might just up and try to kill you one day. I just wish you'd get a wife and kids of your own."

"Mama, I've told you before, women now are too smart for old dummies like me."

"Well, that Elise girl seemed quite the catch," Mama nudged. "She was downright pretty—and she wore dresses with flowers all over them, like I did when I was trying to woo your Daddy. Them dresses worked, by the way."

I quickly steered the conversation to Mama's cats, hoping this would get her off my memories of perfect love. My diversion worked. Mama crooned about her cats as if they were her only children. We played along, as we all knew about her feline will request. Fortunately, I had already straightened it out with the probate official.

Mama also talked about the corns in her feet, the purplish veins in her legs seeming to throb "all the time," the ache in her shoulder, and several other maladies. Five minutes later, she repeated her aches and pains verbatim. Five minutes afterward, she repeated them again. She did this with every subject she discussed.

Peter asked me about Mama's forgetfulness and eccentric behavior.

"As you know, with us Lyons, it's hard to tell what's eccentric and what's just plain crazy," I said. "Mama, though, is losing touch with reality more and more. Maybe that's not so bad, considering what just happened. But yes we are worried about her. Hank tries to watch after her, but it's becoming more difficult for him because she's needing more attention than he has energy to give."

We talked into the early morning hours, as much to get to know each other again as to forget about the loss of our perfect sister. With Daddy and Christine now dead and buried, and Mama going out of her mind, our proud family of lovers was reduced to one son crippled by love, another who had lost sight of love, and a third who had run in fear of love. There was hope among the three Lyons, but not much of it inside the youngest one.

Chapter 28

HOPE RETURNS

$\mathcal{H}$ope blossomed in the spring of my forty-third year in the form of a letter from Elise. She had written a few times in the first couple of years after she had moved to France, focusing mainly on her excitement about her baby and her return to teaching and playing. Then the letters and all other communication stopped. Though thoughts of her were a daily occurrence, I hadn't heard anything from her in five or six years.

Elise, Albert, and their child, Michel, were moving back to Sacramento. Albert's company was sending him to the United States, as he was perfect to head the international unit's west coast "hub" in nearby Folsom.

Elise related her excitement at returning to Northern California. She missed her American experience, especially her friends and "other things" back in Sacramento, and she wanted Michel exposed to a taste of American living.

She apologized for not communicating with me in the past few years, but explained her son had been diagnosed with a form of autism called Asperger's Syndrome. Dealing with his special needs had taken much of her time. She promised to fill me in on his situation when we eventually got together.

And near the end of the letter, she mentioned Albert and her were divorcing.

She would inform me of the details when she arrived the following week.

After knowing virtually nothing about her life for years, this flurry of new information overwhelmed me. I tried not to think about the phone call for which I had seemingly been waiting a lifetime. I threw myself into my work at Hope House, wondering if my excitement would last past our first gaze into each other's eyes.

Still, I found myself thinking about what it would feel like to see her again. Wild, dangerous thoughts of hope were creeping into my psyche. When her call finally came, the ring startled me from a recurring daydream I had been having since her letter arrived. I shook my head to erase the picture of her naked body so I could focus on our conversation.

She had indeed divorced her husband, but there were "complications." Albert was very much a part of his son's life and wanted to stay involved, something Elise not only accepted but strongly embraced. They shared custody and she said they had an amiable agreement as to Albert's role in Michel's life. Michel's Asperger's Syndrome necessitated that he maintain a well-ordered schedule and routine, especially in relation to his parent's involvement. Though they would not be living together, she and Albert agreed to keep as much of their relations with Michel the same as they had always been.

Other parts of Elise's former life in Northern California were coming together. She had a network of friends still in place, as well as a position in the local chamber orchestra. She re-established contacts to begin private teaching once she was situated.

I was the "other thing" at the heart of her return to Sacramento. Less certainty existed about this aspect of her reunion with America. I felt myself holding my breath when she began addressing our situation.

"You once told me I should make decisions about my marriage and my career before I considered what to do about you," she began.

"Yeah, and I was really good at following through on that advice, wasn't I?" was my response. "Those first times you broke away, I wouldn't let you stay away."

"Well, it took a forced separation from you to understand what is important in my life. I'm ready to move forward now."

"Maybe we are finally ready to move forward together," I thought to myself, not daring to speak the words aloud. Though it was a long drive from where she was renting a small home in the foothills forty-five miles southeast of Sacramento, we agreed to meet again for the first time in the McKinley Park Rose Garden near the State Capitol. I didn't mind driving

the fifty minutes to the park from my cabin in the hills above Folsom Lake. I had made the drive countless times in the past to view the au pairs, and then to spend quiet but heated afternoons lying beside Elise under the isolated weeping willow.

We would meet at the familiar tree on a Saturday three days hence, almost eight years to the day we had last seen each other at the fork in the Crying Trail.

Again, I tried not to think of our reunion's next stage. But I had just finished my two-day work shift, and wouldn't have much to keep my mind busy for the seventy-two hours before we were to meet face-to-face. So I kept busy writing thoughts and feelings down in poems, six in all. At the last minute, I decided to leave the poems at home—this time, I would not use my flowery, finely tailored words as a crutch to lean upon.

As I walked into the park and onto the path leading to the willow, I thought of the last reunion we had there, when Elise had run full tilt into my arms. I wondered what the reception would be this time. Deep in thought, I did not notice the slight female figure join me as I made my way on the path. I did not know Elise was beside me until I felt the softness of her hand as she interlaced her fingers into mine. We never even broke stride on our way to the willow, walking together as if neither our hands nor our hearts had ever been apart in the eight years since we parted.

Not a word had been exchanged as we sat down on a blanket I had folded on the ground, the same blanket on which we had made love so many times before. Though I felt the comfort in our bonded hands, I was at a loss for words and longed to fill the empty space with the poems I had left at home.

Sensing my hesitancy, Elise rescued me. Her eyes, bright and vibrant and translucent, filled me with warmth. She softly touched my cheek, and from her dew lips the drop of one sweet word fell, "Honey." I closed my eyes to savor its sound, and I could almost taste the sweet nectar in its meaning. I opened my eyes to take in Elise's beauty once more.

She took my hand and placed it on her breast. The sound of her thumping heart reverberated through my fingers, up my arm and into my chest, joining the chorus of my own wildly beating heart. "Do you feel that?" she asked softly. "The pounding in my chest has been getting louder and louder as the time approached when I would see you again."

She placed her hand on the side of my head and gently guided it to her chest. I heard the sound of a thousand drums and she knew it, murmuring, "you are hearing my love beating out of control for you."

We sat talking, oblivious to the world spinning backward around us. Time peeled off the clock like someone had pushed a reset button. Nothing had changed, but everything seemed different. The same feelings were there, the same depthless passion. But the years had given us perspective and produced more well-rounded lovers.

I sensed a change in her the moment she started talking about her son. Loving him had given purpose to her life and focus to her love. All that had gone wrong had been pushed aside by the one thing she had gotten right—Michel.

When I gave my perspective, she laughed about how on the mark I had pegged her. "Yes, I guess I have found the domestic, nurturing side of me goes beyond caring about children of other people. And I could not be happier by this revelation. When I have been down over the years, all I do is look at my son to realize my worth. I run around looking haggard and spent on some days, but I do not care. I have my handsome son."

"I have, truthfully, never seen you look more beautiful," I said, averting my eyes so she would not see the wonder—and the lust—growing in them.

"There is something different about you," she said, and I knew she had been studying my face for the answer. "I still see the same sadness in those blue eyes, but there is something else about what they contain."

"Maybe what you see is my acceptance of some things as inevitable or unchangeable. Maybe I have finally realized my Don Quixote days are over."

"Stone, I do not think your Don Quixote days will ever end. Your dreams are what make you stand out. No, I think it is something else."

She studied me for a while longer, until her face slowly lit up like a kerosene lamp expanding into a warming glow. "I know what it is," she beamed. "You look as a soldier who has just returned from war. There is a depth of seeing in your eyes coming only from one who has witnessed much suffering and learned a great deal from the experience."

In my mind, I amended her words to "from one who has caused much suffering."

Elise had planned ahead and arranged for a sitter to stay with Michel until later that evening. I thought we would eat a late lunch at one of our favorite cafes around the corner, but we both felt a different kind of hunger gnawing within. I drove us to my place in the hills, recording record speeds getting up the last section of winding road. Where we had shown restraint earlier, our coming together in my bed was like nuclear fusion. I stopped briefly to put on Barber's Adagio, but Elise dragged me back to bed. When I told her of my quest, she said in a breathless voice, "Don't worry, honey, we'll play the music in our heads. Now, climb on top and slide down into me."

In our quest to make up for lost time, we still managed to take a long, slow, and twisting path to mutual ecstasy. We explored new areas of our bodies, as experiences since our last lovemaking had enlarged our knowledge of what we could do to please the other.

Elise was right about Barber's Adagio playing in our heads. The aching in both our bodies resembled the buildup in the music, and the want and desire released in her screams and wails sounded like uncontrollable expressions of repressed grief, mirroring the high-pitched climax of the adagio. Her soft sobs afterward were reminiscent of the calming cessation at the adagio's end.

It was a chilly, breezy spring evening but there was no shortage of heat in my studio. While I sat propped against the stone walls serving as my headboard, Elise reached over and wrote something with her finger on the steamed glass of the window lining an entire wall of my cabin. As she turned and once again slid atop me, I viewed what she had written on the window, "E & S" inside a heart, and copied it on her chest using my tongue.

Our sweat had a salty, primal flavor, reminding me of the sea spray whipping my face at Bodega Head several years before. The taste of the sea seemed to revive my vigor and I ran my tongue across and around Elise's breasts, stopping to lick the sweat from each nipple. She emitted a low moan as I bit each nipple before flipping her over. As I ran my tongue down the center of her back, Elise did not let me get below her waist before turning me over and straddling my chest. As she slid down toward my waist, I watched her eyes flicker and close, then felt a slight shuddering from her as she lowered herself onto me.

We moved our hips in rhythm to the natural music we were hearing, not stopping until the record played over and over through our bodies.

She finally left in the late evening. I did not move from bed until morning, content to smell and feel Elise on and around me throughout the night.

The scene was virtually repeated the next evening, though we had some time afterward to talk. I began the discussion of what my life had become since we had last been together; I had turned my words into verse:

"There was a time when I had no clearer vision of love than when I looked into your eyes. What I saw rang true, and I believed what we had was blessed by the heavens above. It took a while for me to get over this belief. I realized after the weeks wore on, then rolled away, I no longer thought about you and I being together. I thought about you in snapshot images— your beauty, your presence, your hair caught in blurry remembrance. But I stopped seeing me in the big picture, I stopped believing in the two of us as one. Even without hope, I could not let go. I held on to the feeling I had when I was with you, the belief in the perfection of what we had."

"Our love failed," Elise said, her tone soft and absent of blame. "How could it be perfection if it did not last?"

"I guess it was similar to any vision of utopia—the dream was perfection, but the reality was played out by imperfect humans. Our love did not fail—we failed our love."

"You once told me in a letter what we had was a test of true love and our character," said Elise. "You said I passed the character test while you failed."

"Though I still believe I failed to do my part, I now realize our love was not such a test of character but of will and fate. Neither one of us had trust in ourselves and faith in each other to see the fight through. Our doubts allowed fate to eventually intervene."

"I think that has changed," she said. "You always told me it was best to end one thing before starting another. I have done my best to put my first life behind me—or at least to one side. I am ready to begin anew with the person with whom I was meant to spend the rest of my life."

Maybe in the end, our being together was meant to be.

Chapter 29

MICHEL AND THE STONE HEART

After we had re-established our intimacy, Elise felt it was time for me to meet Michel. "Maybe I should have brought you and Michel together earlier, so you could understand his situation before dealing with our feelings," she said. "But with your caring ways and professional experience, I figured you two would hit it off."

Her encouraging words, I suspect, were aimed at making me feel at ease with her son's condition. Though I didn't let her know of my doubts, I wasn't so sure of a smooth connection. I had worked with some of the toughest boys in the juvenile system, but I had heard autistic kids could prove infinitely more frustrating. Social workers who had worked with them told me they presented some of the toughest challenges they had faced.

I thought Elise would give me insight as to what to expect before meeting Michel. When she didn't, I wasn't sure whether to take it as a sign of confidence or a type of test. The only hints she gave were that Michel spoke in an unorthodox manner and was not touchy-feely or overly social. "He is pretty analytical, with certain quirks setting him apart from most kids—like referring to himself and other people in the third person."

At first sight, Michel looked like many boys his age, except for his stunning good looks emanating from his attractive parents. On closer study, I could see the far-away look in his pale blue eyes suggesting his mind was often somewhere else.

I thought hard about how to connect with a boy who seemed to function almost solely on the analytical level. I was used to hot-headed teenage boys who despite all their bluster and posturing could usually be reasoned with after they cooled down.

I bent to give his hand a shake, but he wriggled out of my grasp as if I had burned him. I had read that some kids with autism and Asperger's interpret touch as pain because to them it feels like a thousand tiny pin pricks.

I let him go and assessed my next approach. I couldn't play with Michel the same way I did with other kids, and knew it was even less likely he would respond well to my witty jokes. My strongest tools to relax and earn trust with kids were useless with Michel.

I observed him for a while to get a handle on my next move. He didn't seem too interested in my presence, appearing preoccupied by several model airplanes on the floor. I looked closer and realized they were all passenger planes.

"That's a bit odd," I said, turning toward Elise. "Most kids like fighter jets or Snoopy-like bi-planes."

"Michel keyed into passenger planes one day and they are the only types he cares for," explained Elise. "He knows all the airlines and the models of their planes."

A positive aspect of his minimal range of emotional reactions was his absence of jealousy or other concerns about my attention toward his mom. It didn't appear that Michel was bothered I wanted to date his mother or I might somehow take her away from him. He only seemed worried when I moved too close to his well-ordered arrangement of airplanes, which covered one end of the living room and held most of his attention.

The lack of negativity notwithstanding, I still wanted to make a connection with this distant little boy. In desperation, I thought about teaching Michel sign language—I only knew a rudimentary level of the discipline myself, but I was hoping to convey enough to help him connect and communicate with his mother and vice versa, even if he wasn't sure what feelings were behind the signs. I told Elise of my plan and she said it wouldn't hurt to give it a try, though I should wait until a time his airplane interest waned.

Two hours later, I was still waiting. Finally, his attention floated in my direction.

It was slow going. Michel seemed more fascinated by my fingers than the signs I was forming. "How come you have not fingernails on the tips of your fingers, like Maman and Papa?" he asked.

Puzzled, I looked down at my hands. My fingernails had always been a source of embarrassment for me, as they were perpetually bitten and chewed to an unattractive nub. I turned them over so Michel could see I had some nails left, and was about to correct him, when he adjusted his earlier question.

"Why does Stone have nails like a kid—a baby kid?"

"Because I bite them," I explained, eager to get on to my sign language lesson.

"Bite them?" he said hesitantly, turning his head sideways so as to get a different look at my fascinating nails. "Stone eats them? Stone is hungry?"

"No," I stammered. "I chew them when I'm nervous or angry."

"Fingernails make Stone nervous or angry?" he asked, looking confused again. "Stone is mad at them?"

"No," I replied, my puzzled look matching his. "Why do you think that?

"Because Stone bites them."

I was getting nowhere fast, so I tried to redirect him from my "baby kid" nails. I was able to get him refocused enough to struggle through the alphabet. He grasped the concept fairly well, but seemed to be losing interest. "Here's something to make your mom smile," I told him, as I bent my second and middle fingers into my palm while keeping the other three fingers outstretched, forming the universal sign of love.

"This means love," I explained. "This is the heart sign."

Michel looked at my hand and then at me, and his face was the definition of confusion. Elise had told me he could connect inanimate objects to their meanings, but struggled with identifying feelings or emotions.

"The fingers of Stone look not like a heart," he said, studying my hand more closely. "Maman of Michel says love is what we have in our hearts to give to others."

"She's right," I said.

"Michel does not understand," he said, shaking his head. Then his body stiffened, and his face took on the concentrated look of a genius who had locked into a new theorem. "The heart is a muscular organ pumping blood through the body," he stated in a mechanical, almost robotic manner. I noticed his eyes were fixated on my hand and he was twitching his fingers near his face. "The heart is the power supply of the circulatory system, which is responsible for distributing oxygen and nutrients to the body and carrying away carbon dioxide and other waste products."

"You seem to know a lot about the heart," I said.

Michel kept twitching as he talked. "The human heart has four chambers. The upper two chambers, the right and left atria, are receiving chambers for blood. They collect blood pouring in from the veins. The lower two chambers, the right and left ventricles, are the major pumping chambers. They propel blood away from the heart through the arteries."

I sat silently, not believing what I was hearing from this eight-year-old kid. His choppy grammar of a few minutes ago had been replaced by a stilted, technical delivery sounding like a graduate student assistant trying to impress his professorial mentor—but Michel had the self-assuredness of someone who was not worried about being judged.

"The human heart is shaped like an upside-down pear and is located slightly to the left of center, inside the chest cavity," he continued. "The heart is the size of a closed fist and is made mostly of muscle tissue, which contracts rhythmically to propel blood to all parts of the body. The muscle rests only a fraction of a second between beats. Over a typical lifetime of 76 years, the heart will beat nearly 2.8 billion times and move 169 million liters of blood.

"The heart must beat continuously because the body tissues—especially the brain—depend on a constant supply of oxygen and nutrients delivered by the flowing blood. It is a pumping machine and provides the power needed for life. If the heart stops pumping for more than a few minutes, death will result."

Trying to slow down Michel's pace so my mind could take a breath, I interjected an emotional element to his hard facts. "Aristotle, a famous Greek thinker in the olden days, believed dreams originated in the heart."

Michel seemed puzzled by my contribution and paused in his delivery, as if waiting for more information from the computer files of his brain to download. It didn't take long. "The life-sustaining power of the heart has throughout time caused an air of mystery to surround the heart," he continued. "Modern technology has removed much of the mystery, but there is still fascination and curiosity involving the workings of the heart."

After his short detour into the mystical nature of the heart, he returned to cold, hard facts. "The heart is located in the middle of the chest, behind the breastbone and between the lungs. The diaphragm, a tough layer of muscle, lies below. The heart rests in the pericardial cavity, a moistened chamber surrounding the organ with a durable, double-layered sac known as the pericardium. As a result, the heart is well-protected."

I chimed in again. "Sometimes, though, even a lot of protection isn't enough to prevent pain to the heart," I said, giving Elise a look making it clear I wasn't talking about the physical aspects of the organ. She turned away and looked out a window.

Michel's computer brain started spewing information on maladies of the heart. "A heart attack is an event resulting in permanent heart damage or death. A heart attack occurs when one of the coronary arteries becomes severely or totally blocked, usually by a blood clot. When the heart does not obtain the oxygen-rich blood it needs, it begins to die. The severity of the attack often depends on how much of the heart muscle is injured or dies.

"A heart attack is a process building up over time, usually a few hours. Surviving a heart attack depends on the treatment given within the first hour. With each minute, less oxygen is reaching the surrounding heart muscle and risk of permanent heart damage rises. The sooner symptoms of a heart attack are recognized and appropriate treatment given, the better the outlook for survival—in the near future and over the long-term. Emotional after-affects may also accompany a heart attack. Fear of future attacks, worry about physical activity, and depression are common reactions to the trauma of a heart attack."

"Then, is it better not to use the heart much, so it doesn't get overworked and broken down?" I asked, directing the question more to Elise than to her son.

Michel hesitated at the question, his eyes flickering as if a computer chip in his brain was collecting information. "No," he finally replied. "The heart gets healthier and stronger with more use. Regular exercise and a healthy diet are important in reducing the risk of developing atherosclerosis in one or more of the coronary arteries, thus eliminating a major risk factor in heart attacks. A totally blocked artery is considered less of a threat in terms of a future heart attack than is a partially or almost totally blocked artery."

"Why is that the case?" I asked, genuinely unsure of the reason.

He paused again, and then continued. "Because there is no potential for more damage with the totally blocked vessel. The areas of the heart formerly served by the vessel are permanently scarred or dead, with no need for an oxygen-rich blood supply. A bypass of a totally blocked artery supplying a dead area serves little or no purpose. If the doctor decides there is no path into a blocked artery, he usually decides to help the part of the heart still having a chance to function satisfactorily."

"So," I reasoned, "it's better for the doctor to forget the dead area of the heart and work on the part still having hope."

"What does hope mean?" he said, a puzzled look accompanying his question.

"Sometimes I wonder," I said, more to myself than to him. "I guess it's the belief things will get better no matter what the situation is."

Michel continued like a tape recorder stuck on play.

"The nerves regulating the heart are part of the autonomic nervous system, which directs activities of the body not under conscious control."

"Yeah, I know the feeling of not being able to control my heart," I sighed. "At times, it seems something or someone else has control of it."

Elise directed Michel to his room a short time later, putting on a tape of the Discovery Channel's "Wonders of the Heart" to keep his active mind occupied.

"How does he know all of this stuff?" I asked when she returned to the room. "Did he read the Big Book of Medical Terminology, or what?"

"Actually, he does not read all that well," Elise said. "But he seems to have a phonographic memory for what he hears. He listens to tapes and watches shows about the heart and can almost completely memorize and recite them."

I thought Elise may have slipped when she said "phonographic" instead of photographic, but I didn't correct her. "Is he fascinated with any other parts of the body?" I asked. "How about the brain?"

"No. He just seems to care about the heart."

"How did that start?"

She turned toward me and gave me a look suggesting I already knew the answer.

"What?" I said, understanding her look but not getting the reason behind it. "Why are you looking at me like I know?"

"You know because you are the answer," she said. "You are the reason Michel knows more about the heart than most doctors."

"Me?"

"It can be traced to all the stuff you gave me before he was born," she explained.

"Stuff?"

"Your cards and letters and poems," she explained, "and the books of romantic poetry and the novels and movies about love you gave me."

"And?" I said, still not getting the connection.

"What do you know about Asperger's Syndrome?"

"Not much," I conceded. "I've read a lot about it and autism since you told me about Michel's condition. But the information is kind of running together in my head, so I would welcome clear, concise explanations."

"Considered a milder form of autism, Asperger's is still largely misunderstood," she began. "Evidently, as with autism, the brain is affected in how it synthesizes information. For some reason, a brain with Asperger's lets in certain input while blocking others. In the case of Michel, the part allowing his brain to focus on a specific intellectual area also takes away from other areas, mostly the ones initiating and controlling emotions and sensitivity, especially the ability to recognize and understand non-verbal cues.

"His mind seems to arrange information in a precise, almost mechanical manner," she explained. "The doctors and child psychologists think he has inherited the general mental and intellectual makeup of his father, only to a concentrated, accelerated level."

I understood what she meant. Michel's dad was a brilliant engineer, boasting an innovative mechanical mind to match the creative musical heart of his wife.

"So why do you think his preoccupation with the heart has anything to do with my poems and other writings?" I asked, trying to hide my jealousy of her husband's strong connection to Michel.

"I think it has something to do with what he was exposed to in his first three years, before the initial stages of Asperger's appeared," she said. "He was a normal, happy, smiling baby. He loved it when I read to him, and I used all kinds of resources, from traditional and contemporary books for children to song lyrics and musical games. He seemed to enjoy listening most of all to your poems and letters and cards. I used to read them to him when he became wound up during the day or when he was fussy or irritable just before bedtime. They seemed to calm him down, and he would just lie there, smiling."

"In other words, my stuff worked like a sleeping pill," I laughed.

"No, it was not like that," she smiled. "He would listen closely, becoming relaxed and content. He connected with the rhythm of your words, the way they related to each other. A look of wonderment would cross his face, turning him to putty in my arms."

"I still say my words put him to sleep."

"When the Asperger's began affecting him more and more, he had problems focusing on what I was saying or reading to him. He would rock back and forth, or twist his head from side to side, looking past me toward the wall as if he wasn't listening at all. We thought he might have a hearing problem, but the doctors could find nothing organically wrong. After observing his inattentiveness and rocking behavior, they suggested he might have some form of autism."

"That must have been scary for you and Albert."

"It was devastating. The doctors said his condition could go many different ways. Severely impaired autistics may not talk at all and have little or no concept of socialization with peers or adults. Others will eat inanimate objects or bang their heads to relate anger or frustration. Still others spend long periods looking off into space, blocking out everyone and everything else except what they see in their own secluded world."

As they watched Michel's development over the next couple of years, Elise said they were relieved to find he apparently wasn't affected with the most pervasive elements of autism. Elise explained Michel did not "stem" to the extent of the autistics she described. "Michel tends to 'zone out' for shorter periods of time, and while he has some slight body tics, he does not have dramatic tremors and twitches common to some autistics.

"He appears to have a milder case than most autistic kids and the majority of those with Asperger's. He is extremely verbal and does not stem off visual cues, though he does not read well. It is not that he cannot read; he struggles to focus. The doctors explained some autistics and Asperger's kids have problems hearing and seeing at the same time. It is believed many of them—including Michel—cannot easily focus on more than one thing at a time. In any case, he loses interest quickly, so I have been working with his teachers to improve his concentration. There has been progress, but he has a long way to go."

Elise explained Michel becomes particularly distracted and restless around bedtime. "The only time he stays interested for a noticeable period is when I read some of the romantic stuff you have given me. His fidgeting ceases and he is actually able to look me in the eye for a short time. He is most attentive to anything mentioning the heart.

"The heart?" I said.

"Yeah. Heart was one of the first words he learned to say and the first body part he pointed to on his body. The doctors think he clicked on the word at a very early age and has remained keyed in ever since. Hearing the word or subject matter seems to trigger his cognitive brain into action, blocking out everything except information flowing back and forth along a narrow, focused channel. He can somehow retain most, if not all, of the heart information. The doctors have a fancy name for it, but I call it a 'phonographic memory.'"

"I don't understand how he can connect all the complex words and phrases and make then understandable," I asked. "And his vocabulary is incredible. He doesn't talk this way except when he's talking about the heart, right?"

"He has a stilted way of delivering words, evidently because of the way his brain processes information. But his mechanical speaking manner becomes more pronounced and his vocabulary expands exponentially when he is stimulated to discuss the heart. When he is not locked in, he does not seem to know what most of the complex words mean or how to use them in a sentence. It is like he has a computer in his brain and the memorization file is stuck on the heart."

"Well, even if he is merely memorizing and synthesizing the information, it's still amazing," I said. "You and Albert must be proud of his astounding intelligence, even if it is exhibited mostly in one area."

"Albert was not thrilled upon learning Michel was motivated by your writings, but he thought the interest of his son in the heart was an important breakthrough. He began reading to him from medical books to see where it would go. When he seemed to respond strongly to these sources, Albert decided to get him some related recordings. Michel will listen to tapes for hours, if I do not redirect him. Neither one of us realized he would become a walking and talking encyclopedia on the subject."

Elise could see I was understandably impressed by Michel's mental abilities and confused by her corresponding frustration with it. She offered an explanation.

"We are proud of his knowledge," she said. "And we have learned more about the heart than we could have from any cardiac surgeon. But it is frustrating he cannot connect an emotional tie to what he knows. He thinks of the heart only in abstract, detached terms."

"So you don't think he relates the workings of the heart to anything other than its bodily function?" I asked.

"He never says anything when I tell him I love him," she said, in a low voice I recognized as nearing her sobbing zone. "I can get him to say it, but I have to practically mold his mouth to form the words."

"Well, in that way, he's like the typical insensitive male," I said, trying to ease her pain with a little levity. "That reaction indicates he is normal."

Elise smiled, but her face remained pained and careworn. "I just want him to know the heart as more than a machine or an organ in the body. I want him to have feelings, to somehow know what love is and to be able to show it."

"I think he knows," I said. "I can see it in the way he looks at you."

"I just wish I could hold him and he would hold me back. I would love just one unforced hug."

I thought a moment. "Sometimes love takes a long time to show itself. But I think it's there inside of him. It'll come in time."

"The doctors say not to get my hopes up," she said.

"I know," I said. "But I read somewhere that the emotional blockages affecting kids with Asperger's can open up over time, and many go on to live fairly normal lives."

"I want him to have an extraordinary life," she said, biting her lip at her admission.

"Well, he seems extra special already," I said. "He can't help but be extraordinary with a mother like you. Remember, things in life change and the heart grows stronger with age. Don't give up hope."

"I try not to."

"But something else is bothering you about his condition, isn't it?"

"Yes," she sighed. "However, as with my desire for him to become something more than normal, it is self-serving."

"What is it?"

"Michel has no appreciation for music. He seems to have a dead ear. He does not react when I play or when he hears any other kind of music. He seems to have inherited the intelligence and analytical depth of his father, but nothing from me."

"He does have a strong affinity for the heart," I said. "That says something about your influence."

"You know what I mean. He does not have my interest or aptitude for music."

"That could change," I said. "Music is supposed to be great therapy, maybe the best therapy, for kids who have trouble connecting with others. It helps with adults too as I can attest. Your music changed my life, opened me up to an area I had never known before. I too had a dead ear before I met you."

"You had a lyrical heart," she said. "I just gave you music to put your words to."

"And it was beautiful music."

"Well, Michel does not hear or understand this beauty."

"Remember, he does have an amazing ability to synthesize what he hears. I think that ability came from you. You'll reach him someday, when you find the right key."

Michel was restless before going to bed and none of his mother's bedtime stories or my poems relaxed him. She was a bit irritated herself, knowing our limited time together was slipping away. Michel seemed to sense her anxiety and became more agitated.

"I have a story my daddy use to tell me when I was younger than Michel," I offered. "He got it from his mama, and though I didn't really understand it all that well as a kid, it always seemed to put me at ease before going to bed."

Hopelessness was in Elise's eyes, as she shrugged and mumbled something sounding like, "We might as well try anything."

I sat next to Michel, who was looking at the plastic stars on the ceiling glowing in the muted darkness of his room. He made brief eye contact, and then returned to gazing at the stars and making airplane noises.

I called Michel's name, but received no response. I decided to start my story anyway, hoping he would connect to my words at some point.

"The name of this story is—"

"Stone is not reading this from a book or a paper?" questioned Michel. "Do not all stories at bedtime come from a book or paper? Maman of Michel has twenty-seven books with stories at bedtime, and many pages of other stories."

He nodded at the floor, where all twenty-seven books appeared to be lying. Elise had tried everything in her bedtime arsenal this particular evening, as her spent literary ammunition littered his bedroom floor.

"Not all bedtime stories are written down in books," I explained. "Some are passed on by simply telling them over and over. My grandma told this one to my daddy when he was a kid, and then my daddy told me when I was just a little younger than you are now."

"How does Stone recall the story without the story being written down?" he asked.

"Well, I memorized it in here," I explained, pointing to my head. "In my brain. But I really keep it stored here," I said, pointing to my chest."

"In there?" asked Michel, looking puzzled.

"Inside my chest, in my heart," I said. "Anything that really matters in your life you remember in your heart."

The hairs on the back of my neck began standing on end as I could feel Elise's eyes staring at me from behind. But I also noticed, with the first mention of "heart," Michel had begun to get that focused look I had seen earlier. Was this was a good thing, or would he become transfixed again on the heart and not calm down for some time?

"The right and left halves of the heart are separate—" he began, before I calmly but firmly interjected. "Michel, do you want to hear the story of The Stone Heart?"

He hesitated, and then continued as if quoting a mantra. "But they both contract in unison, producing a single heartbeat. The heart works on the 'all-or-nothing' principle. That is, each time the heart contracts—"

I put a hand on each shoulder and squared my face to his, about a foot away, as Elise suggested I do when trying to get him back on track. "Michel" I said firmly.

"It does so with all its force," trickled out of his mouth, as if his computer was running out of energy. I guess Elise's suggestion worked—I had effectively cut off his energy supply. His eyes flickered, and he stammered, but then his fingers stopped twitching. "The Stone Heart? That is what the story is called?"

"Yeah. The Stone Heart."

"OK. Tell Michel the story Stone has stored in his chest."

And so Stone did.

"It came upon a time long ago in a place far, far away that a landowner of some renown felt it was time his daughter begin searching for a husband. Arianne, as she was called, was a woman of unmatched beauty in the land, with the fairest of skin, like fine porcelain, and long, satiny hair the color of the blackest raven. Her eyes were like jewels of jade and emerald glistening among the ocean waves, and her face...Oh! Her face, when seen by men, would stop them in their work, would cause them to stumble over nothing in particular, would render them mute in mid-sentence."

I turned toward Michel, half-expecting him to be fidgeting or making airplane motions. But he sat calmly, looking past me at his mother, with an intense gaze seeming to analyze every aspect of her face. He looked like he was seeing her for the first time.

"And Arianne was pure in character, showing kindness to most who came her way, especially young children and small animals. She was polite and sweet in her disposition. If the young maiden had a vice, it was her adoration of the lifestyle to which she had become accustomed. She enjoyed beyond measure the

fine possessions her doting father showered upon his only daughter—hand-tailored clothes of softest silk, jewelry made of the finest gems from far-off lands, gardens of the most exotic flowers, and servants to attend her every want and need.

"When word of her desire to take a husband was sent throughout the land, her suitors came from far and near to admire up close her fair face and to vie with presents for her grace and hand in marriage. But the maiden, as unimpressed by false flattery as she was tempted by true riches, spurned the young men and they dispersed a sad lot.

"But one young man remained, standing silent in the shadows. Neither smile nor frown graced his face, as he stepped solemnly forth to offer his trinket to her treasure chest of flowers, baubles, and sweet treats. He held out simply in his palm, a gray stone of little beauty or importance, save for its implied significance.

"At first, Arianne gazed in disbelief at the small rock, so unimpressive compared to the haul of presents lying at her feet. 'What is this, but an ugly gray pebble?' she asked, her voice heavy with disdain. 'You present this, when others have given so much more?'

"'This is all I have to give,' the young man said calmly, 'but it is all you need to have.'

"'I have been given rubies and sapphires, emeralds and diamonds,' she scoffed. 'What do I need with this worthless rock?'

"Undeterred by the fair maiden's brashness, the young man continued holding out the stone. 'Look more closely. See how it is shaped vaguely like a heart. And like a heart, it holds more beauty inside than out. Hold it, and you will feel its power reach out to you.'

"Still unconvinced, yet slightly intrigued by the young man's improbable story and steadfast manner in the face of her challenges, she reached out her hand with no real reasoning in her mind for doing so. He placed the stone in her palm.

"Smooth and cool to her first touch, the stone warmed in her embrace. She moved it to her other hand, where it heated up again and became kindling fire with each caress. She looked now more closely at the rock, hoping to see her face somewhere in the reflection. No picture of her pretty countenance shined back, nor did she sense a message; only a dull grayness and tiny white wrinkles running along its sides giving hint to what shaped its destiny.

"*The young man, sensing the fair maiden's bewilderment, offered a final clue to his romantic riddle. 'Carry this stone with you always and you will have strength. For, it has survived all the world's great floods and wildfires, all its great storms and quakes, and the long loneliness of time. Part of a broken whole, it holds within the wisdom of the ages, enduring strength, and eternal hope.'*

"*Arianne gazed once more at the simple gray stone, her eyes suddenly swirling like tossed waves in an ocean storm. Grasping the pebble to her breast, she felt the powerful gift of undying true love that burned within. Closing her eyes, she felt the suitor's gift of love transferring to her own heart.*

"*Her mouth forming a sweet smile, Arianne understood then the hidden history written in the veins of time along the sides of the Stone Heart.*"

Michel was not yet asleep, but appeared calm and relaxed. I had never witnessed his sleep routine, but I sensed he was ready to nod off.

After softly patting Michel on his shoulder, I glanced up at the mirror beside his bed. In the reflection, I noticed Elise was rubbing something in her hand. I saw it was a gray stone, one of not much beauty or importance, save for its implied significance. She had received the stone from a suitor many years before, and had not forgotten its hidden history. Elise reached to wipe something out of her eye. A tear.

A tear of remembrance, I thought to myself. Or maybe one of renewed hope.

Chapter 30

COURAGE OR FEAR?

The day I got another shot at becoming a hero hardly began in heroic fashion.

I was listless from the moment I awakened. Cool and crisp was the morn in the hills around my cottage, even on this summer day. I knew the heat would rise as morning wended into afternoon, but the eighty or so degrees around my cabin would be nothing compared to the 100-plus temperature blanketing the Sacramento Valley floor a thousand feet below.

Though I enjoyed the coolness of my foothill retreat, I was one of the few locals who also loved the valley heat. While so many others wilted in the stifling temperatures, the molecules in my body expanded and I became a bundle of excited energy.

I was heated up with nowhere to go on this summer day. I hadn't kept in contact with friends, so I didn't have anyone with whom to fish or kick a soccer ball. I didn't feel like heading to Folsom Lake by myself, although the bass bite was supposed to be good.

This indecisiveness was a new feeling. I had long enjoyed being lonely at my own pace. I cultivated this appreciation for aloneness as a kid, playing Tudor electric football and Strat-O-Matic baseball and sorting my Topps baseball cards for hours on end in the comfortable privacy of my room. Though I was sociable with kids in the neighborhood, I also loved playing by myself. I enjoyed countless hours of me-versus-me games of football and basketball, and I perfected a game that involved tossing a tennis ball on our slanted roof and catching it as it bounced off. I made some of the greatest catches in baseball history in my front yard—diving, twisting circus grabs of which my Oakland A's hero Campy Campaneris would be proud. My astounding feats were witnessed by millions of cheering fans who were all in my head. I was a sports legend in my own mind.

As I made my way through adulthood, my attraction to solitude continued. I didn't mind doing anything alone—fishing or attending a baseball game or even eating out.

All this had changed in the last couple of months since Elise re-entered my life and brought Michel with her. I began wanting this exquisite woman and her eclectic son by my side whatever I did each day.

I didn't think of Elise without Michel, and I didn't think of Michel without me in the picture. I had become attached to the kid even though he rarely gave me the time of day, what, with all his hours spent arranging his 747s and Delta M-88s and listening to one program after another about the heart.

I tried to reach him in various ways. I took him to watch airliners take off and land. He loved it—almost too much. I wasn't ready for him to bolt out a side door, down some stairs and onto the runway, all the while pointing to the sky and shouting every known statistic about the United 737 landing in the distance. Luckily, Michel couldn't clearly explain his runway sprint to his mother—one of the few secrets I ever held from her.

I took him to a local American Heart Association office to study life-size models of the heart and listen to tapes and video presentations about his favorite organ.

I succeeded in one area—getting him to calm down at night. I always obliged when he asked to hear me tell "The Stone Heart" tale before bedtime. It wasn't long before he could recite the entire story himself. And he often did, repeating the story softly to himself like he was counting sheep until he fell asleep.

So whereas I used to relish my alone time, I was now filled with emptiness. Once my freedom, aloneness had become my prison.

On this summer day, I felt particularly empty and trapped. Elise wasn't around; her mother and youngest sister, Josephine, were visiting from France, and Elise had taken them to San Francisco for the day to do a "step-tour" of houses in the area. It was Albert's weekend with Michel, but father and son were spending this day doing yard work around

Elise's house. It was a monthly ritual to which both father and son looked forward, though Elise said Michel spent much of the time zoning out toward the sky, pointing out and describing in detail airliners flying in and around the Sacramento area.

Though I understood the importance of Albert's presence in Michel's upbringing, I was irritated it interfered with my movement into his life. Plain and simple, I was jealous.

This jealousy, and my newfound uneasiness with being alone, was why in the early afternoon I found myself driving toward Elise's house. I wanted to watch a father interact with his son the way I now longed to do so myself. Some people might call it spying or even stalking. I preferred the term "practical observer," as I considered this surveillance a learning experience for my expanding role in Michel's life.

For a while, I watched from my parked car as they worked in the front yard. When they retreated to the back yard and out of my sight, I drove up the road toward a dead end at the top of the hill. I pulled off halfway up the ridge, at a spot overlooking the back of Elise's small home. I could see their activities in the back yard without worry of detection.

I had discovered this vantage point one afternoon when I decided to drive up the side road to see where it led. I noticed a guy parked in his car along the side of the road. He gave me a startled look as I passed. As he hurriedly fumbled with something in his lap, then gunned his engine and screeched down the hill, I realized I interrupted something extremely personal occurring in his front seat. As I laughed to myself, I turned to see what view had turned on this pervert.

From his elevated vantage point, Elise's small back yard lay almost completely exposed. And there was Elise, lying on her back on a raised redwood deck, completely exposed and wonderfully naked, working diligently on her European full-body tan.

I watched her silent show for a bit too until I thought I would burst. I twisted down to her place and expressed my excitement in person. I told her afterward about her peep show visitor. She just shrugged and said, "Pfft. Maybe it will keep him from really cheating on his wife or girlfriend."

I watched as Albert cut the grass and trimmed the weeds. For much of the time, Michel was content to sit on the porch and make imaginary flying motions with his arms. I was secretly satisfied I hadn't seen much attachment between father and son.

My satisfaction changed moments later when I realized Michel's arm motions were practice runs for an upcoming flight. After Albert piled the cut grass and clipped weeds together in one huge mound, he walked toward his son. As Albert arrived at the steps leading up to the deck, Michel was just completing a thirty-foot sprint across the redwood platform. As his father reached out, Michel took off from the edge of the steps, his arms held straight out from his sides.

Even from the hill high above their makeshift landing strip, I could see Michel's bright smile as he landed in his father's arms. In one complete motion, Albert swiveled to his side and propelled himself and his son headfirst into the mountainous pile.

I heard their booming laughter twice, first as it roared over my head and then again as it echoed off the hill behind me.

It was the first time I had ever heard Michel laugh.

Turning my head away in self-pitying reaction to this perfect father-and-son scene, I did not witness the aftermath of Michel's third flight into his father's arms. When their laughter went silent, I turned to see Michel standing alone next to the grass pile. Suddenly, Albert rolled out of the pile and started thrashing wildly. I thought he was playing, maybe acting like a monster. Then I realized his hands were around his neck and he appeared to be fighting for air.

A lot of things went through my mind as I flew down the hill to try to save the man who hated my guts. Some of these thoughts I'm embarrassed to admit. I cursed myself for not owning one of those bulky cell phones fast becoming the new rage.

In the two minutes it took to get to Elise's house and hop her front gate, the conflicting thoughts were gone and my mind had switched to my CPR-First Aid mode. I was ready to face whatever awaited me, though I half-expected to end up face-to-face with a fully conscious, safe and alert Albert, who would be surprised and angry I had entered his back yard.

As I surveyed the scene the way I was taught in the forty-four safety courses I had attended in the past two decades, I tried to forget who the people were in the back yard. But I noticed a brief glimpse of recognition in Michel's eyes. "Mr. Stone Heart," he chirped. Then he returned to yelling in a singsong voice, "Papa Delta D-737 is down, 911; Papa Delta D-737 is down, 911," over and over.

I tuned him out and looked down at Albert, who was lying on his side with one hand on the first step of the deck. I noticed he had scratched "call 911" faintly into the wood with a branch before he had collapsed. In his rush or panic, Albert had forgotten Michel did not understand "call" as relating to the phone. That's why he was repeating "911," but had not gone to dial 911 on the phone.

Turning Albert on his back, I tilted his head, lifted his chin, and looked for chest movement. Detecting no breathing, I looked around for Michel, and realized he was standing two steps behind me. I placed a hand on each shoulder, made sure we had eye contact, and said in a calm, but firm voice, "Dial 911. Say '4922 Apple Blossom Lane. Breathing emergency,' to the person who answers. OK?"

"A-O-K, over and out, Mr. Stone Heart," he said in a deliberate manner.

I figured that once the call came in, the emergency dispatcher could automatically key into the address, but I wasn't taking any chances. As Michel raised his arms and flew into his house, I heard him begin to repeat what I had told him to say.

I leaned back over Albert and noticed the area around his lips was turning blue. I retilted his head, gave him two quick breaths, and noticed his chest did not rise. I repeated the process with the same results. His airway was probably blocked by an object. I checked his pulse, then had to recheck it after realizing I counted my own thumping pulse the first time. I detected a pulse on my second try.

I glanced at my watch. "Damn," I thought to myself. "He's been out more than four minutes. A couple more minutes and his brain will be fried." I skipped the next step of rescue breathing, knowing I had to dislodge the object as fast as possible. I prayed my years of redundant training placed the correct breathing repetitions in my head.

I straddled him and gave five quick abdominal thrusts. I turned him on his side and checked his mouth for the object without success, then gave him two more quick breaths, followed by two more. A quick check of his pulse revealed it was still present, but fading.

I tried not to panic, but time was slipping away. I repeated the abdominal thrusts, mouth sweep, double breaths, and pulse check, to no avail. I did it again, trying to keep focused while visions of Elise and Michel's despairing faces raced through my head. I shook my head to erase their devastation, and instead tried to remember the radiant smile I had seen on Michel's face only minutes before as he flew into his father's arms. I was on my third round of abdominal thrusts when I heard the sirens stop out front.

I kept going, hoping something would change or Albert was one of the rare individuals who could handle more than five minutes of not breathing without suffering brain damage. Then I remembered he was an avid mountain and rock climber back in France, so he likely had built-up a resistance to oxygen deprivation.

On the fifth try, as Michel flew around me in circles and the paramedics burst through the back door, I felt something in Albert's throat. With a two-finger scoop, I hooked out a black oak ball the size of a large marble.

I looked at the oak ball for what seemed like an hour, then I leaned over his mouth and felt breathing on my ear. I was about to start rescue breathing, when a deep voice next to my shoulder startled me.

I thought it was a voice from heaven but soon realized it belonged to a dark-haired, solidly built paramedic flashing a quick smile. "Looks like you've done the trick, but could you use some more help?"

"Please," I said, rolling aside as the medic placed a breathing apparatus over Albert's mouth and started pumping air into his oxygen-starved body. "I think he stopped breathing for almost six minutes before the oak ball came out. I hope that isn't too long."

They worked on Albert for nearly a half-hour before loading him into the ambulance. As they wheeled him by, I noticed he had regained much of his natural color. Without identifying myself, I used Albert's phone to leave a message on Elise's cell, letting her know there was an emergency and she needed to go to St. Vincent's Hospital.

I was about to leave, when I realized nobody would be around to look after Michel. I drove Michel to the hospital and waited for Elise to arrive.

Realizing Elise would be frantic by the time she made the two-hour trip from San Francisco, I called her to provide details. I lied. I told her I had been driving up the freeway when I saw an ambulance turn off and head toward a street that led to her neighborhood. "I followed it out of curiosity, and realized that it had stopped at your house. I talked to a neighbor, who said that Albert had apparently choked on something, but the object was removed and he had been taken to the hospital."

"Where is Michel?" she asked.

"He's OK. I brought him to the hospital, so you could come straight here."

"You are a darling," she said. "Tell me the truth though. How is Albert doing?"

She knew I would somehow manage to discern information about his condition, even if I weren't a relative. I had to take a subversive approach. I couldn't very well say I was Albert's wife's boyfriend. Instead, I became her brother. The doctors and nurses gave me updates on the half-hour.

"The doctors were amazed," I said. "He regained consciousness on the way to the hospital and all of his vital functions were practically back to normal within a half-hour of his arrival. They are still watching for convulsions and other complications affecting certain organs, but they think he may even get to go home tomorrow."

I paused for a moment, and then continued. "They told me this guy must be in exceptional physical shape or he must have a tremendous will to live—or both. They also said there must be something or someone in his life he didn't want to give up."

There was silence on the other end of the phone. Finally, Elise spoke in a measured tone signaling she was trying to hold herself together. "I should be there in less than a half hour. Please continue looking after Michel. He needs you now."

Not as much as he needs his mother and father, I told myself as we hung up.

Over the next several weeks, Albert had his difficulties adjusting to life after the near death of his brain. His coordination was shaky and he struggled to remember short-term facts and figures. He recalled nothing after falling into the grass pile the third time. He was unsure who saved him, but was told by nurses and doctors his wife's brother had dislodged the oak ball and restarted his breathing before medics took over.

Albert was stumped, as he knew Elise didn't have a brother. Elise filled him in, but she didn't give him the full story. "A man," she said, "driving up the side road above my house saw you choking in the back yard. He helped you out until the paramedics arrived."

"Helped me out?" shouted Albert, lowering his voice after becoming momentarily dizzy. "Everybody says this guy saved my life. Who was the guy? Where is he? I want to meet him, to thank him for saving me and giving my life back to my son."

Elise did not reply. She had pieced together my identity, starting with suspicions emanating from descriptions given by medical personnel, and confirmed when she heard Michel's repeated references to "Mr. Stone Heart and Papa" playing in the back yard.

I had sworn Elise to secrecy after she informed me she knew what I had done and tearfully expressed her gratitude. "Albert doesn't need to be beholden to me. I broke up his marriage and shattered his life in many ways. I don't want him thinking he owes me. Him being alive, for his son's sake, is enough thanks for me. I don't deserve anything else."

A few weeks later, as we sat on a bench outside Michel's pediatrician's office waiting for his check-up to end, Elise began thanking me again. She said Michel did not appear upset or deterred by Albert's incident; instead, he was making remarkable strides in his behavior and development. Albert was temporarily staying at Elise's house, so she and Albert's mother could more easily tend to him.

"Michel still does not hug me back, but he makes more eye contact and he is starting to use "I" when he refers to himself in a conversation. He is more interested in other toys, and has even taken to putting on a glove and catching balls his father throws to him. He gets so excited, though, he tries to throw the ball on the roof."

I didn't tell her about my sessions teaching him the wonders of "roof ball." But I smiled inside, knowing that the lessons were taking hold.

I shrugged off her repeated thanks for helping Albert. I revealed how jealousy had driven me to the neighborhood, and told her of my conflicting feelings as the situation unfolded. She said she understood and none of it mattered.

I told her the reasons I was feeling that way did indeed matter. "As I stood gawking down at Albert and Michel in the back yard, I realized some dreams belong to others, and so, too, do many of the people in those dreams. I understood then that I had been dreaming other people's dreams, walking down their paths, trying to live their lives."

"It is not your fault Michel and I are in your dreams," murmured Elise, her head buried in my shoulder. "Stone, you are the reason all these dreams can continue coming true. You are the reason Albert is alive. You are the reason one has a father and the other has a son. You are what you have always wanted to be, a hero."

"But I am a hero without salvation," I sighed, pushing her softly away until her face was inches from mine, her eyes and mouth in perfect line with my own. "I was practically stalking Michel and his father. I was only there because I was a peeping Stone. What I did was not heroic. It was no sacrifice. I saved Albert for selfish reasons, because I knew Michel would struggle without him and you would deeply feel his struggles. In my warped mind, I saw us together because of your resulting gratitude."

She tilted her head and looked at me with surprise. "Can you not see that all of what has happened between us shows we are meant to be together? You *did* save my life by saving them. But that is not the reason I want to spend the rest of my life with you."

"It isn't?"

"It is everything we are together, everything no one else has between them. It took me a while to see this, because I could never believe I deserved to be happy—alone or with anybody else. But I believe it now. What we have is the rarest of loves. And your actions did not convince me of my love—that already existed. Your actions just confirmed to me that our bad karma is over. We have the right to be together."

Her words drifted like sweet refrains through my head, and I became woozy from the intoxicating effects of the melodies I had longed to hear. I ran my hands through my hair and held my head steady with fingers glued to my temples. I always dreamed of this moment when I truly believed we beat the odds, breached all obstacles, and convinced the only two people who mattered—each other.

I closed my eyes and breathed in all of the wonderment of true love finally attained. It was everything I sensed it would be—the aroma of roses in spring, the taste of honey from the comb, the feel of silk cool to the skin on a summer morning, the last sound of rain falling on the roof before falling asleep, and the shimmering spectrum of rainbow hues disappearing over the golden foothills following a late afternoon summer shower.

Like the rainbow leading to gold over the horizon, I knew this vision was an indication of riches in love to come. However, as with the fragile reality of a rainbow, I also knew this love was an illusion. Though beautiful and true, this love wasn't real and it wasn't ours to keep. It belonged to someone else.

This feeling had been growing in my heart ever since I had seen Albert and Michel together in the back yard, and I knew what it was telling my mind to do.

I told Elise these things the best way I could. She wasn't convinced. She became mad as only a fiery Frenchwoman can. "This is just an excuse for you to run away," she screamed. "You use your fancy words, but it all means the same. You are afraid."

"I am afraid," I said, turning squarely into her onslaught. "But not of failing. We would have the rarest of loves. But in reaching our dream, we would disturb the balance of love, the parts making up the whole for so many others."

I could tell she wasn't buying my reasoning. I continued anyway, as something inside told me I must.

"I don't know how I know this, or exactly how it all fits together," I said, searching for the right formation of words. "Maybe it's something spiritual. But it's definitely universal. All things happen for a reason; all events and happenings are connected. Everything does matter. And the one thing holding everything together is true love."

"We have true love," said Elise, sounding defiant. "We were made for each other—my musical touch and loving tone matching your way with words and lyrical heart. You are here to lend a voice to my sound and I am here to put melody to your words. Together, we make harmonious music—or at least somebody once told me that fact."

She paused, waiting for the echo of my past words to leave their desired effect.

"Yes, I think we do," I agreed, taking her hand. "But I don't think true love is meant to be mutually exclusive. There can be other true loves in our lives. I know this with my brother Peter. He had a true love with God. He had to find room for true love on this Earth. He couldn't and he's paying a terrible cost. And my sister showed me life could go on after her true love faded, that she could find hope and faith from loving her children.

Talking with her hands as much as with her words, Elise exclaimed, "I am trying; you are the one giving up."

"I'm not giving up," I reiterated. "I'm giving in, to the truth. And to the balance of life and love as a whole. All that has happened to us happened for a reason. This is not fate or destiny. We caused this to occur. Too often we waited, hoping circumstances or fate would dictate our decisions. When we finally acted, our choices changed lives. Your husband is alive and he has reason for living.

"We cannot hold on to what is holding us back. We must move forward. We have developed something more than true love. We have found the truth in our love. The balance is there for you—you have your son, your husband has his son, your son has his father and mother. All that is left to equalize the situation is for both of you to recognize your love for each other still exists and act upon it."

"I love you," she said, thrusting her chin forward. "That is the love I know exists. How do you come out balanced in this scenario?"

"Oh, I'm the most selfish of all. I've never felt better about myself. I am in true love with a fabulous woman, and I am helping her put the pieces of her broken family back together. I've learned about truth in love, so I have a fighting chance to find another form of true love in my life. What more could I ask?"

"I'll go the way of all your past loves," she snapped. Her tone jarred me, and I noticed her impeccable English had slipped into contractions for the first time since I'd known her. "You'll take all the memories of me—the pictures and gifts, the letters and poems—and shove them into a shoebox, tucked away and forgotten."

"I wish it would be that easy," I sighed. "But you needn't worry. I couldn't forget you if I wanted to—and I don't want to. In this remembrance lies my hope and salvation, for you have shown me the way toward true love. I will never forget you, simply because you are eternally inside me. You are my life's blood, with your energy and spirit flowing through me. Your unquestioned love for me, your enlightened view of the world, and your lust for life—they are all inside me, energizing my life beyond mere existence."

Feelings I had kept inside for years poured forth. "You will live in my heart forever. My feeling for you is no longer limited to the tangible, physical realm; it has instead become something ethereal. My love for you is no longer based on your physical presence; I can love your spirit, your memory. My feeling for you is not of this earth. It is a love of the heart, and the heart, at least this one, knows no boundaries of logic and reason, of geography and nature, of spirit and body—none at all."

"Do you think I can just let you go?" she asked.

"Real, true love like the one we have can never be lost. Love finds refuge in our hearts and lives on when we give it to others. You will always have our love to spread to your son and your husband. Wherever you go, wherever your life takes you, my heart will follow. No matter the direction our lives take, I have a love to carry me past life's travails, around all its obstacles and through all my doubts. I will not merely survive because of your memory, I will flourish. My heart and my love will remain yours forever, changeless through all the changing times. This will be enough to sustain me through all the joy and sorrow, success and failure, lost hopes and found dreams to come.

"I will not be haunted by your memories. I will be inspired by them."

Just then, a nurse wheeled Michel through the doorway in a wheelchair, turning wheelies as the youngster laughed in chortling, exuberant bursts.

Turning toward Michel and wiping a tear from her eye, Elise said, "He laughs all the time now. He is becoming a happy boy."

"The doctor is finished with his check-up," announced the nurse, a small, petite dark-skinned woman whose rich, singsong accent suggested Indian descent. "This boy, he knows more about the heart than any book or doctor."

As if on cue, Michel began one of his frequent salutations on the heart. But this one had a twist. "Love is never lost," Michel said, in a straightforward, matter-of-fact manner. "Love finds refuge in our hearts and it lives on when we give it to others."

Turning to his mom, he asked, "But Maman, does it not hurt when you give your heart to someone else?"

"Yes it does, honey," said Elise, turning her full attention toward Michel and giving him a full hug. "But it is the greatest gift you can give." She was surprised at his direct use of "Maman," but was even more stunned by what he did next. After she released her arms from around Michel, he reached up and put his arms around her neck. An awkward, tentative embrace, it was nevertheless the first unsolicited hug Elise had received from her son in five years.

"Tears are good for you, Maman," said Michel, as he reached up and wiped the wetness from his mother's cheeks. "Tears clean out your eyes."

"That is right, Michel," she said, letting him finish drying her tears.

"And Stone says tears are just water leaking from our hearts. Does that mean your heart needs to be operated on?"

Before his mother could reply, Michel turned his cheek toward her and pointed. "Plant one here and see what grows," he said, giving a half-smile in my direction. I winked and gave him the circle OK with my left hand.

Elise stood frozen for a moment in disbelief at the newfound life in her child. As she reached to "plant one" on her son's cheek, she had a look in her eyes I had never seen before, not even when we made love.

Elise confirmed what I was thinking. "It is like I am seeing him for the first time. I know he is still developing, and the Asperger's is still very much there, but he seems different, like he is glowing. It is as if he has been reborn."

"Good doctoring will do the trick every time," I shrugged.

"No, a good man with a caring heart was the hero in this case."

I didn't have to say anything more. Elise was good at reading minds, especially mine, and she knew the word I was thinking. "Balance," she said.

"It's good to realize when you have it," I said.

"You are why the rhythm and balance are there," she said. "But what happens if something throws it off-kilter?"

"When this love thing gets a little out-of-whack, that's when you can remember me. Not to run to, but to refresh your memory on the truth."

I knew it was time to leave, as I was starting to lose the resolve behind my words.

The resolve to leave was further stifled when Michel walked toward me. He held out, simply in his palm, a gray stone shaped vaguely like a heart.

"This is all I have to give," he said. "But it is all you need to have."

I looked at the dull rock and recognized it as the one I gave Elise several years ago, before Michel was born.

"Carry this stone with you always and you will have strength. For it has survived all the world's great floods and wildfires, all its great storms and quakes, and the long loneliness of time. Part of a broken whole, it holds within the wisdom of the ages, enduring strength, and eternal hope."

I rolled the stone in my right hand, feeling its warmth growing. I offered it back to the young boy. "No, Mr. Stone Heart. Maman gave this to me. Now I give this to you, Mr. Stone Heart. It will keep you warm and point you where to go."

I slipped it into my pants pocket. I could feel the burn on my thigh.

"I better go," I said, turning to leave. I felt myself suddenly frozen in place.

I spun around, pulled Elise close and kissed her on the neck, so I could taste and smell her one more time. It would have to last through eternity.

"My heart is yours, but for only one day after forever."

As I walked toward my car, I heard her call my name, heard her say she loved me, first in English, then in French. Her words put a hitch in my gait, and I started to turn around. But I was choked up in the only language I knew and could not form the words leaking from my heart. If I turned now, all I had just declared about love and truth would fall way, and I would succumb again to the lie that felt so good, so right in my heart but so wrong in the real world. I forced my wobbly legs forward. Before I got into my car and drove out of their lives, I held up my right hand and formed the "I Love You" sign with the first, fourth, and fifth fingers upturned. The last thing I heard was Michel yelling, "He made the heart sign, Maman. That means love."

I felt the heaviness leave my heart, as though lifted by the truth—that the rhythm of the world means for a father to be with his son and for a mother to be with the father of that son. I turned the key and started my car with a renewed strength of purpose.

And for once in my life, I never looked back.

As my brother Peter once told me, nothing in this world—no act of kindness or gift of love—is a sacrifice if the giver derives satisfaction or good feeling from the bestowal. We give to feel good. All deeds of giving labeled as sacrifices are, in fact, acts of self-gratification—good-hearted and well-intentioned as they may be.

For all of my eloquent rationalization, walking away from Elise that day was as close to real sacrifice as I have ever known. Satisfaction I was supposed to get from giving Elise's life back wasn't easy to find underneath my flowing tears and aching chest pains.

To survive, I kept reminding myself that love lives on when we give our hearts to others. I hoped mine would help Elise and Michel, and that I could survive without it.

I slipped this note into Elise's purse before I left:

Dearest Elise...

You are tender melody in a world of disharmony, striking beauty in a world disfigured by cruelty. You are God's gift of sublime forgiveness for all my sins toward lovers' past. But now, I understand I cannot accept this present. I have not forgiven myself, even on the oft chance God has. I don't deserve you.

These words are all I have left to give you:
THE DELICATE DANCE
You taught this lonely boy
The necessary part
Each step of the heart
Is taken together
For love is a delicate dance

You took the lead
And showed the way
But I stepped wrong one day
And stumbled too many times
For Love is a delicate dance

You took this boy back
Handing another chance
At good fortune and romance
But still I walked alone
For love is a delicate dance

Sway once more with me
In the moonlight glow
I know now how the steps go
Your lessons have worn through
For love is a delicate dance

But what I know now
I know all too late
Lonely is my fate
And our rhythm an illusion
For love is a delicate dance

Chapter 31

HOPE HOUSE
REDEMPTION

$\mathcal{M}$y grand goal in life beginning at age seven was to live until the year 2000. I knew it wasn't the most ambitious aspiration. I just thought it would be cool to make it to the next century.

I realized this milestone shortly after I turned forty. Four years later, I didn't have a whole lot more to aspire to in life. I had become a hollow hero, with all the women except Mama gone from my life and little else going for me.

Except for one thing—I had my kids.

Though I didn't have a love in my life or children of my own, I had a job I loved—even if the kids I worked with didn't exactly love me back. After my idyllic, pie-in-the-sky view of things when I started a decade before, I had come to understand working with these kids was a grueling, long-term grind and any positive returns—if they came at all—usually occurred far into the future. As my friend Jake used to say, "Any piece of pie given as a reward for this job will be eaten in heaven, cause ain't nothing tasting good coming your way on Earth doing this kind of work."

A few breakthroughs over the years kept me going. Donnie, the "un-adopted" boy, not only found a foster placement with the Ashes, he became a permanent part of their family when they adopted him. He visited a year after leaving the group home, thanking us for our support and talking excitedly about his freshman year of college.

"Hope House really sucked, if you want to know the truth," he told us. "But you dudes were cool. You made it seem like a home, my home. I never had a place or anybody make me feel like that. And Stone, you pointed me to the Ashes. You gave me parents and a family of my own."

When he wrapped his huge hands around one of mine and shook it vigorously, I felt his victory was my own.

Christian, the suicidal kid in black, called the house a couple of years after his disappearance and asked to go to lunch. When we met, he related he was attending school part-time while working at a coffee shop. Focusing on drama and writing classes, he was in the process of writing a script. He showed me an excerpt and it was terrific. He said he was taking his depression medication and doing well, even though he didn't have a girlfriend. I didn't tell him that *not* having a girl might be the reason for his wellness.

He was still wearing black leather, but the makeup and devilish accessories were gone. "Ah, I only wear that stuff on Halloween now," he laughed. "But I still like the feel of leather." The "Satan Rules" tattoo on his neck was covered with a bandage, and he explained he was in the process of getting it changed to "Santana Rules." The "Love" and "Hate" tattoos were still spelled out on his fingers, but he had added a single word to the top of each hand: "Hope?" on his right and "Maybe" on his left.

Christian was still a work in progress, but he was at least entertaining the thought that hope existed in the world. "Don't know if this helps, but I thought a lot about killing myself while on the run, and a big reason I didn't was because you showed me there were people in the world who cared."

It helped.

Several kids crumbled in the weeks before their eighteenth birthday, as virtually no support existed to bridge their path into adulthood. Tracking kids after they turned eighteen was nearly impossible. They blended with the masses of mixed-up, messed-up young adults trying to find their way in the world without many of the tools to do it.

At least with Sean and the others who drifted into anonymity, not knowing their fates left me with some hope they may have somehow found their way in life. There were many kids whose whereabouts and directions in life were known all too well. Charlie, the boy who came from a bruised and battered home, kept true to his belief he would continue the abusive legacy spawned by his father. He spent time in jail for hitting a girlfriend, and then landed in prison for severely beating a man who cut him off on the freeway.

Freddie, the kid who spit in my face and later saved my life, could not save his own. He once told me he dreamed he would die lost and forgotten, buried in an unmarked grave. At last report, his nightmare was becoming reality. According to Donnie, he was panhandling on the streets and sleeping in doorways and under bridges. "I know that boy had problems," said Donnie, "but I didn't think he would become one of those dudes who talked to themselves on street corners and ate out of dumpsters. He looked bad, real bad."

I tried not to think of the ones who were struggling in the world. I chose to recall what Big John told me when I started, about being realistic regarding the impact I could expect to have on these kids. I also realized progress was more common than I first thought. Getting kids through the system alive was a success in itself, and giving them access to tools to handle themselves in adulthood was another triumph.

I passed this realistic, yet hopeful view to all the new counselors who came through Hope House. Jake and Jimbo told me new counselors often pulled them aside during training and asked why I didn't tell them much about how they should do their job. "Stone wants you to figure that out on your own, within your own style," they would tell them. "But if you watch him with the kids, how he talks to them and how he listens, how he does everything, then you'll learn all you need to know."

Hearing praise and seeing the kids every day almost made the blackness in my heart disappear. I remembered what Elise told me, that taking care of her kid and loving him was the only way she was able to get through each day. Now I knew what she meant. After the loss of Elise and my beautiful sister, helping these kids survive from one day to the next was probably the only thing keeping me alive.

Though I had a standing offer to move into management, I chose to continue working directly with the kids. I did move into the newly created house supervisor position, which changed my overnight status to working the afternoon and evening "peak" hours alongside the shift counselor. I enjoyed all aspects of my new supervisory role, especially the opportunity to work side by side with my old friend Omar.

Omar had departed Hope House five years ago to complete his Master's Degree in social work and spearhead the founding of a community activity center in his old Oak Park neighborhood. His efforts sparked a community effort to rebuild and revitalize the venerable area—Sacramento's first suburb and a prosperous city center until it slid into economic and social dysfunction beginning in the Sixties.

Married and with his first baby on the way, Omar returned to group home work to supplement his modest community center salary. His advanced degree and a successful career could have landed him a management position. But the two-day overnight shift met his schedule needs and allowed him to work in the trenches with the kids.

Omar and I agreed that the double coverage was a great idea. Extra coverage in the afternoon and evening helped alleviate the day-to-day tension that often developed between kids and individual counselors. When one of us became worn out dealing with a particular kid or two, the other could step in and cool down the situation.

I made sure we worked as a team, as these kids were experts in splitting people and finding and pushing a person's sensitivity buttons. Realizing physical violence often meant a swift boot from the program, many of them had become astute in using psychological warfare on both peers and counselors. Some did it simply to pass the time and relieve the boredom. Others were more determined and pathological in both approach and execution.

Devin, the kid who had threatened to slice and dice and blow us up, was a master at this passive-aggressive approach. He returned to our house when economics forced our executive director Jerry Stevens to accept tougher kids.

Speaking for myself and the rest of the counselors, I went to Jerry to ask him to reconsider Devin's return. It wasn't that we thought he was a hopeless case—I had learned my lesson with Stevie and others who proved they could make adjustments and flourish within the program. We believed Devin needed twenty-four-hour supervision, a higher level of care than we could provide in our system.

Jerry claimed his hands were tied by the need to make ends meet. For us to survive, he said we had to take the kids other programs wouldn't touch.

Despite our misgivings, we tried not to stack the deck against Devin. We didn't have to. The boys already knew his reputation from other kids in the system. They weren't afraid of his violent threats, but the kids on probation were wary of his tendency to fake injuries and blame kids he didn't like. "Man, you gotta get this dude out of here," said Arturo, a kid with several assaults on his record who had flourished in our program for the past year. "I can't afford for him to tag me for some fucked-up stuff and have my P.O. haul me back to jail. I'm three months away from turning eighteen and gettin' off probation."

Despite our best efforts to welcome him back (while re-establishing firm guidelines for him to follow), Devin returned to his disruptive antics. There were no overt threats or snitching this time. He took a more subtle approach. Belongings started disappearing from residents and turning up in other kids' rooms. Laundry was misplaced and clothes were mysteriously ruined by bleach. He worked the other five kids like a master puppeteer, then waited for them to turn on each other. A couple of the boys suspected they were being played but didn't have the sophistication to deal with his manipulation. As a result, emotions boiled, and tension and turmoil threatened to throw the house into an uproar.

From our perspective as counselors, we could see what Devin was doing. However, we didn't have anything tangible regarding Devin's handiwork to convince our boss.

Omar then stumbled upon a cache of items Devin had stolen from the kids. He had squirreled away cassette players, illegal lighters, clothes, candy, and even pictures of the residents' girlfriends and mothers. He was planning on planting them throughout the house to implicate other kids in the thievery as a way to turn the boys against each other.

Devin blamed Omar, of course, for having a vendetta against him. He promised to get even, especially after Omar led a house meeting to clear the air about the recent spate of missing items. Omar was infinitely more worried about Devin's welfare than his own, as several of the boys let it be known they planned to get even with the young thief.

Later that evening, I talked over the issues with Omar and conferred with the other counselors by phone. We agreed, company survival or not, Devin had to go. Not only had he made a threat against Omar, he had stirred the other boys into a frenzy headed toward vengeful behavior that could lead to threats to his own safety or others getting kicked out of the program. I called Big John, who agreed to suggest to the director that Devin be removed as soon as possible.

The house had calmed by the time the guys shuffled to their rooms at bedtime, but I stayed an extra hour to make sure it stayed that way. As I made one more pass down the hallway to check on the boys' status, I heard Devin's voice from the darkness of his room.

"Why you gotta leave, Mr. House Supervisor?" said Devin. He had taken to calling us by our titles instead of our names, as a not-so-subtle dig for receiving consequences in the past for calling counselors obscene names. "You're gonna miss the ice cream party."

I somewhat understood what he was talking about. A couple of days before, someone had stolen an entire box of Fudgsicles from the freezer. Devin was the prime suspect. He had begged us to get the ice cream bars during the previous shopping trip, yet didn't seem disturbed when they came up missing. We held a meeting to determine who took them. No one fessed up, even when ice cream privileges were suspended for a month.

I didn't know why Devin chose to bring up the ice cream incident just as I was leaving, but I knew he was trying to screw with me. I wasn't in any mood though to be anything more than cool and straightforward in my response. "It isn't going to be much of a party, with all of you guys in bed and Omar doing his paperwork," I shrugged. "Anyway, as you fully know, there isn't any ice cream to have a social."

"Ah, if you have sharp enough eyesight, you can find anything in this house, even what's left of that disappearing ice cream. If ya hang around long enough you'll see the clues sticking out plain as day. Sweet dreams, Mr. House Supervisor."

I felt something more might be behind Devin's comments than just braggadocio. I didn't give it any more thought though as I walked out. The moment I left the haven that was the group home, all my thoughts and feelings drifted back to my losses over the past year. I couldn't get the woman I loved and the sister I had lost out of my heart or my mind.

Hope House was my refuge. Every time I left, I was attacked by my memories.

So I wasn't upset when Big John called early the next morning. I figured he might need me to come in early or cover another shift. I welcomed any interruption of my painful memories. Big John did indeed want me to come in early. I wasn't prepared for the reason.

"There's no real way to say this," he said, hesitating for a moment, as if gathering himself to continue. "Omar is dead. He was stabbed. It looks like Devin did it."

His words, or at least their meaning, did not register at first. Then I thought I had heard them wrong, so I ran them through my brain again. The same deadly ones came up. I tried to say something, but my mouth was like a gun with the safety on.

Sensing I had been rendered mute by the news, Big John continued. "It seems to have happened just before midnight. He stabbed Omar in the office."

My mind raced to the large kitchen knives we kept locked in the office. We had secured the sharp knives since having close calls in our other two houses and hearing of a counselor in another county being severely injured by a knife-wielding resident.

"But we lock up the knives," I said, trying to visualize if we had indeed locked up all of them after dinner. Big John interrupted me before I finished my mental picture.

"He used a homemade knife," he said, explaining Devin had sharpened several wooden ice cream sticks into fine points, wrapped them around *Bic* pens for stability, and lashed them together with glue, masking tape, and fishing line.

I groaned. He had used line from a reel I brought to the house for fishing outings. I groaned again. Ice cream sticks! I recalled what Devin said as I was leaving. He looked me in the eye and told me what he was planning to do, only I didn't pay attention. He had killed Omar with a shiv derived from stuff we had made readily available to him.

And now Omar was gone.

Big John waited for me to collect myself. Finally, he said, "I need your help."

"What can I do?" I said. "Do you want me to come help with the other boys?" Suddenly, I wanted to be back at the only place I felt comfortable, doing the only thing making any sense to me—helping my boys get through one more day of their life.

"No. I'll be here, and Mindy's coming to help with the boys, related Big John. "I need you to find Omar's wife. She wasn't home when I called her house this morning, and I tried the numbers we have for Omar's relatives. I don't want her to find out on the news before we get a chance to tell her. Are you up to telling her when you find her?"

His request hit me almost as hard as the news about Omar. I could handle dealing with the kids, but the thought of facing the wife of one of my best friends with this kind of news scared me to death. I swallowed hard.

"To tell you the truth, I was barely up to hearing it from you. But I'll do my best."

"Someone said she might be going to school at one of the community colleges."

"Okay." Hearing a deep sigh on the other end, I added, "You know, this sucks."

"Yeah," he said. "His kid, his first kid, is due in three months. This fucking sucks."

It was the first time I had heard the straight-laced Bible reader cuss. I guess if there ever was a reason to curse God above or the Devil below, this was the time.

The whole thing fucking sucked.

I thought his wife Mary might be taking classes at the junior college near her Oak Park neighborhood. It was tough getting the information out of the admissions people at River City College, but I wouldn't give up. She was taking business and finance classes, and had two scheduled that morning. I found out later she was hoping to become an accountant, to help her husband's development plans for Oak Park.

I arrived to her first class just after it ended. My heart thumped as I entered her second period and scanned the classroom. I had dined with Omar and Mary many times, and I did not see the petite, strikingly beautiful Filipino woman in the room. Part of me sank, while the other part felt relief. Maybe she already knew and was on her way home or to the police station. I interrupted the professor to see if he knew where she went.

Mary had missed class to visit the doctor. Something about getting a sonogram.

I had no idea how to find her doctor. I called several obstetricians in her area to no avail. As it was getting close to noon, I figured she had probably heard the news by now over the radio or on TV in a waiting room.

I called her house again to see if she had returned. Omar's brother said no one in the family had been able to contact her. I called the group home, and Big John said the place was crawling with cops and reporters, but Mary had not called or appeared.

I sat slumped in my car, stumped. She wasn't anywhere to be found and time was running out. I looked at my notes to see if I had missed anything. Nothing stood out. Then I saw the answer in one word scrawled on a single page of my notebook.

Sonogram.

Jesus. Letting a guy know what his baby was going to be wasn't something you told him over the phone. She wanted to tell him in person, probably as a pleasant surprise.

Jesus Fucking Christ. She was on her way to Hope House.

I called the house and told Big John to be on the lookout and to get to her before the press did. I jetted toward the house, breaking every safety and traffic rule along the way. *"This can't be happening,"* I thought. *"God couldn't let this happen."*

But the Good Lord did.

There was no parking up and down the street when I arrived, so I double-parked in front of the house. Mary arrived five minutes before me, and she had already been engulfed on the sidewalk by seven or eight reporters and a cameraman, who I assumed all thought she already knew about her husband's death.

I overheard their questions as I jumped out of the car. They came in rapid-fire succession. "Did you know the kid used a homemade knife he put together in the house? How many months pregnant are you? Did you know there are reports the kid is claiming your husband sexually abused him? How did you find out he had been murdered?"

Through the maze of bodies and microphones and cameras surrounding her, I saw her holding something in each hand. In one, I saw the brown bag bearing the name of Omar's favorite deli. In the other, I saw a large manila envelope most likely holding the thick piece of film exposing whether Omar's first-born was a boy or a girl.

I shoved the reporters aside and put my arm around the dazed, almost catatonic woman and led her through a gate on the side of the house.

I pulled her close, her limp body melting into mine, and I felt her wrists trembling against my sides. I didn't know what to say. I wanted to apologize for not finding her in time, for not telling her before those blood-sucking bastards stuck their fangs in her. I wanted to say how sorry I was that I didn't stay longer the night before, and for not recognizing what was on the murdering little asshole's mind.

But I was lost in my search for words.

She was lost too. Her eyes searched my face, looking for some kind of answer. Her mouth was open for a long time before any words came. When they finally slipped out of her in a slow, distant manner, they were heartbreaking.

"I brought him lunch as a surprise," she said. "It's his favorite. Lean roast beef, with hot peppers and no mayo. He's trying to lose weight, you know."

"I know," I said, my voice barely a whisper.

"And I brought him the sonogram of our baby. I told the doctor not to tell me if it was a boy or a girl. I want us to find out together."

She had the same unbelieving look my first girlfriend Chandni had on her face in the hospital on that cold December morning long ago. And driving Mary to her house was almost as hard as had been driving Chandni home from that hospital.

On the drive home, Mary slipped the film out of the envelope and stared at the picture of her baby for a long time without saying anything. Finally, she spoke in a calm, measured tone. "It's a boy. Omar is going to be the father of a baby boy."

After her pronouncement, she placed the film back in the envelope and stared straight ahead, saying nothing. She remained silent the rest of the trip, stepping out of my car without a word and walking alone up the pathway to her door, where she collapsed into the arms of her family.

Though I meant to, I never talked to her again.

As I drove home that evening, I noticed that a gray overcast shrouded the sky. "Even the stars are in mourning tonight," I thought to myself. When I reached my door, no arms wrapped me in comfort or held me close. Instead, I was swallowed up by the grim, foreboding loneliness now present at the end of every one of my dark days and nights.

I tried to go back to work, tried to convince myself it was the right thing to do, because the kids needed me. But my heart wasn't in it. They needed a whole man to give them what they needed. I couldn't give it to them anymore.

I realized the ultimate irony of my life. I had dedicated the last ten years to helping children find their way, when in fact the real pain awaits them in adulthood. I taught them childhood was a safe place to fail in small doses, prepared them to deal with the pain and hurt naturally coming along with growing up, and showed them there is hope beyond their early pain and mistakes. Learn from these small transgressions now, I told each of the kids, so the vicissitudes of adult life won't bury you later.

I did all of this only to find that these lessons are lies. None of them matter a damn bit. Nothing can prepare you for the horrible truth and pointlessness of life. Good people like Chandni, Christine, and now Omar die for no good reason. A teenage girl follows her unborn baby into death after her true love turns into a lie. A bright, sensitive woman has her heart ripped out by a man who can only feel in the past tense. A father-to-be dies just before he is to start truly enjoying life.

Jesus Fucking Christ.

Chapter 32

CRACKS IN STONE

Omar's death reunited me with my friends Jake, Jimbo, and Mort. Jake and Jimbo had both married and moved on to jobs providing more monetary sustenance (Jake as the world's toughest fireman and Jimbo as a high school coach and P.E. teacher). Mort had been my friend since I moved here from Alabama; we went to school together through high school, and he was my only childhood connection to Alex and Butch.

I meant to keep in contact with Jake and Jimbo when they both left Hope House four years before. I didn't return their calls, though. Mort took to calling me "Hermit Shell" because of my growing reclusiveness. He tried to keep connected, making plans with me to attend our twenty-fifth high school reunion. I bagged on him a couple of days before the event. Consumed by my involvement with Elise, I lost contact with them and all my other friends. After my final breakup with Elise, I spent most of my time working at Hope House or secluded in my cabin.

My three buddies all left messages on my answering machine after hearing the news about Omar. The concern in their voices and the memories of our friendship made me reach for the phone several times, but something stopped me from calling back. I didn't want to hear Jake and Jimbo try to convince me to continue working with kids "for my own good." I didn't want to hear Mort's supportive remarks. Of all my pals, he knew the most about my pain—the suicides of Alex and Chandni, my breakups, and the deaths of my daddy and sister. I was sure he would try to console me as he had done in the past.

I just wanted to be left alone to wallow in self-pity.

I wasn't even planning to attend Omar's funeral, but some unknown force pushed me out of bed and down the mountain to the service in Oak Park.

As with my sister, an entire community came to honor Omar's memory. I met up with Big John, who had brought the kids. Having not yet told them of my departure plans, I could already feel myself withdrawing from the group home connection.

I might not have made it through the entire service if not for my buddies' arrival. In my extreme state of moroseness, I had forgotten about Jake and Jimbo's friendship with Omar, and Mort's connection to him through his friendship with me. I had forgotten these guys were hurting too. After the service, we decided to commiserate by visiting our old social haunts. We hoped to push aside our pain for at least one night.

I felt better than I had in months, maybe years. Hanging with my pals, recalling the uncomplicated ease of our friendship and the closeness we once shared, made me feel hopeful. Friendship, I realized, was a good thing, maybe the best thing.

But my good feeling could not last, especially when the tequila began to take its overbearing, depressive effect.

The last thing I remember, until I was awakened by cold water pouring over me in my shower the next morning, was excusing myself and stumbling to the restroom in an Old Sacramento sports bar. According to the guys, I walked out of the restroom and just kept going. I headed out the back door and into the night. Jake followed, but could not catch me before I stumbled into a cab and was driven away. At first, they thought I was heading home. Then, Jimbo remembered something I had said during the evening, some rambling nonsense about going to a cemetery to "talk with my daddy." Mort had gone to my father's funeral and knew the location of his burial site.

Worried about things I said as the evening wore on, such as, "I wanna join you underground, Daddy, so we can talk again," they headed toward the base of the Sierra foothills where my father was buried. Though not knowing my dad's grave location, they figured it would be easy to find a drunken man wandering through the headstones.

My friends found me, my palms browned with mud, fingers crusted with dirt, and nails blackened underneath, lying on top of a grave. I was calling my daddy's name through a piece of PVC pipe I had found and driven into the ground near the headstone.

I had lost it in a big way. And when I broke, I came apart in sections like a dam crumbling in God's quaking hands.

The next day, after being brought back to reality by a cold shower, I recalled little of my descent into madness. Jake filled me in, starting with my rantings at the grave. "Did you get the note I left you?" I yelled through the tube. "Talk to me Daddy. No one talks to me anymore, and I can't remember your voice. For some reason, I don't dream anymore."

"I've got one question," Jake said. "Who's this Wilson Lynde guy? Was he a friend of your father?"

"Who are you talking about?" I answered, puzzled by his question.

"Wilson Lynde," he repeated. "You know, the guy whose grave you were pounding on and talking to like he was still around. Were you trying to get this guy to pass on a message to your old man, or what?"

My mind was fuzzy about the graveside incident, as I was probably still feeling the effects of the tequila shots from the night before. When Jake repeated what he said, the picture of the previous night's events came into focus. "I banged on the wrong grave," I thought to myself. "I talked to the grave of some dead guy I didn't even know."

I only thought I was thinking to myself. My words were spoken out loud.

My friends looked at me, unsure of what I meant. When they figured it out, they howled with laughter. I turned crimson out of a mixture of embarrassment and budding anger. Then I just shook my head and weakly smiled. I had to admit that what I did was funny in a darkly comic way. Even in the midst of a nervous breakdown, I had to laugh. And it was good to hear laughter again from Jake, Jimbo, and Mort. They had taken Omar's death hard and seemed equally upset by my downward spiral.

My friends, seemingly warming to the thought of lessening both my edginess and their mourning, attacked my descent into madness with their usual sick brand of humor. Jimbo, mimicking my voice, got the best one off when he said, "I see dead people…just fine. I just wish someone would teach me how to read."

I understood where they were coming from and I laughed with them. But I was not so jovial inside. I realized I had taken the last step into joining the ranks of my crazy family. After years of secretly turning my nose up to them at the same time I was lending a hand, I realized I was no different. I was wacko too.

Worse was the feeling I was missing inside.

Emptiness was spreading within me like a slow-moving tumor. I felt as if I was slipping into some vast black hole sucking the light from my world and dimming my existence toward total and infinite darkness. It had started, I think, when Elise left me broken-spirited on the Crying Trail. The blackness spread when Christine died and grew darker when I walked away from Elise. After the death of Omar, a quilt of gloom covered me. His death stole my last hope at redemption by darkening my desire to help others. I had sunk into a vast, infinite hole of despair from which I could see no way out.

The guys hung out at my tiny place the rest of the day, watching football and watching over me. I put on a good show, laughing as much as I could to convince them I was okay. Mort had his doubts, as he kept trying to look me in the eye and repeatedly asked if I was feeling alright. I avoided looking at him directly and answered his inquiries with shrugs and nods. "Don't you know? When you're crazy, all your worries are gone."

Mort was the last to leave, staying until it started to get dark outside. Sensing the deeper meaning of the looming nighttime darkness, he had offered to stay over. I assured him everything was OK, and he reluctantly left me alone.

Later that evening, I looked into the mirror, and for the first time saw my daddy's reflection staring back. The glass contained a fragile image of the man who had silently shaped much of my emotional destiny. I saw my resemblance in his eyes, not so much how they looked but what they held inside, the sadness of seeing and knowing the pain and futility of the future.

At that moment, I realized the long loneliness that had become my destiny started way before my recent maladies. Beginning with the abortion and punctuated by my daddy's death and Chandni's suicide, everything since had been a miserable attempt to make up for these losses and mistakes.

I thought for the first time about killing myself. It wasn't a firm, formulated plan by any means, but neither was it merely a passing rumination.

I realized my friends also sensed something deeper was wrong with me. I couldn't find any of my pills, not even aspirin or vitamins. I suspected they had slipped everything they could find into their pockets. I further realized that all my scissors and sharp knives were missing, along with my toxic cleaning materials. I hadn't noticed, but my friends took everything they thought I could use to kill myself.

They needn't have worried about me dying that night. I couldn't do anything to cause further hurt to my mama. She had already been through enough. But a plan was illuming in the dark chambers of my mind, the faint flicker of an idea needing only an ill wind to fan the flame into a raging inferno of despair and death.

Two weeks later, this wind blew into my world with the fury of a gale force. While looking through our family photo albums, Mama suffered a stroke paralyzing her entire right side and leaving her barely able to talk. "The doctors aren't sure how much time she has left," my brother said when he called to tell me what happened.

Hank didn't tell me he was the one who found Mama and kept her alive until the paramedics arrived. Others always informed me about my silent brother's heroic deeds.

As I flew down the mountain, leaving my house for the first time since my drunk-induced nervous breakdown, I knew the flames had started and I was headed straight into the maelstrom that would hopefully lead to my final, conclusive end.

Chapter 33

MAMA'S STORIES

*M*ama survived the immediate effects of her stroke, but was confined to intensive care for two weeks before being moved to her own room. The doctors wanted a longer stay in the hospital, but Mama made it clear she wished to go home and a week later got her wish.

I temporarily moved out of my place in the hills and into my mother's house to assist Hank in providing care for Mama. Hank cut down his work hours to spend more time with her. A day after hearing the news, Peter ventured down from Washington and stayed for two weeks. He returned three weeks later for an indefinite stay. It marked the first time in thirty-five years that the Lyon brothers were living under the same roof.

My brothers and I rotated shifts so there was always somebody at Mama's bedside. At first, it was hard to look at my mother during these visits. The stroke had paralyzed the muscles on the right side of her face and body. Her right eye was left perpetually open, an unsettling sight and a condition requiring rewetting drops every few minutes. Her skin was taut on that side of her face, making it difficult for her to speak clearly. Fortunately, as the weeks passed we discovered she hadn't suffered the most severe form of communication impairment, in which words cannot be understood or spoken. Her speech was slurred from the paralysis, not as a result of lost brain function. Her mind was clear.

Each of us hoped we could give her comfort just by being there. We recalled the last days of our daddy's life as he deteriorated in the hospital, and we didn't want to relive that hopelessness. The doctors agreed we could help curtail her depression, but said our presence was important for other reasons. Encouraging Mama to talk could prompt her to employ logic and reason, and stimulate physical improvement in other areas of her body.

In my case, I hoped my presence was enough, because I didn't have much more to offer. I stayed by her side as much for myself as for her. I wanted to find out who my mama and daddy really were, and why they held themselves so distant from their children. I remembered how we had let Daddy slip away without bridging the distance that seemed to separate him from all of us. I was determined not to make the same mistake with Mama.

Even in her weakened state, Mama welcomed the chance to recall long-ago events. "The present isn't too good and the future, well that's not looking too rosy either," she said. "The distant past, I guess, is the best I got to offer."

Engagement was a slow going, even after her slurred speech improved. The short-term memory problems, which plagued her before the stroke, had worsened. She repeatedly mixed up our names and often forgot things immediately after hearing them. But talking, painstaking as it was, seemed to be her best revival tonic, even more than the walks we encouraged her to take and the massages we gave her.

Contributing to her enthusiasm was the condition of her long-term memory, which, amazingly, had been left virtually unscathed by the stroke. She could spin a yarn from sixty years ago with sparkling clarity and sharp attention to the minutest detail. Though Mama was an absent-minded family historian who often told me the same story a dozen times a day, she nevertheless became my link to a past I no longer wanted to avoid. I needed answers to why my life had unraveled and I hoped to find them in the lucid creases of my mama's crazed brain.

My brothers and I were taking part in a family learning experience, not a deathbed vigil. I had heard some of her stories before, including the tattered histories of our grandparents and great grandparents. I knew about the drowning of Daddy's younger brother and the profound effect it had on his life. I had known little about the story of Mama's youngest sister, whose death from cancer at age four broke her father's heart and left Mama with another reason to fear the uncertainty of life. I also gained new information on Mama's oldest brother, who committed suicide by jumping off the Gulfport causeway.

I found out more things. She told me how her mother used to go weeks without talking to her because of some slight, real or imagined. She welcomed those times; otherwise, her mother was on her from the moment she woke up, telling her she better get movin' or she was gonna turn into a "lazy, good-for-nothing dreamer" like her daddy.

"She always said 'dreamer' like it was the dirtiest word imaginable," Mama said. I didn't remind Mama she had said those same disparaging words about dreaming to each of her kids on many occasions.

Mama also mentioned how her mother used to solve their cat overpopulation. "We always had cats running around and I loved them all. They were aggravatin' at times, but not really much of a problem. And they kept the mice and rats at bay. There was one mama cat I really loved, 'cause she seemed to care for her kittens like they were human babies. Each time she had a batch, she never left 'em. She would move 'em, sometimes two or three times a day, to keep 'em from the moccasins, 'coons and other dangerous critters."

Mama would always pause at this point in her story, as if to gather the courage to describe what was coming next.

"Your Grandma went on the warpath one day, shortly after 'Pretty Girl' had another litter, about seven or eight kits. She started rantin' and ravin' there were too many cats, that they were gettin' in the way and eatin' us out of house and home. She did this every once in a while, and then she would usually settle down. I figured this would also happen this time, but just to make sure, I moved Pretty Girl and the kittens to a safer place.

"I don't know how your grandma got wind of what I did, but she got madder than a hellcat when she found out. She demanded to know where they were, but I refused to tell, even though I was scared. I gave in, though, when she took my dollies away. She made me show her where I hid them, behind Daddy's tool shed. She gave me a burlap bag and had me fill it half full of shucked oyster shells, then made me put the cats inside. I figured she was havin' me take them to the end of our property and let them go. Instead, she had me follow her the opposite way. I realized, after a bit, that we was headed toward the bay.

"When we stopped at the pier and she told me to start gatherin' rocks, I figured out what she was gonna have me do. I saw the cats wrigglin' in the bag, trying to scratch their way out while avoiding the sharp edges of the shells. I heard Pretty Girl wailin' like she was some wild animal. But I couldn't do nothin' to stop myself. I was all numb inside. While Mama held the top of the bag open, I put the rocks inside, gently, so as not to hurt them. She had me pull the drawstring tight and told me to carry the bag to the end of the pier, which stretched near fifty feet into the water. I looked at her with my eyes great big, but she just stood there, her arms crossed. She followed close, as I walked slowly toward the end of the dock. The bag was so heavy I had to carry it with two arms.

"I could have let my cats out at any place along the way and emptied the gunnysack of the rocks and oyster shells. Then I could have placed the cats on the bag and pushed it away from the pier, and let 'em float away. I could have saved 'em, and it wouldn't have mattered what Mama had done to me."

At this point, it always felt like my mama was talking to herself. She wasn't seventy-two years old and at the end of her time. She was ten, tawny and tanned from the Southern sun, a Southern girl with the whole wide world in front of her, but was holding the end of it in her shaking hands.

I always hoped the story would end in sweet glory, with her sending the cats floating away clinging safely to their burlap boat, and then marching off the pier in triumph, kicking Grandma in the shin for good measure as she passes!

But the story always ended just as it happened.

"I stood at the end of that pier and waited for Mama to tell me what to do. She didn't say anything for a bit, so I thought she was changin' her mind. Then she told me to wrap the loose end of the bag around my wrist.

"'Jump in,' my mother told me. I stood there, my mouth open, not understanding what she meant and not wanting to understand.

"'I said Jump!'"

"'But the bag…and the rocks…I'll drown for certain!'"

"'Well, child, then you have a choice don't you? You can sink and drown with your precious cats, or you can save your pitiful self. Which is it goin' to be?' I couldn't answer. I was feeling dizzy and my knees were wobblin'. 'You're weak. You'll save yourself. Now jump!'"

"I did as I was told, jumping in feet first. I hit the water and kept going downward. I tried to hold on to the bag as long as I could, but water went up my nose and my mouth took in a gulp that made me choke. I thought of my mama cat and her kitties and tried to hold on to the bag while I thrashed my free arm to swim upward.

"But I was weak and so I let go. I still remember those bubbles coming from the bag as it sank toward the bottom. While I floated upward toward freedom, I never stopped looking at the bag until it was swallowed into total darkness.

"Mama didn't reach down to help me out of the water, and for a time I didn't much care if I got out. But I crawled up onto the pier after a short while, when the coldness started to creep into my bones. Mama never said nothin' when I walked by, just stood there with her arms crossed and a knowing smile on her face. I knew she had won, she would always win, and I would always be weak and scared.

"That bay was pert near my second home, but I couldn't bring myself to go swimming in it for a year after I done what I did," my mama wheezed in a spent voice illuminating her age. "I finally went in again, but I never went very far out. I don't know why. And I never set foot again on that there dock."

When we grow up, there's more to us than who we see in the mirror. Parts of our parents are looking back. Too often, it's the ugliest pieces of them. Or the most damaged.

Every day, when I left Mama's room after being relieved by one of my brothers, I made sure her cats had food and water and a clean litter box. She could leave all her money and the whole damn house to the cats and I wouldn't mind.

After several weeks of mostly the same stories every day, Mama unveiled a new one shedding light on my daddy's tightly held secrets. She must have thought I was finally ready to hear this particular tale. More likely, she was now ready to tell it.

I was the one who initiated her disclosure, though I thought it was just another fruitless overture into a moot subject. I asked Mama again about the "mystery woman" in Daddy's life, the one he had identified in his delirium as his "special one." She had always put me off when I tried to broach this issue in the past, even in her chatty moods over the last few weeks. On this occasion, she acted as if it was the first time I had ever asked about her. "You know, your dad once loved another gal, a Negro gal, more than me," were the stunning words that began her story of the secret Daddy kept from us his entire life.

I didn't know what shocked me the most—Daddy loving someone more than Mama or that the woman was black. Either way, the combination was stunning to every perception I had about my daddy.

"Excuse me, Mama—but Daddy loved another woman, a black woman?"

Mama appeared to enjoy the hand she was holding. Could it be because she held the trump card? Or was it because her old age was playing tricks on her reality?

Either way, she continued the game.

"Well, at first, that's the way he felt. And he would almost die to save her life."

"Okay. Okay. You have me hooked," I said, my astonishment showing in my tone. "Who was this woman and why haven't any of us heard about her?"

"Your daddy didn't see any need for you kids to know. He wasn't proud of himself or his family over what happened with this girl."

"Did he cheat on you with this girl? Is that it?"

"No, No," she said, in a straight voice, but I could see a twinkle in her eyes. She was enjoying my growing exasperation.

"So, he knew her before you two got together, and he couldn't get her off his mind?"

"Well, I guess you could say that's true. He knew her before me and he couldn't forget her. And if I didn't accept her as being part of his life, I think we woulda broken up somewhere down the road."

Daddy's insistence about holding on to his past love sounded a lot like my own preoccupation with true love. "Like father, like son," I thought to myself. "I guess we were alike—in the same sad way."

"In the end," Mama said, "I knew the importance of her being part of the family."

I thought back to Daddy's funeral and I recalled a black woman who stood in the back of the church during the service. She was the only person of color except for two guys Daddy worked with and a couple of my Mexican friends. I wondered who she was, especially after she came up to me afterward and told me Daddy "was a great man, an unforgettable man, and you look so much like him." She was about the same age as my mama, with a light complexion, freckles on her cheeks and reddish-black hair intertwined with gray streaks. What stayed with me, though, were her striking blue-green eyes that held a forlorn sadness within them. Her eyes seemed familiar, and I asked her how she knew Daddy. I thought she was going to respond, but she bit her lip and walked away.

I told Mama of this memory, prompting her to sigh and avert her eyes from mine. "That was her, wasn't it?" I asked, and the thought of my daddy's mistress being at his funeral made me bristle, even more than a quarter century after the fact.

Mama nodded, and continued to look away.

"She had the gall to show up at his funeral, with you and all of his kids there?"

"Well, I invited her."

"What? Why the He—," I stammered, before she cut me off with the wave of her hand to keep me from cussing.

"It was about time we included her in the family."

I had been pacing the room without knowing it. When I heard my mama's last statement, I stopped in my tracks and found myself on the other end of her room.

I glanced at my mama, who looked lost in her own thoughts as she gazed past me and out the window. I didn't have to look behind me to know she wasn't peering at something on the hospital lawn. She was looking back through a window of time before I was born. Her face bore a pensive look and her brow was furrowed clear across. I had seen that look many times in the mirror—it was the telltale Lyon look of guilt.

"Why do you have that guilty look on your face?"

"I think you should take it easy and sit down, son, and I'll tell you the whole story," she said, gesturing toward the chair next to her bed. I slid slowly into the chair, as if trying to sneak up on what she was going to say next. She was still able to take me by surprise.

"I feel guilty because we should have invited her into the family a long time ago. I thought your daddy's sister should be there when he was laid to rest. But before I tell you about DeeDee Washington, you need to know about the world Daddy lived in, the world we all lived in."

As I scrambled to digest my mom's off-hand mention of an aunt—a black aunt—I had never heard of, Mama described the time and place in which she and Daddy were born and raised. "It was a time when whites and Negroes grew up separate, but supposedly equal. Both your Daddy and I could see weren't no truth about that notion. We saw, too, that it wasn't right how most of them Negroes were treated.

"To tell you the truth, Daddy and I didn't do a whole lot to change the way things were when we was growing up. It was tough just to survive, what with your daddy being so dirt poor and gettin' so much grief from his daddy, and my mama and daddy fightin' all the time about not having enough to get by. It didn't change after Shell and I got married; we was strugglin' from the get go for money, and then Hank came along.

"Now, some of them black folks we saw were downright lazy and some were just as mean as any white folks. There were a few didn't deserve no help. But most worked real hard, especially the ones Daddy knew down at the other side of the docks. He used to tell me they worked harder and faster than most men he knew, white or otherwise."

Daddy learned of the black workers' talents after they offered to help when a double load of crab and mullet swamped his processing station. "He hesitated in leanin' on the black workers for help. He couldn't pay 'em 'cause he was barely gettin' anything himself. They understood, and simply hoped to get a bit of the leftover fish. Daddy was OK with that 'cause he knew a lot of the catch was going to spoil if he didn't get no help."

The second reason he hesitated was more seminal to the times—and potentially dangerous if Daddy tested it. His bosses didn't want "no nigger hands" touching the catch, because it would spoil them for eating, at least in their white customers' eyes. Mama says Daddy didn't buy into the spoiling part, but he understood all too well the customers' viewpoint—they were always right, even when they were horribly wrong.

"Now, your daddy didn't have to include the Blacks. He could have gotten some white boys to work overtime. I don't rightly know the complete reason why he done it, though at the time he said the available white workers were neither reliable nor good. A few years later, he hinted at the real reason, when he said he hired them Blacks because he didn't like to see nobody go hungry."

The job wasn't easy to begin with, but the times made things a whole lot harder. The fish and crabs had to be moved to the blacks' processing plant, because any black worker caught in a white-only plant would likely be shot on sight. Working deep into the night under the cover of darkness, they finished the haul in less than a week. Daddy was so impressed with their effort he helped them a few times when they needed an extra hand.

"It was the first time he had gotten to know the Blacks up close, and though he couldn't always understand their words, he could tell they were good people and workers. He introduced some of them to me at night behind the closed doors of their fish processing plants. They were nice folks, and it was too bad we couldn't be friends outside those walls. Your daddy and me weren't ready for the trouble that kind of socializin' would bring."

The restrictive nature of their Southern world became more apparent the day Daddy's half-sister walked up and introduced herself.

"Delores Washington was fifteen at the time, eight years your daddy's junior," said Mama. "She worked in the Black cannery alongside her mama, Mayelle. She asked about your daddy after she overheard that his dad was a fisherman named Orville Lyon."

At this point, I stopped my mama to get everything straight in my mind. For some reason, I had pictured DeeDee as being Grandma Lyon's child. I figured Grandma, at one time or another, had tired of Grandpa's fists and sought comfort somewhere else, anywhere else. The other alternative, that Grandpa was the father, hadn't entered my mind.

"You mean Grandpa was her daddy? And he kept it a secret?"

"Yeah, he was the daddy, but we're getting ahead of ourselves," Mama said, shaking her head. "Stop your interruptin' and let me get on with the story."

"Okay," I said, but I wasn't sure I could handle any more twists and turns. As it turned out there was one more detail I didn't see coming.

"Your daddy was befuddled by the girl's statement, and he didn't know to believe her at first," continued Mama. "When he realized it was his daddy she was claimin' they shared, he demanded to know the details so he could decide if he believed her or not.

"I was in the plant that night and I went over to him to see what the commotion was about. She was this cute little thing, not any bigger than a minute, with dark brown freckles on her cheeks standing out against her light, almost milk chocolate-colored skin. She didn't take well to Shell yellin' at her. Daddy hadn't seen the hurt register on her face when he said he doubted her, and he didn't know she was upset until she started to cry and began walking away. She took a few steps, then turned to face him. Large, pear-shaped tears formed under her eyes before meltin' into straight lines and sliding down her cheeks. She looked plum distressed.

"'I can't change who I is, but I just wanted you to know you had a little sister,' she said, and her talkin' made the tears run faster down her face. 'My mama said you white folks wouldn't believe no Negro girl if'n she said you and her were kinfolk. And even if you believed, you wouldn't want it to be true. Maybe it woulda been better if I never been born. Then that would mean your daddy didn't do that terrible thing to my mother.'"

"With that, she reached in the pocket of her work overall and took out what looked like a necklace. 'I was looking forward to the day I could give this back to your daddy, but you seem to be just like him, so I'll give it to you.' She threw the necklace at Shell's feet, spun around and walked past her mother and out the door.

"Your daddy stood there for the longest time, like he had froze up, till she disappeared out that door. Then he leaned down and picked up the necklace. The chain was one you would hang dog tags on, and when he stretched it out, it made one straight line, like the circle had been broken at one point. I looked at the odd-shaped pendent and realized it was a clipper ship made of silver.

"'I remember this,'" your daddy said, though he looked like he wished he could forget. 'It belonged to Daddy. When I was a kid, he told me Mama gave it to him on their first anniversary. It was missing one day and I heard him tell Mama he must have thrown it in the fire when he was drunk. Then he hit her for asking about it.'

"Now like I've said before, I saw your daddy mad at somebody only a couple of times. I seen him mad at himself more often, but I don't think I ever saw him more miserable with his own self than at that moment.

I wasn't sure if it was 'cause he had made the girl cry, or 'cause he had a half-sister he wasn't sure he wanted, or if it was because he had to face the truth his daddy was a raper. It might have been 'cause he felt all three of them conflictin' thoughts at one time."

Mama said Daddy decided to find out what happened between Grandpa and his half-sister's mother. He strode over to the girl's mother, Mayelle, hoping to find some answers. The woman, who was only about ten years older than Shell, had heard the confrontation and greeted Daddy with what Mama called "a hateful look."

"Shell softened Mayelle's spite by saying he was sorry for what was done to her, and asked if she could please provide details. Mayelle told him Grandpa Lyon often got drunk after coming in from fishing all day. One of these times, he followed her home after she got done with work. She was a young thing, so he probably thought he could sweet-talk her into doing somethin'. But that girl had a pretty good head on her shoulders."

"'I knew what he wanted to start and it wasn't no relationship,' Mayelle told your daddy. 'But I didn't want to tell him 'no' just like that, with him being a white man who could cause me some troubles, and 'cause I saw on the docks he had a temper. So I tried to politely turn him aside by saying I didn't have no relationships with married men. Well, that just made him mad and he started yelling and cussin' at me. I tried to leave, but he hit me hard enough to knock me clear down. I scratched his neck tryin' to push him away, which just made him madder. He slapped me, and then he forced himself on me. After, he cussed me for gettin' blood on his good britches...it being my first time and all.'

"Mayelle's voice had trailed off to a whisper, and she could not look at me or your daddy no more. For the first time, your daddy touched his half-sister's mother, placing his hand softly on her shoulder. This must have given her more strength to continue.

"'I saw after he go I must of grabbed his necklace when I scratched 'im, cause that silver ship was in my hand," explained Mayelle. "I kept it jus' in case one day I might need to prove what happened. Now, I was scared to say anythin' to anybody, so I kept it to myself. Your daddy done leaved me alone, but I heared he found some other girls, both black and white. A few months later, I found I was wit' child. I didn't know what to do, as I was not even seventeen and I didn't have no man. My mama didn't wont to have nothin' to do wit' me, so I went to live wit' some cousins over Apalachicola way. That's where I had Delores, or DeeDee, as we come to call her.'

"'I didn't wont to have her, didn't wont to have no baby wit' me bein' a kid my ownself, and I sure didn't wont no white man's kin. But I come to believe God meant her to be here for a reason, so I loved her like a precious gift from the time she crawled out of me. As you can see, she's a might pretty girl and she's got some spirit, too.'

"Your daddy sighed deep and hard, like he was searching for the right words to say. He finally looked at Mayelle and said, "'It's plain to see where DeeDee got her spunk.'"

"Daddy confronted Grandpa Lyon, out of sight of his mama. I wasn't there, but I think I know what he told him. He knew his mama wouldn't leave the house in which all of her children were born, so he warned Grandpa he would throw him out if he hit, or even touched, any family member, either in the house or across the tracks. She'll put a room together in the back for Grandpa to stay. That's where Grandpa slept till the day he died."

When I got older, I thought Grandpa's room looked a whole lot like a cell. Seems that's exactly what it was. And it was his own son—my daddy—who put him in there.

I'll never forget the last thing Mama whispered into my ear, before asking me to put Pretty Girl on her chest for one last hug. "Maybe I should be telling all of you kids this, but I don't got enough strength but to tell you, son. It's something I should have figured out and said long ago, but I was too blind. It's kinda funny, but now, since I lost most of my sight, I can see things a whole lot better."

"What is it, Mama?"

"I was always good at letting you all know how disappointed I was in what y'all didn't accomplish. It was the easiest thing for me to do, 'cause that was what I was taught by my mama. But I should have let go of Mama's teachings a long time ago, and listened to some of my daddy's lessons. You all might not've been rip-roaring successes, having high-falutin' jobs and making lots of money, but you had a lot of what my daddy had and what your daddy had. You all cared for people, maybe too much at times for your own good. You tried to make others happy, and for that I'm proud of y'all. I just wish I told this to Christine. She needed to hear it a might more than the rest of you."

I told her it was okay because Christine was hearing every word she was saying.

Mama told me she felt as if she was "swimmin' in the sea," and she wasn't scared of the water anymore. "I don't see them cats floatin' nowhere, but I see the colors my daddy told me about. They's all around me—it's like I'm covered in beautiful gems. Turquoise ones, cobalts, and really shiny sapphires. There's Daddy coming toward me with more blue jewels. And now I see Mama too. She isn't holdin' anything, but her arms are open wide. Oh, now I see some cats over there, next to Mama and Daddy. Shell is there too, and I see the twinkle in his eye that lets me know he's excited to see me. And there is Christine too...and she is holding out a slice of watermelon out to me. The light is bright toward their way, so I think I'll swim right over to 'em."

She died, cradled in her youngest son's undeserving arms, before saying whether she reached her cats and all the rest. I'm betting she did.

I wrote down her last words about her kids the best I could remember and read them at her funeral later that week. I kept her closing words about the colors and the swimming to myself. I figured those things were between her and her mama and daddy.

At the end, I couldn't tell her I had lost all the loves in my life, that I had pushed several away and walked away from the truest one. I didn't tell her I tried to talk to Daddy through a plastic pipe stuck in his grave—though she probably would have thought that was funny and asked me what Daddy had to say.

I didn't tell her about my failures in life and love. That's the way it had always been since I told her about Chandni and the abortion. When I was younger, I kept my failures to myself to protect my image in her mind. Later, I did it to spare her additional heartache caused by one of her kids.

I was also protecting her by not telling her of the plan forming in my mind, though she might have been happy to know my pain and heartache would be ending soon. She just wouldn't like the way I was going to end it.

After my mom's funeral, I retreated to my stone studio in the foothills to drown my sorrows in the bottles of tequila that had become my elixir of escape for the past few weeks. For once, I fell asleep without trying.

I awaken to a voice cutting through the darkness. I try to open my eyes, but cannot feel my eyelids lift. Still, a face appears out of the murkiness. Too fuzzy to make out. But I recognize the voice speaking to me.

My daddy's voice. His words are as soft and calming as I remembered them last, so many years ago. They seem, however, to be slightly different in timbre and resonance.

"Son, I am sorry I didn't take the time to talk to you more, about life and love and what to do when things go wrong. Maybe I could have done or accomplished more to make you proud of me. But I don't think it is important what you say, or even what you do. It's the trying that counts most."

"I don't…know…what," I stammer, speaking tenuously, my voice sounding younger and far away, still adjusting to my daddy's dulcet tones. *"I don't know what you mean,"* I repeat, easing into the sound of my own voice. *"I always thought actions speak louder than words or anything else."*

"They do in many cases," he notes. *"Hollow promises break hearts and ruin faith. But actions can hurt just as much if they are not connected to the heart. Action is not always accomplishment and real heroes may not perform visible good deeds."*

My head swirling, I cannot hide my puzzlement as to his reasoning or his sudden appearance in my long-lost dreams. *"I needed you ten years ago, twenty years ago,"* I sigh. *"I've screwed up my life many times. Why have you waited so long to offer your words?"*

"I never stopped giving you guidance and you never stopped learning," he says, his calmness absorbing my frustration.

"You've been dead my entire adult life. I've forgotten your voice, and I haven't followed any of your paths. I had those years just after you died when I dreamed up a complete other life, with you in it. You didn't speak in those dreams, just went on fishing, working and living, the same stuff you did while I was alive. I needed your wisdom in those dreams. But you never said anything, never answered any of my questions."

"Son, you've answered all the questions on your own," he says. *"Weren't you comforted by these dreams? Haven't you adopted my quiet ways with your kids, and then added more communication and displayed more feelings toward*

them, because that was what you wanted from me? Didn't you talk softly and carry no stick at all? Didn't you give them someone to look up to, believe in, count on, talk to, just by being you?"

Daddy knew my answers, knew them without me saying a word.

"You learned everything you needed from me when I was alive," he adds. *"You just needed some time to learn how to use what I taught you."*

"But I wanted to be a hero, like you."

"You are a hero, son."

"What, for saving Elise's husband? That was circumstance, and maybe I had an ulterior motive. Maybe I thought it would help me get back with Elise."

"What you did for him and his son—and her—was heroic. But I was talking about all the kids and their families you helped."

"But I wanted to save somebody. I hurt so many people in my life. The unborn child I denied and the sweet girl I drove to kill herself. The women I cheated on and the family I ignored, until it was too late to help them."

"Son, I watched you suffer enough inside your big heart to pay for the pain you caused others. I saw you do even more to help those around you, especially those kids. The word is you saved a lot of lives you don't even know about, by keeping those kids hopeful enough to help themselves find the right direction."

"But there were so many I couldn't reach, couldn't help enough."

"You always tried and you always cared. That's success. Do you remember what you were told when you started working with kids?"

"What, if I impacted just a few kids out of all I worked with, then I was a success?"

"When I died, I believed I was a failure," he says. *"But I got a chance to look at my life. I only affected a few people, but they were the most important to me. You and your brothers and sister turned out to be caring, loving people, so I feel I succeeded."*

"I've lost everybody, and everything that matters. I have so little left," I reply.

"You have so much more than you think," he counters. *"You can still change the world, and you still have love waiting for you out there. The power to help ourselves is within all of us. I know you have the strength to go on. You have given so much to others. Give something to yourself. Give yourself the best gift...hope."*

As I digest his last remarks, I barely notice his face fading in the distance. I look up to see he has disappeared. I have so much more I want to talk about, so many more questions about the tragedies in his life—his brutal daddy, his drowned little brother, his friend lost to the bottle, his mysterious half-sister.

My eyes open, finally awakening me to the reality that I had indeed been dreaming. I lay there, trying to recreate the first dream I clearly recall in more than twenty years. I cling to my daddy's voice, so familiar now after so many years forgotten. Hearing his words is like recalling soothing refrains from a forgotten song. I remember the kindness in his face, when age had taken the hard lines from his jaws and filled them in with softness. I see his calm, baleful eyes seeming more peaceful and less tired than I remembered.

Not knowing if my dreams are back for good, or if I'll be visited by my daddy again, I write his words down so as not to forget them.

Try as I might to hold on to the hope offered by his appearance, the uplifting feelings I felt from his words fade. All I feel is...nothingness.

I decide to move to the coast and find a peaceful, desolate setting affording me the solitude to write a memoir of my family's ill-fated battle with love. My mom and sister had each left me a little money, just enough to let me quit my job and flee to the coast for the few months I would need to complete the project.

I find the ideal place on the first weekend of my search. Advertised in the *Mendocino Beacon* as a "cute, romantic cottage with a breathtaking ocean view," I didn't care that reality revealed it to be a tiny, abandoned fisherman's hut that had been converted from a tool shed. Definitely a hole-in-the-wall joint, it suited me just fine since the "hole" was actually a large window looking directly off the cliff and across the Pacific Ocean. It is the most beautiful place I can think of to plot the end of my life.

Chapter 3 4

THE CLIFF

*H*ere is the final chapter of my journey to nowhere, the last entry in the journal of a life running down like a broken and battered child's toy.

As I look out at the crashing waves and swirling foam and roiling green water, I cannot see the natural beauty of it all. I don't feel the wonder throughout my body as I once did. Stretched out before me are only rocks and water and sky; the mystery behind their ancient history and enduring symbolism—which used to excite and enthrall me—now means nothing. I don't see any stone hearts on the beach below, only weathered driftwood and dried out shells lying on the sand.

The world around me is empty because all the women in my life are dead or gone—Chandni and Elise, and so many others whom I loved with a flawed romantic heart, and Christine and Mama, whom I loved completely without complete understanding.

Since my tragic failure with Chandni, I battled bad karma throughout my love life. For all the good that came from loving others, I cannot get past the memories of those I deceived or drove off. In the same manner as a cold-blooded assassin, I thrust a stiletto quick and clean through women's hearts, a blade of hope run through, then extracted as they fell.

Was all the loving and losing worth it? Did loving one woman beyond all reason make sense? I once thought the oft chance of finding true love was worth taking, that living without risking pain was a life missing real love, and a loveless life is one not fully lived. I believed struggling through all the lies and bullshit to find true love was the only meaningful fight in life; anything less was merely shadow boxing.

Now I have seen too much damage done in the name of love to believe the heart-to-heart combat is worth it. I am done with love and all the crap that goes with it.

I no longer have the resolve or the conviction to continue the battle. I have found no one to replace the loves of my life and their memories, and I am too tired to look any further. Only hurtful things have happened in the past few years, and there is nothing else to look forward to except ending this crushing pain in my chest.

I hope my love-struck brothers fare better. After years of self-imposed isolation, they have ventured back into the world of love by tentatively extending their wary hearts. Hank says he met someone while on vacation at the dude ranch; hopefully he will find the answer with her. Peter wrote in his last letter he was trying to make his marriage work. "You were right, little brother. I am the problem. I'm not sure Carma wants me anymore, but I'll move heaven and Earth to get her back."

I am saddened I will not be around to see the results of my brothers' quests for second chances at love. I wonder how they will handle my passing. They have survived the ravages of love and loss before, so maybe they will survive one more family failure.

How does a man kill himself? More to the point, how does this man do it?

I rule out a messy ending—no hanging or shooting myself. Too much pride in my looks? Partly. Afraid of guns? Decidedly so. Take a bottle of pills and just let my world slip away? No, I'm still hurting from Chandni's last breaths taken in my arms. Cut my wrists? Seen too much blood in my life already. Jump off a bridge? Too clichéd. Besides, I'm scared of heights. I push these choices aside, because they don't symbolize what I want to leave behind.

I spend my days writing on a wooden table in my shack. On most nights, I sit bundled in a chair on my back porch, my breath coming out like puffs from an old steam engine while I gaze into the vast blackness of a cloud-covered ocean. One evening reveals a view different from the others.

I am sitting at cliff's edge watching the vibrant white light of a nearly full moon vanquish the stars to mere twinkles, which are all but lost in the moon-washed background. The waters of the Pacific are black, except in the tips of their wave crests flickering like candle flames. Illumed by the lunar lamp, I spot a small skiff no longer than ten feet moving slowly across my watery screen. I am reminded of Grandpa Tyler's little rowboat Mama used to tell me about. I pick up my binoculars and focus on what looks like a little girl of six or seven, sitting on the lap of an elderly man. He has his hands over hers on the oars and they are rowing in a choppy, but straightforward motion.

"What the Hell?" I say to myself, adjusting the binoculars for a telescopic look at their faces. When I look again, the duo has vanished. They are nowhere to be seen as I sweep the lens back and forth across the shimmering water below me.

After my three tequila shots earlier, I don't know whether what I saw was reality or a mirage. But I realize what it means. As with my mother, who in her last moments retreated to the bay of her sweet childhood, this hollow, discarded Shell Junior needs a return to the salty brine of his youth.

Fuck my fear of heights. I will make the ocean below my grave.

With a sprint and a jump, I can merge with Mama and Daddy in the salt water so much a part of our early lives. It will complete my journey, which has been spent mostly on the run—from the Alabama harbor home of my childhood to this California coastline cottage at my life's end. I have nowhere left to run but into the Pacific Ocean waves.

On the last day I will write in this journal, I sit in my deck chair, looking into the distance at the most pristine view eyes can possibly see. But I am blind to the exquisite beauty stretching across the horizon. I feel...

Empty.

Searing pin points press on my temples, stifling any urge to change the emptiness holding me hostage to this wooden chair. There is a dullness in the center of my stomach, and I feel it eating away at me, spreading through my limbs, into my fingers and toes. The ends of my body—even my eyelids—feel like they have lead weights dragging them down. I am like a mythical prisoner in medieval times—a betrayed prince or fallen king, banished to a remote castle's forgotten dungeon, hanging from chains in hopes of a savior.

There is no saving grace for this vanquished Lyon, as the nothingness in my heart tells me so. The midday sun extends its shimmering radiance onto my face, but I am dead to its rays, with my eyes closed and my heart an ice block. Having not moved since sitting down five hours ago, I will not budge until the sun disappears from my sight.

As the sun dips toward the distant horizon, the sky lights up in a dazzling display of yellow and orange and red in brazen defiance of the coming night. A fierce fight ensues, with the brilliant hues stretching in buffeted layers across God's canvass. As the golden orb drops lower, the battle takes an ominous turn. Backlit by the retreating sun, the clouds transform the sky into deep purples and rich burgundies, the real color of blood spilled from a slashed heart. A faint, rust-colored glow can be seen just above the darkened horizon as the last gasp of daylight resists the coming of the long loneliness of night.

As I sit facing the immense Pacific Ocean and watch the sun dropping slowly out of sight, I realize this is the final blood-red battle between day and night I will ever see.

When the light of day finally loses to the blackened sky, I think of the early morning struggle for which I used to yearn. I visualize the duel that will resume in the dawning twilight, as the sky wrestles its way out of the grasp of darkness and triumphantly spreads its bright colors as far as my eyes can see. But I drop my head, for I have not the energy or the desire to see this epic battle repeat itself.

A short time later, I look up and am awestruck. The moonless sky is a glittering kaleidoscope, surely van Gogh's "Starry Night" vision come true in shimmering black and white. Countless constellations and scattered stars stretch further than eyes can see, like an infinite dream.

I take a small hand mirror from my pack and gaze at my face. Though the stubble on my chin and cheeks is darker than his reddish tones, I catch much of my daddy staring back. I think about the limited possessions defining my accomplishments and determining my place in the world—many of them are stuffed in my bag, waiting for this journal to join them. Newspaper and magazine clippings of real-life heroes I had written about; gifts I received from kids with whom I had worked, and letters and poems to and from lovers. These papers and objects define my success and failure.

I am reminded of my high school English teachings on T.S. Eliot, and his feeling of when a man is ready to go to his rest.

"To do the useful thing, to say the courageous thing,
to contemplate the beautiful thing, that is enough for one man's life."

I have done all these things and they must be enough—because I have nothing left except memories of the painful things.

All the losses in love and life file through my mind, an ugly parade of failure and death. So much of life dying in my arms—Alex, too young to handle his broken heart and spirit; Christine and Mama, the two women who knew me best but, thankfully, did not know my worst, and my first love, Chandni, who didn't see my betrayal coming and couldn't handle my going.

And my son, who never made it to my arms but remains the deepest part of me.

I am done with this world.

I have prepared well to leave it behind. On the table is a cassette recorder containing a tape of my last words to my brothers. Hank and Peter, you can add these words to my journal or choose to keep them to yourselves. I'll leave that to each of you to decide. I am dressed in the same clothes I was wearing when I last saw Elise and her son Michel, down to my favorite (and only) French Faconnable boxers.

Hope is a bad thing, maybe the worst thing, because it imprisons you in a false world. But losing hope once and for all is the greatest freedom. No more illusions and dreams hanging just out of reach. Reality is the only thing you can hold onto, the only thing one can control. I embrace nothingness. I am ready to die.

I will close this journal now and place it in the burlap bag with the other stuff. These words of damned wisdom are yours. Do with them what you wish.

I am on the edge, my breath on this frigid night drifting in aimless puffs over the ocean below. My baby boy is floating in front of me, formed in my

image and suspended, effortlessly, just beyond my outstretched arms. I look to the stars above for answers, squinting to see the ones I have named for my lovers in so many rhymes I penned for no reason. Dense fog, though, has rolled in and my vision heavenward is blurred. Damn! No last connection with the women I loved. No surprise.

I check to see if I have my wallet, so that I can be identified should the tide wrestle my body from the shallows, past the breakers and into the open sea. Damn! Left it inside! I stalk back into my hut and grab my billfold and shove it into the front pocket of my jeans to ensure it stays with me—as my back pockets of these jeans are loose and not reliable to hold my wallet.

I feel the blackness that is my despair taking over and I slide toward the edge, reaching again for my baby boy—but he is no longer waiting for me. Like all the others, he is gone. I feel a veil of darkness cover me and begin to creep deep inside. I am chilled to the bone by the foggy mist and the ice surrounding my heart.

I feel nothing from the constellations above that once connected me to my distant lover. I simply don't fucking care. I walk toward the edge to end my pointless purpose on this Earth. I stop, as I realize my wallet is sticking out of my side pocket. I shove it down, only to feel resistance. Something is blocking it. I don't want the billfold to fall out, so I fish into my pocket to determine what is delaying my departure.

Damn it! Just let me die!

I feel something small and hard, and in my fumbling to dig it out my wallet and the object fall to the ground. "Fuck!" I scream, as I squint in the darkness and spot the contents of my wallet strewn on the crest of the cliff. I drop to my knees to gather the pieces, wondering why my wallet is at all important as I'm about to kill myself. "A fucking idiot to the end," I spit out. I'm about to blast myself again, when the blackness around me suddenly lifts. The moon has decided to re-enter, through a break in the fog and clouds, casting a white-hot glow around me like a spotlight on a Broadway stage. The full moon's silver sheen reveals what has conspired with my wallet to stall my death—a damn rock! Probably something stupid I found on the beach below on one of my aimless walks. I grab it with intent to cast it into the sea, with me to follow.

Off-round but familiar to my hand, the uncommon shape reveals it to be something I know by feel— and feeling. It's a stone heart, the one handed to me by Michel in our farewell meeting! Hidden in these pants ever since, it reveals itself to my wondering eyes.

Lit by radiant moonshine, the stone glows like molten kindling, the last cinder in a fire refusing to go out. Its pale gray sides gain light from the moonscape, exploding with bright whiteness in my hand. I feel the stone heart igniting, sending lightning bolts up my arm and into my neck and head. In the glow, I see Michel's face, and turning, I catch Elise's emerald eyes supplying their own fire to the scene. My head feels flushed, and the brilliance of this rush makes me stagger sideways. My world starts to spin, and I stumble wildly toward the edge.

I stop in mid-spin, realizing I am balanced on my left leg while an arm and a foot are suspended over the edge. Glancing down, I am startled to see the bleached white beach waiting 150 feet below. I shake my neck, trying to clear my head and regain my balance, and again I catch sight of the beach lit up in a kaleidoscope of vibrant white light, revealing a million tiny stone hearts shining back up at me.

As I grab a bush with my free hand, my left leg slips from under me. The force yanks my hand from the bush and I tumble over the side, rolling sideways several times before I grab an exposed root and a jutting rock with each hand. My lower body is jerked downward, leaving my legs and feet dangling like loose shoe laces. I realize my goal of dying is but moments away.

As I hang, a misbegotten man on a misbegotten wall, I am struck by the stark silence surrounding me. I am truly alone in a lonely world. Why all this fighting to hang on for dear life, when life is no longer dear? Why can't I just let go? Why is my heart beating like it will never stop?

I understand no one is here to save me except my own flawed self. I think of those I couldn't save—Chandni and Alex, and Christine and Mama, who all reached out to me when death staked its claim and received nothing in return except my weak arms.

I recall those I helped at Hope House, including Christian, Donnie, and Jesus, who walked into the unknown with hope and a stronger belief in themselves. I think, too, of the boys who loom ahead, all in need of a concerned heart—one hardened by the long loneliness into a shield these kids can count on for strength and protection. A stone heart like mine, holding on to life with fierceness that cannot be wrestled away by hopelessness.

A stone heart that must keep beating!

I don't wanna let go! I don't wanna die! I wanna live!

Memories of all those affected by this stone heart fuse into my arms, giving them the strength to hold on to the jutting rocks, until one foot and then the other finds rest on large roots sticking from the wall. The climb is slow and deliberate, one hand up to a higher hold, followed by the same-side leg, and then the same for the opposite side. A deep sigh and then a nod to the vision of my dad's face now level with mine, his matching pale blue eyes staring in silent support of my stone heart's fight to live. Re-energized, I do the same movements with the other limbs. All moves are aided by the moonlight above and the reflection off the washed-out sea shells and stone hearts below.

The first hand, then the second claim holds on rocks half-buried in the ground near cliff's edge. One foot, then the other step upward, raising my head and shoulders above cliff level, and I reach one more time to grab an exposed root for my final pull up and over the edge.

The midnight dew has moistened everything in its reach, and my left hand loses its grip on the slippery vine, sending that side of me flailing backward. My other hand is yanked from its rock hold, and my entire body slides over the edge. Suddenly, I have hold of nothing and begin a free fall feet first toward my namesakes below.

I fall ten feet or so before clasping my right hand on a jutting root, nearly yanking that arm from its socket. Feeling tendon and muscle straining toward their tearing points, I dangle precariously, a pendulum swinging between life and death. I no longer have the want for death—living is the only thought on my mind as I reach for another root with my left hand. As my right arm and hand lose their strength and grip, my left arm takes up the fight, and I pull myself close to the wall, giving my feet chance to find rest on twin dirt knolls. Now the moisture of the night is my ally as my boots dig into the dew-soaked earth. I hold on for a minute, giving time for my right arm to rally enough to grab another root, so my left hand can grasp onto a shallow ledge.

In three thrusts of my legs and arms, I push to the crest of the cliff. I feel for the rocks on top before committing to a firm hold, and then I pull myself over the edge.

I turn onto my back and lay flat on the ground, exhausted and gasping for air, but feeling more alive than I can recall. I laugh at the stupid man I was and never intend to be again. I think of where I have been and where my

choices have taken me. I am once again in my English class, with Master T.S.
Eliot guiding me:

"We shall not cease from exploration and the end of all our exploring will
be to arrive where we once started and know the place for the first time."

I laugh at myself again. In reality, I am right where I started before I
intended to leap off this cliff. I am still alone and lonely. Only, the hope I now
have is stronger than the loss and loneliness I feel. This thought of what could
be is a beacon bright enough to guide me away from the edge and out of my
darkness to—anywhere!

I shield my eyes, as the morning sun's first rays peek above the eastern
horizon, the shimmering shards signaling another light of day's triumph over
the darkness of night. I celebrate the sunlight victory as my own. The long
loneliness no longer lies heavy upon my chest, and I take in deep, glorious,
unchallenged breaths.

Did the dream I just have really happen? Was it true I headed toward
the edge without a hope or care left? Did I really hang on to the side of
that cliff and become a hero by saving my own life?

I don't know if I'm a hero, but the persistent aching in my right
shoulder reminds me that I did indeed hold on for dear life after I finally
decided I wanted to. I open this journal one last time, to pen the final entry
into what was once my will, but is now simply my testament—to exactly
what, I'm not sure.

Three or four months have passed since I conquered my fear of life,
and I have left Elk and returned to my cottage above Folsom Lake. I dream
often now, and I recall many of them in vivid detail. The vision above,
of my failed attempt at dying and successful effort to continue living, has
been repeated so often that I routinely wake up more exhausted than when
I went to bed. But I always greet each victorious morning with a grin.

My other dreams leave me with a smile, too. Mama is there, watching
over me like she did so long ago on that first day of school in my new world
of California. Looking across the street at me sitting alone on a playground
bench, she closes her eyes and wishes the best for her baby, sending all her
energies to protect the Stone Heart of the last of the Lonely Lyons.

I now realize that my sweet mama has always been there for me, for all of us.

My daddy also appears in these dreams, his voice feathering softly down to me. "Son, you're on your own, but you're not alone." Simple statements, just like the man.

In the wind echoes of the canyon I hear his laughter, and in the mirror of the lake I see his smile. His silence is no longer my bondage—in his voice I have found my own. It is my bond to his legacy and my connection to a world I am just coming to understand.

I no longer limit myself to fishing and swimming in lakes, with their safe banks and static currents. I seek the fast-running streams, relishing the freedom and energy of their swirling waters as they flow toward the seas. I yearn to fish and sail upon the oceans—their open-ended vastness no longer intimidates me. Within the tides and currents, the twisting eddies and rolling waves, I see an infinite number of possibilities.

I will never abandon the lakes of my youth. They taught me the importance of boundaries—and when to step beyond them. I will return to Far Away Lake, a kid once again with dirt on my face, a faded Kelly green Oakland A's hat on my head, and a rod and reel in hand. But when I look down at the watery mirror, I will see a man looking back, one not unlike my daddy. And I will stand proud.

I am still running, but it is no longer in wayward directions or down aimless roads. I'm heading toward what I want and who I desire.

Love has been a tough road, a long, thin line broken and twisted in many places. I have left a trail of shattered hearts and gathered the pieces of my broken one along the way. Now I travel the path of hope that leads through the winding way, toward home.

Her home.

After a lifetime searching, I know who she is. I hear her voice calling in my dreams. I see her face just as clearly. I feel her moving in the wind. And I recall her name.

Elise.

Sweet Elise!

I no longer have a journal of memories to shield me from the present or excuse my future. I am exposed and unsure of what comes next. I have but one certainty—hope.

Make that two certainties. I know where my next steps are going.

Seventeen hours ago, I stepped on a plane in San Francisco and began flying to the other side of the world, to a country where I have never been. I land in Lyon, home to my unsteady birthright. The shuttle driver laughs at the last name on my passport, as he takes me to the Grenoble station. I catch a train and then a bus, which stops in Annecy, the *Pearl of the Alps*, as it is called in my brochure. The scenic city is gateway to majestic Lake Annecy and many small hamlets and villages shadowed by the surrounding mountains.

In search of a certain chalet on the outskirts of Duingt, a quaint village not far from Annecy and set on the waning slopes of Mount Le Taillefer, I walk down a promontory that splits Lake Annecy. My path stops short of dividing this massive body of water, as the *Grand Lac* and *Petit Lac* are actually one with each other. I see a castle in the distance—*Chateauvieux*, which the brochure notes was the subject of a painting by Cezanne and guards the strait separating the two lacs. Castles and lacs, and rolling hills dwarfed by the legendary Alps—I am in a place that until now has been to me but folklore and a dream.

I am in France, *la terre de l'amour* (the land of love) and home to my true love.

Using a local map, I turn a corner and head down a dirt path that turns into stone, my shaky steps leading me toward the cottage where an exquisite woman lives with her remarkable son. I carry nothing but a small gray stone worth nothing except for its power to save a dying man's life and restore its purpose.

Though my journey to self-discovery has convinced me of my worthiness for both life and true love, I have no idea if Elise will share my new awakening. I will tell her of the stone heart—how it represented hope and dreams and life in my battle against desperation and despair and death. And how its magic led me back to her.

Though emboldened by a true heart, I still worry she will interpret my words as simply a plea thrown her way by a drowning man. Fearing rejection, I didn't contact her before jetting across an ocean and two continents. I leave my fate to the chance of hope.

Measuring steps in time with the wild beats of my heart, I turn into her cobblestone driveway rimmed by beds of purple roses and come to rest at her front door. A local has informed me this traditional Savoyard chalet, with its rough stone walls and triangle-shaped tile roof, is some 300 years old. A lump forms in my throat in reverence to the history around me and the beauty that waits behind the rustic wooden door. I barely find strength to lift the heavy metal clacker, and its hard thud against ancient wood startles me.

As the door opens, I close my eyes and inhale the crisp mountain air in a failed attempt to slow my vibrating heart. My eyes slowly open to a view filled with languid pools of vibrant green. The setting sun peeks its lasts rays over my shoulder, the reddish gold light landing on Elise's eyes. I am lost in layers of color—drawn in by the golden surface reflection, pulled under aqua shallows and swallowed into her emerald depths.

All that I have prepared to say has vanished from my being, and I feel the Hallelujah drawn from every part of me.

"Oh. I really, want you to know, uhh, what I mean is—" I stutter, searching for the words to win back this exquisite woman, while half-expecting her to slap me and slam the door. She stops my struggle for words, gently pushing a finger against my lips.

"Shush," she says, smiling as a tear rolls down each of her cheeks. "I knew you would be back."

"But…how did you know? I didn't even know until a few days ago."

"I always knew. Just shut up and get in here! *Now!*"

"But I have so much to say…"

"I can see everything I need to know in those blue eyes."

"But you are so calm—"

"Calm?" she laughs, and her familiar deep, raspy voice shakes me to the core of my being. "Put your hand here."

She doesn't wait for me to comprehend her invitation, taking my hand and placing it on her left breast. I feel the pounding of her heart all the way down into my soul.

She offers her arms and we dance right there on her doorstep, to music that can only be heard by the two of us. Though I haven't danced since we last saw each other, her lessons are still inside me. When our dance ends, she walks past me and toward her front door, pausing to turn around and extend a hand toward me. I take her hand and she leads me across the threshold and into her home.

Elise sees my eyes searching past her and reads my mind. "Michel is over at his dad's place this weekend. It is just us for a now, if that's okay with you."

"Dang!" I said, my shoulders slumping to show my disappointment. "I flew halfway across the world to see the little man. And he's not even here!"

Her punch on my shoulder is playful, but hard enough to get my attention pointed directly back into her emerald eyes.

"Actually...I *did* come here to find both of you. His rock and your memory...saved a man's life. That man sent me here to repay—"

"Stop right there, silly man," she says, putting her finger to my lips again, this time holding it there."

In silence, I hand her the stone heart, which I have attached to a thin gold chain. She takes the stone without a word, but her eyes dance as she holds it cupped in her two hands. I lift the necklace and drape it around her neck, placing my heart next to hers.

I can't help but ask again about the lack of surprise I saw in her eyes when I arrived. "Someone somehow tipped you off, right? You knew I was coming, didn't you?"

"No. I just knew you couldn't stay away."

She nods toward a wall on her left, to a framed sheet of binder paper filled with handwritten material. Looking closer, I realize the writing is in my hand and forms "The Delicate Dance," the poem I tucked into her purse as I walked out of her life.

I read the poem, sighing as I recall my fatalistic view of finding love again. But something seems different, more upbeat about the ending. I reread the poem, realizing she has altered my last few lines to fit her wishes.

For the ending that once read, *"But what I know now/I know all too late/Lonely is my fate/And our rhythm just illusion/For love is a delicate dance,"* she has substituted:

Let us glide across the floor
Together, arm and arm
Hold me, shield me, from harm
I will do the same for you
For our love is a delicate dance

Let us sway our lives away
Twistin' and turnin'
Lovers forever in motion
Lovers for ever and ever
For our love is a delicate dance.

At times, the faith of one must be strong enough to power the broken hearts of two.

As I pull her close and bring her lips to mine, I feel not the comfort and satisfaction of love finally attained, but the wild, pulsating excitement of true love's infinite possibilities...as plentiful as the millions of tiny stone hearts reflected in the vibrant white light of a full moon.

EPILOGUE

*T*oday is different than yesterday.

At first, this difference may not be so apparent. Two decades have passed since I last wrote in this journal. The skin under my chin sags like molten wax dripping from a candle. Years have melted one upon the other, their significance buried under layers of forgotten moments. Wrinkles run like delta rivulets from my eyes, which people tell me still hold a sparkle despite all that they have seen.

My right shoulder—the one nearly pulled apart on the wall—stiffens on cold days, or when dark clouds on the horizon portend a change in the weather. My lower back aches more days than not, though not from a lifetime of lifting. Long nights bent over a desk, putting down my aimless, but heartfelt thoughts on paper, have done the painful trick.

My hands are gnarled garlands bent and twisted with age. The undersides of my fingers, though, are smooth. Hidden from the sun and other elements, they have survived the ravages of time gnawing at my body. The insides of my middle and index fingers of my right hand are like polished oak, rubbed flat and shiny by pen and pencil over their sixty years of use. My right thumb is smoothest of all; massaged to the pink sheen of a baby's cheek, it scarcely holds a print. This is my writing hand, the one that opens the secrets inside me.

My journal has not lain abandoned. I have read part of it—sometimes a hundred pages and sometimes just a paragraph—almost every day since I decided it would be my testament, but not my will. The skunk trainman needn't worry—I don't use the words to wallow in the past, just to remind me what my family of troubled lovers has been through.

The diary helps me recall my younger years, when I didn't worry about the consequences of my choices. Back then, if I missed a sign and headed down a wrong path, it was easy to turn back. My steps were shorter and I usually never wandered too far astray. This journal won't let me forget my later years, when I stumbled often, missed turns, and almost ran off a cliff into oblivion.

I am older now and my steps are slower, but I have become more sure-footed with the wisdom I have gained. Still I sometimes wonder if my feet are headed in the right direction. Often I am awakened from restless dreams by a voice I cannot place. I soon recognize it as my own, but it has a different resonance each time—sometimes it's me as a child or a grown man, while other times I'm cast as a father or a lover. In the stillness of the night, I close my eyes and hope the voice tells me the truth.

Most of the time, the voices tell me the right way to go. I no longer fear the word "hope," nor do I cling to the daytime light and fear the long loneliness of night.

I am the last of my beautiful, tragic family of lovers. Hank died of lung cancer a few years ago when his taste for cigarettes caught up with him. But he breathed his last breath a sober man for almost two decades. And he died in love, as a husband and a daddy.

He had met the second love of his life at the dude ranch in Montana he traveled to on the first vacation of his adult life. Stacey, the ranch's "dude" trainer, taught him to ride a horse once again. A vivacious, spirited blonde with eyes the color of translucent turquoise, she also showed him that love still existed in his heart.

Peter passed on peacefully in his sleep just a year ago, on Mama's birthday. He never gave up his spiritual fight, but after outliving several end-of-the world deadlines he changed his mission to helping people live spiritual lives day-to-day. Most of those he helped were part of his own family. With his wife Carma and three children, he shared their sprawling 120-acre enclave in the high desert forests of Eastern Washington with nine grandchildren and numerous aunts, uncles, cousins, and other assorted "relatives."

On some days I still feel the pain life has dealt me. During these times, I recall the night my daddy came to me in my tequila-induced dream. His words are now mine, and I will not forget them because I know them by heart. I am still comforted by his words and the final lesson he taught me—the power to save ourselves exists within each of us.

Helpful, too, is listening to those who love us and learning from both their frailties and their wisdom. I found my voice and direction with help from Mama and Daddy, my sister and brothers, my friends and lovers—and my "kids."

When past wounds ache in my chest, I examine my life and realize my deepest hopes and dreams have come true. I am greeted every day by three miracles—Michel, now twenty-nine, and my two adopted jewels, Emerald Chandni, eighteen, and Shell, fifteen.

Though at times I feel like my children's grandpa, I'm reminded of the wonderful, no longer frightening fact of fatherhood by one word from their mouths—"Daddy."

I haven't progressed in some things, including my career. I returned to working with troubled kids, becoming possibly the oldest *educateur en foyer* (group home counselor) in France. The kids get a kick out of calling me *Papi* (Grandpa), and listening to my scrambled French, delivered with a Southern drawl I don't have when speaking English. I still get a blast out of showing them things can get better, and seeing hope and dreams reflected in their eyes.

I tell them my stories if they ask. I speak of Christian, who waded through the dark reminders of his childhood and now directs a small theatre company in San Francisco, and Donnie, the unadoptable kid who found a loving family in the Ashes and his place in the world as a teacher. I point out Sean, who never found his mother, but whose quest led to finding someone else—himself. He became an advocate for the homeless, working in shelter agencies in both San Jose and San Francisco. He resurfaced in Oak Park after hearing of Omar's death, and became a force in seeing that Omar's plans for the area were realized. He even tracked me down online ten years ago to make sure I returned to the States to attend the dedication of the Omar Lewis Community Center.

I tell them about Freddie, the boy who spit in my face and later saved my life. Sean found Freddie living under a bridge and brought him to the

Oak Park Humanity Shelter. Freddie did the rest on his own. He cleaned himself up and went to work for the shelter, becoming an outspoken champion of the homeless and misplaced. Attaining a local and national reputation for his tireless efforts, he was featured on "60 Minutes" and in numerous newspapers across the country. He didn't slow down after he learned he had AIDS a few years ago. He never stopped working to help others until the day he died.

Freddie didn't die "lost and forgotten and buried in an unmarked grave." His funeral drew almost a thousand people, most of who had been touched by him in some way.

I was one of them.

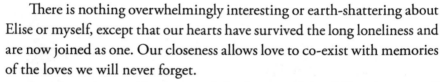

There is nothing overwhelmingly interesting or earth-shattering about Elise or myself, except that our hearts have survived the long loneliness and are now joined as one. Our closeness allows love to co-exist with memories of the loves we will never forget.

In sojourns toward lovers past, I think most often of Chandni. I recall her when the sun's first light creeps above the majestic Alps towering over our cottage in Saint Jorioz, or when I watch its evening flame extinguished after crashing below the western horizon and sinking into nearby Lake Annecy. Chandni's spirit resides within me and is reflected in the middle name and milk chocolate eyes of my sweet daughter.

Michel has grown into a capable young man, coming out of his social shell and displaying an amazing interest and aptitude for music. "After you left," explained Elise when we reunited, "he became even more fascinated by recordings of beating hearts. On a hunch, I started playing music heavily laden with drums. His resulting interest prompted me to buy him a drum set. He wore out two sets in six months, before I decided to get him a top-of-the-line set. His rhythmic touch expanded, until he became a percussion prodigy."

And he hugs his mama and "Mr. Stone Heart" every chance he gets.

Elise finally found the right key to reach him.

As beautiful and different as each one of my days are now, filled with a remarkable woman and three children who love me completely without complete understanding of who I am, it is still the nights for which I long.

Since the visions of my daddy returned and my years of darkness vanished, I now have long, vivid dreams filled with striking colors and vibrant images.

In some of these dreams, a young siren with hair of cocoa brown and skin and eyes of melted caramel dances a minuet that makes my soul rejoice. I am held close by this sweet woman of substance, who believes in me despite the pain I caused her. I can see it in how she looks at me, even in the dark with both my eyes closed.

This is the dream I hold close.

In other visions of the night, an exotic lady with eyes of polished jade and hair the shade of blackest coal flowing to her waist plays haunting adagios on her flute casting spells on my heart and firing my desires. I awaken sweating and exhilarated, then close my eyes once more to remember the feeling.

This is the dream for which I live.

CPSIA information can be obtained
at www.ICGtesting.com
Printed in the USA
LVOW07s1324201117
557016LV00004B/156/P